THE RICE DRAGON

A Selection of Recent Titles by Elizabeth Darrell

AND IN THE MORNING
AT THE GOING DOWN OF THE SUN
WE WILL REMEMBER

SCARLET SHADOWS *
UNSUNG HEROES *
A VICTORIOUS PASSION *

* *available from Severn House*

THE RICE DRAGON

Elizabeth Darrell

This first hardcover edition published in Great Britain 2001 by
SEVERN HOUSE PUBLISHERS LTD of
9–15 High Street, Sutton, Surrey SM1 1DF.
Previously published 1980 in Great Britain by Macdonald Futura
under the title *Dragon of Destiny* and pseudonym *Emma Drummond.*
This first hardcover edition published in the USA 2001 by
SEVERN HOUSE PUBLISHERS INC of
595 Madison Avenue, New York, N.Y. 10022.

British Library Cataloguing in Publication Data

Darrell, Elizabeth, 1931-
The rice dragon
1. Love stories
I. Title
823.9'14 [F]

ISBN 0-7278-5655-3

Except where actual historical events and characters are being described for the storyline of this novel, all situations in this publication are fictitious and any resemblance to living persons is purely coincidental.

Printed and bound in Great Britain by
MPG Books Ltd., Bodmin, Cornwall.

Author's Note

The "black sheep of the family" is a phrase that is out of fashion, but in the Victorian era there was one in most well-to-do hierarchies. They could be out-and-out villains or mere nonconformists to tradition, but the passing of time and the demands of popular fiction have made "black sheep" irresistible, and endowed them with winning qualities that dilute their reprehensible actions. The loveable rogue, in fact.

When I first wrote *The Rice Dragon* in 1980, I decided to reverse the theme. I made my hero the one white sheep in a family of black ones, who are not in the least endearing. During the development of the novel, it occurred to me that while a man's virtues never cancel out his children's wickedness, a father's sins invariably bedevil those who come after him.

So if you are a parent!

Prologue

The most terrible aspect of a battle, Rupert realized, was the inhuman noise. He had dreamed of the honor and glory; the fear and pulsing excitement. He had faced the prospect of sudden death and, perhaps worse than that, mutilation. But it was all forgotten in the tumult of the day.

All around him was the din of men at war—the thundering, shuddering roar of cannon on the Russian redoubt; the subterranean thuds that rolled in waves against his ears; the crack of rifles sharp and clear amid the rumble of heavy guns; the high whistle of shot and the baritone song of shells flying overhead. Then there were men's voices, hoarse and urgent like his own as he shouted yet again to his company not to yield.

For a moment Rupert checked his advance, shocked at what lay ahead. Around the foot of the great outer defenses of Sevastapol lay a mound of red—the scarlet-coated dead of renowned British regiments that had endured so much during the Crimean campaign. Clambering over them were their comrades, driven on by their officers to climb the scaling ladders from which the dead had tumbled. They, in turn, were falling.

"Forward, men, forward!" he heard himself cry before running to the walls half-hidden by smoke and dust. His boots felt the pliancy of that scarlet carpet before he jumped for the rungs of the ladder; then all was forgotten as the gray shapes at the top became hostile men. There was no time for planned thought; instinct took over. Many fell immediately, unwary or petrified by unacceptance of what they saw, but Rupert parried, twisted, leaped, and thrust at the milling foe while, miraculously, enemy bayonet and sword failed to find their mark on him.

His arm ached; his sword became leaden. Smoke irritated his eyes and gave an even rougher edge to his voice. All sounds had merged into one—the drumming of his heartbeat. Men dropped to the ground around him or jerked forward and lay limply across the gabions. Faces both strange and familiar swam across his vision—all moist, pale, and with red-rimmed eyes. Then the familiar ones were gone, leaving only bearded strangers with dark eyes and foreign curses on their lips.

Now no scarlet coats were to be seen other than those on the backs of the dead. The Russians came at him, three together. He dispatched two with his pistol before the bayonet of the third pierced his side as he twisted away. Losing his balance, Rupert fell to the muddy floor of the redoubt and waited to feel a mortal wound in his back. It did not come.

Turning his face away from the dank earth, he saw a fresh wave of soldiers from his own regiment appear over the top. Yet, even as he watched, the Russians were pushing the ladders away, sending those clinging to them crashing down onto the bayonets of their comrades below. After dragging himself to his feet, he stumbled forward to where a ladder lay against the gabions, as yet undiscovered by the Russians. He fought for possession of it with all his failing strength, until the number of red coats in the small redoubt equaled the gray. He continued fighting until the position was taken.

Only then, when he was leaning against the sand-filled baskets in breathless pain, did one sound rise above all others: English bugles were calling the retreat! He would not believe it; he could not accept it. For half a lifetime today he and those beside him had fought to take the fortifications, and yet now that victory was theirs they were being ordered to relinquish it!

Rupert thought the order mad, cruel even, until after climbing down the ladder and crossing the plain once more, he could view the whole scene. Whereas he and a small number of men had won through, there were many who had not and were still groping their way to the British lines through the shower of shot and shell pouring from the Russian guns. The assault had failed.

Hundreds were dead, and nothing had been gained. To make retreat even more bitter, it was evident from the tricolor flying triumphantly from the Malakoff that the French had stormed it with great success. Pride and honor had been lost today in front of their allies, and Rupert felt the pain of defeat along with the pain of his wound. It took more courage to return across that plain than it had taken to advance in the face of the enemy.

So this was battle! Not all his study of warfare, his avid attention when old soldiers recalled their experiences, his dreams of being called to duty had prepared him for the mud, smoke, and heat; the courage and fear of man; the pain and inhuman noise. Neither had they prepared him for defeat. Yet, as he stumbled back over the uneven ground, giving a word of encouragement here, a helping hand there, he experienced an inward drive that urged him to continue until the day was won. The testing time had come and not found him wanting. In the midst of defeat he had achieved personal victory—he knew he was a true and instinctive warrior.

Two hundred feet from the British lines he collapsed and knew no more until he regained consciousness in the field hospital. He was not really *in* it since the large tent bearing the medical flag had for months been inadequate to accommodate the wounded, and patients lay everywhere up to fifty yards away; mercifully he had been placed beneath a tree and so had escaped the additional discomfort of having the afternoon sun blazing down upon him.

It was a long day filled with half dreams that flitted through his mind when the cries of those around him became unbearable, but at last the medical team reached the place where he lay. He knew the surgeon well, and so he did not mince his words when the man began to sew up his side.

"Have a care with that damned needle, Theo. I am not one of your little Nell's rag dolls in need of a stitch or two."

"Aye," was the placid reply, "but if it's fancy work you want, I'll hand you over to Lady Dorothy. I hear she's a neat stitcher when the mood takes her." He nodded at the cup held out by an orderly. "Take a dram, will ye? Then lie still."

Rupert ignored the rum. "Keep it for some poor devil with stronger need for it."

The surgeon gave him a quick glance before concentrating again on his bloody work. "Ach, drink it down, man. When you have been here as long as I have, you'll lose some of those scruples and be glad of anything that improves the daily grind."

Rupert felt a particularly sharp twinge of pain while he listened to the doctor's words, but he gritted his teeth and continued to ignore the spirits offered him. When he summoned enough resolution to speak, he asked, "What is the news?"

Bushy eyebrows rose. "The same as always, laddie: We go again tomorrow. This time I believe they mean it. The French are holding the Malakoff and will never let it go. Puts us in a wee predicament, does it not?"

Rupert, now throbbing from head to toe with pain, said, "If they go, I want to go with them."

The doctor's answer was slow and considered. "Aye, ye're hotheaded enough and have a strong body. Ye'll no come back, mind, but that's your affair. Many's the man who has rushed off to avenge his friend and been the cause of another man's doing the same." A hand rested for a moment on his shoulder. "We're all sorry about Edward. After all this time it is sad when a man goes at the end of a war, for there's no doubt the Russians are all but beaten now."

All pain was suspended for a moment. "Edward?"

The surgeon paused in the act of wiping his instruments on his apron. "Had ye not heard, laddie? I had to take off both his arms when they brought him in . . . but it will na save him. He is dying."

Cold and suddenly shaking from head to foot, Rupert put out his hand. "I'll have that draft, after all."

It was fully half an hour before Rupert was able to go in search of his friend Edward Deane. The regimental chaplain, who was sitting with the young officer, was glad to see him, saying he had only a moment before sent an orderly with instructions to locate Rupert.

"Mr. Deane is most anxious to speak with you, Captain Torrington. . . . And time is growing short," he added under his breath. Rising from the wooden box, he took Rupert's arm. "You look more in need of a seat than I, dear sir. I will wait outside." He gave an understanding smile. "My duty is to forgive sins, not listen in on a man's regrets that he will no longer be able to commit them."

With that he ducked his head and pushed through the tent flap into the night.

Rupert turned his attention to his friend lying on the trestle bed lit by yellow light from the lantern swinging on a pole. A blanket was pulled to his chin, mercifully hiding the stumps that were now all that remained of his arms. Edward did not look like a dying man. His cheeks were stained bright pink, his blue eyes danced with reflections from the lantern, and he spoke with animation.

"By God, Rupert, you look devilish seedy and yellow around the gills."

"That cheers me no end," said Rupert, shocked into giving an automatic response. "You always were the frankest of my friends, Edward."

"Coming from you, that remark is almost effrontery, old fellow. If I had a sovereign for every damned insult you have issued under the guise of frankness, I should be a wealthy man."

With a mind full of the horror of that day and the words of the surgeon still ringing in his ears, Rupert forced a grin that gave him more pain than the wound in his side.

"And every sovereign would have found its way to the gaming table, no doubt."

Edward sighed. "Yes, no doubt . . . but I would not have needed to write so many notes of hand. I always disliked it—especially when it involved my friends."

"Nonsense! A gentleman's note of hand is accepted anywhere."

Rupert wished the pointed roof of the tent, gilded and softened by the glowing lantern, did not suddenly resemble the inside of a church.

"Ah, what is a gentleman?" reflected Edward. "Have you ever thought about it, Rupert? I have been doing so this past hour. To the fair sex he is someone who hands them into carriages, sends posies and trifling presents with absurd verses attached, and nourishes an overriding passion within his breast that must never be expressed other than threatening to put a pistol to his brains if he does not receive a smile from the loved one.

"To men he must be fearless and honorable, respect the wives and daughters of other gentlemen, yet have an unflagging virility with women of doubtful virtue. He must risk his neck on the hunting field and his fortune on the toss of a dice. He may cheat and deceive his wife, but never his friends." He turned his head restlessly on the pillow. "To his men he must be a leader, set an example, show courage in the face of death."

A terrible silence followed as his blue eyes began to glisten with moisture. "Would you wipe my brow?" he whispered hoarsely. "This damned sweat is affecting my sight."

It was then that Rupert realized the high color was due to fever and the vigorous manner was caused by desperation. Edward Deane really did have very little time left to live. Sick and shaken, Rupert took up a towel from the bedside and wiped his friend's brow.

"On the day of reckoning," Edward continued thickly, "I suppose it is only what a man is to himself that really matters, eh?"

Holding on desperately to his own self-control, Rupert said, "You have no fears on that score, my dear fellow."

Blue eyes looked anxiously from a face too youthful to be contemplating such things. "I have not been the best of brothers. . . . No, I have not, I see that now." The confession was jerky with emotion. "It cannot be easy for a female, Rupert. Try to put yourself in a woman's place. If there is no one to lean on, to act in defense, to make the decisions . . . I spent so little of my time at home, and when I did, I followed a man's pursuits, you know. I was not there to support her when our father died, and my diligence in letter writing has been deplorable this past year."

"Any man can be excused that, under the circumstances," Rupert said through lips grown stiff. A scarlet stain was beginning to spread across the coverlet, and he prayed his friend would not notice the ominous sign. "Your sister must have heard how things are out here and understood that you had more to do than write letters."

His friend appeared not to have heard. "There is my gold watch, and a miniature of Mama, a tiepin or two—things like that. When you take them to her, will you explain how things were—ask her forgiveness?"

Rupert nodded, not trusting himself to speak.

"There'll be nothing for Harriet when I am . . . when I am . . ." His voice rose, and the tears spilled over unashamedly. "Before God, Rupert, you are the only man who could hear this. I am afraid as I have never before been afraid. I shall never see another morning, and the thought fills me with terror. I had rather they had blown me to pieces out there than *this*. I shall slip away like a leaf that has dropped from a branch. I . . . I have no hands to hold on to the living, to clasp life until the sun comes up again. It's the darkness. . . ."

Rupert called raggedly to the chaplain and then took Edward's shoulder in a firm grip. "I won't let you slip away, never fear. Daybreak is only an hour away," he lied desperately.

He did not relax his hold throughout the time the churchman took to give his words of hope and salvation. Gradually the young officer grew calm, and with him his friend. The experience affected Rupert profoundly—more, perhaps, than the greater events of the day. In that small tent yellowed by the grime of the

Crimea and the flame that was now burning low in the lantern, and listening to words of a life beyond life, Rupert saw in great clarity the need for human compassion. Holding onto a man no older than himself whose life was tragically ending, he found himself vowing to live life to the full for as long as he was compassion. Holding on to a man no older than himdeeply, so that when the chaplain cast him a look that conveyed an unmistakable message, Rupert took Edward's other shoulder in a firm grip and smiled without effort.

"The branch is still here, old fellow. There is nothing to fear."

The pale lips moved, and his words were barely audible. "You have been the best of friends, Rupert . . . but I was on a losing streak, you know."

With seven hours still to go before the dawn, Edward Deane died.

Part One

Chapter One

That afternoon the silence in the parlor seemed to be telling Harriet something—something that had been bothering her increasingly as the days had passed. She looked up from her embroidery to where Nanny sat dozing in a chair. It had become her habit of late, and Harriet realized that the woman who had reared her was growing old. Her exact age had never been mentioned; she had always been "Nanny"—the same when Harriet's father had died two years before as when her charge had entered puberty. But her own recent restlessness made Harriet more aware of all that was going on around her.

While Nanny had been a pleasant companion during Professor Deane's lifetime, now the motherly soul's company was not enough; Harriet felt the need for stimulating conversation, as steel on which to sharpen the blade of her wit. Many times she and her father had argued fiercely for the pleasure of exercising their minds. Nanny had never approved; she could not accept that it was right for a female to put herself forward in such manner to her papa—or to anyone else, for that matter. As to a young woman's wishing to improve her intellect, it was, in Nanny's opinion, both alarming and dangerous. With the passing of her father, Harriet had lost all the sparkle in her life. She might as well don a muslin cap and doze away her day like Nanny, despite her four-and-twenty years.

Society already had her a confirmed spinster, and there was nothing in her existence to suggest otherwise. Yet Harriet could not believe there was no more to life than stitching, keeping household accounts, and receiving morning calls from declining spinsters. Admittedly she had her father's work to copy in a fair hand—an unfinished study of indigenous races—and there were the dogs to exercise, but there was still a large gap to be filled.

She wished to marry—what female did not when the alternatives stared her in the face? But young men bored her, and older men had become embarrassingly free with their paternal pinches on her cheeks and pats on the arm. The death of her father had not only left her bereft of stimulating companionship but made her position an unenviable one.

The Deanes were not wealthy; the family fortune had been spent by the past three generations on disastrous projects. Harriet's great-grandfather had invested a huge sum in an expedition setting out to find a trade route from India to Persia which would bring untold riches to the West. All it brought was death to the white explorers and untold riches to several tribal chieftains. Grandfather Deane had invented countless expensive gadgets that invariably burst into flames or flew into fragments on their first demonstration, and Professor Deane had been a philanthropist, distributing money he could not afford to spend.

Thankfully Edward had shown signs of steadiness

by purchasing a commission in an infantry regiment, and Harriet hoped his future sons would benefit from his decision. Unfortunately it meant he was absent a great deal just when his presence would have given some comfort. He had been en route to the Crimea when their father died so suddenly, and Harriet had had only spasmodic letters from Balaklava since then. She missed Edward badly. Harum-scarum he might be, but the warmth and generosity of his nature made him very lovable. In his company she always felt life should not be taken too seriously. If only he had a wife, someone she could visit in his absence.

The ticking of the clock took on a greater significance than the mere working of wheels and cogs; each tick marked another second of her life passing, and yet all she could do was sit silently while putting colored silks onto a square of cambric in delicate patterns.

Thrusting aside the embroidery, she rose swiftly and walked to the silken bell rope, her abrupt movement bringing Nanny awake with a jerk.

"Whatever is the matter, Harriet?" quivered the aging lady.

"I have rung for tea."

Nanny looked shocked. "It is nowhere near four yet."

"What has *that* to do with it?" challenged Harriet.

"It has everything to do with it. We always have tea at four."

"How unbearably dull we are, in that case," was her brisk answer. "Do you not think it disgraceful that two females should celebrate the Lord's gift of each new day merely by taking tea precisely at four?" She began pacing, the skirt of her black-and-white-striped crinoline rocking on its huge cane frame. "Are you aware, Nanny, that women in China gather rice while standing knee-deep in water, and those in the East Indies kneel beside rivers to wash their clothes beneath the noses of crocodiles. Imagine that if you can! The snap-snapping of great jaws only inches away from the laundering of a camisole." She stopped in front of the bewildered old soul. "*They* do not take tea precisely at four each day. Life is not passing by outside their parlor windows. They are a part of it."

Wrinkled hands straightened the muslin cap as Nanny gave a deep sigh. "Oh, dear, you have one of *those* moods on you again."

The door opened to admit a small, dumpy girl in a brown sprigged dress, starched apron, and cap. Her hair escaped from the cap in wisps that were quite plainly used to being free, and the little pinched face beneath was made comical by two enormous eyes which made her look like a dormouse just awoken from hibernation. She bobbed.

"Yes, madam?"

"We will take tea, Bessie."

The girl's eyes cast a furtive glance at the tall clock.

"It is three twenty," supplied Harriet.

"Oh," said the girl.

"What time did you imagine it was?"

"Four, madam."

"Mmm. If I asked you to bring breakfast, what time would you think it was?"

"Nine in the morning, madam . . . except I'd know it wasn't because you had your luncheon at twelve thirty."

"For the only reason that the hands of the clock told us that we should, no doubt," was the crisp comment. "What would happen if all the clocks stopped, Bessie?"

The dormouse eyes grew larger. "I'm sure I don't know, madam. Cook would be in a rare old spin."

Harriet sighed. "Yes, I daresay she would not be the only one. That will be all, Bessie."

The girl bobbed quickly, hesitated, and then said, "Am I to bring tea or not, madam?"

"Yes, indeed. I have set my heart on it, and the day will be quite ruined if I am thwarted."

The maid left the room with a delighted smile, saying under her breath, "This'll shake up Cook, and no mistake."

"My dear," said Nanny as soon as the door closed, "was that wise? The servants will think that you are growing eccentric, and once that happens, your chances will be even less."

"Chances of what?" challenged Harriet, in a provoking mood. "Making a suitable match?"

"If you wish to put it that way," was the placatory answer. Nanny pulled her shawl closer around her shoulders and fastened it with a jet brooch. "Winter will be hard this year. My bones tell me so, and they are never wrong."

Harriet sank onto a papier-mâché stool facing her companion. She saw a woman with a thick waist and iron gray curls drawn into clusters at each side of her crepelike neck. She saw eyes that were peering ever closer to what they sought and ears that had to be turned to the speaker in order to hear clearly. She saw a face that reflected years of patience, resignation, and loneliness. She saw herself in years to come.

The vision frightened her. Edward would marry and have a family. He would be loving and kind, but she would be regarded as eccentric Aunt Harriet by his family. She would be pitied, and although she would be invited to make her home with them, the children would imitate her behind her back, more in awe of her than fond, and Edward's wife would make tactful arrangements to ensure Harriet was not at home when persons of influence called.

Yes, the vision frightened her, but what did she want of life? A marriage like so many she saw would be quite as bad as the life she had just imagined, and she had never felt the slightest devotion toward any gentleman who had come her way. Her looks were no more than pleasant, and although her figure was envied by many a plump contemporary, she did not have the power to attract the male interest that was essential if a female was to have her pick of suitors. Those few who had been drawn to her had invariably ended up provoking her into one of her outbursts, and sentimentality flew in the face of rage.

What she wanted was someone whom she would instantly recognize when he came upon the scene. Yes, she thought ruefully, it was a *he*, that much was certain—but was he a husband, a replacement for her father, or a companion like her brother for whom she sighed? Whatever the answer, she prayed he would come soon. Her twenty-fifth birthday was less than four months away, and Nanny already thought her eccentric for having tea forty minutes early. She did not even want tea—just a reason for breaking the pattern of what her life had become.

Unable to sit still, Harriet rose again and walked to the window. Outside, the November dusk was gathering, and it served to increase her restlessness and melancholy. The autumn of a day as well as a year—warmth, brightness . . . *youth* had gone. She had made no more of that day than she had of that year, of her twenty-four years.

Turning away from the scene outside, she said with forced brightness, "I hear Madame Bourgoni is to sing at the opera next month. I thought we might take a box for the performance."

"I do not know why opera is considered so entertaining," confessed Nanny. "So much screeching and wailing. They are all of them far too gross for strutting about in such clothes, and I cannot approve of young women masquerading as gentlemen, for whatever cause."

Harriet felt her color rise, "It is a great art. One has to study for years to perfect such a fine voice."

"That's as it may be, but it does seem most unnatural to me, besides touching on the vulgar."

It occurred to Harriet that a character in an opera might well tear her hair and throw a pot at the stolid woman still trying to arrange her shawl to the best advantage. Schooling herself with difficulty, she walked back to the fire, hoping the warmth from it would disguise the flush of temper that was already staining her cheeks.

"I trust you will take more kindly to my wish to visit the National Gallery this week. The exhibition of

Dutch masters cannot fail to please, and I know of your fondness for interiors."

The graying head nodded. "True, my dear. In my younger days I often enjoyed a visit to the gallery, and I still marvel at the ability of an artist to put such richness of sheen upon material or sunlight through a window with merely a brush and colored pigments." A short reflective pause led to a negative movement of her head this time. "Alas, I find the corridors excessively long these days. I recall my last visit to such a place. I was hard put to complete the viewing and suffered for several days after with the swelling in my feet. Age takes its toll of pleasures, Harriet."

"Only if one allows it to do so," flashed the girl. "We shall take as long as we wish over the visit, and you may sit as frequently as you feel the need. There are benches provided for the purpose."

"As I know to my cost," was the plaintive answer. "They are all situated in the path of severe drafts from the windows, which do the greatest mischief with my bones."

"Why do you not state clearly that you wish to do nothing that will take you from that chair beside the fire?" cried Harriet angrily. "We have given up our morning drive in the park because the November mists do not suit your disposition, evening visitors are discouraged because you drop into a doze soon after they arrive, and the pleasure of a stroll around the bandstand is at an end because the volume of noise gives you the headache. It is my belief that you wish to do nothing more than contemplate your ills while taking meals at exact times during the day."

This outburst brought crumpled distress to the aging face and doused Harriet's quick temper immediately, although her regret at having injured Nanny's sensibilities was tempered with a strong feeling of justification for her words. They were true enough!

"I do not deserve your kindness," Nanny told her in quivering tones. "Where should I have gone if the professor had turned me away when you left the schoolroom? My best is not enough for you, my dear. You should have a companion of your own age, a woman with similar tastes—not an old nanny who is merely a burden to you. You have little enough, goodness knows, without feeling an obligation to someone who has outlived her usefulness. If only—"

"Hush!" said Harriet firmly. "There is not the least need to become upset. You have not known me since childhood without experiencing my hasty tongue and learning to disregard it. I beg your pardon," She patted the soft, flabby hands, at the same time fighting down her annoyance at the need to placate Nanny.

Fortunately Bessie arrived with the tea tray to provide a diversion, but Harriet still burned with the need to express her longing for life and fulfillment of herself as a person. Truth to tell, she could not afford to employ a companion such as Nanny described. . . . Her future certainly looked black the way things stood.

While Bessie arranged the teacups, Harriet walked to the window to draw the curtains against the beckoning world. Reaching it, she stood for a moment shaken by disbelief and then by the joy of knowing she *could* believe it. In the street below, a carriage had drawn up outside her front door, and alighting from it was an officer in scarlet regimentals wearing a black shako and swinging cloak.

"Edward," she breathed. "Oh, thank God!"

Turning in a rustle of silk skirts, she cried, "It is Edward home from the war! Did I not tell you he would be here now Sevastapol has fallen?" She began to run across the room. "How like him to arrive with no warning. I shall give him the most tremendous scold for this."

Her appearance suggested anything but a scolding, for her face was alight with pleasure and a smile turned up her mouth most attractively as she pulled open the door and ran, skirts held high, along the balustraded landing to the curved staircase. She could hear the jangle of the bell and Bessie's hurrying feet as she ran, then deep masculine tones as she flew down the stairs to greet her brother in the small square hall.

"Edward," she cried.

He swung around to greet her.

Within three steps she halted, releasing her skirts automatically. The man standing before her was a total stranger.

He took off his shako and bowed. "Miss Deane?"

A tremor ran through her. It was as if blazing light had sprung suddenly in a shadowed cloister. The combination of rich brown eyes and creamy fair hair was startling enough, but the sun-darkened aggressive face was completely arresting. Most men would have swaggered in a uniform as handsome and snug-fitting as his; he seemed unconscious of it to the point of nonchalance. He appeared utterly out of place in the genteel surroundings of her small house. He gave no smile of greeting, made no pretense that he had not seen her undignified descent; his expression merely had a gravity that did not accord with his vigorous physique. He seemed to loom before her in the entrance hall, as if it were not large enough to contain him.

He approached the foot of the stairs, ignoring Bessie, who was waiting to take his tasseled shako. "Miss Harriet Deane?" he asked again in a strong voice.

"Yes," she managed. "I am Miss Deane."

"Rupert Torrington, at your service. Perhaps your brother mentioned me?"

For once unsure of herself, Harriet remained where she was, three steps above him. Never before had she felt such weakness—as if her headlong flight had brought her up against a solid object that knocked the breath from her. As she gazed down into dark, burning eyes in a face of almost native brownness, her galloping thoughts gradually settled, allowing her to remember Edward's letters.

"My . . . my brother wrote of you with great enthusiasm, Captain Torrington," she murmured, trying to regain her normal composure. "It is a pleasure to meet you. Pray forgive my rushing at you as I did, but I saw your arrival from my window and thought it must surely be Edward come home."

Before she could move, he had mounted the stairs to stand beside her. "Can it be that the news has not reached you? By God, they had all of eight weeks!"

His use of an expletive in her presence betrayed his emotion, and his expression changed from grave to grim. Something inside her shriveled up, leaving her icy cold. She knew then why he had come.

"Edward will not be coming home," she said more to impress the fact upon herself than to save him the task of saying it to her. "I regret it has been left to you to bear the news, sir."

He coaxed her down the stairs to a chair beside the hatstand. "The intrusion of a stranger at such a time is unacceptable. May I instruct your maid to fetch someone to you?"

She took the seat gratefully. Her legs had turned rubbery, and a stone seemed to have lodged in her throat. "There is nobody to fetch. Nanny will be cast low by the news, so if you would kindly remain until I am sufficiently in command of myself to support her, I should be most grateful."

"Of course, anything you wish . . . but is there no one who can be of comfort? A person who is close to you?"

She looked up at him. "You were close to Edward. That is surely more important." Suddenly the sight of him in his scarlet jacket beneath the cloak reminded her all too vividly of Edward running down the steps to his carriage as he went off to war. Her eyes filled with tears.

"Did he die in battle, Captain Torrington?"

"Yes . . . most bravely."

"Was . . . was his suffering very great?"

"No," was the reassuring answer. "Death was instantaneous."

"I am glad." The relief of knowing he had not been in agony on some foreign field while she had been engaged in a meaningless task designed merely to pass the time helped her to accept his death. "He was proud of his profession. I must believe that he gave his life willingly."

"We must all do that, Miss Deane, or leave the army," was the unexpected reply.

She looked at him through a mist of tears. "Edward was but seven-and-twenty."

"I know, but there were many who had not even seen twenty. War takes no account of age, I fear."

He was expressing none of the customary condolences, and yet his stark words brought her comfort. Edward's departure from life did not seem such a terrible lonely journey.

"Was he accorded Christian burial?"

"They were all accorded Christian burial unless"—he broke off sharply and then continued in a firm tone—"unless they could not be traced. Your brother's grave lies beheath a tree. I ensured there was a stone cross erected before I left the Crimea."

"You have been a good friend, I see that."

He reached into his cloak and brought out a package that he placed in her lap. "I came today to bring these. It was Edward's wish that you should have them, Miss Deane."

She stared at the small parcel but made no attempt to open it. That was something she must do in the privacy of her room. It was a moment or so before a thought struck her.

"How is it you knew of his last wishes if his death was so immediate?"

"He also knew mine," he answered without hesitation. "Every soldier accepts that he might not survive the coming battle and charges his friends with duties such as this. I should have written my condolences except that I was taken with fever for three weeks following the battle. My visit today was intended to explain why I had not done so and to offer my services, insofar as I am able."

"You are very kind," she murmured, the daze of shock making her suddenly tired.

He must have nodded or made some sign to Bessie, for the girl was suddenly there, helping Harriet to her feet, and he was preparing to leave.

"Here is my card. If I can be of assistance to you in any way, please do not hesitate to send for me."

He seemed to have imparted a lifetime of friendship in the short while he had been with her, making her feel that his departure would take away the very prop she had sought for so long. Yet all she said was: "What is there to be done? No funeral carriage, no flowers, no grave to be tended . . . and what is the point in going back into black gloves eight weeks too late?"

He took her hand in a strong hold that somehow sent a flow of reviving confidence through her. "You knew Edward even better than I. He hated the thought of all that. This way you will remember him full of life and youth . . . which is how he would want it."

He must have let himself out, for Bessie was there, helping her up the stairs. Her brain was a jumble of thoughts and memories, but her legs had regained strength enough to walk steadily into the parlor, where Nanny had dozed off again. For a moment or two she stood uncertain in the silence broken only by the ticking of the clock, and then she moved to the window.

The street below was empty now. Mist was beginning to creep up from the river, swirling around the portly figure of the lamplighter as he moved from lamp to lamp with his long pole. It was so desolate a scene she turned from it quickly as emotion overwhelmed her. The movement brought Nanny awake, blinking several times while she tried to recall the situation just prior to her doze.

"Where is Master Edward then?" she asked.

Harriet took a deep breath and then became aware that she was holding something in her hands. She placed the small packet gently on the lid of the piano but kept the visiting card in her left palm. It was impossible to know why, but just holding it gave her courage, as if he were still there to steady her.

"My dear, there is something I must tell you," she began. . . .

The Gaiety Theater was its usual garish, colorful self. Onstage the burlesque girls were strutting and posturing, flashing their fleshy silk-clad thighs and warbling risqué songs in voices that made what was vulgar seem attractive.

Rupert and his two companions strolled around the horseshoe-shaped promenade, dividing their attention between the heavy opulence of the preformers and the daintier but no less voluptuous charms of the courtesans with whom they were mingling.

The gentlemen were on a spree and high on champagne already. The aftermath of war left them all with a decided need for comfort, luxury, the good things of life . . . and feminine solace. But they also needed excitement and action, so they steered clear of society balls and the opera houses where their own set could be found indulging in genteel and civilized amusement. Their fancies did not lie with demure virginal creatures quivering with the hope of discreet dalliance at fingertip distance. The laughing, beckoning women of the town offered what they sought, and half the enjoyment of the evening lay in their making their final selection.

The scarlet coats of the military caught the eyes of the fly-by-night girls, but those seeking lasting and greater financial rewards for their services concentrated on the opera-cloak and silk-hat brigade. Army officers were dashing, unrestrained, and fickle—an irresistible combination—but better to lose paradise than one's heart. With a vacuous man-about-town or an aging roué there was less chance of heartache and more of permanent comfort.

Strengthening the case for the three officers, however, was the insignia of their regiment, which proclaimed them as heroes of the Crimea—a fatal blow to those young or foolish enough to possess susceptible natures despite their way of life.

Rupert was trying to decide between a golden-haired Diana with bold eyes, and shoulders that set him craving to stroke their milky white softness, and a sultry gypsy-dark creature with a bosom of remarkable proportions compared with the slenderness of her body. He was still undecided when a vision cut across the scene around him, and he groaned inwardly. It was more than two weeks since he had called on Harriet Deane, and yet he could not banish her from his mind. With tears glistening in her dark blue eyes, she had looked very much like her brother as he had gazed up from his deathbed. *It cannot be easy for a female, Rupert. Try to put yourself in a woman's place.* How could he possibly do such a thing when he knew little or nothing of the home life of a gentlewoman? He had no sisters, and as for the females he knew intimately . . . he supposed that their lives could not be described as *easy*, but he had never ill used any of his paramours, and he rewarded them handsomely for their favors.

Lost to his surroundings, he fell back from his companions and leaned on the plush rail running around the promenade, staring at the actor quoting verse who had replaced the chanteuse in purple tights. Filling his mind was the memory of the emotions that had crossed Harriet's face as she tried to accept the truth. He could not recall any young woman of his acquaintance who would accept the news he had unwittingly taken her with such control and fortitude. That she had been devoted to Edward was evident from the manner in which she had sallied down the stairs in order to greet him. It must have been the cruelest of blows that followed, yet her first thought had been that Nanny—presumably some old retainer—would need comforting.

Was there really no one on whom the girl herself could lean? Edward had said she would have nothing when he was gone, but surely he had been exaggerating. The house could be best described as shabby-genteel, in an unfashionable part of town. An unattractive façade prepared the visitor for the interior, but Rupert still puzzled over the worn carpet and the wall coverings that had seen better days. Edward Deane had been a wealthy man, gambling with large sums of money; why should his sister choose to live in such humble surroundings? She had not seemed the uncaring type—brisk and capable would be his estimate of her character—so why had she let the property deteriorate so badly in her brother's absence?

His unseeing eyes missed the fun when a cabbage was thrown at the departing actor, and he did not hear the audience's jeers and their advice that the man should return only at his peril. His conscience was troubled, much to his annoyance. He had been through a kind of hell on the battlefields of the Crimea. Why should the dowdy spinster sister of his dead friend demand his thoughts when he had every right to indulge in selfish pleasures?

He moved away but by only a few feet to the next section of red-plush-covered rail, where he leaned again in uneasy recollection. It did not seem right that a young woman, however capable, should have to bear the burden of bereavement alone, and in fact, Edward had asked him to look after his sister's welfare. But, as she had said, there was no funeral to arrange, no visiting relatives in black who must be given hospitality, no grave to tend.

All at once the particular sadness attached to the distant passing of a beloved soldier and comrade gripped Rupert. He had lied to save the girl further grief. Would she have drawn more comfort from the truth and from knowing Edward had spoken of her at the end? He saw again that tent and a young man without arms struggling to face the terror of the unknown. No, he had been right to lie.

"Whatever it is that is troubling you, Captain, I know how to make you forget," said a voice beside him, and a white-gloved hand touched his sleeve gently.

Still half-absorbed in his thoughts, Rupert turned to see a face that should already have made the girl a duchess. Her black hair was drawn up into a knot interwoven with flowers. Her eyes were black, soft with desire, and reminiscent of pagan goddesses. In the lamplight her skin was flawless—creamy olive against the velvet of her gown. Returning slowly from the past he found his gaze locked with hers while ghosts and battlefields faded.

"Been to war, haven't you?" she asked softly.

"Yes."

"That's what I thought. There's something about you—a loneliness. Are you lonely, Captain?"

Excitement began to mount in him as he studied her voluptuous form, and warmth rushed in to replace the coldness that his thoughts had conjured up. With a wicked smile he took her gloved hand to his lips. "Not any longer, my dear."

She laughed throatily as he tucked her hand through his arm and began to lead her from the theater. They had supper in a discreet restaurant, where he drank two glasses to her one. Then they took a carriage to her rooms. The heady quality of the evening increased when he saw the ornate bed supported on gilded legs and covered with vivid brocades, and the walls hung with strange objects of mystic design. Here was the perfect antidote to boredom, the best way to forget the agony and noise of Sevastapol.

She gave him a drink before going in to an inner room. He waited impatiently, for she knew how to tantalize a man to the point of desperation; by the time she reappeared in a loose robe of scarlet and gold Rupert had reached that point.

It was a night such as he had never spent before; in the morning he realized that there had been more than champagne in the glass she had given him, for he had been a king among men with her.

The following two days he spent in hunting with a fellow officer, the evenings being fully occupied at the gaming tables or at cards. Unable to restrain himself, he returned to the girl on the third evening, finding drug-induced paradise once more. A private party held by a friend which ended with a drunken race around the grounds holding a shrieking girl in the saddle was the perfect way to let off steam, and a weekend spent visiting casinos proved a financial success.

It was when he was in the carriage driving once more to the Eastern-style room of the girl called Moona that the thought of Harriet Deane returned, and he realized that his feverish activities of the past week had never entirely banished her from his mind. Yet again he told himself that she had his card and an invitation to call upon his services if she needed him. Despite his close friendship with Edward, he had no real obligation to the sister. It was not as if they were truly acquainted; that one short meeting had not entailed any personal exchange, nor had it constituted a formal introduction. He had been an agent, that was all. His duty was clearly done. The young woman must be left alone with her grief.

The carriage halted, but he remained inside, lost in thought. That she *was* alone was something he could not forget. Damn the girl! In two weeks' time it would be Christmas. How could he relax and enjoy that merry time if her image were going to intrude every time he laughed or hailed his friends? A girl and an aging nanny. What would it be like for Edward Deane's sister when the season of merrymaking and hospitality arrived?

Shaking himself free of such contemplations, he reached for the door handle, but his hand remained on the metal bar without turning it. He had alighted from this same carriage on an errand of duty and condolence only to be met by a girl with skirts gathered above her ankles as she rushed down the stairs, eyes and cheeks glowing with laughter and affection. How would she survive in that unimposing house with a carpet that competed with the leather chair for the description "well-worn"? The gloom of that November scene in her hallway descended on his spirits. She might as well be shut away in a nunnery!

"We're 'ere, Captain," said his driver in a voice made rough by too many nights on the box of his carriage.

"Eh?"

Rupert frowned at the shadowed archway through which could be seen the green door. As Edward had lain dying, it had been easy to vow to live life to the full in gratitude for being spared, but Moona no longer seemed to be the way to fulfilling that vow. She was just another wanton—and damn it, he needed none of her potions to make him virile!

"Drive on, Medkins," he said heavily. "I have changed my mind."

* * *

The servant girl looked at him from around the door as if he were a fugitive from a Bow Street runner. "Oh, Lor', sir, I can't let you in, not now, I can't. And there's no one will make me."

"Whyever not?" he demanded, stepping past her into the dingy hall.

She swung round like a headstrong mouse confronting a tomcat determined on disturbing the peace of the night. "Miss Deane'll go for me good and proper when she sees I've let you in."

"That is a risk you are paid to take," he told her with some amusement.

"Not at this time o' night, I ain't. It's past ten!"

"So?"

"They've already retired, Captain."

"Good God . . . at *ten*!" he said with incredulity. "Are they all indisposed?"

" 'Course not," replied the indignant girl. "But you'll have to leave. They never receive guests at this hour."

Taken aback, regretting the impulse that had brought him there, he was about to turn to the door when a light voice from above halted him.

"Good evening, Captain Torrington."

Harriet Deane was standing on the landing, regarding him from over the banisters. Even in that dim light it struck him anew that there was a commanding dignity about her that was unusual. He saluted, looking up at her with an apology on his lips.

"I have called at an inconvenient time."

"Not at all . . . it was kind of you to break into your evening. Will you not come up, sir?"

He handed shako, cloak, and gloves to the servant

girl, who was stiff with disapproval, and then went up the curving staircase to the girl in a simple gray silk gown. She had obviously decided on half mourning for the brother who had been dead two months before she knew of it. He took her outstretched hand and gave a slight bow.

"I trust I find you well."

"Thank you, yes. Please come into the parlor. The fire is still glowing, and you have brought in the November chill."

He followed her along the landing, full of surprise at the flush on her cheeks and the vivid glow that was not only in her eyes but somehow in her whole being. Why had he remembered her as plain? The minute he walked into a room lit by only one dimmed lamp he knew the servant had been right. Harriet Deane began lighting others with a taper until there was brightness enough to see that she was very nervous beneath the outward calm of her welcome. There was no sign of a chaperone.

When she turned to face him, he found himself saying gently, "You were on the point of retiring."

After only a moment's hesitation she replied with breathless honesty, "Yes."

"Then I beg your pardon. A year in the Crimea has made me forgetful of civilized habits," he said, as if it really were the fashion to go to bed so early in the evening. "It was merely my intention to give you this." He took a card from his pocket. "Perhaps you have mislaid the other one."

She gazed at his hand as he held out the card and then looked into his eyes with such a look of desperation that he felt moved.

"I have not mislaid it. If you but knew the number of times I have taken up my pen to send word to you."

"Yet did not . . . why?"

A little frown creased her forehead. "You have only recently returned from the battlefield. Your family . . . wife and children . . . would welcome every moment of your company. I had no justifiable reason to demand your presence here."

"Enough reason to be forced to deny the impulse on many occasions, it seems," he said, putting the card back in his pocket. "I would not have pledged my assistance if I had no intention of keeping that pledge. I have already spent a few days with my father in Sussex. As to wife and children, I am blessed with neither."

Her smile made him glad he had abandoned his night of sexual delusion.

"How glad I am that you did not wait for a summons, Captain Torrington. My companion would like to meet you. Can you stay long enough for a glass of Madeira?"

"Of course. It would be most welcome."

There followed a scene that had him completely bemused and in some way conscious that it was more stimulating than the night of passion he had planned. An elderly retainer was brought, protesting, into the room, wearing a large plaid shawl over an obvious nightgown—snatched from her bed, no doubt. The comical servant girl was sent for the Madeira and tea tray for the ladies with a swift aside from her mistress—an order that threw the girl into a paroxysm of glee as to what Cook would make of it all.

It was like being part of a stage farce, and Rupert

would have found it hilarious had he not felt a strange compassion for his friend's sister. She must live a life that daily stripped her of her youth and spirits. Is that what Edward would have wished for her?

The old nanny submitted to his determined pleasantries with ill grace, but he had her measure and soon rendered her silent. Was the old woman wrapped up in her real and imaginary illnesses the only companion Harriet Deane had? Good God, she must be at her wits' end!

The servant girl returned with a tray containing a bottle of Madeira and one glass. She went to her mistress and bobbed. "It's took me four minutes, madam, and Cook is crying like misery-me. She says she'll end up in the river if you turn her out tonight. The tea tray's outside. I told her you might think more kindly if the tea was ready at the same time." She put the Madeira on the table, swung around, and hurried out, to reappear carrying a heavy oval tray set with tea things. She bobbed again. "Begging your pardon, ma'am, but if I could tell Cook four minutes wasn't too long, it would make things easier downstairs."

"Of course I shall not turn her out, Bessie. Tell her quickly before we have the kitchen awash," was the strained answer.

"Very well, madam."

Casting an accusing look at Rupert, the girl hurried off, leaving behind her a sizzling silence.

Rupert grew more disturbed. The household smacked of Bedlam. Whatever had Edward been about to leave his sister in such straits? Lost in far-off visions, he returned to the present to find Harriet Deane looking at him in flushed confusion.

"It is no use, Captain Torrington. You see how unrelated to life we are," she said with a candor that went straight to his soul. "One unexpected guest throws us into a muddle. Whatever must you think?"

He frowned. "I think it is time your relations with life improved. Do you ride, Miss Deane?"

"I have not done so for some time, I fear. Miss Frisby is no longer able to accompany me," she said in something of a daze.

"Then grant me the pleasure of doing so. If we ride in the park, your companion could sit comfortably in the carriage, could she not?"

"Unfortunately the moist chill at this time of the year makes her reluctant to venture out," was the reply he was sure came with automatic regularity.

Her reply annoyed him for some reason, and his tone was brisk with authority in consequence. "With a hot brick at her feet and rugs over her knees, I feel confident she will be comfortable."

They both turned to the elderly woman. The advanced hour and the warmth of the fire had been too much for her. She was soundly asleep, her gray head hanging forward, her feet stretched toward the warmth.

Harriet turned quickly toward him, and the becoming blush on her cheeks was not due to the fire glow. "There is my ultimate betrayal, sir," she said with touching candor. "My chaperone is so seldom needed she sleeps soundly at ten every night."

Knowing it was strictly against the conventions of society, feeling that he was putting her in an impossible position, he nevertheless asked, "Must I go now?"

She seemed completely unprepared for the words

and just sat looking at him for a moment or two with growing disbelief in her eyes. "I . . . I cannot think that you would wish to stay longer, sir, but if you do, it will save the evening from complete disaster."

"Saving disasters is my forte," he said with a smile as he rose to his feet. "I was offered Madeira, I believe." Having poured some into the glass, he held it out to her. "This will improve your relations with life far quicker than tea."

She hesitated. "There is but one glass."

He pressed it on her. "My months in the Crimea also taught me to take my wine in whatever vessel that offers itself. A teacup will suffice, believe me." He poured some into the flowered cup and held it aloft. "Your very good health, Miss Deane."

Her smile warmed him more than the Madeira. "If Nanny should awaken to see me in a convivial mood and with a glass in my hand, she will be scandalized," she told him in breathless amusement.

"It does not take much to scandalize her, I would venture to guess," he said a trifle sharply as he sat down opposite her. "Quite the wrong companion for a young woman of your disposition, Miss Deane. Why do you spend your time with her as sole company?"

She averted her eyes from his for a moment. "Because I am hers."

"Oh?"

Her gaze came up again, and he realized she was the most vital person he had ever met.

"If I turned her away, she would be quite alone in the world. After her lifetime of service how could I show her such ingratitude? As a soldier you must know something of duty and self-sacrifice. Nanny's life has been all that. Would you abandon your men after such loyalty?"

"We do."

They sat for a long moment in the sweet intimacy of the fireglow, seemingly loath to say more, yet wanting the moment to go on and on. He could see it written in her expression with the honesty he found so irresistible in her and felt it in his own breast. Eventually he said, "Why did you not send for me long ago?"

She took a deep breath. "I think because I was afraid you would not come."

Chapter Two

Harriet Deane and Rupert Torrington were taken by storm in the days that followed—each in a different way. The young man, used to indulging in the wild pleasures of those forced by convention to put on an outer coat of virtue, found himself fighting that which was fast overtaking him and becoming a helpless loser. And the spirited young woman well able to cope with most situations capably found herself in the only one she was ill equipped to handle.

Harriet could run her household with sense and economy; she could supervise servants and companion with firm consideration; she could put down insolent young men with a word and deflate pompous old ones in an instant; she could face disappointment without wringing her hands and despair without weeping. But love and overwhelming physical desire were new emotions, and they ruled her instead of her ruling them.

Inexperienced, and with no one in whom to confide her new state, she gave her heart and soul unreservedly to the man who had walked into the blackness of her life and illumined it with a brilliance she had not believed possible. The young woman for past years obliged and accustomed to take command of her household and those around her found the natural dominance of Rupert's masculine personality thrilling, and she succumbed to it willingly. As an adolescent in the throes of first love finds it easy to gild the loved one's every action with the glow of her own hopes, so Harriet loved so deeply it was possible to accept that a man like Rupert Torrington—a strong-willed, determined fellow spirit—could feel about her as she did him.

In love, as in every other aspect of her life, Harriet was honest, vigorous, and wholehearted. It did not matter to her one jot that he had come from humble origins. She reread Edward's letter from the Crimea telling of his first meeting with the man destined to become his friend.

> *I have come across a capital fellow amongst those regiments who have come out as reinforcements. He gave me a cheese, for which I was most grateful, not having seen any for several weeks. We formed an instant rapport, and it was only later that I discovered his family is in* TRADE. *One would never guess it, for he has the most pleasant manners and there is not a trace of it in his voice. Of course, he went to all the right schools, and the Torringtons are reputed to be one of the wealthiest families in England (I hope to win some of it from him at cards), but there are those who cold-shoulder him. I intend to disregard his ancestry. I cannot see what it should have to do with whether I like the fellow or not. All the more credit to him that he can play the*

gentleman when his grandfather was no more than an eel fisherman. (I can imagine the lift of your eyebrows at that, but I promise you he is most unexceptional and could grace even a duchess's salon.) I hope you will meet him when we return from this tiresome war.

The fact that her brother had been so close to Rupert made her own love for him more precious—as if she were continuing a triangular bond. As for the stigma of trade, there were a good many blue-blooded people she knew who imagined their ancestry allowed them to behave like fishermen and be treated as nobles. Her own family's distant links with aristocracy had never influenced Harriet's relations with people. Her frank nature had led her to treat others the way they deserved to be treated—whoever they might be. In her estimation Rupert Torrington deserved the highest respect and admiration in all that he did—not, as many felt, because of the Torrington millions but because she saw in him the qualities she had searched for and never found in others.

As winter faded into spring, Harriet's life and personality became full, and the fact that she was as passionate in love as in anger began to color her every moment. Mourning for Edward prevented her from attending many social functions; that meant that the couple had more time to spend together and grew close quicker than they might have done. Morning rides in the park, afternoon strolls to feed the ducks on the lake, visits to galleries and exhibitions kept them free from the restrictions imposed by large gatherings and hastened the onset of something for which both had been unprepared. The sexual overtones of their moments together began to torment Harriet, who had had no previous experience of such attraction, and in typical fashion she made no coy protestations over his advances. Completely trusting and honest, she responded eagerly to every touch of his hand, every lingering kiss on her fingers, every fiery glance from eyes as brown as the darkest amber.

However, while Harriet had rushed willingly into love, Rupert resisted it as long as he could. Between their meetings he still visited courtesans, gaming houses, and those of his acquaintance who could be relied upon to uncork the champagne bottle and raise the roof. But he always went back to Harriet. As a born soldier he would not easily admit defeat, but almost against his will he found his mind more and more occupied and stimulated by his dead friend's sister until it was clear to him she had undermined his defenses so completely he could only surrender or be destroyed. Always a man of action, he made his decision.

Pagoda House stood at the end of a long drive bordered by palm trees that looked immediately incongruous in the heart of Sussex. The mansion itself—if it could be thus termed—further surprised the visitor, for it was a replica of a Chinese house of considerable grandeur.

Rupert had always disliked it intensely. It had been built on a whim of his grandfather—a madman, in Rupert's opinion—but mad or not, he had made a fortune in the East Indies and, later, in the Far East. He had also left his descendants with a legacy that gave them wealth but a family reputation that was hard to live down. Reckless, unscrupulous, pirating the high seas and other men's business outlets, Garforth Torrington had established the Battle Trading Company, named after his home village in Sussex. If the business had prospered, it had been at the cost of making enemies. Like many a shrewd and brilliant businessman, Garforth Torrington had used any tactic necessary to achieve his ends, looking on those who suffered at his hands as fools for letting themselves be so duped.

Aubrey Torrington had inherited his father's free-and-easy manner, but the strict Victorian society into which he made his debut as a merchant dictated a more restrained attitude in his dealings with others. As a result, the Battle Trading Company was respected, and it also flourished in its new role as dealers in high-class silk from China. If a little of the stigma of the founder still remained, Aubrey's conventional methods did much to overcome it—even if the man himself was an obvious son of the notorious Garforth. Rupert, of the next generation, fought his hardest to remove the last stigma of Garforth's deplorable legacy, and he possessed a very strong sense of integrity that astonished Aubrey, who ascribed it to an unfortunate twist in the nature of a boy who had heard too much for his own good when young. Only Rupert knew how wrong his father was.

He drove toward Pagoda House on a day in early spring, viewing it with renewed distate. Aubrey found the place exotically beautiful, but Rupert was quite open in his opinion of it.

"When you are gone, I shall sell the damned place," he had once warned his father. "Much better leave it to someone who will appreciate it, sir."

The last occasion on which Rupert had visited Pagoda House was on his return from the Crimea the previous November. He hoped his father had not gone off to China during the intervening four months. His visit to Sussex was being made on impulse, and his father would not be expecting to see him again so soon. Father and son maintained a relationship that was pleasant rather than dutiful, each man treating the other more as a friend than a kinsman.

They had had a serious confrontation when Rupert showed his determination to buy a commission in the army, but the son had a stronger will than the father, who had to acknowledge his son's right to follow his own heart's desire.

"A good manager will run the company far better than I until one of my sons takes over," he had told Aubrey seriously.

"Very well," had been the resigned reply. "Just ensure that you produce all those sons before getting yourself killed on some foreign battlefield."

On the whole, Aubrey was resigned to having a military son but was not averse to deploring the fact when company seas were stormy, and he was vastly relieved to see his son return unharmed from the war. It was on that occasion in November that Aubrey had referred to the sons Rupert had so far made no effort to produce. Because of that, Rupert was doubly anxious that the merchant had not decided to sail off across the world on company business just at the time when it was most important that he should be at home.

A liveried footman admitted him and expressed his pleasure at seeing Captain Torrington again. Rupert did not know his name—the servants all looked alike to him—and went straight into the lacquered morning room, instructing the manservant to inform his father he was there.

In no time at all he was invited to the first-floor study. To reach it, he passed through corridors lined with enormous pots and vases, urns and plates, bowls and grotesque animals—all treasures brought from India and China. The walls of the landing that ran around four sides of a huge square hall below were hung with vermilion silk, but Rupert passed by the display of a fortune without noticing it. He had more important matters on his mind.

Aubrey Torrington was at his desk and looked up with a smile crossing his handsome but weary face as his son entered.

"Rupert, why did you not let me know of your intended visit? I am off tomorrow to a silk convention. Do you stay long? Have you had luncheon, my boy?"

"Thank you, sir. I ate a tolerable meal at the inn. I intend to take no more of your time than an hour or two. How are you today?"

"A great deal irritated by the post. Here are three reports from my manager in Canton that make me distinctly uneasy. Those damned Chinese are up to their tricks again. I tell you, Rupert, there is not a more calculating country."

"They probably say the same of us," murmured Rupert.

"Eh? Nonsense! We have made quite plain to them our wishes with regard to their country. After a war with the rogues we signed treaties with them that indicated our intentions and their approval. Those treaties apparently have no meaning for them whatever." He frowned at Rupert's apparent lack of response and left his seat to come around the ornate desk toward him. "I know you don't give a damn about the company, but as an Englishman you must be aware of the situation and feel angered by the insults they are dealing us."

Sensing belligerence, Rupert gave an answer that was defensive. "I am watching events with a clear military eye, naturally. If the company and others like it are treated with aggression, it will be the army that will fight on their behalf." He half sat on the back of an ornate chair. "Forgive me, sir, but we are always rushing to defend others who cannot handle their affairs."

"The deuce you are!" exploded Aubrey. "Just how do you suppose merchants should handle this affair? We do not go around waving swords and firing guns at everyone to get our own way, as you do. Fight on our behalf, do you?" he raged. "Well, let me tell you, that is the easiest part of it. The army tramps into the situation with numbers in thousands, cannon roaring, and men swarming all over the place, cutting throats and hacking bodies to pieces, until the victim agrees to anything that is demanded. After that you all swarm off to do the same thing somewhere else, and *we* are left to cope with the aftermath. *We* have to live there; *we* have to deal with those who have been filled with hatred by your methods; *we* have to mend relationships and build up trust and goodwill again. If we fail, this country would not have enough wealth to maintain an army at all."

"Sir, I simply said–"

"How would your regiment fare without a colonel at its head, for that is as good a comparison as you will understand? We set up trading companies which will bring the Chinese wealth in exchange for their silk, tea, porcelain, and all kinds of sundry goods; we use our own armed ships to patrol the coast where pirates still fight for control of the seas; and we bring them the example of our own civilized way of life, yet they treat us as inferior creatures, call us barbarians. *Barbarians*, mark you! They show us plainly we are there under sufferance."

Rupert knew his father was venting all his pent-up rage on him as the first person to come in after he had read unpleasant news in the reports, and he tried to take interest.

"In my opinion, the situation will continue until we have ambassadors at the court of Peking," he ventured.

"My dear Rupert, that piece of wisdom has been expressed by one hundred and one men before you," he said bitingly. "At present the Chinese ignore our envoys with a serenity that suggests they do not exist. And now look at this." He waved a hand toward the reports. "The hoppo at Canton is trying to bleed us dry. Already we pay huge bribes so that he will not take our name from the lists of the best silk traders in the city and to stop him from impounding our unregistered cargoes. Bedford writes that one of our ships has been discovered taking in a private cargo of clocks—something the Chinese find fascinating—and the hoppo has made it clear he wants them for himself. If Bedford refuses to hand them over, he must pay an exorbitant fine for some trumped-up transgression. He has no choice but to hand over the clocks. That, on top of the bribes we are already paying. How can one deal with such people?"

"By calling their bluff," said Rupert swiftly. "Good God, you will never extract recognition from them if you meekly comply with their demands. You call them rogues; you are the same if you resort to bribery."

Aubrey flared up. "There speaks the voice of ignorance. You know nothing of trading practices. It is the only way these people will trade."

"Then withdraw. There are other lands and merchandise."

"Not nearly as financially rewarding as the China trade. But you would not know that."

"No, sir . . . but I do know that it is often necessary to gain one's ends through some small sacrifice."

"*Small sacrifice!* Have you looked at your bank balance of late? Without the China trade we would be ruined. Garforth made his mark there when it was opening out to only those men with courage, cunning, and ruthlessness enough to stay in the field. To pull out now would be the end for us."

"Oh, surely not, sir," he protested in his ignorance. "But while money overrides all other considerations, no acceptable and lasting code of practices will ever be achieved. I can still see the army being called in before long. The Chinese will not ignore guns, however great their serenity."

"The remark of a typical military man," said Aubrey in disgust. "Blast them into acceptance!" He came up to Rupert and also stared out of the window. "Think of it this way, man. If one of your privates wanted to get an important request to his colonel, he would get nowhere if the NCO refused to pass it to you or if you threw any such request in the wastebasket. He would be quite helpless to make his wishes known to the one person who could help his case. If he decided to get his way by rushing at the colonel's door, breaking it down, and standing over him with his rifle until he listened, it might get him what he wanted at that moment, but his future would be short indeed."

"All right, if the use of armed force does not appeal to you, what is your solution to the problem?" said Rupert, growing irritable with the discussion of something so serious when he had come to broach an important personal matter. "You and your associates appear to have tried everything else with no success."

Aubrey turned to him and sighed. "What use is it trying to discuss it with you, Rupert? You see things through entirely different eyes." He walked back toward his desk and fiddled with one of the reports from Canton. "These documents concern your future and that of those who will come after you, yet all you can talk of is your damned guns. The company has given you everything you have."

It was Rupert who sighed then. His father must be very worried indeed to take such a line. "I know that, sir. I have never been ungrateful."

"Just careless of something you take for granted." Aubrey turned and waved a report at his son. "You would find this completely incomprehensible. From the time you could crawl it was toy soldiers, castles, wooden swords. You were obsessed with battles and strategy, Napoleon and Wellington, cavalry and infantry, storming the heights and undermining the defenses. I suppose it is Garforth's aggressive spirit coming out in you in a different way, but I wish to God you would use some of your strength of personality to further the source of your income. Your captain's pay alone would not keep you for a week."

Feeling guilty, Rupert said, "The mercantile streak is not in me, as you have just said. I would be useless to the company. I know nothing of business matters or of silk."

"And have no wish to know." He put up a hand. "Oh, keep your protest to yourself, boy. I am no fool. Not only have you no heart for trade, but you despise it."

"Sir!"

"Yes, Rupert, in your heart you are ashamed of your heritage." He stroked his chin thoughtfully. "By some quirk of nature I was blessed with a son who has an innate nobility of character and who fiercely resents his lack of noble background. You see your grandfather as a villainous rogue—and maybe he was—but he took himself from a hovel on a Sussex beach into the homes of maharajas and mandarins, to exotic places of the world, and to an opulent mansion like this by his own effort and ability. He was a brilliant and courageous man, no matter what else is said about him." He looked around the study speculatively.

"I benefited greatly from his endeavors and worked hard to mitigate some of the evil effects of his rise in society. Because of that, you were able to buy a commission in your regiment rather than take the queen's shilling along with a pack of cutthroats and ruffians. The only thing your grandfather could not buy was a pedigree . . . and you suffer from that fact. As Mr. Torrington, silk merchant, it would not matter that your money had passed through dirty hands. Unfortunately you have chosen a profession that stands on its dignity and regards its members through a monocled eye." He stared at Rupert for a moment or two, then gave a faint smile. "I see the truth of my words on your face, my boy. You bear your vast wealth in the manner of a gentleman, but they will never totally accept you, you know. The mark of trade is stamped on you forever—as it will be on your heirs."

Something inside Rupert stung with the pain of salt on an open wound. "I was accepted into the regiment," he said stiffly.

"After being turned down by five others," Aubrey walked back to the window. "See how defensive you have grown at the very mention of social rejection." His hand fell on Rupert's shoulder. "You have all the fine qualities missing in my father and me. If only you would accept your inheritance, the company would have a distinguished future. But you must go chasing after something that gives you as much pain as pleasure." The fingers gripping his shoulder tightened. "I have seen the way they sneer, my boy, and wonder that you with your fighting spirit submit to such treatment."

"They do not matter," was the husky reply. "At Sevastapol they did not sneer."

"No, Rupert, I do not suppose they did. When it comes to laying down one's life for queen and country, they will allow anyone to do so."

Suddenly the afternoon seemed chill. Rupert felt as he had when a childhood playmate swept the toy soldiers from the table, declaring them to be silly in comparison with his sailing ships.

"Why did you not press me into the company's service if you feel so strongly on the subject, sir?"

Aubrey's handsome face lost a few of its formerly harsh lines.

"That nobility of character I mentioned just now would have been a great stumbling block to your career in the company." He sighed. "Loath though I am to admit it, you have chosen for yourself the perfect life for a man of your temperament."

"So I believe," said Rupert firmly, hoping it was the end of the matter.

He was wrong. Aubrey walked back to pick up the reports and stood staring at them in contemplation. "You never met young Bedford, did you?"

"Your agent? No, but I have heard of him and that affair that set him fleeing the country. I wonder that you care to trust such a blackguard."

His father looked across at him with eyes narrowed. "Yes, Rupert, you probably do. Here is the perfect example of what I have just been saying. You have joined the ranks of your fellows who frown on any man who does not play the game. It is my fault, I suppose, for sending you to those highfalutin schools and turning you into the perfect officer and gentleman. No, you would not approve of Bedford, but starting out as a highborn young officer, he has become a highly successful mercantile agent." He waved the reports at Rupert. "You will not find it easy to do the reverse, I think. Watch that your high ideals do not bring you down one day, that's all."

Having heard such warnings before, Rupert grew impatient. "I did not come here today to discuss my failings, sir. I think I know them well enough."

Aubrey relaxed upon hearing his son's sharp tone, and he held up his hands in surrender."Do not jump down my throat, my boy. It is just that I cannot accustom myself to having a son like you. You must be a changeling to spring from a long line of uncultured rogues."

Far from mending the situation, his words only increased Rupert's agitation further.

"Perhaps I am nót a Torrington. When you went back to China leaving your son not much more than an infant, perhaps two children were switched. After all, you saw no more of me until I was sixteen."

There was a moment's silence. "I never knew you felt that separation so strongly, my boy. Why have you never spoken of it before?"

Feeling cornered that he had been forced into an admission against his better judgment, Rupert struck out, "I was merely reminding you of it in the context of your disapproval of how I have turned out. I was left in the hands of schoolmasters and other disinterested authorities, and it is rather too much of you to have expected your son to have been raised as an uncultured rogue to suit your own requirements."

Aubrey flushed and straightened. "Oho, that is a little too much to the point, don't you think?"

"No more than some of the things you have said this afternoon. You have made me out to be a social climber of the worst kind, a military oaf who blunders into every situation with cannon blasting instead of intelligence and understanding, and a man spoiled by wealth he makes no effort to earn. I'm sorry if I do not live up to your hopes . . . but neither of us had any choice in our relationship, had we?" The bitterness of his own words surprised Rupert, as did the emotions he thought he had long forgotten. "If I had remained with you in China, I might have grown into a facsimile of Valentine Bedford. As it was, I had to develop along lines chosen for me by institutes and scholars."

"Lines that apparently encourage young men to resent paternal strictures," was the swift reply. Then Aubrey gave up his stand in the face of Rupert's greater staying power. "I'm sorry. That is a pompous remark to make to a son who has proved himself a man in the cruel rigors of war." He put a weary hand to his neck. "Oh, drop your guard, my boy. The hostilities are over." He eased the stiff muscles of his shoulder, saying, "I have no wish that you should be like Bedford . . . but he was a godsend when my doctor told me I must leave the debilitating climate of China for a while. His knowledge and expertise have enabled him to run the company with the greatest success these past three seasons."

Rupert was disarmed when a pang of guilt penetrated his anger. Aubrey had been very ill indeed when he returned to England, leaving his agent to run the Chinese end of the business, a task that should have been undertaken by the Torrington heir, of course.

"I shall go back before the next season begins," Aubrey went on. "Can't leave this state of affairs for too long, you know. A man should be there to run his own company."

"But will your health bear it, sir?"

"Oh, yes . . . yes," was the effusive reply. "Hong Kong is getting more civilized and plague-free every year."

They both fell silent for a moment. Then Aubrey said quietly, "You know why you were left in England, don't you? I visit your brothers' graves every time I visit Macao. Pathetic, tiny, so far from us or your poor mother just here in the churchyard. I think she never forgave me, even on her deathbed. She accompanied me to Macao only because she was afraid I would take other women at the end of the trading seasons, but she hated every day she spent there. I am a lusty man, Rupert, but she never gave me much affection. A hard, uncompromising woman she was, and when you were born, she did not even take you in her arms. I suppose the loss of two infant sons made her afraid to love the third . . . but there was no reason to reject me. I was not responsible for the yellow fever that took so many English infants that year, and I mourned them quite as much as she." He looked at Rupert in appeal. "I can't risk losing your good opinion also, my boy, I need affection, you know."

Rupert felt uncomfortably affected by the admission and found himself trying to console the older man in the only way he could think. "So I am persuaded on the occasions I meet you in the city."

A chuckle proved his success. "Ah, the little creatures are only too willing to cheer the lonely hours of a man in his prime. But I have not noticed any reluctance on their part to console you, either. They can never resist a scarlet coat."

Rupert laughed in relief. "I think it is a little more than the coat, sir. When I take it off, I have not noticed that they run away."

Now in a relaxed and genial mood, father invited son to take a glass of brandy. They left the study and walked together along another opulent corridor, all thoughts of China forgotten for the moment as they discussed the merits of various ladies of their acquaintance. It was only when both were comfortably settled that the older man asked what had prompted his son's visit.

Resting his glass on the side of the leather armchair, Rupert said, "I thought I should advise you that I am contemplating marriage. I have every confidence that my offer will be accepted."

The confession left his father with a suspended expression that slowly turned to one of high merriment. "You tell me *that* after the discussion we have just had? By God, you are the very devil, Rupert! Who is she, eh? Some saucy minx who has you by the coattails or the virtuous daughter of a noble, who will turn a blind eye to your amours?" He leaned back, ready to be entertained.

"Neither sir," was the slightly stiff reply. Suddenly,

with regard to Harriet Deane, he found his father's ribaldry unwelcome.

"Well . . . come then," Aubrey encouraged with eager curiosity. "Who is the young woman?" When his son was slow in answering, he continued, "I trust she *is* young. You have not made a fool of yourself over a fascinating widow, have you?"

It was then Rupert realized how very rakish his father had become of late. It was not going to be easy telling him of his future daughter-in-law.

"Miss Deane is the sister of a friend who was killed in the Crimea. I believe she is five-and-twenty years old."

"Mmm, I see. No schoolroom miss who has wrapped you around her little finger." Aubrey Torrington considered for a moment. "A good thing, perhaps. A bride who is fully matured is not likely to disappoint you within several years." He gave a knowing smile. "A discerning beauty who has finally succumbed, I take it?"

Anger began to flare in Rupert's breast. "I would not say so. Neither is she flirtatious, provoking or willful. Her looks are no more than pleasant. She has no dowry whatever, and there are a number of my acquaintances who would benefit from a little of her common sense and capability."

His father was puzzled, and it was a second or two before he asked, "But—but why have you chosen to marry her?"

Rupert replied in a determined but somewhat dazed manner. "I think because life without her would be unacceptable."

* * *

Mr. Adolphus Harkins was the middle partner in a small but reputable firm of solicitors. Professor Deane had always spoken highly of him, and Edward used to refer to him as "a good sort." But Harriet found him difficult. He was a man of rigid ideas, one of which was that females were brainless, fragile creatures who provided a necessary accessory for gentlemen—and nothing more.

When Professor Deane was alive, business was conducted through him, although it was Harriet who ran the household and accounts. After her father's death the solicitor had looked upon Edward as head of the family and consequently sent all correspondence through him. Since the regiment moved from place to place, letters took a long time to catch up with the young officer, and he sent them all back to Harriet when he thought of it.

Harriet was understandably incensed over such a ridiculous procedure, but nothing she did could budge Harkins from his opinion on what was not fitting for ladies. One morning in spring, however, she was full of martial spirit and determined to impress upon the man that like it or not, he must now acknowledge a lady as his client and do as she asked.

The cause of her present annoyance was a series of bills that had been presented yet again by three local tradesmen, requesting payment of accounts outstanding from the beginning of January. When they had arrived on Harriet's desk last month, she had sent them on to Mr. Harkins with a firm instruction to settle them immediately. She disliked being in debt and was annoyed to discover they had not been settled the first time. That morning they had appeared for the third time, and it was all too apparent the solicitor had ignored her letter. Being a woman of action, Harriet decided a personal exchange was necessary if the man were to be convinced, once and for all, that she was the only member of the Deane family left and, therefore, his only client.

During the short walk to the business premises of Podmore, Harkins and Belvedere, Harriet grew increasingly anxious over her financial position. Eight years ago, when she had taken over the running of the household to save the expense of a housekeeper, she had had to learn economy. As time passed, they were able to live in comfort as a result of her excellent management, but once her father had died and the solicitor had taken to sending everything to Edward, Harriet had found it difficult to keep her books in any kind of order. Gradually she had lost touch with the exact amounts remaining in the account, and she economized even further to compensate.

All her representations to her brother to speak to Mr. Harkins on the subject had produced no result. Edward had been a happy-go-lucky man who did not seem to understand the running of a household. Nor did he wish to try to do so. Nagging at the back of her mind as she walked briskly along the street was the knowledge that her economics had taken a setback recently. Since she had decided to go into half mourning last November, it had been necessary to purchase several new gowns in gray and lavender, plus—since Rupert had broken into her life with such devastating results—several bonnets and an outdoor shawl. She longed for much more than that, for he was followed by female glances whenever they walked in the park or rode together, and Harriet felt that she, in her somber gray and the same bonnet day after day must ill compare to the pretty, flirtatious creatures. But thrift had to be put before vanity. Small wonder that the prospect of unpaid household bills made her most anxious to thrash out the matter with the man who ran her affairs. Increasing her pace to the extent of making Bessie run to keep up with her, Harriet vowed determinedly to transfer her business to another solicitor if Harkins still refused to acknowledge her right to his attention.

On reaching the discreet offices occupied by gentlemen engaged in a discreet profession, Harriet marched up the indented wooden staircase to the second floor, ignoring the stares of those who watched her bold progress. Bessie scurried behind her, her face such a picture of dejection that her mistress could not help being amused.

"My dear girl, you are not being led to the scaffold," she chided.

"No, madam," agreed Bessie miserably. "But I always get the mulligrubs in such places. They remind me of the orphanage. The smell of old offices is the same no matter where you go. The beadle always made us wait outside till kingdom come just so's we'd be shaking in our shoes by the time we went in."

Harriet smiled. "Mr. Harkins will not keep us waiting, that I promise . . . and it will be he who is shaking in his shoes by the time I have finished."

"Yes, madam." Bessie sniffed, quite as dejected as before.

The plump, pale-faced clerk turned red when Harriet swept in, demanding to speak to Mr. Harkins. He muttered immediately that it was out of the question.

"Why, pray?" she demanded coldly.

"He is not here, that is why." His bright pink tongue washed over his puffy lips.

It was an obvious lie and incensed Harriet further. "Then I shall wait until he returns. Kindly fetch me a chair."

Since the only chair in the room was the one occupied by the clerk himself, it posed him a problem—one she knew he would be forced to solve in the way she wished. With fumbling haste he moved it from behind his desk to the center of the room, excused himself, and vanished up a half staircase and around a corner to knock on a door. Harriet was irate but satisfied to hear a voice bid him enter. She would deal with Harkins in like manner if he refused to see her. She glanced up at the cringing Bessie and smiled.

"If there is one thing gentlemen cannot bear, it is a woman sitting in the middle of a room watching them while they try to be busy. It completely unnerves them."

"No more than it does me, madam," Bessie assured her, the little pointed face very straight. "When I sees a gentleman behind a desk, I turn into a blancmange straight off."

"Pray do not do so today, or it will completely destroy the possibility of my winning the day. Gentlemen remain behind desks only because they feel the need for something to protect them, you know. I am willing to wager that Mr. Harkins will not venture out from his position of safety while I am with him. Mark my words, Bessie, while they might be prepared to face a barrage of cannon, they find an enraged woman too much for them."

"Hmph! There's one gentleman I can think of who does not," she said with feeling.

Harriet gave a small laugh. "Captain Torrington cannot be classed with other gentlemen. He does not run with the field."

"Oh," was the faint comment, the servant girl not understanding the phrase but recognizing the glow that sat upon her mistress at the mention of his name. Her trembling stopped, but she grew very pensive until the clerk returned to inform them that his employer had, in fact, just come in but regretfully was engaged for the remainder of the day.

"If Madam had made an appointment . . ." he tailed off awkwardly.

"I did," said Harriet promptly. "That is why I could not believe Mr. Harkins was not here. I assured him I was always punctual." She glanced at the large fly-blown clock on the wall. "We have already wasted five minutes. I would be obliged if you would remind him of my appointment immediately."

The little obese man was torn by indecision. It was clear he dared not discount the possibility that the visitor *had* made an appointment, and Mr. Harkins could well have forgotten it since he had been a trifle absentminded of late. It was even clearer that he wished to be rid of a lady who was proving so embarrassing. After a comical ritual of changing from foot to foot that suggested he could not decide which way to go, he lurched desperately in the direction of the stairs once more.

Harriet followed him, emboldened by growing anger over her treatment. As soon as the clerk knocked and entered, she swept into the office, a tall, slender creature in dove gray silk, gray bonnet trimmed with purple, and matching gloves.

"Good afternoon," she greeted the solicitor with sweet determination. "The weather is delightful for the time of year, is it not?" Looking pointedly around for a chair, she indicated one in the corner with her parasol and smiled at the clerk. "Just here will do nicely."

He moved the chair to the spot indicated, and she sank gracefully onto it to face the solicitor, who was still crouching half in, half out of his seat with an indescribable expression on his egg-shaped face.

"I cannot spare too long for our discussion," she went on, "so I shall state immediately the reason for my visit. It concerns the accounts from Roberts, Meddleton, and—"

"Miss Deane!" intoned Mr. Harkins, in shock. "This is most . . . most . . ."

"—kind of me to call? I thank you for saying so," said Harriet smoothly, "but since you did not appear to have received my directive concerning the matter last month, I felt it best to broach it in person."

Her dominance of the scene ended then as Adolphus Harkins recovered from what he regarded as eccentric behavior from a female. A curt nod of dismissal sent the clerk back to his desk, and then the solicitor prepared to end the interview very summarily. Coming around from behind his desk, he said, "I see that the tragic death of Lieutenant Deane so soon after the loss of the esteemed professor has left you sorely tried, Miss Deane, so please allow me to send for your carriage."

It was a determination, not a plea, and Harriet had no intention of being ushered from the office in such rapid manner.

"My brother's death was tragic in the extreme," she agreed firmly, "but I believe I have survived it with tolerable composure. As I am now all alone in the world, I am obliged to handle my own affairs, and it is to this end that I feel we should have some discussion. As the one remaining member of the family your good services must be directed toward–"

"Ah . . . no, Miss Deane. I am happy to say your fears are groundless." He smiled thinly, with a trace of condescension, rocking back and forth on the balls of his feet. "Having had the honor of serving a distinguished family for a number of years, I would not find it in my nature to neglect my duty when adversity struck, dear lady."

Harriet saw he was preparing to make a lengthy speech and read in his tone a pity that renewed her anger. The man was suggesting that grief had made her distracted, not responsible for her invasion of his sanctum. It was clear to her that he *must* be made to accept her competence as mistress of her own life.

"I am sure you have served the family most diligently, Mr. Harkins, but I do not have overmuch time to spare and would be obliged if an explanation of these could speedily be given to me." She put the accounts on the desk before him. "Why am I being pestered for payment when I sent instructions to settle the matter over four weeks past?"

His pale eyes registered neither confusion over nor interest in her words. Indeed, he did not even glance at the papers she produced. She felt suddenly as if the whole scene were unreal—the dusty ill-lit office, the aging man in black formal attire—and her anger changed into a strange apprehension.

"I am awaiting a reply from Mr. Dominic Ralston on several matters, one of which is the settlement of accounts still outstanding. Everything is well in hand, Miss Deane."

Her feeling of unreality increased. "Mr. Dominic Ralston?" she repeated vaguely.

"The remaining male relative of Professor Deane." Harkins smoothed his lapels. "I pride myself on my diligence in tracing him."

Harriet swung around on the small chair to follow his progress to the door of his office. "I should know my own family, sir, and I am all that is left of it."

Harkins stopped, his fleshy face showing his distaste for the forcefulness that was being shown by one of the gentle sex and also his annoyance at being obliged to continue the unwelcome interview.

"By dint of much industry I was able to trace Mr. Ralston to his present abode. He is a gentleman of some six-and-thirty years, the one surviving son of Professor Deane's second cousin."

Harriet found herself at a loss for the right words. "I . . . Mr. Harkins, what has . . . this gentleman of six-and-thirty . . . what has he to do with my affairs?"

"It behooves me, Miss Deane, to refer all business to him, as the sole male relative," said Harkins righteously.

"The son of my father's second cousin!" she exploded. "That is ridiculous—quite out of the question! In all my years there has been neither sight nor mention of a second cousin or of his sons alive or dead. If this man truly exists, then he had best remain where he has always been—completely divorced from the Deanes." Bosom heaving, Harriet rose, clutching the handle of her parasol with some force. "Are you telling me that my household accounts are being referred to this . . . this . . . *complete stranger*? How dare you do so?" When Harkins made no comment, she went on, "Where does Mr. Dominic Ralston live, if you please?"

"Smithson's Creek. *America*," he finished hesitantly.

If she had felt a sense of unreality before, Harriet then wondered if her wits had altogether left her. Swallowing hard, she said, "Am I to take it that since my brother's death all family business has been forwarded to America? I do not believe it—*cannot* believe it. The prospect is too near to lunacy."

Harkins was looking exceedingly flushed by now. "Legal matters to a lady, if I might venture, are often incomprehensible. That is why—"

"Ho, do not give me that!" cried Harriet in a fury. "I understand well enough your reasons for this. There is nothing in the world will make you acknowledge me as your client if there is a gentleman anyway remotely connected to the matter. May I inquire what Mr. Ralston feels of the situation, or may I not even be consulted that far?"

Harkins drew himself up. "Naturally, it took awhile before I was successful in tracing the gentleman, and mail takes some months to reach the extremities of that continent. However, I am hopeful of receiving word from Mr. Ralston by the autumn."

"The *autumn*, Mr. Harkins!" she cried. "No, this is really too much. I have already suffered from the inconvenience of having correspondence follow my brother's regiment all over England and the Balkans only to be redirected to me, but I will not wait until *autumn* for this far-distant colonial to tell you what I can say plainly at this very moment. I am my father's child and, as such, the only person concerned with matters pertaining to the Deane family now that my brother is dead." So great was her passion she found it difficult to retain a steady tone. "I would not care if there were *fifty* sons of my father's second cousin scattered over the globe. I'm of age and in direct line of descent. My money is my own to deal with as I think fit."

"There is no money, Miss Deane," he said with some force and undisguised regret at the disclosure.

For a moment or two Harriet stared at the man while her fury abated somewhat.

Mr. Harkins was now a sympathetic and embarrassed figure. "I had hoped Mr. Ralston—" He broke off unhappily. "Colonial gentlemen. Often amass great wealth, Miss Deane."

"It was your duty to have informed me of this . . . indeed, it was," said Harriet in a daze. "No money? Where has it gone?"

Harkins looked most unhappy. "Lieutenant Deane was at the war . . . a strain on any young gentleman, I venture to suggest." He tugged at his tight, starched collar. "The inaccessibility of the battlefield, the loss of mail packets at sea . . . it is not to be wondered at if your brother had no notion of his latest affairs of finance. With no other pastime to lighten the grim days . . ." He tailed off, delicately refraining from mentioning a subject unsuitable for a lady's ears.

A woman she might be, but Harriet was sufficiently acquainted with worldly matters to recognize what she was being told. Edward had gambled away his fortune and her future while he gambled with his life. Dear, gentle Edward, the last person to wish her to suffer, had little thought there would be no tomorrow on which to recoup his losses. Her throat tightened with grief. Always the optimist, Edward would have fought a war believing his life charmed. Thank God he had died instantly, or his last hours would have been tormented by remorse.

"So my brother lost heavily at games of chance," she said to Harkins. "Then there is nothing to be done but redeem the trust bonds left to him by my father," she continued in tones that were meant to hide the flutter of apprehension in her breast. She had been frugal before; how would she manage now? "It is a pity they have to be surrendered, but I will have no debts on my hands. See to it directly, if you please."

The elderly man flushed a deeper red, finding it difficult to meet her eyes. Regrettably Lieutenant Deane surrendered the bonds some months ago when I wrote to inform him of the state of his personal account and remind him that there was little to his credit but the trust bonds. Little did I expect to receive an offhand missive directing me to use them to settle any outstanding personal debts." He looked at her with apology. "Your brother added that he was shortly expecting an encouraging increase in his fortunes. I mistakenly took it that he meant a payment of back salary from the military. In wartime the paymaster often finds it impossible to trace . . . I mean, so much moving about and young gentlemen exchanging into other regiments—" He broke off miserably at her disparaging look.

"So the bonds are gone forever in payment of gaming debts?" Trying to remain calm in the face of calamity, she went on. "Well, it is useless to brood on things that cannot be remedied. It seems the only course left open is for me to sell the house and live in something smaller—a cottage, perhaps. Such a residence is too big for two spinsters, after all, and a move would be an advantage."

Here Harkins underwent an astonishing change into aggression, and she could not at first think why.

"Miss Deane, your . . . your *insistence* on entering my office this morning, and your . . . *determination* . . . to oblige me to reveal facts I strongly feel are Mr. Ralston's concern means I have to tell you your house was fully mortgaged last year on the instructions of Lieutenant Deane. Perhaps you will now understand why I am endeavoring to my utmost to find your distant relation before the most dreadful of fates overcomes you."

The most dreadful of fates? Harriet began to tremble. What was the man suggesting?

"If my brother mortgaged the house to the full, there surely must be—" She broke off at the swift guilty flush that flooded Harkins's face. "Sir, is there nothing left, nothing at all?"

"Miss Deane . . . ma'am . . . you must understand that between gentlemen debts of honor are regarded as the first to be settled. It is a matter of principle that I well understood, and Lieutenant Deane relied upon my devotion to duty in this matter." He grew more and more prosy, as if by doing so he would put off an evil moment of revelation. "One would not expect a lady to understand such things, in the normal course of events, but since you have made a point of—"

"What are you trying to find the courage to tell me, sir?" said Harriet in dangerously quiet tones. "However unpleasant it might be, I wish you will get to the root of it."

The color receded from his face, leaving it the unpleasant shade of candlewax. "The loan on the mortgage is almost run out, ma'am. Lieutenant Deane lost heavily with the greater part in trying to find a run of luck that would enable him to redeem the mortgage. He died before that happened." Here he fiddled with some files on the shiny surface of his desk. Then he decided on delivering the final blow. "Regrettably I am responsible for further reducing the sum, albeit unwittingly. Your brother lost a great deal of his fortune to the same man—a fellow officer—whose banker is the type of man of business I fortunately do not often deal with. Sharp, pushing, lacking in finesse, he presents his accounts with unmannerly speed on the first day of each month and presses for payment if I show the slightest sign of tardiness." He looked at her then with sincere regret in his eyes—the first sign that he possessed the normal human emotions toward a client that he had given her. "I . . . I settled one such account only after he had accosted me at the club and mentioned the matter, but it was only when you sent me the tragic news of your brother's death that I realized the transaction had gone through *after* the date of his demise. Believe me, Miss Deane, if it had not been for the fact that the sad bulletin arrived so long after the event, that last sum would never have been paid."

He clasped and unclasped his fat hands in distress. "I give the other man credit for not knowing the truth either, but debts of honor are normally canceled when a man falls in battle. His speed in presenting the account and my own dislike of his methods led to the sum changing hands too soon for the situation to be saved. I . . . I blame myself for being hurried into something that is normally treated with courteous consideration between men of business."

Harriet felt numbed, but one thing he had said stuck in her mind and filled her with strong revulsion. "You said my brother lost mostly to the same man—a fellow officer?"

Harkins nodded, still very unhappy.

"Then he *would* have known when Edward fell, would have been there during that same battle, would surely have canceled debts there and then? Who—who is this man?" she asked through a dry throat.

"A Captain Rupert Torrington. The deeds of your house are held by the Battle Trading Company, of which he is a major shareholder, and unless we can raise the money to redeem them, you are liable to pay rent to him which you cannot afford. Now you will see why it is imperative to contact Mr. Ralston as soon as possible."

His voice faded away as Harriet felt her body turn icy cold. The solicitor turned into a dangling puppet without a voice, even while his mouth formed words that were never uttered. The door opened silently, and her feet made no sound on the wooden staircase as she floated down it. Bessie was waiting in the outer office and ran after her, opening and shutting her mouth like a mute, costumed mouse. Out in the street carriages ran on soundless wheels, the horses seeming to trot on tiptoe along the cobbles. A dog ran past, throwing its jaws open and shut in silent barking. The plaintive cries of peddlers were given by dumb vendors. Laughing children had lost their vocal cords. There was only one sound in that otherwise-noiseless world: the sobbing of her broken spirit.

Chapter Three

Rupert left Pagoda House in a thoughtful mood. His father had been less than delighted at his description of Harriet, cautioning him to think seriously before rushing into an unwise alliance at the early age of twenty-seven.

He had to admit that there was much truth in his father's words. It was very unlike him to seek the company of a young woman of Harriet's type. His heart did not bleed for the fair sex as a rule, and yet concern for a brown-haired spinster with no claim to beauty had sent him to her door again and again. Could it simply be that she resembled her brother too strongly for his peace of mind?

No, no, no. Perhaps that first evening, when he had thrown her into confusion by his late and unexpected visit, perhaps that time he had been driven there by allegiance to his dead friend. But never after that. In four short months he had come to realize his life would be empty without her. Starting with admiration, compassion, and a sense of incredulity at finding a woman who so complemented him in every way, he had grown to love her, heart and soul. Her face was not beautiful, but it shone just for him; her eyes held the glory of honest adoration; she smiled, and everything he did was just for her.

Having taken a healthy interest in women for the past ten years, he had grown accustomed to bringing about their surrender in the shortest possible time, then waving good-bye. This time he wanted to stay and discover all that time would reveal about a woman he found so compelling. He fell into a reverie, and when he arrived at his destination, all his father's warnings had flown, leaving thoughts of Harriet lying sweetly on his mind.

The village was some fifteen miles from Battle on the road to London. Rupert had discovered the old mill on his return from the Crimea, and from that discovery had sprung an idea—an idea that appeared in practice to be working. He drove into the millyard, immediately approving of its tidy state and the sounds of industry from within the building. He grinned as he leaped from the seat and made his way toward the door, now neatly repaired. The familiar roar of Sergeant Knott's voice could be heard from inside the lofty mill. With Knott in charge, Rupert need have no fears for the efficient running of the place.

Entering the mill, he was further cheered, even if deafened, by the noise of cogs, ratchets, and grinding plates, all driven by the great waterwheel. The air was thick with pale, powdery dust that set him coughing, but he followed the sound of his ex-sergeant's voice until he came upon the man castigating a strapping young lad with one ear missing and the whole left side of his face and neck puckered like a purple prune.

Sergeant Knott broke off his remonstrations concerning the careless spillage of a sack of flour when he spotted his visitor. His face smiled with genuine pleasure, and so did that part of the lad's face that could still move.

"Captain Torrington, you should've let us know you was coming, straight you should. Come outside, sir. This place sounds worse than a field kitchen at dinnertime."

"Actually, I want to take a look at the entire place," shouted Rupert above the clatter.

"I'll take you around in a minute," promised the sergeant as he led the way out into the sunshine. Turning at the doorway, he explained, "There's one or two things to tell you first, sir, and it's quieter out here."

Outside, Rupert lowered his voice to normal as he inquired after the man's wife.

The weather-beaten face softened. "Mrs. Knott's fine, sir. There's color in her cheeks now, same as there is in young Wixby's girl—and it's all thanks to you. Now, just a moment, sir," he continued as Rupert shrugged off his words, "I know you ain't the kind of gentleman to want flattery—never have been—but you must let me speak straight on behalf of us all. We know where we'd all be now if you hadn't done this. We serves our country; then, when we aren't fit to carry on no longer, the army pays us off and forgets us."

"Times are changing, Knott," said Rupert quietly. "The repercussions from the Crimea are being felt in very high places. Things will be different before long."

Knott walked with ease on his wooden limb as he led Rupert across to a small whitewashed cottage. "Mebbe, sir. I don't have your intelligence . . . nor your faith. But I do know my wife would more'n likely be in her grave from the consumption by now and little Meg Wixby would've starved if we had depended on the army for help." He stopped and faced Rupert with unashamed emotion. "What you've done here, sir, is like a miracle."

"It's an experiment, not a miracle, man. All I have done is made it possible for you to come here. If you don't make it work, the whole scheme will be abandoned. I told you that at the outset." He looked around at the peaceful rural scene and smiled. "But I am very impressed with the start you have made. Are they all working well?"

"Now that I have put the fear of God into Wright . . . yes, sir."

"Oh, what is the fault with Wright?" Rupert asked sharply. "He was a good enough soldier."

"Ah, that he was . . . but he figures he don't *have* to do as I say now there's no army regulations to back my orders. Not pulling his weight, he wasn't, so I up and told him we was all here through your generosity and each dependent on the other. I sez to him that if he let us down, he'd be letting *you* down—spitting in your eye, so's to speak. I sez it wouldn't take much for us all to be back where we was when you found us—wimmin and nippers, too."

"Mmm . . . and he took it to heart?"

Knott grinned sheepishly. "Well, sir, there's another thing as happened that might better account for it than my words. Corporal Stoke's widow arrived here after the train ticket you sent her, and Wright has taken a real shine to her. Working like Mother Malone he is, just to impress her." His grin broadened. " 'Tis astonishing what a good woman can do to a man."

Rupert grinned back happily. "It certainly is."

"If they decides to get married, sir, is it all right for them to have Mabbs's old cottage?"

Rupert's smile faded. "Yes, of course. It's a great pity about Mabbs. You've heard no more of him, I suppose?"

The burly man shook his head. "Quiet he was, and thought the world of that girl. It broke him up proper when she went off with that traveling peddler. Todd him to his face, she did, that she couldn't do with half a man any longer."

Rupert's thoughts flew immediately to a tent at Balaklava, and he thanked God Harriet had never seen her brother as "half a man." Hot on the heels of that thought came another. Would she turn from him if he ever returned to her as these soldiers here had returned from battle? Could he ever bring himself to face her if such a thing happened?

Knott broke into his tormenting thoughts. "Mabbs knew it was best for us all, and that's why he went. He knew this scheme is no charity home, as you keeps pointing out, Captain, and we can't afford to keep those who are afflicted inside their heads."

They had reached the cottage door now, and Knott said, "You'll take a cup of tea with us, sir? Mrs. Knott'll be real pleased to see you."

Rupert smiled his assent and dipped his head beneath the low lintel before stepping into the spotless room.

"Have you traced Private Smithson's widow yet, sir?" asked Knott as he followed his former company commander indoors. "We could do with another woman about the place to help with mending the sacks."

Rupert turned quickly. "Yes, a piece of great good fortune led me to follow a lead her brother gave, and the poor woman was found in a cellar in Manchester, very ill indeed. She is recovering slowly, and I trust she will be fit enough to travel here within the month. My agent reports that she is very willing to join you. There's no guarantee that she will be suitable or that she will fit in with the group. That will be for you to decide, and I'll try to find employment for her elsewhere if you say she cannot stay. But Smithson was a stickler for the rules, and I should imagine the widow would be amenable."

"God bless you, sir."

Rupert shook his head. "Not me—all of you here. You have taken your opportunity and worked hard. I admire you all. Mine has been the easy part of the scheme." He turned as a thin, prematurely gray woman walked in. "Good afternoon, Mrs. Knott. You are looking much better than on my last visit."

The careworn face became radiant. "Captain Torrington, it is a pleasure to have you in my kitchen again. It so happens I have made one of my ginger cakes you like so much."

Rupert laughed. "Is there ever a time when you do not have one of your excellent ginger cakes in reserve? You are a remarkable woman, Mrs. Knott."

* * *

When he left the mill, Rupert was feeling elated. His visit to Sussex had filled him with confidence and happiness. Time would persuade his father that Harriet was the perfect partner, and the experiment with the mill was proving successful.

He spent the remainder of the journey back to London lost in thoughts of the scheme whereby he had enabled some discharged and disabled soldiers, and soldiers' widows, of his company in the Crimea to survive the penalty of war. Strongly against the present system that cast such people aside, he had used his great wealth to put into operation a plan to offset hardship and offer a useful and productive livelihood to those who would most likely end up in the gutters otherwise. Sergeant Knott was the son of a miller and knew the business. Under his command, the ill-assorted and crippled group had become a contented community, each of its members knowing he must contribute to the best of his ability or leave.

As Rupert had said, his part had been the easy one. Dipping his hand into his pocket made little difference to his bank balance, but those limbless or disfigured men, or lonely bereaved women, had had to work to get along together and to cope with the limitations that went with their disabilities. If they failed, there was no other chance for them. It was amazing how the country air had built up the men's strength and put roses in the cheeks of the women and children. It was also amazing how quickly Knott had taught them to become miller's apprentices.

Although he knew that these were still early days and that problems were bound to arise, Rupert thought seriously of looking for another suitable place—a blacksmith's and farrier's forge, perhaps. There were many crippled cavalrymen who might be suitable candidates for such a place. He sighed. If only he could persuade the authorities to try such a scheme! But shortage of funds made it impossible—even if they would listen. Regiments were clamoring for money to keep themselves running. What use was it for him to campaign so strongly for new weapons and, at the same time, put forth ideas for charity schemes? Of course, the guns must come first . . . and they must come quickly if the British soldiers were to maintain their fighting superiority. At any time there might be a war in China and the need for a crack force.

His father had suggested that the situation was worsening in Canton, and any man with sense could see that all it would take would be sufficient provocation to set the Western powers on the road to force the Chinese into final acceptance of their treaties and diplomatic representatives.

His heart leaped at the thought of the regiment's possible journey to China, and for a while he mused on the prospect of war in the East. Would they be ready? What of the depleted regiments—their outmoded guns and unsuitable uniforms?

At some stage in his reverie it occurred to him that a call to war would mean he must leave Harriet in England when he sailed off for a year or so. The thought dampened his enthusiasm for action, and he thereupon decided there was no reason to delay his proposal of marriage. If the regiment should be sent away, it would be far better for his beloved to be happily and comfortably settled as his wife than left in her present drear and lonely situation until he came back. *If* he came back!

At that, his mind went back to those women he had left at the mill. Better for Harriet to be his widow with the Torrington name and wealth to protect her than a spinster waiting forever for a man who would not return for her. So strongly did he feel the need to assure her of his love and protection that he made the decision to speak to her on the following morning.

Once he was determined on such a course, it was a severe setback to be told that duty would demand his presence at barracks the following day. He requested, wheedled, bribed, swore and threatened, but the adjutant refused to allow him to apply for the colonel's permission to miss the previously unexpected visit of a royal duke. The adjutant—heir to a title—did not like Rupert, but even had they been the best of friends, it would have made no difference. Preparing for a royal visit was like preparing for battle—immaculate dress, swords well sharpened and gleaming, alertness to any emergency, and every available man ready for action. Rupert knew his case was hopeless; but he had prepared himself for proposing marriage to Harriet that morning, and any delay was unacceptable.

But accept it he must. It did not help that the heavens opened ten minutes before their visitor's arrival and did not cease sending down cold, gusting rain until everyone on parade was drenched to the skin. But worse was to come. The duke, having been assisted into dry clothes by his aide, had to be entertained by thirty-eight officers, in slowly drying and steaming uniforms—gentlemen who made a brave show of ignoring their discomfort and the smell of wet barathea.

It was early evening before Rupert was free, and his mood drove him to seek out the woman he loved without further delay. He was nervous, however. Certain that Harriet loved him and would accept his offer with the greatest joy, he wished the actual asking were over and she happily in his arms. The practiced seducer found it difficult to decide how to make an honorable proposal to one of the fair sex.

When he finally pulled the bell at the front door, he was still undecided about what she might expect of him in such a situation. It did not help that the servant girl glowered at him as she held the door partially open, as if to prevent his entry. Pushing her firmly aside, he stepped into the gloomy hall and began loosening his cloak.

"It's not a bit of use you coming in," was the surly comment.

"Too late. It is a *fait accompli.*"

"A fetter *what*?"

He regarded the little figure with exasperated amusement. The girl made no secret of her disapproval of him, and yet she appeared to be the maid-of-all-work devoted to her mistress.

"Did no one teach you French?" he asked in mock sternness.

"In the orphanage the only thing they teached was scrubbing floors, washing and mending clothes, and—"

"*Taught,*" he corrected.

"Beg pardon?" she queried suspiciously.

"The only thing they *taught* . . . except you went on to mention a whole list, so it should be *things*, you know," he said, trying not to smile at her open-mouthed stare. "What *is* your name, girl?"

"Bessie Porridge . . . sir," she said with a sniff.

"Bessie . . . By all the saints, *nobody* is called Bessie Porridge!"

Dormouse eyes gleamed in challenge. "I am."

Still greatly amused, he continued, "Very well, *Bessie Porridge*, inform your mistress of my arrival."

"Miss Deane is indisposed. She won't see no one."

His amusement faded swiftly. "She is ill . . . really ill?"

The little pinched face showed bewilderment. "Not laying-in-bed ill, if that's what you mean. She's gone away, like. I've never seen her like this before."

Rupert knew immediately what ailed his beloved, and his heart leaped. A person as volatile and fiery as Harriet would also be passionate in affection. At their last meeting there had been a moment when he would have kissed her on the lips if Miss Frisby had not chosen to turn their way and call to them to observe a duckling entangled in the reeds. Harriet had hastened to free the creature, but the near embrace had tinted her cheeks with delicate pink and given a sparkle to her eyes. Small wonder she was lovelorn and remote today.

Flooded with confidence, he knew his instinct to hurry to her had been right. Doubts fled along with the rehearsed formal speeches. He made for the stairs.

"I will announce myself," he cried over his shoulder.

"No, sir," was the scandalized cry. "Miss Deane is alone in the parlor."

"Good," he said gaily. "In my carriage there is a bottle of champagne. You may tell my man to bring it in."

He took the stairs two at a time, his athletic body tingling with energy, and rapped loudly on the door with the impatience of a lover. Her invitation to enter was faint, but he already had the door open when she spoke. Fortune was with him all the way. She was sitting alone in the room lit by only one lamp. The soft golden halo around the walls, the leaping flame light from the fire added a romantic intimacy that filled even his experienced soul with the haunting sadness that accompanies excessive joy.

She looked up and then grew completely still. "*You!*"

It was said with such passion that Rupert knew he had been in her thoughts as she sat there. The realization halted him for a moment; then he went forward to drop on to one knee before her chair and take her hand to his lips in passion.

"You see before you a fool," he murmured ardently. "All day I have been trying out speeches, learning lines I thought were expected on such an occasion, yet now that I am here, I know they would not do for you. Honesty is all that you have ever wanted." He kissed her fingers again and sighed with happiness. "I love you, my dearest—more deeply than I can bear. You fill my mind when you are not in my sight, and there is no future for me without you. I went into Sussex yesterday to tell my father of my intentions and have spent today in a fever to escape from onerous duty in order to come to you." In his fervor he held her hand against his heart so that she might feel its beating. "I am alive only when you are beside me. You know I have no noble background to offer you, but all I have will be yours. I shall surround you with every luxury and fill your life with interest and excitement, I swear. With you as my wife there is nothing I shall not be able to do, and my undying love and devotion will be yours . . . as it is now."

He raised himself to draw her into his arms, but she was out of the chair and standing behind it before he realized. Her face was white, her eyes brilliant blue and enormous with fiery emotion.

"If I had known you were at my door, I should have barred it against you," she cried. "How dare you walk in with such effrontery!"

Rupert was immobile with shock, frozen with the bizarre unreality of the moment. His words of love still hung in the air; his arms were still half-raised for an embrace as he stared at the virago she had become.

"You came here with condolences, fond recollections of a dead friend and comrade, and offered to be of service to his bereaved sister. Yet all the while you were stacking away his money in the vaults of your bank." She gripped the back of the chair with fingers seeking support in her fury. "As you so rightly said, you have no noble background," she told him icily. "Neither have you nobility of character. You come from nothing and remain nothing. Ill-gotten wealth might have bought you a place in society, but it cannot buy those qualities society demands. All it has done is endow you with an insatiable appetite for still more wealth—at *any* cost."

He must have moved, for she backed away and cried, "Do not dare to touch me again. I am not witless, as you are well aware. I know, from Edward's letters, that a man's gaming debts are canceled when he falls in battle. Debts of honor are revoked by men of honor. Not so *you*," she flung at him in great passion. "From your alleged friend, a fellow officer, you claimed every sou, even from a man in the grave. To drive a man to stake more than he can afford is despicable enough, but to claim his last penny, the bonds left in trust by his father and the mortgage on his house, simply to satisfy a lust for wealth is the action of a man unfit to be called gentleman. Are your millions not enough that you must break a man who thought you a friend?" Her voice faltered with emotion she could no longer hold back. "Before God and by my brother's sacred memory, I would have refused to allow you to set foot in this house had I known what you really were. I weep with shame for these past four months. I bow my head at my betrayal of Edward and my beloved father."

Her fists beat a demented tattoo on the chair. "I cannot pay you rent, for I have nothing—but you may take the roof from my head with my blessing, for I would not live in a house owned by a Torrington." She came around the chair to face him. "As to my becoming your wife, I would sooner die."

As she stood before him, he saw in her blue eyes bright with tears another pair full of fear and seeking reassurance. Her face, gilded by flame glow, looked so like Edward's as he had lain in that pointed tent yellowed by one single lamp. *I have no hands to hold onto the living, to clasp life until the sun comes up again. It's the darkness. . . .*

It was, indeed, the darkness. Pain greater than the anguish of his wounds at Sevastapol had overtaken him . . . greater because these wounds were inside.

Because of it, the man who spoke was a creature apart from himself.

"I think you have no choice. You are alone in the world, and no matter how blue your blood, there is no one will take you in save as a servant or governess. Would not the memory of your father and brother be more dishonored by that circumstance? If you have no money to pay the rent, it will mean debtors' prison. Will your pride suffer that?" He stood wreathed in the humiliation of her words. "As my wife you will have access to that money you claim should be yours. I will give you three days in which to come to terms with the inevitable."

He left immediately, because the real Rupert Torrington was struggling within his body like a madman fighting to get out, creating a thudding in his temples and a feverish heat in his body. Taking the cloak from a hand that appeared before him, he was about to go out into a street shining with puddles when a voice intruded, saying, "Your champagne, sir."

His hand reached out and smashed the bottle againt the wall—the wall of a house he had not known he owned.

During the three days that followed, Harriet went through mental anguish. Time and again she asked herself how she could have been so completely taken in—she who had wits and years enough not to fall headlong in love with the first personable man who came her way. Times without number she wished she had sent him away that night when Nanny had fallen asleep. Over and over again she recalled those things about him that had so completely charmed her, and she found her cheeks flaming. How it must have amused him to watch her react with wide-eyed trust and gratitude and fall so easily for his soft words! Dear God, she had even admitted to him that she rarely needed a chaperone. How loudly he must have laughed at the dowdy middle-aged spinster who believed so easily she could attract an experienced man-about-town! And all through those invigorating mornings, magical afternoons, and gossamer evenings he had known that her debts were piling up and that the house in which she lived belonged to him.

When he had walked without warning into her parlor with such histrionic professions of love on the evening of that day of truth, her control had vanished. She would have struck him had he not left when he did.

For two days she had become almost feverish with plans for her future. She would, indeed, become a governess; it was unlikely anyone would take her as a servant even had she been prepared to consider such a course. To settle her debts, she would sell those things Edward had sent her from the Crimea.

The plans to become a governess soon fell apart when she remembered Nanny and little Bessie Porridge, whom she had found in an orphanage. What would become of them, who would give them a home if she followed such a course?

Harriet desperately sought another solution that would ensure a happy outcome for her two retainers. She would finish her father's study of indigenous races, which she was copying for publication in a book. But she soon realized that even if she worked by day and by night, it would take her half a year to complete the work, and the process of publishing was very slow.

On the second day her fevered brain and fingers were compiling columns of figures to estimate the possibility of starting a small establishment where she, Nanny, and Bessie could undertake sewing for the middle classes. It was not long before she flung down her peneil in despair. One could not start a sewing establishment without premises, and Rupert Torrington would certainly never allow her to use his house for the purpose—not that she would ever ask him. With characteristic frankness she also owned to herself that Nanny's fingers were stiff now, and her own expertise at stitching was debatable.

Throughout that day she was distracted and unable to eat, causing distress in those she was trying hard not to abandon. They could get nothing from her as to why she was so afflicted, and she was so worried by their scolding concern she sent them both away in tears. When Harriet went to bed that second night, it was with the conviction that there was nothing to be done but face debtors' prison with the fortitude she had always tried to maintain in her life. Nanny and Bessie must take their chances in the world, for there was nothing she could do for them.

A note had been delivered from Mr. Harkins that afternoon to say he had received notice from his colleague in America advising him that Dominic Ralston had set out on an expedition into the interior of the wild Indian country to the west and could not be contacted until he returned. Mr. Harkins now regretfully believed it would be a great deal later than the autumn before Mr. Ralston replied to his letter. That note caused Harriet's last hope to fade, and she faced the night with all emotion spent, filled with cold hopelessness.

For several hours she lay with prayers on her lips, and then she fell into sad memories of Edward. But when she traveled on in thoughts to those days when she and Professor Deane had argued, expounded, and explored all aspects of human behavior, a vastly different kind of mortification swept through her. She saw him so clearly, heard his beloved voice.

One should never try to compromise or escape the inevitable, my dear, but go out to meet it and turn it to one's own advantage. How else do you imagine mankind has lasted so long? The world is not there for one's amusement but to test one's strength.

With clarity of memory came clarity of vision, and the past two days fell into perspective.

All her anguish, her absurd plans for the future, her ridiculous martyrdom had been caused by selfishness. If she cared anything at all for the memory of her father and Edward, if she indeed had true concern for her elderly companion and orphaned maid, her solution was all too plain. Marriage to Rupert Torrington would save her reputation and the family name from disgrace. It would allow her to complete her father's work and publish it for the world to read, and Edward's regiment would never know he had staked everything and died penniless. As for the two women who now depended upon her, they would remain in her service in her new life.

Her two days of anguish and misery had been due to no more than stiff-necked pride. For the first time in her life a man had reached her heart and exposed it to an emotion that flattered and shattered with equal devastation. Rupert Torrington had done no more than many men had done to women since the beginning of time, but she had been behaving as if her personal bruised pride, her sensation of mortification, her misplaced trust in a person she had known such a short time were of earthshaking importance.

Unable to lie in bed any longer, she reached for her shawl, drew aside the heavy curtains around the bed, and hurried to the parlor, where she lit a lamp and curled up in the large wool-covered armchair. This was not the first setback she had had in her five-and-twenty years; it must be met with her customary resolution. She *would* marry Rupert Torrington. He was arrogant in his insistence that she become his wife; she would see to it that he married her on her terms. It would not be an easy marriage, as he would find to his cost . . . and he would never hurt her again!

It was soon after ten o'clock the next morning when Bessie hurried into the parlor to announce that Captain Torrington was in the hall. She asked Harriet what she wanted done with the captain.

"*Done* with him?" she repeated sharply. "You will show him up, of course. And kindly ensure that Miss Frisby does not quit her room while he is here, for I do not wish to be interrupted."

Bessie's eyes widened considerably. "Will you be all right, madam? If he's in no better mood than last time, I doubt you are safe. All that champagne down the wall!" she finished in a disapproving tone.

Harriet, taut, nervous, and overtired, was in no mood for her maid's opinions and snapped, "You are paid to do as you are told, without comment. Show Captain Torrington up immediately."

"Yes, madam," was the resigned reply, and the girl swung around, muttering under her breath, "Pale as a pumpkin, he is, and set to pick a fight with anyone who so much as *sniffs* in the wrong direction."

Harriet changed seats twice in frantic indecision concerning the best place to be sitting when he entered and then waited with fast-beating heart as she heard footsteps approaching. When he walked in, all her notions that the interview would be easy fled. He was as pale as Bessie had described, and he seemed to have aged overnight. There were harsh lines on his face that had never shown before; the dark, surprising eyes looked bruised and fathomless. There was none of his former assured strength in the way he held himself, no glimpse of the gentle determination she had so admired.

Perhaps the original Rupert Torrington had been love's illusion; perhaps she now saw him for what he was . . . but the sight of him standing within her parlor again hurt her beyond measure. Great emotion dies a progressively slow and agonizing death, and hers was yet in its first stages. She found herself trembling as the wound of disillusionment reopened and began to bleed.

He gazed at her for some moments before saying quietly, "It was good of you to consent to see me."

"You said 'in three days,' did you not?"

"I . . . yes, I believe so." He came a few steps farther into the room, and she saw the strain on his face highlighted by the pale morning sun. "I am not precisely certain of all that I said, truth to tell."

"Then it is as well that I recall it very clearly," she told him in a manner that halted him where he stood. "You informed me that I must become your wife or prepare to enter a debtors' prison for failure to pay your rent."

He winced under her forthright repetition of his words and put up a hand as if to speak. Before he could do so, she continued. "You are right. There is no alternative. There is only one condition I impose—that my companion and maid be allowed to remain with me. I trust you will not object?"

"No . . . no . . . of course not," he murmured, taken aback by the speed with which she was dealing with the matter. Then he seemed to realize to what he had agreed. "No, I cannot . . . naturally, the choice of a personal maid is your own, but I cannot have Miss Frisby as a permanent member of my household." He passed a hand over his brow in confusion. "It might be . . . I had thought . . . before, I mean . . . I had thought of the cottage on the Sussex estate where your companion could live out her days in the congenial company of my old nurse." He put out a hand in appeal. "Harriet, all this, when I must first explain—"

"That sounds very suitable," she put in quickly, striving to keep command of the situation. The sooner the details were decided and he was no longer there to put such pain within her breast, the better. "When am I to prepare Miss Frisby for her removal to Sussex?"

He tried again to halt her verbal attack. "Harriet, please, there is something you do not understand. I have to make clear to you—"

"I believe you made everything abundantly clear two nights ago, sir. There is nothing more to be said on the matter," she told him in throbbing tones, rising from her chair and going to stand by the window, where she did not have to look at him.

The silence that ensued went on so long she could not resist turning back into the room. He was even paler than before, and a fiery light had now appeared in his eyes, giving him back a little of his old look of command.

"As you wish. Your period of mourning will be over shortly, so I suggest the first week of July for the wedding," he said with a crispness that made it sound more of an order than a suggestion.

"July is but three months ahead," she exclaimed. "Will it not be thought unconventionally rushed?"

"What reason is there to wait? And I had thought you cared not a fig for convention."

This reminder that she had revealed her thoughts and opinions so openly to him led her to retaliate. "I take it you have already decided the venue also."

"Unless you have objections, the most suitable place is the parish church in Battle. I am known by the rector, and the setting is delightfully rustic." When she made no comment, he added tautly, "As your silence suggests agreement, I will put my plans forward. As you have no family and few friends, it will be a quiet ceremony."

In her overwrought and sorely tried state Harriet read into his words a taunt that she was friendless, alone in the world, dependent on his protection, and she lashed out at him. "I have friends, sir, I assure you. If you have not met them, it is, perhaps, because they move in higher circles."

He drew in a sharp breath, and his lips tightened further. "In that case, it must be a full society wedding with an escort from my regiment to form an archway of swords. I shall insert notices in all the necessary publications and have cards printed. If you will let me have a list of your guests, I will see to it that they are sent invitations."

She was caught well and truly, for the last thing she desired was an ostentatious flourish made over the affair; besides, misty veils and a uniformed escort smacked too much of romance. The screw turned to heighten her pain at the thought of how much she would have wanted all those things only three days ago. She looked at the face she had thought so full of strength and character and saw only a man who had destroyed her trust.

"Let us have one thing straight from the start," she said with passion. "I am embarking on this marriage for no other reason than desperation. Showy pretensions and the flaunting of wealth are quite out of place."

A muscle moving in his jaw betrayed his emotion, if it were not already apparent in the incredible tenseness of his body. "My wealth is my own affair, I will have you realize."

"I agree . . . but do not attempt to use it to buy *me*, sir, or you will rue the day."

"As you have already pointed out, ma'am, I am no gentleman—so do not expect me to behave like one. And let us have another thing straight. Whatever might be your reason for this marriage, *in public* you will give no hint that it is anything but happy—or *you* will rue the day." He gave a swift nod and turned for the door, but with his hand on the knob he slowed and glanced back at her.

She turned and went to the window, dismayed at the loss of her control in so short a time with him, for she almost longed to beg him to stay. It seemed an age before the click of the door told her he had gone. For a long while she stood with heaving breast and whitened knuckles; then, incredibly weary, she rested her burning head against the smooth wood of the windowframe and closed her eyes.

"Papa, oh, dearest Papa," she breathed. "I am facing the inevitable, but it does not promise to be easy to turn it to my advantage."

Chapter Four

It was a fine clear morning in mid-May when Rupert brought his bride-to-be to Sussex to meet his father. He did not look forward to the overnight visit, for the pride with which he would once have presented the woman he loved was overshadowed by the antagonism between them. Aubrey had been unenthusiastic from the start about the proposed alliance. It would serve only to convince him of his doubts when he was brought face-to-face with a sharp-tongued, aloof young woman with no more than passable looks.

It did not help that Pagoda House was fashioned on ostentation and betrayed the immense wealth of the family more blatantly than any other aspect of his life. He grew tenser with every mile, knowing Harriet would see in the silk-hung walls, the pagoda towers, the Oriental gardens a flamboyance that bordered on vulgarity. As for Aubrey Torrington himself, his free-and-easy manner and roving eye would suggest to Harriet a roué of provincial cut.

Harriet was doing nothing to ease the strain of this duty visit. Although her six-month mourning period was over, she was wearing an unattractive gown in fine gray wool. On greeting her that morning, he had stifled an instinctive protest; at least he had the satisfaction of knowing he was denying her an opportunity to tell him the gown still had a deal of wear in it.

He was learning just how fiercely determined his betrothed could be. That independence and strength of personality he had so admired from the start were now turned against him with a vengeance. An expert in managing horses, Rupert had tried similar handling techniques on his bride-to-be and had been thrown heavily. His own determined nature led him to try again, but he was a strong man with one vulnerable spot . . . and Harriet Deane had hit it with unerring marksmanship once too often.

The love that had led to his proposal of marriage was now overshadowed by guilt, shattered pride, and the desire to return to her all she had accused him of grasping with greedy fingers. There he had underestimated *her* pride. An impasse had been reached. His compulsive need to lavish wealth on her was met by her unyielding resistance to it.

The large sum he had transferred to her name for the purpose of buying the many requisites of a young woman facing a marked change of circumstances had been used merely to settle outstanding tradesmen's bills. The remainder lay untouched while she continued to wear the unflattering gray and mauve of half mourning.

He had sent a jeweler with a case of rings so that she could make her choice; she had told the man that as the engagement was to be of short duration, she saw little point in wearing a ring to signify the event. Furious, Rupert had selected a large diamond surrounded by emeralds and sent it with a brief note expressing his direct wish that she should wear it during her visit to Sussex. It was on her hand now but looked showy and in bad taste against the puritan gown.

Small wonder he sat in the carriage opposite Harriet and Miss Frisby wondering gloomily how soon he could decently quit his father's house the following day. There seemed little chance of the visit's doing more than showing him up as a fool who had allowed himself to be shackled by a competent bluestocking with a ravishing figure who dared any man to touch it at his peril.

The horses turned in at the gates of Pagoda House and made their way along the extensive and imposing driveway. Rupert wished once more, and a great deal more heartily than usual, that his father had flattened the fairy-tale building and erected a less exotic edifice to leave to his heirs.

Miss Frisby's face was a picture of consternation. "My goodness, what very strange trees, Harriet!" she exclaimed in an undertone that was clearly heard by Rupert. "And . . . oh, my . . . just *look* at that! I have never before seen the like of such a place."

"That is not to be wondered at," replied Harriet in normal tones. "I doubt there is another of its kind in England. As a reproduction of Chinese architecture it is very fine."

"*Chinese!* Oh, Harriet, you do not mean to tell me that—"

"No, and I pray you will not be so nonsensical. Your cottage will not be in the least Chinese. Am I not right, Captain Torrington?"

Rupert stifled a strong urge to suggest that it would be a pagoda staffed by Chinese servants, but Harriet's matter-of-fact acceptance of his grandfather's whimsy had taken him by surprise. She seemed anything but disparaging, and he was too busy pondering the fact to bait Miss Frisby further.

"I think you will find it in every way like any other cottage," he said. "I have arranged for you to meet Miss Thurston, with whom you will be sharing the place. Jennings will drive you down to take tea with her this afternoon."

The old woman's face flushed with the embarrassment such consideration afforded her. "So kind . . . I do not know what to say, sir."

"Then there is little point in trying," replied Rupert absently, his gaze on Harriet's face as she absorbed the full bizarre glory of his father's home.

Her cheeks were softly pink from the gentle spring breeze that fluttered the pale feathers in her bonnet, and her dark blue eyes that so clearly betrayed her feelings were alive with the dancing lights that always signified her pleasure in anything. Something stirred within him. Was she really as relentlessly frigid as she made out?

He watched through narrowed, speculative eyes as she considered, oblivious to his presence, the entire façade of the house as it became visible through the palm trees. Starting with the vivid red pagoda towers that rose from the top roof in irregular clusters like chimneys, her gaze wandered over the ornate turned-up corners of the three graded roofs, along the elaborate carved lintels and multitude of miniature wooden balconies that ran riot over the many levels and mock balconies that complicated the upper regions of the house. Then, down over the sloping canopies, gilded and decorated with heavy carvings of beasts and serpents, to the lower floors protected from sun and weather by more wooden canopies in green and red and gold. The windows were all elaborately shuttered or decorated with carved openwork panels, and on every available corner or pinnacle was a burst of exotic embellishment.

The main entrance was reached by passing through an open-sided pavilion covered by a carved roof that flew out in upturned curves supported on pillars of lacquered red. Before the house lay an ornamental lake of great beauty, crossed by a series of bridges that were perfectly mirrored in the still water and enhanced by the flat green leaves and the buds of water lilies. As far as the eye could see in the vast grounds of the estate stretching behind the house were banks of azaleas and masses of pink and white cherry blossoms.

Rupert saw the picture Harriet had been watching as the carriage swung around, and he felt, as he always did, that a stately house in the same setting would have completed the beauty of the grounds. Yet as the carriage drew to a halt, Harriet's gaze was still riveted on the showy pseudo-Eastern house with obvious fascination. He began to feel a strange resentment. She displayed bewildering perversity by taking an interest in something he himself felt to be vulgar and pretentious and yet, at the same time, rejecting his ring, with the finest stones in a tasteful setting.

They exchanged no word as he helped her alight. He could have been the coachman handing her from the carriage! Their silence continued as they entered the grand hall, where even in dimness caused by drawn shutters and carvings over the windows were revealed priceless treasures acquired from Eastern lands by his ancestors, all shown to advantage against walls paneled with yellow silk brocade embroidered with exquisite delicacy.

Harriet selected a dark ornate chair near the window of the morning room, where a view of the grounds occupied her full attention. Miss Frisby appeared to feel she had entered a den of vice, judging by the look on her face as she gazed fearfully around her strange surroundings.

A servant sent hastily on his way by Rupert's terse instruction soon brought Aubrey Torrington, anxious to meet his son's choice of bride.

"Ah, my boy, the train made good time, I see." He came across with his hand outstretched. "It's good to see you, Rupert."

"Thank you, sir. The journey was a little tedious for the ladies but tolerably comfortable. The new rolling stock is quite impressive, I must say."

As he shook his father's hand, Rupert could not help noticing the strong scent of his Macassar oil and the rakish cut of his plaid tailcoat. His heart sank further, and his introduction was brusque in consequence.

"Sir, it is my pleasure to present Miss Harriet Deane, who has consented to become my wife."

Aubrey allowed himself to glance in the direction he had been longing to look, and Harriet turned her head. She presented a charming and seductive outline against the latticed window, but the shadow cast by her bonnet prevented a clear view of her face.

Aubrey went forward. "My dear Miss Deane, it is a proud moment when a father sets eyes upon the beautiful creature without whom his son has said life would be worthless."

Rupert winced and wondered wildly why he had resisted the impulse to inform his father that the situation between himself and his future bride was not quite as he had described it on his previous visit. But then, what could he have said to explain the marriage? It was far too late now, for Aubrey was well into his speech of welcome.

"Rupert has always been a trifle wild and self-willed, but I never doubted for a moment that he would choose as his life's partner a young woman with a heart of gold."

"Yes, sir, I well believe no other kind would do for him," was the cool reply to his unfortunate phrasing. "How do you do, Mr. Torrington."

Reaching Harriet, the sophisticate took her outstretched hand to his lips in extravagant manner. "Welcome, my dear, to the bosom of the family. Now I have been accorded the privilege of meeting you, I can see why my son would not rest until he had your promise."

Rupert's heart sank further. The smooth, flattering words were quite, quite wrong, and he could imagine Harriet's opinion of them and the speaker. He groaned inwardly. There were another twenty-four hours of the visit to get through somehow.

"Thank you for your welcome, sir," Harriet said in level tones. "As for my giving my promise, your son knew there was no doubt of that from the start."

Uncertain how to take a remark that should have

been coy and yet was spoken in crisp tones, Aubrey innocently jumped deeper into the mire.

"Ah, your brother had written of Rupert, no doubt . . . in glowing terms. My sincere condolences on his tragic demise. How great a blessing that my son was at hand to console you in your loss. He was a very close friend of Lieutenant Deane's."

"Closer then I had dreamed possible," was the reply in even crisper tones.

Not understanding the true impulse behind such words, Aubrey looked puzzled. "It is not unusual in times of conflict and peril for men to form deep friendships in a very short time, dear lady. I daresay it is difficult for a female to understand such things, but the association between two gentlemen is vastly different from that of ladies, who are used to a series of morning calls and very proper observance of manners. In times of danger it is quite unexceptional for young men to dispense with formalities; indeed, it is often necessary to put one's life and trust in some stranger. It means that kindred spirits are drawn to each other in an instant." He smiled reassuringly. "I understand Lieutenant Deane found in Rupert a companion to help him forget the terrible winter months in Balaklava. Your brother was happily enriched by such friendship before he was killed in battle."

"No, sir," said Harriet in trembling tones. "I have reason to believe it was quite the contrary."

Aubrey was taken aback and lost for words. He sensed that the young visitor was hostile, but he was not in a position to understand why.

Rupert had begun to grow angry. Harriet was behaving badly, and yet he could understand that his father's unwitting words confirmed her advance opinion of the Torrington family. Surely his father could see Harriet was not the kind of young woman to be taken in by a smooth approach? And surely Harriet could allow that Aubrey was in no way responsible for her own present poverty?

He intervened swiftly. "Sir, you have yet to meet Miss Frisby, Miss Deane's companion."

"Eh?"

Aubrey looked startled at being interrupted in the midst of his puzzling conversation with his future daughter-in-law—the young woman he hoped would provide the sons to run the business his own son so determinedly shunned. Rupert received a darkling look that spoke volumes before his father turned to face the shrinking elderly nanny, who regarded him as if he were an evil magician in a castle of Oriental iniquity.

"Miss Frisby," he said in distant tones, "I trust you will find your new life on the estate comfortable and less taxing to your health than the hectic social round of London's season."

"No, sir, not at all," came the hesitant response. "Miss Deane and I have always led a most sedate and secluded life. Indeed, we have no time for those who . . ."

She quickly caught sight of Harriet's fierce glance, and her words tailed off in embarrassment.

Aubrey looked sharply at Rupert. His expression said quite plainly, *You have landed me with these two impossible females; now take them off my hands as speedily as you can.*

Rupert rose to the occasion immediately, saying, "It

has been a tiring journey, sir. I feel certain the ladies will wish to retire to their rooms for a while before preparing for dinner."

Harriet rose at once and walked toward them. "Miss Frisby will certainly wish to prepare for her visit to tea with Miss Thurston, but I should not care to fritter away such a beautiful day by shutting myself in a darkened room until evening." She looked at her host. "Do you have any objection to my taking a stroll through the gardens, sir?"

"No . . . not at all, but I regret I have . . . er . . . urgent business to which I must attend," he replied. "Forgive me if I do not accompany you."

Harriet gave a faint smile. "It was not my expectation that you would do so, Mr. Torrington." Her glance swung to Rupert. "The short time it will take me to change my gown will allow you an interval of conversation with your papa." She gazed straight and clear at Aubrey. "I am sure you are most anxious to have a few words with Captain Torrington, sir."

In an atmosphere that could best be described as vibrant with silence a servant was summoned to conduct the ladies to the upper floors. No sooner had they departed than Rupert announced to his father that he wished to freshen up after the journey and made for the door.

"Now just a minute, my boy," Aubrey began in a manner that suggested that he needed a great deal longer than a minute in which to say what was on his mind.

But Rupert decided instant retreat was the best move and halted in the doorway just long enough to say, "Your urgent business matters, sir . . . you have not forgotten them, I hope."

He left the room and consolidated his advantage by taking the stairs two at a time—something his father could not emulate. But he was still angry enough to tackle Harriet on her behavior the minute they were out of earshot. She had taken a surprisingly short while to don a gown of soft lavender silk, and the pale shimmering material, the lacy shawl, and her brown curls free from bonnet or cap gave her a softness of appearance that affected him strongly—and perversely increased his anger.

They strolled along a maze of stone paths, for the grass was damp, and the atmosphere was disturbingly seductive with the spring sunshine, distant birdsong, the swish of silken skirts, and the somnolent buzzing of bees dotting the blooms that rose in banks wherever one looked. They had not spoken since setting out—Harriet appearing lost in the beauty of the gardens—but when she finally put up a hand to smooth a tendril of hair, the flash of the diamond on her finger—*his* diamond—made him say, "I have complied with your one condition of this marriage. Miss Frisby is even now setting out to survey her new home. Is it too much for you to bow to mine? You made no effort to ingratiate yourself with my father or to suggest that you were a willing bride. He cannot be blamed for what I have done."

She turned to him as if his voice had rudely shattered her isolated tranquillity. "He did not like me. That much was clear from the outset," she told him coolly. "There seemed little point in making a fruitless effort after that."

"Fruitless effort!" he exploded. "You set out to be as disapproving as your nature allows. Deny if it you can."

"I do not deny it," was her infuriating reply. "If my nature allows me to be disapproving, it also allows me to be scrupulously honest—something of which you have no understanding." The flush upon her cheeks deepened as she added, "He had prepared a welcome for the bride he expected you to choose. His manner was gushing, conciliatory, typically masculine in his presumption that any woman would flutter delightedly at such flattery. When he realized his mistake, there was no doubting his consternation . . . or the glances demanding that you should immediately relieve him of my presence." Her eves flashed. "I do not care to be taken for a brainless butterfly—plainly the type of female normally favored by you."

"Do you not?" he grated angrily. "Well, I mean to have my way over this. While you are here, you will present every semblance of being happy with your circumstances . . . and the type of female I favor is none of your concern," he added with finality.

The fire in her eyes increased. "Indeed, it is. I cannot present a picture of blissful contentment unless you also make it known your taste has undergone a complete reversal, something Mr. Torrington clearly did not understand. I trust you will now make him aware of the fact."

The born soldier brought up his big guns. "When you are my wife, it might be considered that you are entitled to give your opinion on my actions, but for an unmarried woman to do so suggests a forwardness of manner unacceptable to society. It also suggests a partiality that could be challenged by rivals."

The arrow found its mark, and her cheeks flamed at his implication that she cared for his good opinion. "I was coerced into this alliance, but you will discover I hold my independence more dearly than all your Torrington millions," she flung at him. "You will never hold me in pawn, as you did Edward."

He held onto his control with difficulty. "I would advise you to further your knowledge of gentlemen's pursuits, for it is plain you are unacquainted with the rules of the game. No man plays against his will."

"Maybe," she flashed back, "but you have a way of making certain people do as you wish. I think you do not care a jot about the rules of the game so long as you get your way."

"Then you understand me very well," he snapped. "Tonight, when we have a guest at the dinner table, you will do well to bear that in mind. I shall expect to see a charming countenance full of smiles and an expression of prenuptial contentment each time you look my way."

Despite their bitter clash during the afternoon, in which he felt he emerged the victor, Rupert viewed the evening with reluctance.

Since Miss Frisby was an old retainer rather than a true companion to his young guest, Aubrey Torrington had been obliged to provide a matron to act as hostess and chaperone during dinner. Rupert had been told that the lady would be the wife of Grenville Dornacre, a great friend of his father who lived on the neighboring estate. Mr. Dornacre was also involved in finance, and the couple were such close friends with Aubrey that Pagoda House was almost a second home to them. Unfortunately Caroline Dornacre would be alone since her husband was in the north of England for several days, but she had been only too happy to chaperon her friend's future daughter-in-law.

Rupert had never met the Dornacres—his visits to Pagoda House were brief and infrequent—and he did not look forward to a gathering that would include a father still irate because he had been unable to thrash out the situation with his son, an icy fiancée who could not be relied upon to do as he had instructed, and a society matron. Heaving a sigh as he dressed for dinner, he wished heartily that the damned visit were over and he were back with his regiment. There he was always welcome, even if one or two aristocratic ramrods still turned their backs in his direction.

It was in a reluctant state that he eventually ventured downstairs, and he was considerably surprised to find his father in the withdrawing room entertaining a ravishing creature no more than his own age. The pair turned at his entry, laughter soft on their faces, and he went forward greatly intrigued. His father had not mentioned a Dornacre daughter.

"Ah, Rupert!" exclaimed Aubrey jovially, arm outstretched to draw his son into the warmth of friendship. "Allow me to present you to Mrs. Dornacre."

Rupert took her graceful outstretched hand to his lips in undisguised surprise and pleasure. She was stunning!

"I had thought you to be *Miss* Dornacre," he murmured gallantly. "The evening is ruined now that my hopes have been dashed so cruelly."

Green eyes dancing with zest and lively appreciation of his masculinity widened with an experienced show of innocence. "There is only one other gentleman of my acquaintance who expresses such wicked flattery with such innocent candor. You could be no one other than Aubrey's son." Her gaze flickered over him from head to foot, and her mouth curved into an irresistible smile. "I knew you must be handsome, Captain Torrington, but this is really too much. Where did you get those devilish eyes with such fair coloring?"

"I am a changeling, ma'am," he said, responding instinctively to her provocation. "It is said we possess strange powers over mortals. . . ." He kissed her fingers again more lingeringly, as he gazed deep into her eyes. "I have never yet known them to fail."

She laughed in delight. It was an enticing, throaty sound designed to make any man's pulse quicken. With her silver fair hair drawn back into a complicated mass of curls and swaths, her complexion of breathless beauty, and a décolletage that revealed pale, swelling breasts against the rich crimson of her dress, Caroline Dornacre presented a challenge he could not resist.

Without taking her gaze from Rupert's she said softly, "Aubrey, are you going to allow your son to flirt so outrageously with me?"

The older man slid his hand down her arm and gently disengaged her fingers from Rupert's to pat them possessively. "My dear, Rupert has been charming ladies since he could walk. I fear it is too late to attempt to school him now."

Her eyes challenged laughingly. "What have you to say to that, Captain Torrington?"

He accepted the challenge with practiced ease. "I confess my fickleness, ma'am . . . but *you* could school me within a very short time."

She sighed. "Let us hope your bride can also do so, or she is in for . . . an unhappy time."

A slight readjustment of her gaze made him sense another presence. He turned to see Harriet standing a few feet within the room, watching the scene with acute contempt.

"I am a little late, I fear," she said coolly, "but I think I have not been missed."

Rupert went across to her, fully conscious that he had been caught red-handed in a situation not likely to impress her with any need to comply with his demands of the afternoon. A guilty feeling made him angry rather than repentant as she deliberately looked away from him when he reached her. This whole visit was a mistake. Why had he not arranged for a fellow officer to send an urgent message recalling him to duty an hour after they arrived? Any man in his right mind would have done so.

Putting a hand beneath Harriet's elbow, he led her across to the other two, saying, "Mrs. Dornacre, allow me to present my future bride, Miss Harriet Deane."

"Miss Deane." The visitor smiled in a superficial manner that did not disguise her astonishment at what she saw or the pleasure of discovering that the beauty stakes still remained in her own hands. "May I wish you every happiness in your forthcoming marriage."

"Thank you, ma'am," was the controlled reply. "You cannot long have been a bride yourself, I think. I look forward to hearing your further advice on what will assure my happiness with Captain Torrington. There is no doubt of your own."

The other woman covered the moment with brittle laughter. "Show me the woman who would not be happy in the company of two such handsome men." She glanced saucily from father to son. "Aubrey is an old and valued friend . . . and Captain Torrington plainly follows the tradition of the gallant military, whether on the field of battle or in the ballroom."

"He also appears to shine in the withdrawing room," said Harriet sweetly and then, as Rupert was about to speak, turned to his father. "Good evening, sir. My stroll in the garden was pleasant, but I have to confess it is the house that claims my full attention and admiration."

The older man's expression underwent a swift change. "Oh, indeed? I had not thought to hear that from you, Miss Deane."

"Why is that, sir?" came the pert question.

"Eh? Er . . . most young women appear to prefer the garden." He grinned wickedly. "At least, that is what Rupert tells me."

"No doubt," was the crisp reply.

Caroline did not like the manner in which Harriet had dominated the conversation since her arrival and remarked swiftly, "The house is not liked in the village, and Aubrey is considered something of a heathen for living here. They have never forgiven Garforth for building such a place right in the heart of England."

"Stories have grown up concerning Pagoda House that describe it as anything from a pagan temple to a kind of Hellfire Club," said Rupert. "I have to say I agree with them."

"Poor Aubrey is considered an evil force," said Caroline with amusement, "although I cannot think how they could imagine such a thing of him."

"Rural communities always have their witch, Mrs. Dornacre," Harriet told her calmly. "It is a throwback from the days of truly pagan religions and provides an outlet for their fears and suspicions. In one sense, it ensures the survival of the community, for the people pour out all their aggression onto one person rather than undermine their combined strength by quarrels among individuals. The owner of a house such as this would be an obvious choice . . . but it is a pity the villagers do not appreciate what they have in their midst. The house is an extremely fine example of Chinese architecture—something they would normally have no chance of seeing in their lifetime."

Rupert could not resist saying, "You always make the mistake of imagining that everyone has your own intense interest in culture and the arts. I hardly think the people of this village would care that they have an example of Chinese architecture in their midst."

She looked up at him quickly, lost in an excess of enthusiasm. "Then it is a great pity someone does not attempt to educate them." Turning to Aubrey, she asked, "Have they ever been invited to see the house other than from the end of the driveway?"

He looked startled. "See the . . . you mean, come onto the estate and wander at will?"

"Oh, no," she said immediately. "That would be unthinkable. But if your manager were to speak to them as a group, point out the virtues of the construction, show them the meaning of the embellishments, tell them a little about the country where such houses are commonplace, their ideas of sorcery and evil would vanish."

Aubrey was regarding her with shrewd eyes. "You are well informed on country matters for a town-bred lady. Where did you acquire your knowledge, my dear?"

"From my papa, a professor of great repute in the study of the human race. He was working on a book concerning indigenous races when he died. It is my intention to finish it from the papers he left."

" 'Pon my soul . . . finish a book on—" He broke off to look at Rupert. "Did you know of this, my boy?"

He gave a small sigh. "Yes, sir. I spoke of it to you when I last visited."

"Did you? Well, I had a lot on my mind that day . . . bad reports from Canton and so on." His attention returned to Harriet. "I do not know that I agree with you, but yours is an interesting theory. Invite them all in, eh?" He caught sight of Mrs. Dornacre's face and drew her closer with an arm about her waist. "What do you think, Caroline?" he asked in teasing manner.

She smiled a trifle thinly. "I think none of them would venture here. They are too afraid of what might befall them in your presence."

"Ah", his eyes lit up—"what of that, Miss Deane? How do you solve that problem?"

"Only you can solve it, sir," she told him with her

first smile of the evening. "If you present an eccentric face to the world, you must learn to accept the consequences. My papa rarely took a walk without children pulling their noses and dogs worrying his trouser legs."

Beneath Rupert's bemused gaze his father burst into hearty laughter, saying, "I shall look very carefully at children from now on and avoid passing dogs, I assure you." Then he took one of Harriet's hands to his lips in a swaggering gesture as his eyes, twinkling with amusement and admiration, gazed into hers. "We shall get on famously, my dear, I see that clearly. You see me as an eccentric, eh? Well, well . . . it is certainly not the role in which I am usually cast by young ladies." He chuckled anew, then tucked her arm through his as Miggs, the butler, signaled that dinner was ready. "Let us go through, my dear Harriet." Over his shoulder he said, "Caroline, Rupert will offer you his arm. You will find my son not nearly as eccentric as I—he refuses to live in this perfect example of Chinese architecture."

Still laughing heartily, he led a smiling Harriet from the room.

Rupert was so engrossed in watching them he almost jumped when a hand touched his arm and Caroline Dornacre said slyly, "You have chosen for yourself a formidable partner, Captain Torrington. Will *you* be able to school *her*, I wonder?"

He looked down into the lovely provocative face that was so like dozens of others he had kissed and saw her for what she was.

"I have not the slightest wish to do so. I find her irresistible just as she is."

Filled with the heavy truth of his statement, he offered her his arm and led her into the dining room.

Dinner was served on Oriental china in a room hung with hand-painted silk and furnished with dark, heavily carved tables and chairs. Lacquered screens inlaid with mother-of-pearl stood around the large salon, and lighting was provided by globular lanterns hung about with scarlet silken tassels.

Rupert scarcely noticed what he ate, although the conversation demanded little of him. His thoughts were completely taken up with the astonishing rapport that had now sprung up between the girl he loved far too much and his rakish, sophisticated parent. He could not believe that two people poles apart in temperament could take such obvious delight in each other's company, especially after their disastrous introduction.

"You spoke of Canton, sir," Harriet was saying. "Is it truly the city travelers would have us believe?"

"Ah, one must see a city like Canton to appreciate it . . . but the damned Chinese refuse to allow any of us within the walled city. We are confined to factories, y'know, throughtout the trading season. There is a tiny garden area where we take exercise, but that is the limit of our exploration. Foreign barbarians we are called, and we are treated as such. It gets deuced monotonous, I can tell you. Hong Kong ain't so bad, but then that is a British colony run by men with sense and education. *Civilized,* d'ye see?"

"Come, sir, I am astonished at such a remark," said Harriet, much to Rupert's amusement. "The Chinese civilization is far older and more complex than our own. Here you sit surrounded by evidence of the fact, and yet you will not acknowledge it."

Aubrey stopped with his fork halfway to his mouth and then lowered it slowly.

"See here, young woman, I know these people. I have seen what they can do to other human creatures. It is they who are barbaric."

"So were the ancient Egyptians, the Romans, the Greeks, but their civilizations were splendid . . . and, sir, I have heard of barbarism amongst our own ranks. Your son can tell you of the Crimea, if you dare to hear of it."

"That was *war*, Miss Deane," added Caroline Dornacre, not to be ignored.

"That was *inhumanity*, ma'am," was the spirited reply.

Rupert felt a surge of pride go through him. Harriet was at her very best when enthusing on a subject dear to her heart. She held them all around that table in the palm of her hand, as she had held him since their second meeting. Her blue eyes sparkled, her face became vividly attractive, her slender body moved gracefully as she emphasized various points.

"I think my father was referring to diplomacy, protocol, and liaison between the two nations," he said. "The Chinese are certainly not civilized in that respect. They will not acknowledge Western superiority."

She turned her blue-fire gaze onto him, in that moment forgetting what was between them. "Oh, come, that is not worthy of you, for I know you are well aware of their culture. Their emperor is divine—a god incarnate. How can they regard anyone, least of all a sinful Westerner, as superior to such a being?"

"You sympathize with their attitude?" he challenged provocatively.

"How could I do so when I know there to be one true God? But I understand why they think as they do. Is it so very different from the attitude of local villagers to this house and its owners? Something strange and foreign has intruded into their ordered lives. They do not look upon your papa as superior—merely sinister and evil."

Before Rupert could remind her that the villagers maintained constant hostility whereas the Chinese showed one face while wearing a different one behind European backs, Aubrey rapped the table with a pepper pot.

"I do not attempt to trade with local villagers, miss. It is very well telling me they believe the emperor divine, but he is human enough to ignore treaties that have been signed between his own and two of the greatest nations in the world. It is impossible to do business with such people."

Harriet smiled with endearing sauciness. "Do you not think that is what they are hoping to imply? Their culture forbids them to tell visitors to leave their country, so they simply make it impossible for them to do what they came for, in the hopes that they will leave of their own will."

"Damme, we shall not," declared Aubrey. "They must be shown that the rest of the world will not kowtow to them."

"That is just how they regard us—they are the nucleus, we are 'the rest of the world,' " said Harriet gently. "I understand the emperor regards Queen Victoria as one of his lesser officials who rules a barbaric, far-flung outpost of his kingdom."

"That is insulting," cried Mrs. Dornacre shrilly. "Aubrey, how can you have intercourse with such people?"

"Mostly I do not, my dear," Aubrey told her as the servants removed the fish and brought in a haunch of venison with buttered vegetables. "I leave most of the business to my agent in Hong Kong, young Valentine Bedford." He surveyed the food with satisfaction. "Ah, yes, this looks most appetizing. Something young Bedford would appreciate at this moment, no doubt."

"No doubt," echoed Rupert dryly. "Except that he dare not set foot in this country again. I wonder you trust that confirmed scoundrel with such responsibility, sir."

"Well, you know," his father began, more interested in the venison than a subject he did not wish to discuss, "a fellow has to be given a second chance—which is why his family sent him out there. One mistake does not make a person a villain for life."

On irresistible impulse Rupert turned to Harriet. "What is your opinion on that viewpoint, I wonder?"

The sparkle, the animation gradually drained from her face to leave it as cold as it had been when she entered the room and saw him flirting with Caroline.

"As you said yourself, sir, one should not trust a confirmed scoundrel."

Silence hung heavily over the table while vegetables were served, and Rupert cursed himself for a fool. She would not be won over so easily, and all he had accomplished was to prove to those at the table that he and his future bride were at odds with each other.

"My cousin is in Hong Kong," said Caroline, seizing an opportunity to assume her role of hostess and chaperone now that the "young ingénue" had fallen quiet. "Her husband holds an important post in the administration of the colony, Captain Torrington."

"Indeed?" he commented politely, still feeling the sting of the moment of direct confrontation that had ended so badly. "I would not have his responsibility."

"No more I," she agreed. "I receive long letters of their life out there, and I must say it does not appeal to me. So hot and dirty . . . It would not suit me one jot." She laughed lightly. "I am much too fond of luxury and the niceties of life. Is that not right, Aubrey?"

The deep smile and the possessive pat on her bejeweled hand Aubrey gave her as it lay on the table caused Rupert to wonder at the manner of his father's friendship with the Dornacres. His father's next words increased his vague feeling of concern.

"My dear Caroline, Hong Kong would not do for you at all. The excessive heat would dim those cheeks, and the noise and vulgarity of the port would offend your nice notions. This is the place for you, Caroline . . . and think how lonely I should be without you so near."

"And Grenville," she prompted, wide-eyed.

"And Grenville, of course," he agreed with a roguish smile. "I hope he will have returned in time for the soiree I am giving for my colleagues in the silk trade."

"Oh, yes," she assured him, "but I fear I shall be

deserted again shortly afterwards, when he visits Belgium." Her pretty nose wrinkled. "The sea voyage always affects me disastrously, so he says I may remain at home this time." She turned her wide-eyed gaze upon Rupert. "Shall you be down for the soiree, Captain Torrington?"

"Good Lord, no," he said hastily, still uneasy at the interchange between his parent and the brittle young flirt. Grenville Dornacre must be senile or singularly stupid to leave such a wife alone so often!

Aubrey continued smoothly. "My son, Caroline, is a soldier, body and soul. Anything in the least to do with trade is abhorrent to him. He steers away from it with the greatest dexterity."

"Yet it has provided him with so much," protested the matron.

Aubrey laughed. "Maybe, but Rupert could have an excellent living from the gaming table. He holds the luck of the devil. Is that not so, my boy?"

"So everyone is quick to tell me," he said stiffly, avoiding looking at Harriet.

"Then you shall show us your skill tonight, Captain Torrington," declared Caroline in delight. "But only for penny points. I have no fancy to be cleaned out by you, sir . . . do you, Miss Deane?"

The changing of plates for the next course distracted her and Aubrey from noticing the fact that Harriet had made no reply to a disastrous question put so innocently, but throughout the remainder of the meal Rupert remained conscious of the barrier it had created. When the ladies left the gentlemen to their port and cigars, Aubrey made it plain he had no wish to linger.

"Drink up, Rupert. Can't leave the dear creatures too long without entertainment . . . although I doubt they are anxious to see your deuced long face again. I'm sorry to see it, my boy."

"Eh?" said Rupert absently.

"She is the most delightful and entertaining young woman I have come across in a long time. I never guessed you would have the sense or inclination to choose so wisely, in the light of your past record. But I must admit to being greatly disappointed that it is only your money she wants."

"What's that?" Rupert came out of his reverie as if someone had snapped fingers before his eyes. "My money?"

Aubrey looked hard at his son. "Well, it's plain as the palm of my hand she don't like you one bit. What other reason could she have for marrying you if not to get her fingers on the Torrington wealth?"

Chapter Five

September 8—the anniversary of Edward's death—and Harriet had been married to his treacherous friend for two months. On the whole, the days had passed pleasantly enough. Their rented house was tastefully decorated and had everything she could have wanted. Since she had declined to select furnishings and color schemes, Rupert had sent in a man who specialized in such things. Bills and household accounts never appeared before her now, but she could guess that the cost of refurbishing a large house in the style Rupert approved would have shaken her to the core.

Everywhere she turned there was evidence of Torrington wealth. Wall coverings were richly embellished with raised velvet designs; curtains of finest brocade hung in great folds from rings of heavy brass. The rooms were filled with ottomans, great hide sofas, velvet chaises longues, papier-mâché tables, antique desks, tallboys, lamps, busts, porcelain ornaments, Sèvres bowls, jade, ivory, and the best lead crystal, while every floor was covered with the finest Indian and Chinese carpets. There was an extensive library, mostly consisting of Rupert's books but enlarged by those volumes previously owned by Professor Deane that Harriet had not been obliged to sell. On the silver tray in the reception hall were deposited daily the visiting cards of the nobility and the wealthy; invitations poured in.

Rupert had ensured that the wedding had been a major society affair that had been reported in all the influential publications, and she had been forced to invite the well-bred friends of which she had boasted, most of whom she could not tolerate for their snobbishness.

Her choice of a plain gown had been eulogized as an example of pure good taste, and tears had been shed willy-nilly by foolish females who were affected by the vision of the chaste and modest bride standing with her gallant Crimean hero in his splendid gold-encrusted scarlet uniform beneath an archway of swords held by more gallant Crimean heroes. If the bride was not exactly ravishingly lovely, she made a suitably fragile feminine contrast with the strikingly attractive, six-foot-tall blond protector who was taking her into his keeping. In short, everyone but the bride and bridegroom felt the wedding in the beautiful parish church on a cloudless July day was the embodiment of romantic and spiritual perfection.

No doubt, society in general still considered them as an ideal couple on the rosy clouds of marital bliss. Harriet had done all that was expected of her in public, not because her husband had enforced his one condition of the marriage but for her own sake, for her father's, and for Edward's. She would not let society know it was only because she was penniless that she had agreed to a marriage they all considered so romantic.

Face the inevitable and turn it to one's own advantage. She had followed the first instruction without shrinking, but now she was left wondering what came next, for the advantage was all hers already. She had comfort beyond anyone's expectations, an abundance of acquaintances, no lack of entertainment, no worries over unpaid bills; in short, a life that was full of opportunities to do all those things she had been unable to do as an unescorted spinster with a frail and aging chaperone. Best of all, she had a room of her own in which to work on her father's random notes. The only thing she did not have was a loving husband . . . and that was the one thing she did not want!

It was of her husband that she was thinking on that sad anniversary as she waited for Bessie to bring the tea tray. Outside the window was a vista of trees the leaves of which were on the point of turning with autumnal colors, and she was reminded of the day she had seen an officer emerging from a carriage and believed him to be Edward returning. The memory put a twist in her stomach. The man who had arrived that day had appeared so . . . so *fine* and had continued to give her that impression during the four months that had followed.

Turning from the September beauty outside her window, she rose and walked restlessly to the opposite window, one that overlooked the lake in the park. Her instinct had been wrong—so wrong. Since their marriage he had behaved in a manner that confirmed her later condemnation.

Rupert's profession was his life. When he was not at the barracks, he was visiting fellow officers, studying manuals, writing letters to *The Times* concerning outmoded firearms or disgraceful commissariat administration and hospital conditions in the Crimea. He talked endlessly to his friends of army reform and the need to train men for emergencies. He reveled in reviews and military steeplechasing.

But with those same military men he was drinking heavily and spending night after night at the gaming tables. At least, that was what she had thought until that morning when she was driving in the park with new acquaintances. As a result of their gossiping, all afternoon Harriet had been in the grips of an emotion she could not name or decide how to handle.

Their two-month-old marriage had been stormy. They maintained a front in public, but at home their relationship was vastly different. Rupert spent money extravagantly, to Harriet's alarm; she made prudent economies in the household that incensed him beyond all proportion. He insisted on summoning dressmakers with bales of silks and satins; she would not wear the expensive gowns they made her. She condemned his gaming; he spent his vast winnings on jewelry and costly presents for her, which she put into a drawer and neglected.

They continually struggled to live apart from each other and found it could not be done because their lives overlapped constantly. As a result, Harriet was growing edgy and restless, wanting to crusade against her lot and yet finding the advantage was already hers. She wanted to punish Rupert but seemed to be taking the punishment herself. She did not enjoy the times he was in the house and yet resented the long hours he was away from it, leading his rackety life.

Rupert, on his part, seemed hell-bent, on showering

her with jewels that grew more extravagant and costly with each gift and on recklessly filling the house with everything he thought she could possibly want. From society gossip she learned that he was playing for impossibly high stakes and yet continuing to win. Some said it was as if he were challenging his luck, *wanting* to lose and to do so disastrously . . . but what man in his right mind would want such a thing?

A knock fell upon the door, and Bessie entered with the tray. After two months she still looked ill at ease in the formal black dress, starched apron and cap, and squeaking black boots.

Harriet looked at her irritably. "Can you really do nothing about that noise, Bessie?"

The pinched face turned up from studying the arrangement on the tray. "No, madam. I'm sorry, reely I am. It fair drives me to Bedlam's gate, but I've tried everything from goose grease to thumping them with a drubber." The mouse features turned crafty. "Mr. Bowker says it's on account of me having a sinful disposition . . . but I've settled his hash by leaving *his* shoes under the dripping tap in the scullery. Today he's squeaking like a moggy with fifty kittens."

Harriet sighed, but not without a twinge of amusement. Bowker was Rupert's valet, and a Very Superior Person who did not approve of Bessie's being in the household. In that respect, man and master were of one opinion.

"I wish you would not fall foul of Bowker," she told the girl.

"I try to keep out of his way, madam, straight I do. But he's got it in heavy for me. There's not a doubt it's him who's behind the captain's telling me to go."

Harriet had reservations on that score but did not voice them.

"That's as may be, but it will not do for you to put his shoes under the tap, you know."

The overlarge eyes looked back at her, full of innocence. "They was there on the floor, madam, *very* near the tap. All I did was move them along a bit until the toes was under the drip. It wasn't like putting them there of a purpose." She went about arranging cups and saucers with the plates on the circular table. "I've brought two of everything, madam. I see the captain's shack-ho on the stand and thought mebbe he'd be up for tea with you."

No sooner had she finished speaking than the door opened with a crash and Rupert strode in, looking straight at Harriet on her window seat.

"This time you have gone too far, by God, you have!"

Harriet found her heart thudding, and she cast a significant glance toward the servant girl, who had dropped a plate of tiny sandwiches in her nervousness.

He pulled up short and took in the scene quickly before making an attempt to control himself. Tugging his tight-fitting red jacket into creaseless perfection, he said to the girl, "What are you doing here? I dismissed you yesterday."

Bessie stood her ground, albeit a trifle shakily. "Miss Deane said I was to take no notice of it, Captain."

Harriet could have shaken the girl. How many times had Rupert chastised her for using her mistress's maiden name, yet she had to do so when he was very obviously in a rage. The next minute she remembered her morning ride in the park. If she were to lay hands on anyone, it would be Rupert!

At that moment he was towering over Bessie like a god of wrath.

"If I hear you refer to your mistress once more as anything but Mrs. Torrington, I will personally throw you out into the street without money or good character. Now go before I do it this minute."

"But . . . the samwiges, Captain," she wailed, feeling her reputation would be lost if she did not clear up the spilled plate.

His response was immediate. Seizing her by the large starched bow of her apron strings, he ran her out of the room and closed the door behind her none too gently.

When he turned back into the room, Harriet snapped, "She is not one of your soldiers."

"Neither is she part of my household. I have dismissed her three times, but your campaign of interference undermines my authority on every possible occasion—as I have come to demonstrate to you. I want that girl out of here by tomorrow. She is insolent, aggressive, and unsuitable."

"She is also an orphan and completely dependent on me," Harriet told him coldly. "I took her into my care when she was about to be sold into a house of disrepute at the age of twelve. Is that what you wish to become of her?"

"I do not give a damn what becomes of her."

"No, I do not suppose that you do," he said in a significant manner, feeling the emotion that had ruled her all afternoon becoming more painful now he was standing before her. "In common with most men, you think only of your own desires and pleasures."

He studied her for a moment while changing lights in his eyes indicated the deepening of his anger into an emotion that shook her confidence.

"Do you consider that I have neglected you? Is there something you desperately need that you do not have?" he asked bitterly. "Perhaps I have not understood fully the requirements of a wife, but since you put all my gifts carelessly into a drawer, I believed your own desires and pleasures long ago satisfied."

Disliking the disadvantage of being seated when he stood, she rose quickly, and yet he still seemed to present a formidable opponent.

"I did not speak of material things. You are well aware, I think, that wealth has never ruled *me*!"

"Perhaps because it has never been your misfortune to suffer from it. But I have no intention of living like a pauper to please your nice notions of virtue."

She felt her temper rising disastrously. "I would not attempt to speak to you of virtue. I refer to natural compassion and humanity. You ride roughshod over anyone who is less fortunate than yourself. You flaunt your immense fortune by filling this house with priceless flummery and set the town on its ears with your excesses. There is not one indication that you care a jot about anything that money cannot buy."

Even as she said the last words, she knew they were unjust, but for once, her honesty would not allow her to apologize. This quarrel was different from others they had had. Today she wanted not only to hurt him but to strike a mortal blow. Her thoughts were uncharacteristically confused as a result.

"I think you have said enough," he told her savagely. "I will not have my character torn into shreds because of a sniveling servant girl. I suggest you examine your own compassionate tendencies before you condemn mine. You are my wife, remember."

Suddenly Harriet's pent-up emotion burst through her usual aloofness. The sight of this young and blatantly virile man made her long to strike out.

"And you are my husband, I will remind *you*," she cried passionately. "A pretty speech you made about presenting an image of marital contentment to the public. *I* have kept to my part."

"What is that meant to imply?" he asked, growing still.

She took a step nearer, as if her words would deal him a physical blow by her doing so. "The story is all over town. There is not a person who has not heard. When two vulgar and preening women spoke of it within my hearing today, I must have been the last to know."

"Indeed?"

His lack of response infuriated her further. In the grips of one of the worst rages she had ever experienced, she began to move around the room, clutching the sides of her crinoline with feverish hands.

"How dare you . . . how *dare* you make me the subject of ridicule and scorn? It is an insult second to none. After a mere two months you are conducting public amours. Not one, I was led to understand, but several women of the night enjoy your attentions." She was beside herself with a passion that frightened her with its intensity as she swung around and flung at him, "I was even provided with the name of one—

Moona. A creature much favored by rakehells and wealthy dissolutes." Leaving him a moment in which to digest that, she pounced once more. "You look shocked. Did you think ladies would not speak of such things, would not be aware that gentlemen were anything but the noble creatures they would have us believe? Well, these were not ladies, but the wives of some of your lower-born acquaintances who drive about the park and viciously tittle-tattle."

With a muscle jerking in his jaw he said, "And you are behaving just as they hoped."

She could not bear to look at him any longer and turned to the table, where the sandwiches lay scattered between the Wedgwood cups and saucers.

"How, may I ask, would you expect any wife to behave under such circumstances?"

He was a moment or two in answering. His voice was quiet now, and it held a strange echo of something she had almost forgotten over the past months. "I cannot speak for other men's wives . . . only my own. As a student of the human species I would expect her to understand the simple needs of a man—not an impossibly noble creature but an ordinary man. Especially one who has, but a year since, been through the horror of seeing other men blown to pieces, frozen to death, fall prey to disease; who has suffered the disillusion of knowing his country did not appreciate his endeavor and is prepared to forget it now. I would expect her to realize that he still has dreams that haunt him, faces that float before him when he closes his eyes, an uneasy certainty that he will do it all again anytime he is called upon to do so.

I would expect her to know there is a reason why he behaves as he does."

She made no answer because she could not speak through the thickness in her throat and the hot rushing pain that constricted her chest.

"I am sorry you were subjected to the tongues of brainless females who have nothing better to do than act like fishwives," Rupert continued in a more abstract manner, "but when you decide to make them unnecessary, my amours will cease."

With quickening pulse and flaming cheeks she swung around; but the door was closing behind him, and she was left with the silence of an empty room as well as the ghosts he had left behind.

The light hurt his eyes, his throat felt as dry as dust, and the marks on the cards danced before his strained vision. He had started at the dice tables and then retreated to a private and discreet parlor where men had made or lost fortunes on just one hand. Once more the cards had gone his way, and he was richer by 10,000 guineas already that evening.

The small group called for a fresh pack of cards and several more bottles of brandy. During the bright conversation made by rich young men nervous and keyed up by the uncertainty of Lady Luck, Rupert sat staring at the green baize tabletop. Another quarrel with Harriet, and a damnable one this time. His father had accused his own dead wife of being hard and unrelenting; were all women like that?

Only a fool would stake every penny he possessed when there was a chance there would be no tomorrow to win it back. How could he have known Edward

Deane would take such a risk? A man did not insult his close friend by asking if he could afford the money he laid down as a stake. Even allowing for the fact that the packet ships taking mail to the Crimea had been infrequent, the sacks of letters sometimes lost completely, thus making it difficult to keep a check on one's bank balance, Edward must have known he was tossing away his sister's future with every card.

Oh, he could understand all too easily the desperation suffered by men like Edward during that autumn and winter before his own and other regiments arrived as spring reinforcements, and he could understand the need to blot it out with reckless steeplechasing, drinking, and games of chance. But Edward should not have participated in games where the stakes were so high.

Someone refilled the glass at his elbow. He reached for it absently and downed the brandy in one draft. It did not help to clear his vision or his thoughts, but the fiery warmth in his throat and stomach gave him a touch of bravado. It was not *his* fault that Edward's debts had been settled after his death. It was all the fault of the damned communications system that swiftly delivered accounts of the debts or winnings of officers too busy fighting to keep accounts of their affairs but that managed to delay within its complications the vital notification of a man's death for two months so that even his sister did not know of it.

It was also the fault of his own man of business for pressing for prompt payment of debts. Rupert paid little attention to his banker's lengthy and precise accounts. He took for granted that notes of hand were eventually redeemed by those with whom he played—they were all honorable men—and his wealth was such that the exact amount standing to his credit did not much matter. But his banker had been taught by Aubrey to "keep at" any debtor until the amount was paid—a hardheaded and ruthless practice begun by Garforth Torrington—and had pressed for settlement of Edward Deane's debts by his solicitor, Harkins.

Only after Harriet's terrible condemnation, flung at him at a time when he was swamped with the need to make her his own, had Rupert summoned his banker to account for the charge and found, to his horror, that her words were true. His man had presented the account, and Harkins had settled it with the last of Edward's mortgage loan, neither man being aware that the young lieutenant was dead and the debt should have been canceled. But Rupert, who had been present at his friend's death, knew of it only too well, and Harriet believed he had been party to the transaction.

He stared broodingly into his empty glass. That she should so quickly have believed such a thing of him had led him to lash out with his tongue; if a man had made such an accusation, he would have knocked him down. When he had made his visit three days later, the terrible facts in his possession and full of desperation, she had refused to allow him to explain and cut him short with biting words and forced him to take an attitude that had worsened the situation between them. There and then he had vowed she could go hang for an explanation. And he was damned if he would give her one until she showed some kind of remorse over her injustice.

The brandy strengthened that resolve. No, he was damned if he would plead his case when he was not guilty. Let her think him a greedy, grasping rogue if that was what her uncharitable nature dictated!

It did not help his mood when one of his companions clapped him drunkenly on the back at that moment and said, "Why so pensive, Rupert? It cannot be due to a letter from your banker. The only things he sends you are notices of the present number of millions to your account."

"Yes, what does it feel like to be the wealthiest man in your regiment, old chap?" asked another broodingly.

Rupert tipped up the bottle. "It does not seem to matter when the bullets are flying," he said with sudden savagery, and then drank another long draft of brandy. "Come on, do you play or not?"

"It really is damned unfair," complained the dark-haired heir to a title. "Here am I with name and estates to uphold, while you have nothing on which to spend your money except your excesses. I wish my father were in some lucrative trade instead of prattling about reform in the House and letting the estate fall to rack and ruin. The confounded thing is entailed, so I will have it as a stone around my neck all my life."

"If your father were in trade, old fellow, there would be no estate to keep up. Torrington knows that. All he stands to inherit is a frightful Chinese monstrosity."

The sneer in the voice set Rupert rounding on a man he had never liked overmuch. "Pagoda House is a fine example of Chinese architecture. It is a great pity more people haven't the wits to recognize it."

"Ha!" countered the other, as drunk as any man in the room. "That is a change of tune from you. I understood you abhorred the place."

"Oh, come, Bart," said a meek-mannered captain of cavalry. "It's weally most pwetty."

"Pretty . . . *pretty*! It's a damned pretentious example of bad taste. But what can you expect from the son of an eel fisherman? That *was* how your grandfather began, wasn't it, Torrington?"

Rupert only resisted the urge to smash his glass in the fellow's face by clenching his hand around the brandy bottle and pouring himself another. Rupert had heard it all before and knew he would hear it again. It was true, and no words of his would alter facts publicly known. His father had expressed surprise that his son could accept such treatment, but he did not know what burned inside Rupert's breast.

The greatest desire in his life had been achieved when the regiment allowed him to buy a commission in its ranks, and retaining it was all that mattered. His wealth allowed him to live like a gentleman; his uniform and rank gave him the appearance of one. The years would dull the memories of those who held his ancestry against him; his own valor would override all other considerations. At the Crimea he had been commended for gallantry; a start had been made. He had no intention of throwing it all away by acting like a merchant's son. If they thought to drive him to it, they were mistaken.

He looked around the small smoke-laden room at the faces reddened by inebriation. "I suggest we double the stakes," he challenged, as if all that had gone before were of no consequence. "That should sort out the daring from the fainthearted."

There was a shocked silence; then the sneering voice said, "I find my interest in the game completely vanished. I have no wish to cover money that smells of eels. No amount of it will ever distract from its odor."

Before he knew it, Rupert was on his feet, sweeping cards, bottles, and glasses from the table in a surge of anger.

"One day you may cry out to me for help in the heat of battle, Merridew. I wager the smell of eels will not trouble you one jot then." After kicking his chair out of the way viciously, he walked unsteadily to the door. "I'll seek more congenial company—and she will not be one of your damned aristocratic fillies with an overlong nose and virginal loins. This one does not care for a man's background, only his virility."

He arrived at Moona's door in a state of despair. He had lost his temper after all, and they had achieved their purpose in ridding themselves of someone who did not measure up to their standards. At least, that is what he thought as he waited for the girl to send away an unwanted visitor. While he waited, he drained the contents of another bottle, and when she reappeared, it was with a sense of deep gratitude that he took her in his arms to ease his frustration with desperate embraces that should have been for Harriet.

He remained with her all night and eventually slept very heavily. Moona had no desire to hustle away one of her most attractive, exciting, and considerate clients, and it was only because she had a royal visitor due that afternoon that she finally woke him and sent him on his way.

He went straight to his club to shave, take breakfast, and get his uniform pressed. Because of the lateness of the hour, there were few members present, and since he ate in his room, he had no conversation with anyone. He did not want company. There was too much weighing heavily on his mind.

His two months with Harriet had been worse than he had feared. Nothing he did made her relent in the slightest. Knowing quarrels only worsened the situation, he still lost his temper on numerous occasions when her unyielding determination clashed with his own. Unhappy in her company, he played harder and drank more than was wise in an effort to defy the woman who haunted him all the time. He cursed himself as a fool to want her so much and yet was damned if he would invite rejections of his advances, and doors shut in his face. From the day of the wedding he had made no attempt to make love to her, and if she locked herself in at nights, he did not know because he had never tried the handle of her door. On that one thing he was adamant: She must come to him.

Yesterday had been the first time the subject had been mentioned between them, and he had felt immediately that his words had sounded like a plea. In consequence, he had left the house angry with himself and loath to give her the satisfaction of believing him to be in his room waiting in hopes of her knock.

He sighed heavily. Was he a man or not? Any other would tell him he should end all the nonsense, be master in his own house, march into her boudoir, where he had every right to be, and teach her submission. But he knew instinctively there would be no happiness that way. Harriet's emotions ran deep, like his own. She had been hurt to the point of numbness; brute force now would destroy any chance he might have of regaining that love she had once felt for him. The truth was, the situation was beginning to break him. He did not know how much longer he could go on before resorting to doing that which he knew would alienate her for good.

His mood was not improved on reaching the barracks, for the officers' mess was practically deserted, and those who were there were not being sociable. In fact, they left a minute or so after he walked in, giving him no more than a nod—not even that in two instances. When he summoned a steward to fetch him a drink, the man looked at him, frankly astonished.

"I didn't think as 'ow you'd be in today, Captain Torrington."

"Changed my mind," he murmured absently. "I want to try that new steeplechase pony of mine."

"Yes . . . yes, I see, sir," said the man in such a funny tone that Rupert looked at him in irritation.

"Don't stand there looking as if you have seen a ghost, man. Fetch me that drink."

"Right away, sir," said the soldier, jumping into action.

The drink did not make him feel much better. Since the mess remained deserted, Rupert left and made his way past the administration offices toward the stables. Rounding a corner, he came face-to-face with the adjutant and another officer, who stopped, reddening.

"Good God, Torrington!" cried the adjutant. "I hardly expected to see you here this morning."

The other officer said nothing; he simply stood looking very discomfited.

Their attitude annoyed Rupert. "I believe I have every right to be in my own regimental barracks when I choose. Soldiering is my profession, after all."

"There is no need to take that line," said the adjutant with a trace of hauteur. "It is natural enough for a fellow to believe you would not care to be seen here under the circumstances. But since you have decided to brazen it out, you had better go straight to the colonel. He wants to see you at the first opportunity."

Disliking the man as he did, Rupert did not dwell on his words, simply registering that the colonel was anxious to see him. It could be one of two things: a comment on the paper he had submitted on the failings of the rifles used extensively in the Crimea, or there could be promotion up for purchase. Both prospects were strong enough to drive away his earlier preoccupation, and he turned away from the two men to cross the wide avenue, anticipation giving him a welcome feeling of zest.

The assistant adjutant, a spotty-faced subaltern, also turned red when he saw him enter the office, but he always did so when confronted by a senior officer and Crimean veteran, so Rupert saw nothing significant in it. The boy had joined the regiment only since its return from the Crimea and stood in awe of men who had actually been in battle.

"C-Captain Torringt-ton," he stammered. "I did not expect . . . I mean . . ."

"I appear to have taken everyone by surprise this morning," said Rupert dryly. "I understand the colonel wishes to see me."

"Y-yes, sir . . . but we did not expect . . ." He ran his hand nervously down his trouser leg. "I am not certain he is ready."

"Ready?" repeated Rupert tartly. "Either he wishes to see me, or he does not. I think you had better find out instead of standing there looking like a stallion who has just discovered he is a gelding."

The boy blushed even redder. "He *is* most anxious to see you, sir. I'll tell him you are here."

"Thank you . . . and, Paynton, if you hope to make anything of your career, you must be prepared for the unexpected."

The young man bolted down the corridor and returned in a short while, still painfully flushed. "Will you go in, Captain Torrington?"

Rupert smiled to himself as he approached the commanding officer's door. The boy was looking at him much in the manner of a new boy at public school who comes face-to-face with the hero of the cricket team. He was still smiling faintly when he entered at the colonel's invitation and saluted smartly.

"Good morning, sir."

His senior looked extremely serious and yet, at the same time, almost ill at ease as he replied, "Good morning, Captain Torrington. I did not expect you in today under the circumstances."

Rupert grew puzzled, and the earlier remarks of his colleagues now assumed importance. Why was everyone so surprised to see him—no, not surprised—in some way *embarrassed*? While rapidly reviewing all he had done recently that might explain it, he asked, "*Under the circumstances, sir*? I do not quite understand."

The colonel's black brows drew together, and his face, still sallow from prolonged Crimean fever, folded into lines of perplexity. For a moment he studied his officer and then said, "Good God, can you possibly know nothing of it? *The Times* this morning at least?"

"I regret I have not yet seen the newspaper, sir." He dismissed any wild notions of war having broken out in some far-flung part of the world to which they were to be sent immediately, for in such an event they would expect him to report to barracks, not be astonished that he had done so. "I'm sorry, Colonel, but in what way does this morning's *Times* affect me so particularly?"

By way of answer, the senior man heaved from the chair his portly figure encased in a uniform meant for a man of a more slender physique and walked across to a bookcase, where he picked up a copy of the newspaper and held it out.

"Take your time, Rupert. This is no longer an official interview." He cleared his throat noisily. "Page five."

Rupert's puzzlement changed to chill apprehension, but he was wildly off course in his thinking. In that silent room of austere formality he read the long account that caused a crescendo of pulse beats in his head until he was oblivious of his surroundings and his silent companion. It was impossible to put a name to what he felt—sadness, defensive anger . . . regret? His relationship with his father had always been one of undemanding friendship, mutual understanding, rough affection. If he had not been so self-absorbed that day at Pagoda House, he might have been more awake to the truth, but could he have prevented the outcome? Probably not.

Even in the dignified language of *The Times* the affair sounded sordid. Wealthy financier Grenville Dornacre had returned unexpectedly to his home in Sussex to find his beautiful young wife being attacked by the couple's close friend and neighbor, Aubrey Torrington, millionaire silk merchant. The seducer was caught *flagrante delicto* by the betrayed husband, who took up his rifle, wounding him in the shoulder. He then horsewhipped the partially clad intruder across the grounds of Dornacre Park and threw him off his property. Dornacre was bringing a court action against his neighbor for the assault upon his terrified wife; Torrington was bringing a cross action for violent assault while under intoxication.

The words ran into each other as Rupert ceased to see them, even though he still held the folded newspaper as before. What he actually saw was that beautiful face with upswept silver fair hair and green eyes that dared a man to want her. He had wanted her himself in those first moments, but his response had been to a woman supremely ruled by her known prowess of sexual attraction. Women like Caroline Dornacre ruined men as part of their self-indulgence, and there was no doubt in his mind she had drawn his father to her house as a spider draws a fly to the center of its web. It was probable that her husband's return had been as much a shock to her as to her lover, but the episode would only enhance her sexual reputation. Man was the villain; woman the pure and helpless victim—always.

Rupert's hold tightened on the newspaper as he thought of his father's humiliation at the hands of an elderly man who could not hold a selfish and amoral wife. Oh, God, what a mess! Why had his father not remained content with courtesans—acknowledged courtesans? He had laid himself open to imprisonment, professional ruin, the loss of his good name. What madness had led him to fall so completely under that woman's spell as to forget honor and the strict rules of society?

"Did you really know nothing of this?"

He looked up at his colonel as if he had still not awakened from the drugged state of the night.

"No, sir. I—I met the lady just once—when I took my wife to Sussex to meet my father."

"Yes . . . well, it is a damnable business, there's no mistake," said the colonel gruffly. "It's all around the regiment, of course. Can't stop it." He walked back to his desk and fiddled with some papers on it. "A damnable business," he said again.

Rupert was too shocked to reply and stood looking at the desk littered with papers, lost in his thoughts.

"Of course, the thing would have blown over, in time . . . but court actions!" The colonel shook his head. "The papers will be full of it. *The Times* is discreet enough, but there's no knowing what some of the others will make of it. Court actions drag on—gossip, public scenes outside the courtroom, that sort of thing. It's bad for the regiment."

"Bad for the regiment?" echoed Rupert uncomprehendingly. "How is the regiment affected?"

The black brows met again in a frown. "You will be dragged into it. Your whole background will be laid bare for society to read. 'Captain Torrington, an officer of that illustrious regiment of foot' . . . and so on. Of course, the regiment will suffer." He fiddled with the papers on his desk once more. "Your fellow officers were understandably concerned and . . . and shocked. Many of them are connected to the noblest families in England and Ireland. They feel—as I do—that the regiment should be protected at all costs. We have a glorious history—that of a proud regiment and a valiant one. Its officers are gentlemen of honor and gallantry. There is a standard to be maintained. . . ."

Rupert was rushing back to full comprehension and remembered the officers' mess that had suddenly emptied when he walked in, the red faces at his unexpected appearance this morning. By God, they all thought he should have slunk away like a cur with its tail between its legs!

"Sir," he began with quiet anger, "are you trying to tell me you are dismissing me from this regiment?"

The colonel's sallow face feigned horror. "No, no . . . I have no grounds for doing so. But . . . but under the circumstances I feel sure you will want to do the gentlemanly thing."

Holding onto his control with difficulty, Rupert said, "No, sir, I'm damned if I will. It is my father who has committed this folly, not I. I have served the regiment honorably, and until I am forcibly removed from it, I shall continue to do so as one of its officers."

Chapter Six

"Rupert, we cannot," cried Harriet immediately. "It is but three days since it happened. We *cannot* attend the regimental ball tonight."

"I have tickets. What else could preclude us from being present at this splendid occasion held by my own regiment?"

She sat at the breakfast table with her husband and knew at once that this was one occasion on which she would be forced to give way. Rupert was still shocked and defensive, as he had been ever since the scandal had broken.

Things had been difficult enough before, but he had grown almost frighteningly unapproachable at a time when she felt . . . well, she did not exactly know what she felt, but his manner did not help her to find out. After his disturbing defense of his visits to women of the night he had left the house and not returned until the following afternoon, by which time they had both heard the disastrous news.

Rupert had been pale and uncommunicative ever since, and she had seen little of him. He had gone into Sussex to see his father, curtly telling her, when she offered to accompany him, that it was an affair into which women should not be drawn. Her spirited reply that it was surely one of her own sex who had precipitated it was met by the uncharacteristic reply that he had given his views on the subject and the matter was now closed. And closed it was! He returned from Battle, went straight to his club, and had not mentioned the visit since.

Harriet could not dismiss the sad affair from her mind as he appeared to have done. For three days she had been unable to settle down to anything, listening all the time for Rupert's comings and goings and feeling incredibly lonely. A quick bond of friendship had formed between herself and Aubrey Torrington after they had sized each other up, and she felt more than somewhat affected by his gullibility concerning a woman who had plainly been provocative. There was no one to whom she could confide her feelings. Little Bessie Porridge was loyally sympathetic in the way she fussed around her mistress, but one could not admit to a servant that such scandalous things had even happened. Nanny was in Sussex, where she was doubtless shocked to the core and smugly justified in her belief that allowing a gentleman in at ten o'clock one evening had led to all she had predicted. As to friends, her old ones all appeared to have left town; her newer acquaintances seemed not to notice her when she passed.

But by far the worst aspect was that Rupert had become remote. He treated her with uninterested formality, brooking no argument and going about his life as if she were just an accessory. It left her with a feeling of bereftness that was even worse than what she had felt when she first discovered his treachery. Then she had been able to strike back.

She looked at him now as he drank coffee and ate his breakfast with a heartiness that suggested he had not a care in the world. Wearing an expensive frogged velvet jacket that sat across his shoulders perfectly, with his blond hair carefully brushed into gleaming neatness, he gave his usual impression of strength and assurance, but his eyes always betrayed him, and Harriet saw hovering there enough to make her try to dissuade him from what she felt was an unwise decision.

"Your friends will not expect us to be at the ball under the circumstances . . ." she began, meaning to intimate they would sympathize with his predicament.

He looked up quickly and snapped, "Why should they not expect us? We are, neither of us, indisposed, and you are finally out of mourning clothes, I am glad to note," he added pointedly.

She tried again. "The details are universally known, Rupert. Why do you pretend they are not?"

He set down his knife and fork with exaggerated care and then took a sip of coffee before replying. "I take it you refer to that affair in Sussex. What has that to do with our going to the regimental ball?"

"It has everything to do with it," she cried, feeling her frustration turn into a rise of temper. "*He is your father.*"

"And an adult male of some eight-and-fifty years who runs a prosperous trading company with astuteness and expertise. *I* am not responsible for his actions."

"Of course, you are not responsible . . . I did not mean to imply that you were. But this will reflect upon you—"

"I do not agree," he put in quickly. "When Aubrey Torrington made that record-breaking voyage from Canton to Woolwich, did anyone clap his son on the shoulder? When a certain royal princess charged my father with an order for silk for the entire wedding wardrobe, did the honor of her patronage fall upon *me*? Why then, because there is now something to his discredit, should you fancy I shall be any more concerned than on those other occasions?" He went back to his breakfast. "Now will you kindly say no more on the subject?"

She rose from the table and stood looking at his downcast head while a curious feeling of intense gentleness assailed her.

"If I did not know you for a man of great intelligence, I *would* say no more on the subject. If you go there tonight, you will be subjected to further distress over the affair. I do not believe you are as immune to it as you make out."

His dark glance nearly burned through her as he looked up quickly, and she grew more angry. "You do not know how cruel society can be."

"Do I not?" he retorted bitterly. "For most of my life I have been the recipient of sneers, supercilious condescension, and reminders that my forebears were of lowly stock." He got up, flinging his napkin onto the table so carelessly that it landed in his cup. "Do you think I am not aware that they tolerate me only because of my millions? Do you think I regard them as friends? I use them, as they use me; that is all. My real friends—like your brother—are few, and valued because they see only me and not my history."

He kicked his chair out of the way. "Oh, yes, ma'am, I know how cruel society can be. Even my wife denies that I am a gentleman." He strode to the door and turned to say, "The regiment is the most important thing in my life, and I will allow nothing to take it from me. Be ready at eight. I expect that you will be dressed as befits the occasion . . . and wearing one or two items you have cast into your drawer in disparagement. You are a captain's lady, I beg you remember, not an impoverished noblewoman in half mourning."

After he left, she took the napkin from the coffee cup with as much care as if it were so fragile as to break in her trembling hands.

It was a sight to stir even the most cynical observers of society, for the Victorians had a strong dash of sentimentality in their formidable characters. The assembly of clear-eyed, manly defenders of the queen, together with those pure, delicate creatures who upheld the morality of a country dedicated to enlighten and rule the heathen, could draw only a feeling of pride from all those present.

The great hall had been decorated with silver-gauze fish to commemorate the regiment's nickname, The Fishers, given to it during the war with Napoleon, when it had come upon a company of Frenchmen easing their aching feet in a stream and had pulled its captives out by means of ropes. It was a noble building with a vaulted roof famous for its painting of the great fire of London, and fluted columns of Italian marble that divided the area to provide a series of cloisters on each side that were attractively situated for those who wished to converse more privately or spend a thrilling moment or two away from the eyes of chaperones or jealous husbands.

The regimental band was conveniently placed above the assembly on the minstrels' gallery and was already playing a lively march when the Torringtons made their entrance. Harriet was impressed. She had once met the colonel and knew a few officers of Rupert's closer acquaintance, but the circumstances of her mourning and the swiftness of her marriage had prevented her from attending previous occasions such as this one.

She saw at once why Rupert spoke with pride about his regiment. The hall epitomized its past glory and present distinction, and the dress uniform—embellished with gold braid, the jacket cut to emphasize broadness of chest and shoulders but slenderness of waist, and the blue overalls with double scarlet braid on the seams fitting so tightly on the leg that it was possible to see a man's thigh muscles ripple as he walked—brought home to Harriet the justification of her fears. This ball was not only a social occasion but an extension of military life. The Fishers were not going to take kindly to the presence of Aubrey Torrington's son and his lady at such a time.

Harriet glanced up quickly at Rupert. Indeed, he had as much right to be there as any other man—his strong body set off the uniform to perfection, and he looked far more the gentlemanly Victorian hero than many to whom nature had been less kind—but she could tell by a tightness around his mouth that he was there out of defiance.

Even as they were about to set out, she had made one more appeal to his common sense, but he had silenced her sharply and commented instead on her lack of jewelry when he had particularly asked that she should wear it. Her quiet remark that she had felt it unfitting that particular night caused no further remarks from him, and she had entered on his arm, wearing a gown of palest apricot satin trimmed with bronze lace and seed pearls. It was one of the new crinolines she had previously refused to wear, but she had selected it now, needing something to give her confidence.

At the moment of their entry she knew they should not have come. They were soon spotted, and the news of their attendance rippled around the room, causing the gentlemen to raise their eyebrows and their partners to stare rudely. It was humiliating and uncomfortable to find the entire assembly expressing disapproval so plainly, and Harriet began to burn with anger. Then her thoughts became more occupied with a strange truth. Her natural impulse had always been to toss her head at ridiculous moral confrontations, and so her present desire to withdraw was merely to prevent Rupert from being lashed by unjust censure.

As she walked beside him toward a small group, she was shaken to the core. It was quite absurd to feel protective toward a man of Rupert's character after all he had done to Edward and, through him, to herself. Yet there could be no other reason for her reluctance to face these people tonight. She cast another quick glance up at her husband and now, realizing the astonishing fact, felt a surge of painful warmth at what he was about to do.

"Good evening, Chalfont . . . Mrs. Chalfont," began Rupert with a smile. "It must be all of six months since we met, ma'am." He drew Harriet forward into the circle of unsmiling people. "Miss Deane has since become my wife."

Harriet forced herself to smile at Mrs. Chalfont—a pretty brainless creature with a monotonous voice, she remembered. "We spoke of trimmings, as I recall. I trust you found what you wanted at the small emporium I recommended."

Mrs. Chalfont turned pale and looked at her husband, who bowed stiffly and spoke on her behalf. "My wife is indebted to you, ma'am. Now, you must excuse us. We have promised to speak to Major and Lady Harrington."

They moved away, leaving an elderly captain, his wife and daughter, and two subalterns standing in acute embarrassment. Rupert left them no time to invent excuses and presented Harriet. The matron and her daughter hardly moved their lips in response. The subalterns giggled nervously, conscious that Rupert was the senior officer, even though Captain Clair was twice his age. They were in a difficult position professionally and hardly knew what to do.

Rupert made it worse for them by asking to write his name in Miss Clair's card, while indicating Harriet's. "My wife is an accomplished executor of the quadrille," he told the two young men. "I am persuaded you will wish to secure such a partner before her card is filled."

"My daughter does not dance the waltz, Torrington," blustered the elderly father, very red in the face.

Rupert flicked his glance down the names on the well-filled card attached to Miss Clair's wrist by a silken cord. "Dear me, then all these gentlemen are doomed to disappointment—Ponsonby, St. John, Lord Crawford . . . even the colonel—all promised to waltz with a young lady who does not dance it." Quick as lightning he turned to Mrs. Clair. "You must be well versed in the steps of the waltz, ma'am. Will you not grant me the pleasure of the next dance?"

Her much-folded face stretched and folded into another pattern that was easy to read. "I do not care to extend myself this early in the evening, sir."

Checking her anger, Harriet gave the woman a bright smile. "I regret my husband, having tragically lost his mother at an early age, is unfamiliar with the needs of elderly ladies, ma'am. But I have to confess your loss is my gain, for duty done, he is now free to dance the waltz with me." Slipping her hand through the crook of his arm, she looked up at him with a smile."The opening bars are already being played."

They walked away, leaving Mrs. Clair, who was nowhere near an age that could be called elderly, feeling she had been put down by a young woman vulgar enough to deserve the family into which she had just married.

Her temper still smoldering, Harriet moved into Rupert's arms to begin the dance. She held her head high but avoided looking directly at him as he began circling, guiding her with a hand behind her waist. The music was haunting, evocative; the twirling panorama of scarlet jackets and pastel crinolines was romantic;

the glittering chandeliers cast prismatic reflections upon walls and ceiling, but Harriet could think of nothing but the scene that had just occurred and the way Rupert's hand on her waist trembled.

She might have been oversensitive, but it seemed to her that other couples managed to avoid dancing near them, and those sitting or standing around the ballroom spoke confidentially among themselves while their eyes were fastened on just one dancing couple. Much as he might brazen it out Rupert was as aware of the atmosphere as she. It was obvious from the stiffness of his body, the unnecessary tightness of his grip, the way he kept swallowing in nervous fashion.

Suddenly she could stand it no longer. "Rupert, they are being impossible. You can see that they are."

"Clair is a pompous bore, and Mrs. Clair a prig—they always have been," was the toneless answer.

His hurt was her hurt, and she could not keep back her plea. "Let us go home . . . please."

He looked down at her with eyes that were stony, and his hold on her tightened. "What, run away at the first setback? You forget I am a gamester; I continue until I hold the winning hand."

"Or until you are ruined," she flashed back. "What are you hoping to gain by this?"

"Respect," was the immediate answer. "Which is something I shall not earn by skulking in the corner like a man who has no right to a place in society. I have done nothing of which to be ashamed. I have served this regiment with honor, and the sooner they realize—" He broke off sharply. "I have already told you the matter is closed. You will oblige me by removing the frown from your brow. You have just now indicated to the Clairs that nothing would give you greater pleasure than to dance with me."

He drew her closer, and she found herself swung around faster and faster as the music accelerated to a conclusion.

Thanks to Rupert's determination, Harriet did not lack partners, but the evening dragged along as she danced with tongue-tied ensigns afraid to defy a captain's orders, even in a ballroom; with bachelor captains, who leered at her as if *she* had been seduced by Rupert's father; and with tottering majors, who went from partner to partner, not knowing or caring who they were but enjoying the thrill of holding a woman rather too tightly for her comfort.

Through it all, Harriet watched with the ache inside her increasing as Rupert continued to pretend there was nothing about the evening that was different from any other. He found a few of his fellows who would stand and chat for a while and several dashing widows who found it thrilling to dance in the arms of a man so closely concerned with a scandal of passion.

But backs were still turned toward them as they strolled past. Harriet felt the situation becoming more intolerable with every minute; but Rupert continued to throw his gauntlet of defiance at their feet, and she was obliged to act out the charade with the fire within her damped down with a great effort of will.

It was three dances before supper when she was brought face-to-face with a handsome bachelor who was flushed with wine and contempt. He led her onto the floor for the waltz with an unmannerly flourish that suggested it was a Parisian night spot rather than a grand ballroom. His loutish treatment of her drew glances and fanned the flames of her anger, so she was ready for him when he breathed into her ear. "You dance divinely, Mrs. Torrington. Quite the lady. Who would have thought it?"

"Certainly not you, sir," she replied clearly. "It is quite obvious to me that *thinking* is something you seldom do."

A shadow passed across his face, and he swung her unnecessarily roughly around a corner of the hall. "As to that, I imagine dancing is something *you* must seldom do. I hear your gallant husband is more often away from home than an officer of the Royal Navy."

His remark hurt because he spoke the truth, but she was not prepared to let him see she was the slightest bit affected by his words. "Yes, indeed, my husband is one of the few officers of this regiment who is very conscious of his professional responsibilities," she snapped.

He leered in her face. "So are the ladies of the demimonde who enjoy his company."

She drew in her breath sharply but managed to remain outwardly composed. "I doubt even a female of that nature enjoys yours, sir," she told him tautly.

With that she pulled free and walked very deliberately from the center of the ballroom, forcing couples to fall back to allow her passage. The scene had attracted a great deal of attention, but as Rupert was nowhere to be seen at that moment, Harriet took a seat near two matrons, who viewed her with distaste and said in audible aside, "Disgraceful behavior—quite disgraceful."

Turning to them on the instant, she said, "I quite

agree, ladies. Absolutely disgraceful. I am used to mix with *gentlemen,* and it surprises me that my husband's regiment allows into its ranks someone who does not know how to conduct himself in society."

The aging faces grew openmouthed with horror, and Harriet's temper rocketed. "All too often blue blood is used as an excuse for every kind of rudeness. My papa always used to say a true gentleman does not need a title to advertise the fact; it is stamped upon him for everyone to see." Then, seeing outrage growing on their self-righteous faces, she added, "He also claimed there was many a duchess among the peasants and many a scrubbing maid among the duchesses."

That they did not succumb to the vapors was amazing, for the shock sustained by their systems in those moments was enough to conquer their delicacy of constitution, but one had retained sufficient command of herself to cast an imploring look at a nearby captain deep in conversation with a pale creature hung about with diamonds. He noticed her appeal and rose quickly to take command of the situation.

As he approached Harriet recognized him as Captain St. John, the adjutant, who was another embryo noble. With the bit now firmly between her teeth she prepared to take him on also.

He approached her, hardly executed a bow, and said, "Allow me to take you to your husband, ma'am."

"Oh," she said, "has he sent you for that purpose?"

The man stiffened at the suggestion that he was at Rupert's beck and call. "I was under the impression that you had been . . . hem . . . abandoned . . . and required his company."

She smiled with false amusement. "My dear sir, my . . . hem. . . *abandonment,* as you so delicately put it, was by my own choice. As it must be to any unfortunate female who finds herself committed to dance with the inebriated Honorable Digby Canfield. I think it is he you should be escorting from the room before he can further lower the tone of the company tonight."

The young noble flushed, finding himself obliged then to maintain impeccable manners toward a young woman whom he felt should never have been present at the ball.

"If you have been offended in any way, Mrs. Torrington, I am profoundly sorry. All the more reason, I feel, that you should join your husband, who will offer his protection. Please allow me to find him for you."

Harriet rose and looked him straight in the eyes, for he was a short man. "But you do not know him, sir. When we bowed to you earlier this evening, it was plain you had never set eyes on us before."

He flushed a deeper red and grew agitated. "Mrs. Torrington, I beg you, do not create a further scene. Already so many eyes are turned in this direction."

"That is very strange, for I had the distinct impression that they were all turned very determinedly in the opposite direction until now," she said icily. "Do you suppose it can be *your* behavior that is causing the phenomenon?"

At that moment a pink-faced ensign hurried up and said in tones of great drama, "Captain Torrington cannot be found, sir. I have searched everywhere, except the further stretches of the garden. I . . . er . . . hardly liked to. . . ."

"Yes, quite so," said the adjutant with such meaning Harriet could not help understanding what he suggested.

The matrons nearby reached the same conclusion.

"Shocking! But two months married," clucked one.

"What can one expect from that family? They are all tarred with the same brush," pronounced the other.

Harriet had had enough. She would not stand there listening to them discussing Rupert in such manner. Nor would she remain in the company of prigs and poseurs a moment longer. In the full blaze of her strange new protection of a man she had treated with the same contempt, she said to Captain St. John, "I will be obliged if my carriage is called."

He looked intensely relieved and turned to the hovering ensign. "Mr. Calthorpe, see to it at once. Mrs. Torrington is feeling indisposed."

"On the contrary, sir, I have seldom felt better," she told him in throbbing tones that were designed to reach the matrons' and any other interested ears. "I simply find myself unable to endure one more moment of this abysmal evening. If my husband is, indeed, in the further stretches of the garden, I heartily sympathize with his desire to put as great a distance as possible between himself and an assembly that is unmannerly, full of its own importance, and most decidedly *dull.*"

Her anger raged throughout the solitary journey home, and as an aggressive Bessie undressed her and tidied the room of her ball accessories, Harriet admitted to herself that while she had been launching a fierce defense of a man she professed to hate, he had been making love to some siren in the seclusion of the garden. The thought fanned the flames of her mixed-up emotions, and she walked the room, unable to calm herself.

After sitting down heavily on the velvet boudoir seat, her fist beat gently on the squabs of the chair. Why did she slay him with her own tongue, yet leap to his defenses when others did the same? Rising, she resumed her pacing. Why did he not return? Surely he had emerged from his garden flirtation? They were engaged to take supper together, so it was not possible that he was unaware of her stormy departure. He could not mean to remain without her! Then she put her hands to her temples as it occurred to her that Rupert might well have gone straight to one of his mistresses, having no intention of returning to the house until midday on the morrow.

"Oh, madam, do let me bring you some tea," wailed Bessie yet again. "I know you've snapped me head off twice already when I mentioned it, but you won't never get calm this way."

At that moment there was the sound of a door slamming far off in the house, and Bessie's eyes enlarged with apprehension.

"Ooh, there's the captain now. I won't leave you, madam, never fear," she assured Harriet with great pluck. "Shall I bolt the door?"

"Go to your room," snapped Harriet, her own heartbeat thudding loud enough to awaken the dead. "You are being absurd and impertinent."

Bessie remained unabashed. "I won't go to my room, madam. I'll be outside within call."

With her hands once again to her temples Harriet cried, "Bessie, Captain Torrington will almost certainly be in a great rage. He would not dare lay hands upon me, but if he catches sight of you lurking in the corridor, it is very possible he will wring your neck and toss your body from the window. Then I shall have no servant at all."

The girl went scurrying from the room without another word, and Harriet was left staring at the door as she listened for Rupert's footsteps. He must have run up the stairs, for she was unprepared when the door immediately burst open without a polite knock.

She had seen him angry before but never like this. In the dim light from her one lamp his face was shadowed, but his dark eyes were burning with the fire of the accuser, the man who has been betrayed. He gave an impression of immense strength as the lamp glow caught the sheen of his pale hair, the gold embellishments of his jacket, and the whiteness of his teeth. She caught her breath at the thought of those women who knew him as she did not.

He walked toward her, kicking the door shut behind him. "I asked only one thing of you in this marriage. I thought you had pride and courage enough to accede to it." He flung down the white gloves he was carrying. "It has pleased you to tell me on every possible occasion that the accident of my birth has put me out of your league, that my wealth has not bought me equality of breeding, that my way of life and the gifts I offer you are pretentious and in bad taste. You are not the only one to think so. Three days ago I was invited by my colonel to 'do the gentlemanly thing' by resigning—selling out."

"*No* . . . oh, Rupert!" she exclaimed in quick sympathy, but he swept on with all that had gathered inside him since the scandal broke.

"I told him I was damned if I would ruin my career over something my father had done and set out to prove to them that my skill as a soldier was more important than my family history."

"They will never give you the chance," she cried. "You saw how they were tonight."

"Yes, I saw," he said savagely. "Do you think *I* was crushed by their ridiculous puffed-up superiority . . . a gathering of titled fools who cannot see beyond the end of their aristocratic noses? All I care about is those common soldiers, as rough and villainous a crowd as you could meet, looking up to me for strength and courage when death yawned ahead of them. They trusted me, believed in me, knew I would not let them down. They saw me suffer and endure what they suffered and endured. When their comrades fell all around them, and the regiment scattered in disorder, they saw me still there and rallied. It did not matter to them that I wore no coronet. They saw only a man who kept his head and knew what he was doing in the midst of confusion. They knew I was prepared to die for them."

He took a pace or two toward her, raising his voice. "I am who and what I am, that is all. I am not my father or my grandfather; I am not a millionaire merchant's son or a commoner aspiring to be a gentleman. *I am a damned good soldier* . . . and that is all that matters—all that should matter. Tonight they turned their backs on Aubrey Torrington, on Garforth Torrington who made a fortune from piracy and exploitation. They turned away from a young man whose wealth and education have given him the opportunity to be where his birth forbids him to be. But as for Captain Torrington, honorable veteran of the Crimea—they dare not turn their backs on him or they would be turning them on queen and country."

He took a deep, steadying breath. "You did that tonight. When I asked for your support, you failed me. You, whom I loved for your honesty and courage in the face of adversity, would not help me. You joined their ranks by walking out on me tonight."

The injustice of his words, the realization that he believed she had taken a cowardly way out increased the pain within her.

"*No!* Did they not tell you why I left?"

"They had no need to tell me," he flung at her bitterly. "From the start of this marriage you have shown your contempt for all I stand for. You have been no wife to me in any respect."

"Nor you a husband," she flung back equally bitterly. "At the time I was making my stand against those you forced me to join tonight, *you* were in the garden, pressing your kisses on some other man's wife."

He seized her arms with punishing fingers. "You will take that back—before God, you will."

Shaken by his display of physical violence against her, she said heatedly, "They knew—they all knew why you were in the garden."

"They did *not* know!" he raged. "I was in the garden talking privately with the one man who believes in what I am doing."

Too far gone in passion to understand the turbulence of emotion, fighting for prominence, Harriet hit out yet again. "Then it says much for your reputation that everyone thought otherwise."

He shook her fiercely, his fingers gripping the flesh of her arms until they hurt. "What does it say for *your* reputation, do you suppose? A cold, ungenerous wife? It is time you realized we can destroy each other very easily, tied to each other as we are." His hands dropped to his sides, and he sounded unutterably weary as he added, "Pride can become destructive unless it can bend . . . and you do not know the half of what you are doing to me."

He made for the door, and Harriet stood watching him, her hand pressed to her stomach in an effort to ease the thudding pain that made her breathless with yearning.

"Rupert . . . please. Tonight was a terrible mistake," she began, but he was already going out and merely looked back at her through the open door.

"Tonight is over. It will not stop me . . . *nothing* will stop me from remaining an officer of my regiment."

But Fate had other plans. On the following morning Aubrey Torrington was found dead with a bullet in his brain.

Chapter Seven

News of the suicide was soon all over the country. The newspapers, still trying to keep alive the four-day-old scandal, seized on the bizarre conclusion with joyous hands. Reporters soon invaded the peaceful village of Battle to emerge with titillating details of an affair that shocked the nation.

The full history, lavishly embroidered by newsmen's imaginations, of Aubrey Torrington and his rascally father was brought into the open, those even more determined than their comrades unearthing reports and comments from years back and interviewing anyone who had been remotely connected with the colorful trading family. In consequence, nonagenarian rivals or conspirators gave lavish and exaggerated accounts of the birth and growth of the Battle Trading Company, starting along the Coromandel Coast of India and then moving to the China Station, where Garforth Torrington, son of an eel fisherman, used his lifelong association with the sea to indulge in piracy and smuggling.

Aubrey gradually brought respectability to the company by concentrating solely on silk, although he had smuggled opium with the rest on occasion. But if he was a more orthodox businessman than his father, his private life was just as wild. Fellow merchants spoke of Chinese concubines, outrageous parties in Macao, and a marriage that produced three sons, two of whom lay as infants in the cemetery at Macao. Rupert's mother was represented as a long-suffering paragon of all the Victorian virtues, who stoically endured long years in the pestilential climate of Macao, her husband's infidelity with native women, and the death of two babies before expiring after the birth of a third in the lurid and eccentric Pagoda House built by Garforth Torrington in the heart of Sussex.

It was inevitable that, those two dealt with, attention should then be centered on the heir to the Torrington millions, who was presently a captain in a well-known regiment of the line. Here the newsmen had to exercise care, for their victim was alive and liable to sue, but it did not prevent them from presenting the facts so as to hint that he followed the style of Torrington men. By concentrating on his partiality for the gaming table and the gay life where ladies were to be found in large numbers, they gave an impression of his being a wild young man of the day who had no deeper side to his nature. A fleeting reference to his presence in the Crimea made no mention of his two recommendations for gallantry during the assault of Sevastapol or of his campaign waged in the columns of their own newspapers against ineffective firearms at present issued to the regiments.

The two-month-old marriage was mentioned with a certain amount of reserve. Someone had been astute enough to inquire into Harriet Deane's background and come up with a family as eccentric, if not as rascally, as the Torringtons. But pens were reluctant to do to a lady what they happily did to her husband. Most papers were content to mention in passing that the remarkable Deanes had gone through a fortune because of their interest in inventions and philanthropic works. Now Mrs. Torrington devoted her time to preparing for publication her father's lengthy study of indigenous races of the world. In that short sentence they managed to imply that she was an eccentric bluestocking who was too studious to know or care about her husband's rackety life outside the marital home.

Having dealt thoroughly with the principal actors in the drama, the reporters then set the scene that led to the sensational suicide. Aubrey Torrington, after being horsewhipped from the house of the man he had betrayed in the worst possible way, had faced the wrath of villagers who had never taken kindly to the family—father and son—that had erected a monstrosity in their beloved countryside.

Faithfully reported word for word were accounts of "odd goings-on" at Pagoda House. Villagers solemnly affirmed to seeing strange people moving about the grounds at night and strange Oriental animals that roamed at will within the walls of the estate. They agreed unanimously that the pagan spirits ruling the area were responsible for droughts, ruined harvests, outbreaks of disease in farm stock—even for village maids who found themselves pregnant.

All in all it was evident that it was only because of the squire's friendship with Torrington that their hostility had been curbed for so long. On hearing of the assault on Mrs. Dornacre, the villagers could no longer contain their wrath. The beautiful carp in the ornamental lake of Pagoda House were poisoned overnight, windows were smashed by stones and rocks, the magnificent banks of azaleas were hacked down and trampled upon, a small wooden pavilion was burned to the ground, and worst of all, three dogs were killed and pinned to the ground by stakes through their hearts.

Aubrey Torrington, weakened by the gunshot wound in his shoulder, deserted by his servants and friends, and facing professional ruin, took the only way out. His doctor found his body when making his daily visit to the house. He also found a note addressed to Captain Rupert Torrington, which the police delivered to the home of the young officer. It was understood to contain a confession of suicide and a plea for forgiveness that he no longer had the courage to face his accusers.

The articles concluded with a sugary-smug regret that Captain Torrington, when called upon to give a statement, was unwilling to see anyone. However, several of his fellow officers said they believed the captain had handed his resignation to his colonel and put his commission on the market, so it appeared he was intending to salvage what he could of the company he had inherited. They asked their readers a rhetorical question: Is a soldier the best man to run a fleet of merchant ships?

Nobody appeared to think so, for shares in the company fell to a disastrous low as news of the scandal spread. The smart town house rented by the young Torringtons was besieged by newsmen and sensation seekers, the latter shouting insults and, in one instance, heaving a brick through a front window. The police had to be called to keep away the crowd and to protect servants and tradesmen as they went about their daily business.

It was a nightmare period that took its toll of the young couple. Rupert was stunned and saddened by the death of his father under such circumstances and went around in a state of disorientation after the surrender of his career. There had been no choice this time. The colonel had regretted to tell him that the junior officers all refused to serve under him and senior officers declined to have him in their command. That fact, coupled with the realization that he would no longer be admitted to clubs and public places where military men were expected to be seen, made it impossible for him to continue to hold a commission in that or any other regiment of the queen.

The board of directors of the company was pressing him for an assurance of stability to calm the shareholders and bombarding him with questions and suggestions on something about which he knew very little. The French, who had great trading interests in China, were already planning to jump in and take over the lucrative business at the first sign of a collapse of the administration of their rivals, and Rupert was forced to decide which of his directors he should trust and which had their own interests more at heart than those of the company.

For Harriet it was a week of oppression. She could

not go out and felt like a prisoner guarded by the police. Aubrey's death had upset her greatly. That an individualist of great charm should have been crushed by that very society he chose to enliven with his personality seemed, to her like spirit, a tragic blow. That Rupert should now be defeated by that same society saddened her even more.

On the night of the ball he had awakened her to a side of his personality she had not before suspected, had not attempted to discover. Somewhere along the road of their isolated partnership she had begun to realize that the man she had been forced to marry was more complex than she had imagined. Now it was all too clear that he was as much of an individualist as she . . . and she felt his defeat as much as if it were her own.

They traveled to Sussex by train on the day of the funeral. It was a harrowing ordeal. Aubrey Torrington was to be buried in the grounds of Pagoda House, and those who found excitement in tragedy were there for a day's outing. At the railway station a rowdy mob tried to surround the two principal mourners and to prevent their reaching the carriage awaiting them in the yard. Those directors who had traveled from London with them did their best to surround the couple. When one bold lout tried to lift the heavy veil from Harriet's face, Rupert struck out at him with his cane. It did not improve the mood of the crowd, and they stood in the rain as the carriage moved off, shouting abuse from mock-pious mouths or giving lewd invitations to Rupert to sample their charms.

Harriet sat in the carriage trembling. She had not

believed people could be so cruel and vicious. Then she realized that this was no different from Rupert's being forced to leave his regiment, people showed their disapproval in the only way they knew—but they always delivered the same message: Conform or be punished!

A group of leering youths was preventing the carriage from getting under way, and Rupert leaned forward to shout in a hoarse voice, "Whip them out of the way, or by God, I will do it myself."

It did the trick, but the sightseers sensed more drama to come and piled into carts, ready to follow them all the way to Pagoda House. Harriet's heart seemed to thud in time to the beat of hooves, and her mouth felt dry. The man beside her sat silent and withdrawn, his face set in rigid lines that showed too clearly the strain he was under in those moments. Yet she could say nothing by way of comfort. Sharing their carriage were two directors respectfully clad in black for the funeral that could not be held in the normal way. They sat in silence also, and so she stared from her window at the dripping trees and hedges as they passed. Today Aubrey would be buried . . . and, in time, forgotten. But what of those who were left?

In a quick surge of apprehension she glanced up at Rupert, but he was leaning forward to stare at the distant gates of Pagoda House. A carriage drawn up before the gates was being prevented entry by what looked like a line of hostile villagers.

"That is the rector's carriage," said Rupert quietly. "They will not let him in to conduct the service."

Harriet was appalled. A man was dead. Whether they liked and approved of him or not, he should be allowed to go before his Maker to receive judgment. But these men and women of the village, rough, work-worn, and riddled with superstitions, were forming a barrier across the gateway. It was clear they were not content that someone they regarded as evil was being denied burial in their churchyard; these village people resented their rector's speaking holy words over the dead man.

"Pull up!" commanded Rupert so crisply that Harriet jumped at the sound of his voice. Hardly had the carriage slowed than he was out of it and striding toward the scene, a tall figure in black holding a silver-knobbed cane. Harriet watched through her thick veil, wishing she could be out there beside him in that moment, yet knowing he did not need her help.

The villagers guessed Rupert's identity and reacted accordingly. Whereas they had been immobile and silent before, they now tightened their grips on the farming implements they held as weapons, and their leader shouted, "Keep away, and there'll be no 'arm done."

Rupert took no notice. Stopping a mere foot from them, he called to the gateman to open up at once. The man replied faintly that they had threatened him if he did so.

"If every man who was threatened for doing his duty meekly complied, this country would now be in the hands of Napoleon," snapped Rupert. "Open those gates, and be quick about it."

The spokesman for the villagers shuffled forward, holding a large scythe. He had a blunt, ignorant face with ears that stood out beneath his cap.

"We don't care 'oo else goes in there," he said, jerking his head toward the house, "but no man of God is going to set foot in that heathen place and then come out and taint us with the touch of the devil."

There was a chorus of agreement, and they all moved up in support of their leader, raising pitchforks, scythes, and flailing sticks in a threatening manner.

"Mr. Torrington, sir, please have a care," called the rector in trembling tones from his carriage. "It will not do to cross them. I know these people. They are acting from strong feelings of fear. They are liable to become ugly."

Rupert turned his back on the small army and walked several paces to the window of the rector's carriage. His voice carried clearly to Harriet, who recognized in it the same tone he had adopted with her after the ball. He had had almost more than he could take.

"Are you still prepared to conduct my father's funeral service, sir?" he asked of the dithering churchman.

"Prepared? I have always been prepared to . . . but you must appreciate that it is out of the . . . these people will never allow it."

At that point everyone's attention was directed toward the arrival of the carts that had followed them from the railway station. The occupants, seeing a prize situation, threw themselves into the spirit of it by adding their jeers to those of the villagers. Harriet found her carriage surrounded by jostling spectators. Her quick anger rose, and it was tinged with fear for Rupert. Crowds were unpredictable. They could turn from noisy to aggressive in a flash . . . and Rupert seemed a very lonely figure out there in the circus ring formed by his opponents. She found the scene blurring and swiftly lifted her veil. Her vision was no better; her eyes had grown misty with tears.

She watched, hand to mouth, as he walked to the heads of the rector's horses and slipped his hand through the bridle ready to lead them forward.

"The fool . . . he'll be cut to pieces!" exclained one director, forgetting the man's wife was present.

"He'd do better to drive it—mow 'em down," commented the other, as intent on watching the scene as his colleague.

Harriet hardly heard them. In everything but physical presence she was out there with Rupert. She felt his heartbeat, his anger that made him discount fear, his solitude. The noise grew. Raucous voices called down curses on his head and those of his sons, condemned him as another heathen, called him an adulterer. The villagers prepared to attack, and the horses whinnied loudly, frightened by the noise and pressing crowds. Blinking away her tears, Harriet watched with bated breath as her husband moved toward the now-open gates of the house that was his by inheritance. He coaxed the horses forward with quiet words, while the rector dived out of sight of his parishioners as the carriage neared their lines.

It seemed the man in the carriage was right—Rupert

must surely be set upon and cut to pieces by the hostile villagers. Yet he walked on as if the yelling crowds brandishing weapons were not there. Suddenly a young man in a stained shirt and trousers hurled a horseshoe from the back of the crowd, hitting Rupert's temple with a sickening crack.

Harriet gasped as his black hat fell to the ground and rolled beneath the feet of the crowd. Blood began to ooze from a cut beside his eye, and a roar went up from those watching—a cry of excitement at the first sign of violence. Clinging desperately to the side of the carriage, Harriet kept her gaze on the one man who stood taller than the rest as he drew nearer and nearer the gates.

It was then she heard a voice near her yell. "Go to it, Captain Torrington. Show them a taste of Sevastapol, sir. You did it then—you can do it now!"

The speaker was a burly man with a wooden leg. He was sitting with a thin woman in a miller's cart, and his continuing encouragement caught the attention of those around him. Incredibly they began to join him—cheering on the underdog—until the chant became a roar.

A shaken villager brought his whip down across Rupert's shoulders, but the line began to break before the man leading the carriage without faltering. They lowered their weapons, and at the gates the carriage passed between the two sullen ranks without hindrance. It was over. All too plainly they believed the devil was looking after his own.

Through her tears Harriet saw Rupert struggling

back through men and women who were slapping him on the back or trying to kiss him. He paused at the miller's cart for a second to shake the man's hand before pushing on again. At last, disheveled and bareheaded, Rupert scrambled into the carriage as it began to move forward, and Harriet turned her head to the window so he would not see her weakness.

"My word, sir," enthused one of the directors on the opposite seat, "that was a masterly performance."

Harriet heard the labored quality of his breathing as Rupert said with savage bitterness, "I am not here to entertain, sir, but to bury my dead father. I think everyone has forgotten that."

All through the ceremony Harriet could not forget what he had done or his words afterward. As they stood around a grave dug in a shaded grove which would be bright with azaleas in the spring, the rain on their umbrellas seemed to counterpoint the painful sadness within her. The poignancy of this funeral made her think of Edward, also lying in an isolated grave beneath a tree that would bloom in spring. Rupert had erected a cross above it, as he would do here.

They left the graveside and walked over the sodden grass, a silent and ill-assorted group. For so well known and successful a man as Aubrey had been, it was a dismal gathering, but Rupert thanked them all for coming to honor his father's memory and expressed his gratitude to the rector for performing his duties under such trying circumstances.

Harriet's gaze never left him, even when she presided over the cold collation, and her concern increased as time passed. He looked in danger of collapsing, although he did all that was expected and necessary. Far too often his eyes stared from the window out into the rain-sodden garden, and she had the instinctive feeling that he was seeing more than the late roses and banks of poinsettias.

Sometime later, when she had been drawn into conversation with an elderly couple who had known Aubrey in China, she looked up to find that Rupert was missing from the room. Excusing herself immediately, she ignored the voice that told her there was a simple explanation for it and preferred to trust her intuition. Through the lower floor she hurried from room to room, then, lifting her black crinoline skirt, ran up the stairs, her apprehension mounting.

Among the upper corridors she ran, past jade griffins and priceless vases on pedestals, pausing only to look through each doorway as she passed before rushing on. At the end of the second corridor was Aubrey's study, and it was there she found him, sitting in a leather chair with his head in his hands. The sight brought her to a halt, holding her in the doorway for a long moment while he remained unaware of her presence.

It was more than she could bear. When she had been left alone in the world, he had comforted her. She remembered the strength he had imparted when everything around her had collapsed. She thought of the miracle of his late visit one night when she had heard his voice in the hall and looked down to see the one person who had cared enough to come back a second time.

Going into the room, she sank down before him, putting out a gentle hand to touch his. His head came up quickly, betraying him before he could help himself. He looked old, drained, and incredibly lonely. A bruise had swollen on his temple in a purple-yellow lump, the clotted blood covering a cut that narrowly missed his eye. The pain and desperation that were reflected in his eyes and showed a vulnerability she had not seen in him until then brought a thickness to her throat that would not allow her to speak. All she could do was grip his fingers tightly while her other hand ran with a feather touch over his hair, down across the contusion until her fingers rested against his mouth. The gestures were meant to tell him that he was not alone, that she cared, but the contact brought to her a flare of desire that took control of her body and senses before she knew it. With it came a longing to hold him and be held.

As they looked at each other, the pain in his eyes cleared to be replaced by a look that echoed her own desire, and he dragged her hands to his lips with a soft groan.

"At last, dear God, at last."

Breathless, aching for the touch of his hands on her body, she allowed him to pull her to her feet with him. Reading in the fire in his eyes an unmistakable message, she whispered faintly, "No, Rupert."

It was far too late. His mouth was on hers, and nothing could then stop what they both knew was inevitable. She clung to him, digging her fingers into his shoulders, hating him for all his kisses given away, for making her alive again to that love she had thought dead.

He picked her up in his arms and began walking from the room. Giddy with thoughts of surrender, she still managed to protest in a whisper, "No, Rupert."

The light of need and elation that had put youth back into his face made nonsense of her denial, and he carried her to his room, saying thickly, "Nothing would please him more than this. He wanted us to be man and wife."

From the moment he kicked the door closed Harriet had no more thought of the funeral or the guests below. As he took the mourning black from her body with impatient hands, she throbbed with the passion of a hundred days and nights. Her responses were fevered and more demanding than she had dreamed possible. She thought of his infidelity and wanted more from him in that moment than all his other women had had from him in the years he had been seeking his pleasure.

Their passion rose in matching crescendos until, right at the threshold of possession, he held her in exquisite agony, saying, "If I take you now, it must be with everything forgiven between us."

"Yes, yes . . . everything," she cried, begging him to end her agony of surrender.

He took her on a journey to the realms of physical exhaustion. They fought a battle that vanquished all those things that had kept that moment away from them for so long. She shed tears of jealousy, accusing him of being thus with so many others; he showed his passion for her was far greater. He demanded unconditional forgiveness; she gladly gave it. She made him pledge fidelity; he showed her what would ensure that pledge.

Finally, as they lay with fingers entwined, gazing at the truth in each other's eyes, a faint sound of crunching gravel outside broke through their bemused senses.

"My dearest love," she whispered dreamily, "the guests are all leaving."

"Splendid," he murmured through the hair that lay across her breasts. "Now I can have my bride to myself."

Rupert left the company offices and stepped into his carriage late one afternoon during the first week of December. His brain was full of confused thought and the unwelcome knowledge that he did not give a damn about shares, sailing times on the China run, or raw and graded silks.

As the carriage moved off, he remained chasing the medley of facts around in his mind as he stared absently from the window. The company was still shaky, despite the massive sum he had injected into it, partially from his own pocket but mostly from the proceeds of the sale of the contents of Pagoda House. He personally did not care for Eastern art, however priceless, and the unique pieces had fetched a double fortune that shored up the business while it struggled to survive the scandal. The house itself was to be destroyed. He had commissioned an architect to build him a gracious mansion more suited to the setting, but it would be well over a year before he and Harriet could move into their new home.

After two months the scandal was beginning to fade from the public mind, but there were still occasions when people stood outside the house, hoping to see the Torringtons emerge, or shouted at them in the street as they passed. But society had not forgotten. Life was being made next to impossible by attitudes that died a slow and cautious death.

He sighed as a couple strolled past arm in arm, gazing with the joy of lovers at each other. Thank God for Harriet! She had gone to him at the moment he had felt utterly destroyed, and their love was now as vibrant and passionate as he had hoped it would be. She drove him to joy he had never reached even with Moona's Oriental potions, and her passion was as free and honest as her personality.

As the carriage made its way through the West End, despair beset him once more. Passionately in love they might be, but he and Harriet were each of them too volatile to endure life as it was at present. There were no personal invitations, and if they went to the theater, they were snubbed. Doors were closed in their faces; events had shown their true friends to be just three in number. Pride and independence were being strained by social rejection, and the battle was being lost. Each put on a pretense in front of the other.

Deep inside Rupert was desperately unhappy. Having to relinquish his commission had almost broken him. The one thing that made his blood sing had been wrenched from him, leaving him with something he had always hated—hated even more now that it had seized him by the throat with a hold that would never loosen. After two months he still felt the knife twist that men he had fought with and shared a tent with on a battlefield had turned their backs on him. There had been times when only the smile of a fellow officer kept a man sane; times when he had looked through red-rimmed eyes, seen another shouting with raised sword as he urged his men on, and taken courage from the sight; times when he had stood on guard in sleet and rain, sore in body and soul, and been cheered by the arrival of one of those men to take over the dangerous duty. How could they forget all that, hold against him all that had not mattered then?

He gazed unseeing at the squabs on the seat. He was no better than those at the mill who had been used, then tossed aside. The world had got its values mixed. He remembered Sergeant Knott at Aubrey's funeral, who had not cared about scandal—only the man he knew as his captain. The man who had been at Sevastapol.

He leaned forward, pulse quickening, at the sight of two scarlet-coated officers strolling through the early evening throng. For an instant he believed himself one of them again. Then his spirits dropped further. He was finished—Captain Torrington was dead; Mr. Torrington, silk merchant, had replaced him. The Battle Trading Company was a stone around his neck forevermore. Somehow he must accept himself as a trader, a dedicated businessman, yet everything within him cried out against it.

His gaze followed the scarlet jackets until he could see them no more. He remembered Sevastapol, the noise of battle, the agony and the fury. He remembered his own confidence and the men who had placed their trust in him. The sprung comfort of the carriage faded away, as did the noise of Piccadilly and the view from his window, and he was back in his beloved environment again.

His suspicions had been proved right. There was trouble flaring in China, and it would surely be a matter of days before the decision to send troops was made. Only that morning the newspapers had reported a new incident in the persistent clash between Chinese authorities and Western merchants.

The Chinese did not want foreigners in their country. They believed China was the nucleus of the world and, therefore, superior to any other nation. The emperor ruled with divine wisdom and was obeyed with slavish devotion on pain of death. Western adventurers seeking to open up trade routes were, naturally, not prepared to adhere to this belief, and so, as the best way to treat this tricky problem, the Chinese ignored them. Such treatment led to constant frustration for Western diplomats, who negotiated—with the aid of military force, if necessary—firm treaties and stuck to them, and Chinese mandarins, who signed the treaties and continued to do as they had always been doing.

The greatest trouble was that Europeans were not allowed to have direct contact with the emperor, were refused admission to Peking, and were treated as inferior beings in a land that did not want them. No emissaries were received in the Forbidden City; no messages were allowed to be sent direct to the emperor. All discourse was left to the discretion of the local mandarins in Canton, Macao, and other trading posts reluctantly opened to Westerners after several small wars. Only the mandarins had direct contact with Peking, but they, fearing the Silken Cord of Displeasure of their emperor—upon receipt of which they were required to commit suicide to remove their offensive person from the kingdom—wisely refrained from sending their master any message that would displease him. In consequence, the requests of foreign nations were reworded to make them into something acceptable to the emperor, or they were delayed, tossed aside, sent by unreliable couriers, or just simply ignored by local officials.

Two recent incidents, however, had enraged the French and British authorities to the point where they would not easily be appeased. The Chinese had captured and tortured to death a French missionary for preaching Christianity, even though the terms of a recent treaty allowed such teaching, and Chinese soldiers had stormed a British ship in the absence of the master, hauled down the flag, and arrested twelve Chinese seamen on a charge of piracy. The British consul in Canton had demanded the immediate return of men guaranteed British protection under another recent treaty with the Chinese, and when this was not instantly done with the apology he felt was due, he contacted the governor of Hong Kong. His superior, long feeling it was time the Chinese were made to toe the line, decided a demonstration of force was called for. In this, the French were willing allies.

Acting on his own authority, the governor had sent Royal Navy ships upriver to Canton, where they captured four fortresses and shelled the trading city. Any man with interests in Eastern expansion knew nothing would be permanently achieved until ambassadors were allowed in Peking with direct access to the emperor . . . but they would have to fight their way there.

Rupert saw this only too clearly. The news had aroused interest and excitement in him. His interest, however, was not that of a merchant, and his excitement was at the thought of the regiments being sent to reinforce the tiny garrison of Hong Kong. God, what he would give to be going with them!

The remainder of the journey was spent in visions of assaults on Oriental forts standing in vast stretches of wild land; of scarlet jackets pressing forward in waves, driving the enemy before them; of triumphant troops marching into the hitherto-unseen city of Peking, viewing the wonders of imperial China with the eyes of victors; of comradeship, understanding, achievement in the company of men with similar interests. His pulse began to throb painfully, and a desperate longing filled his breast. The swaying of his carriage was the ship taking him to that far-off land; the horses' hooves beat the ground like the sound of military drums.

"We're 'ere sir," said a voice above him. Then again: "We're 'ome, Captain Torrington."

"Eh?"

He crashed out of his reverie to see his coachman peering down at him from the box. The truth returned to him, and he stood frowning at the pavement when he left the carriage, feeling bereft. For a moment it seemed he did not know where he must go, and then he went thoughtfully up the steps, handed his overcoat to Merryweather and turned toward the parlor, where Harriet always awaited him.

She rose the minute he entered and ran into his arms; but he was still preoccupied with his thoughts, and it was merely his unhappiness that put strength into his embrace.

She kissed him with passion. "Beloved, I have been counting the minutes to your return. I have news that cannot fail to—Rupert, what is amiss?"

"Eh?" he asked with a frown, not having heard her speak until then.

She touched his cheek gently. "Is something wrong? You are far away from me in thoughts . . . so far away you might be on the other side of the world."

It began as a small bubble but was soon a great fount of excitement as the visions returned with great clarity. "Yes, that is it, my dearest. The other side of the world," he echoed in a dazed voice. "China, to be exact. Now that I have put affairs in order here, there is nothing to prevent our departure for Hong Kong."

"When . . . when do you propose that we should leave?" she asked with commendable steadiness.

"At the end of the month. One of the company's ships is sailing then," he told her as if the plan had been formed long ago. Only then did he become aware of her wide, startled eyes and parted lips.

He pulled her close again and kissed her gently, then murmured into her hair, "It will be best for us to get away for a year or so—allow this dreadful business to be forgotten. Besides, there is likely to be trouble brewing in Canton. As head of the company I should be there to see to my business interests."

He said it as if he truly believed it.

Part Two

Chapter Eight

"A child in four months' time!" Rupert exploded. "You must have known about it before we left England."

He sat up in bed, cracking his head on the forgotten low beam, all ideas of passion driven away now by Harriet's soft-spoken announcement. He swore heartily, putting a hand to his crown to feel for blood. There was only a fast-rising lump, and the sickening pain of the blow made him more angry.

"You knew of this and have kept me in ignorance of the fact deliberately," he raged, flinging back the bedclothes and stepping onto the rolling deck, still with his hand to his head.

Harriet was smiling, her face shining with joy, supremely sure of herself in her exclusively female role. "I wish I had not told you now, for you are taking the news in a most unflattering fashion. I am your wife, Rupert, not a mistress who will confront you with a bastard."

He staggered on the unsteady surface, thinking savagely that the cabin of a pitching and tossing ship was the worst place in which to discuss a matter such as this.

"You have chosen the wrong moment to have one of your frank and humorous moods, Harriet. This is extremely serious."

She gave him a provocative invitation with her eyes. "How can I be serious when you are standing before me naked? Do come back to bed."

As she held back the sheets, he saw quite clearly the fuller curves of her once-slender figure and called himself a fool for thinking the fresh air from the seas had been responsible for increasing her appetite at mealtimes. His anger flared anew. He could not be expected to think of such things; it was a wife's duty to tell her husband.

"I am the father and had every right to have been given the news the moment it was known," he informed her, snatching up underwear and scrambling into it as best he could in the motion of the ship.

The next minute she was before him, holding his hands that were fumbling with buttons, and pressing her naked warmth against his chest. In her eyes was a look that normally weakened every resolve in him.

"Dearest, you were but a moment ago vowing to pursue me around the cabin with your carpet slipper because I had grown plump," she murmured, her lips traveling over his bare skin in a manner that should have set him on fire again. But he was in no mood for such things.

"And if I had not threatened that, no doubt I should not have been told even now." He put her away from him with gentle firmness when he longed to shake her. "You are wasting your time if you think to placate me by seduction. You have not been clever, Harriet—merely deceptive and disloyal."

She turned and snatched up a coverlet to cover herself, and he saw that her teasing mood had vanished. "Very well," she cried, swinging back to face him. "I knew of the child on the very day you told me of your intention to visit China. You were certainly in no mood to listen to anything I had to say."

"Our own child . . . *my* child!" he cried. "By God, what kind of man do you make me out to be? Is anything of more importance?"

She studied him for a moment as the ship rode an unusually long wave. "That is what you would have said then. I would never have been allowed to set out on this voyage."

"Of course you would not," he agreed hotly.

"You would have completely canceled your plans?"

"Naturally."

She moved closer until the perfume of her skin reminded him of his recent desire. There was a strange sad challenge in the deep blue of her eyes that made him strangely uneasy.

"No, Rupert, you would have left me behind to follow after the child was born. *Nothing* would have made you change your plans."

"That is nonsense," he protested, feeling the lie take him by the throat.

She shook her head. "No, my dear. Even now you are afraid the war will start before you get there."

Her perception frightened him. He felt exposed, vulnerable. He realized once more how total was the emotion that drew them together, how strong the power each had to make or break the other. She must be afraid of it also, or she would never have deceived him over the child.

"The war?" he echoed in a harsh pretense of surprise.

"You knew all too well that troops would be sent to China and you could not resist being there," she cried.

"How could I have known? My decision was made before Parliament gave permission for troops to be sent."

"You are a soldier heart and soul, as your father once said to me. Your mind works the way of a military man, and you knew it would be only a matter of time before war was inevitable."

"It was necessary that as owner of the company I should look into its position there," he said, knowing that the feebleness of his protest would be obvious to her.

"You have no heart for trade. All the company did was provide you with the perfect excuse to sail ahead of the troops, if only to stand on the sidelines and watch the battle." She tossed back her hair with a fierce gesture. "I have seen the way you come alive at the sight of a scarlet jacket. It has never been the fact that society shunned you that you could not withstand; it was the fact that they flung you out of your beloved regiment."

The truth hurt him beyond measure; it always would. He could hear again the colonel's blunt words and remembered the faces of his fellow officers as he vacated his office and arranged for his horses to be removed from the regimental stables. He recalled his last sight of the mess anteroom with its large paintings of battle scenes, silver trophies, and atmosphere of camaraderie. Harriet was right: They had flung him out . . . for something he had not done.

He had thought his pain well hidden, his longing known only to himself. Through the porthole he could see the early sun on the swell—bright light that flashed across his eyes each time the vessel dipped into the troughs of waves. Between the blinding flashes he saw Harriet through dazzled eyes—a woman who was so much a part of him he would never be a free man again. Their liaison brought him deep joy and excitement, but there was also an element of apprehension. The greatest means of fulfillment in his life had been taken from him, leaving him raw and vulnerable. If Harriet should also be lost, then so would he be. He could not take that risk.

"Yes, there is to be a war; it is inevitable. It is out of the question for our child to be born in a place torn by battle. You have not seen it as I have. At Singapore you must leave the ship and return to England. By taking the overland route, you will be at home in ample time for the birth."

"No," she cried immediately, grabbing at the bed rail to steady herself. "I will not go back."

"I say you will," he insisted heatedly. "You are my wife. It is time you realized it is your place to obey me."

She stared at him as if she were seeing a stranger. "You can send me away? After all you have vowed these last months, you tell me it will not matter to you if we are apart for a year or so?"

"I have not said . . ." he began, but she was truly caught in the passion that never slept.

"I have lain in your arms and heard your wildest demands; I have wept with you at the pain of our shared joy." She flung back the coverlet and stood naked. "Look at me and tell me that it has meant so little to you that you can send me away."

Head still aching from the blow on the beam, he tried to maintain common sense. "Just now I thought you knew me too well," he told her unsteadily. "But I see you know nothing of my love. Your body and the joy it gives me are only part of the whole."

"Love?" she challenged passionately. "How can you speak of love when you give your orders and demand my obedience?"

Her attack was desperately bitter, but he could think only that she carried his child and had not told him until now.

"Suppose you had been ill on the voyage . . . did you consider that when you remained silent? Did it occur to you that I could have lost you and the unborn infant through the lack of medical assistance on this ship? Was *that* love—to risk taking half my life from me forever?"

With quick steps she was against him, pulling his head down to kiss his mouth. "I could not bear to lose you again so soon after finding you."

He pulled her arms from around his neck. "The situation in Hong Kong is too uncertain." He began thrusting his legs into his trousers, trying to ignore her nearness. "I shall have to be away in Canton during the trading season. The Chinese are rushing through the streets attacking Europeans, setting fire to their homes." With angry movements he snatched up a shirt. "We heard, at Cape Town, of poisoned bread that was delivered to the Westerners and those who were near to death as a result. We heard of servants being bribed to leave their European employers, going in the night and leaving families without food or water." Thrusting the tails of his shirt into his trousers, he confronted her then. "Against such things I could probably protect you—but *enceinte*, or mothering an infant, it would be highly dangerous."

She was flushed and bristling with pride. He thought she had never looked more compelling.

"What of those who are conceived and born in such a country?"

Avoiding a direct answer, he snapped, "We are in a position to choose between safety and uncertain danger. Our child is not. I am the father and decide for him. At Singapore we shall stay long enough to hire a physician and put you on a ship for England."

"And you?" she asked breathlessly.

"I . . . I must go on, now I am so near." His voice had grown husky, and it was not easy to tell her something inside him compelled him to be there, even if it were only on the sidelines, as she had said.

"I see." She seemed almost broken by his decision. "Well, I will not go back to hostility and gray loneliness again without you. Do you love me so little?"

Shaken though he was by her distress, he would not give way. "It will be the same for me."

"Oh, no, Rupert," she cried with fire. "It will never be the same. Consolation will always come easily to you in the arms of other women."

It was a moment or two before he realized that she had no intention of crying that she did not mean what she had said or of asking his forgiveness. When he left the cabin, she was still standing there defying him, her nakedness somehow giving her a dignity many a woman never achieved in the most ravishing of gowns.

The smell of tar and rope, of breakfast cooking in the galley, and the fetid waft from the animal pens belowdecks further discomfited him. He struggled up the steps leading to fresh air and open decks, thinking how much he hated ships. The warm tropical breeze caressed his skin and lifted his hair from the crown of his head as he looked around at the desolation of the never-ending sea. Walking toward the bow, he fell over some coiled rope and swore loudly. He understood nothing of sailor's jargon and even less of the workings of the vessel. What was more, he had no desire to learn.

For all of three months he had been tied to a small floating prison that heaved up and down and poisoned the air with noxious black smoke. The longing to gallop across wide fresh fields on a spring morning, to laugh with his fellows over breakfast in the mess, to hear the tramp of boots and the ringing bugle calls at dusk filled him with a pain that tore at his breast.

Having slowed his steps, he leaned on his forearms against the rail. Yesterday he had been happy at the prospects of nearing his destination. Now he had no choice but to send Harriet home—any responsible man would do the same. It would tear him apart to say good-bye to her. She also knew well he could not go back. It would tear him even more apart to return now that he was so near to escape.

She also knew he would not remain celibate until they were reunited. It would mean nothing to him, but Harriet was an intensely passionate woman who was soon roused to jealousy. He looked at the ocean rolling in great swells of deepest blue out into the distance and saw his own life stretching ahead—soaring up, then plummeting again. He knew, to his cost, how unrelenting Harriet's censure could be. Would it drive them apart again? He clenched his fists. She had given him no choice. If only she had told him before they had left England!

For some while he stood trying to come to terms with the sudden turnabout of the situation until a hand touched his arm. Harriet was dressed in a gown of deep blue that made her eyes vivid enough to catch at his senses. The breeze stirred her curls and flicked the delicate lace collar around her throat. Her face displayed a serenity of beauty that he now associated with the news she had given him.

"You did not even say if you were pleased," she said softly, by way of bridging the gap.

He found it difficult to speak for a moment, and then he took her hand. "Is there any need for me to put into words what you know to be true?" He played with her fingers, then lifted them to his lips. "You know that my two brothers lie in the cemetery at Macao. Is that what you want for our child?" he asked quietly.

She kissed his hands as they held hers and looked into his face with a trace of desperation. "You asked me earlier if there was anything more important than our child. He will grow in our love, then leave us. That is how it should be. A mother will always lose her child . . . but if I should lose you, there will be nothing."

"And if I should lose you?" he asked thickly, hating

what he was saying. "Better for a year or so than forever."

The blue eyes blazed. "I will not go back."

He loosed her hands and moved away, the tension from his pent-up desire that had been dashed that morning making him lash out at her. "For once you will do as you are told. I have made the decision, and that is the end of the matter."

But it was not the end of the matter. When the ship docked in Singapore, the European quarter was abuzz with news of a bloody mutiny that had broken out in India in which British women and children had suffered horrendous deaths at the hands of crazed mobs. So terrible were the tales that it took Harriet no more than five minutes to persuade Rupert it would be more dangerous to travel to England via India than to continue on to Hong Kong.

Her success might have been partly due to the fact that he was avidly concerned with the details of Indian regiments that had slaughtered their British officers and the news that the troops heading for Hong Kong had been diverted to India as reinforcements. Their vessel was well on the way to Hong Kong before Rupert realized Harriet had achieved her aim and given him the added responsibility of protecting a third Torrington in their new island home.

The Torringtons were to be met in Hong Kong by the company's agent, Valentine Bedford, who had been instructed to see that Aubrey's house was vacated by the present tenants and prepared for new occupation.

But it would be a turbulent island colony in which the young couple would be setting foot.

The French and British retaliation for acts considered treaty breaking had enraged the Manchu overlords in China—in particular, the viceroy of Canton, Commissioner Yeh. Yeh was clever, cruel, and typical of his race in that he hated the "foreign barbarians." As the man most useful to the merchants striving to achieve greater freedom of access to ports and expansion of trade, he was wily, obstructive, and vengeful, wanting only to see the backs of those he looked on as immoral bearded rogues. Where his cooperation might have eased the tension of the East-West confrontation, he continued to inflame it by his complete lack of insight.

The situation at the start of that second half of 1857 was one of uneasy withdrawn hostility. After the naval action in which warships had shelled Canton and overrun the fortresses guarding the city, the force had to withdraw, being too small to capture and hold their prize or to guard the European trading factories against hostile Chinese from the inner city barred to Westerners. In fact, the firing of some of the factories, during which a member of the British consulate was burned to death, compelled the traders to abandon the remainder of that season and return to their homes in Hong Kong.

But vengeance had followed them there. Arson persisted; murders occurred in the streets; servants were paid to shun the houses of Europeans. The governor of Hong Kong had increased the strength of the island's police force and recruited help from French and American naval commanders on the spot. With the mainland of Kowloon so short a distance away there was always the prospect of their being overrun by Chinese under Yeh's dominance.

Spasmodic fighting continued between naval gunboats and the war junks up the river toward Canton, but they were losing impetus for want of land forces to capture and hold strategic vantage points. Hopes had been high until the outbreak of the mutiny in India had made a greater demand on troops heading out from Britain.

So it was that when the Torringtons' ship docked, the colony was threatened by fire, murder, and an edict that offered a substantial reward for every European head surrendered to Manchu officials. It was also a colony in which merchants grew increasingly worried over the lost months of the last trading season and the next due to begin in October. With Canton still closed to them, trade would be at a standstill. The Battle Trading Company stood to lose, along with the rest.

To the new arrivals, none of these hazards and difficulties was apparent, apart from a surplus of ships lying idle at the company's wharves. Harriet stood alongside Rupert as they inched toward land, as eager as he to get her first glimpse of the legendary colony. Singapore had fascinated her, but this was to be her home for a few years.

The deepwater natural harbor was excitingly blue against the island that rose up from it in hills of reddish brown earth cloaked thickly with lush foliage. Clear-cut and beautiful against the skies reflecting the

South China Sea, Hong Kong appeared a fitting jewel in the Empire's crown.

Harriet soon discovered that the natural beauty that had so excited her an hour offshore was part illusion. Those heavenly blue waters bore heaving layers of drifting rubbish, rotting food, sewage, and animal carcasses as their ship steamed slowly past the waterborne colonies of tiny, bobbing, hooded boats that clung to the coast like leeches to their host. She had read of them in her father's notebooks.

"Just imagine living one's life from birth to death on a tiny vessel, tied, as those are, to each other to form a floating village," she enthused to Rupert, not taking her attention from the sight.

"No, I thank you," was the firm reply. "It is the last thing I wish to imagine. The stench alone is enough to drive one away."

She glanced up at him. "Where is your sense of romance?"

He grinned wickedly. "You stand there swollen with my child and ask such a question?"

Her cheeks turned pink as they always did at his unrestrained wooing, and she chided him affectionately. "You are come to Hong Kong to make it your home for a while. Do you not think you should take an interest in such aspects of local life?"

"I cannot believe I shall be in any way enriched by aspects of that nature," he told her strongly, "and all I am likely to gain are lice, rat bites, and plaguey diseases."

She sighed with exasperation. "Rupert, I sometimes despair of you."

He grinned again. "Yet continue to find me irresistible." He drew her close to his side and brushed her hair with his lips. "My sweet wanton, I am a self-confessed and unashamed Briton. The indigenous races of the world I leave to you, the expert."

"No," she countered wistfully. "I only wish I were." Once again she glanced up into the dark fascination of his eyes. "But I do mean to educate you in some facts of life of which you seem to be unaware."

"Splendid," he murmured ardently. "I look forward to it."

The pink of her cheeks deepened as she looked away from him. The advanced state of her pregnancy had made them strangers to passion for a while, but he could stir her unbearably with a word, a look. Enjoying the present comfort of his arm around her, she took pleasure in the scene growing more and more distinct as the ship drew alongside the wharf.

The harbor presented a picturesque bustle of shipping activity. The graceful tea clippers rode the water side by side, arrogantly confronting the squat large-bellied junks with their lurid decorations on the flat prows and their great ridged brown sails. Colliers slunk low in the water, dirty, noisy, and purely utilitarian, and the busy upstart Hong Kong–Kowloon ferries brashly announced their importance with shrill whistle blasts as they approached the pier. Amid the barkentines, barges, tugs, water boats, trawlers, and merchantmen moved a teeming fleet of sampans, proas, and tanka boats, the occupants of which offered their wares to sailors in return for a handful of small coins.

The Torringtons were not on one of the oceangoing passenger ships, and so they entered the harbor at the busier, noisier mercantile section. Harriet drank in the scene avidly, finding all she had read about now spread before her in rich reality. For a brief moment she recalled a November afternoon when she had rung for tea forty minutes early as a protest against the dull routine of her life—the day Rupert had walked into her life for the first time.

In a rush of love she smiled her thanks up at him, but he was intent on studying an artillery battery perched high on an overhang with an excellent command of the harbor. She felt a tug at her heart before she lowered her gaze to the jetty at which they had arrived. Amid the scurrying pigtailed coolies stood a man in fawn trousers, cream-colored frock coat, and a strange type of hat the like of which Harriet had never before seen.

"Rupert, that must be Mr. Bedford," she said, touching his arm.

"Eh?" Her husband's glance left the gun-emplacement reluctantly. "Yes, I suppose it is. I had hoped he would be older."

"My dear, you knew very well before we left England that he was no more than five-and-thirty. You surely did not expect him to become senile in six months."

"He does not look like a man able to hold such responsibility," he retorted moodily. "I would take him for a young rake as he stands there."

"No doubt he is thinking the same of you at this moment," she teased, guessing the reason for his sudden irritability. "You look far too young and rakish to be the owner of an entire trading company."

"I was never meant to be."

His reply was curt and designed to dismiss a topic he did not wish to discuss, so Harriet wisely said no more on that or any other subject as the tugs pulled the ship alongside the company's jetty.

A gangplank was lowered soon after Harriet and Rupert went to their stateroom, one kept for use of the owner should he ever want to sail in the ship. It was only a matter of minutes before a knock fell on the door.

Harriet was eager to meet the man Aubrey had entrusted to conduct the vitally important part of the company's affairs. Her common sense told her he must be astute, trustworthy, and capable, but she also knew of the scandal that had obliged him to leave England fifteen years before.

The son of a highly respected and aristocratic judge, Valentine Bedford had been a cornet in the Life Guards when he took part in a private challenge to race his horse over a difficult cross-country course against a fellow subaltern. Wild and hot-tempered, Bedford had been so incensed at losing to an inferior rider that he had accused the man of veering from the agreed course and taking a shortcut. The duel that resulted had been unavoidable, although illegal. Despite the fact that both duelists were bad marksmen, Bedford had escaped unscathed, but his own bullet took out the eye of his rival and brought him dangerously close to death.

Judge Sir Lowry Bedford had carefully turned his back while his friends had hurried his son across the Channel, over Europe to the Mediterranean, and thence to the newly established colony of Hong Kong, where it did not matter what lay in a young man's past. By the time Hong Kong began to flourish and grow respectable young Bedford had been befriended by another rascal—Garforth Torrington.

Denied the hope of ever returning to England, Bedford had devoted his considerable intelligence and determination to advancement in the Battle Trading Company, and Aubrey had had no hesitation in making him the Hong Kong agent and manager when he had been warned not to spend so much time in the East.

The young man had not been in the day cabin more than a minute or two before Harriet realized it was not only his knowledge and capability that had been behind his success. Valentine Bedford was full of irresistible charm that made her glad that he had escaped his fate in England.

"Welcome to Hong Kong, Mr. Torrington," greeted the manager, offering his hand with a smile. "You had a good voyage, I trust?"

"Tolerable," replied Rupert stiffly.

"She's a marvelous ship. I've known her do the return in only a little more than a hundred days . . . and that's with a full cargo."

"Indeed?"

Because of her husband's patent lack of interest, Harriet put more warmth in her smile than she would normally offer a strange young man when Rupert presented him. "It has been a long voyage, Mr. Bedford, but one that was full of interest. However, I cannot wait to see the colony about which I have read and written so much."

Bedford bowed over the hand she held out to him, and she could not help admiring his thick dark hair that lay so sleekly against his well-shaped head.

"I trust Hong Kong will not disappoint you, ma'am." His green eyes looked candidly into hers as he straightened. "Your father's reputation is known, even this far from home, Mrs. Torrington." A smile played around the corners of his mouth, and humor deepened his voice attractively. "But I had not dared hope you would be his disciple. To a lady with such insight this island will be a constant source of pleasure."

"Ah, sir," she replied lightly, "a theorist and student is not to be compared with one who has practical knowledge. I shall count on you to complete my education on the colony."

"It will be a privilege, ma'am, but I warn you that this place is a great deal more odorous, savage, and distressing than books suggest."

She smiled broadly. "I have already found that to my cost. One cannot travel half across the world without knowing words are a mere shadow against the evidence of one's senses."

"I understand you received the message concerning my father's house," put in Rupert impatiently. "I believe we are ready to be conducted there, Bedford."

The agent turned with easy grace. "I had expected you to take luncheon on board. The servants have been instructed to prepare for your arrival late in the afternoon."

"Are they so badly trained that they will be thrown into confusion by an earlier arrival? A discouraging start, I must say."

Harriet hastened to ease the tension. "We could take luncheon here, my dear. It surely does not matter one way or the other."

"I think it does," he said in a light tone that did not fool her for a moment. He was digging in his heels. "After the tedium of gazing at these walls for months on end I feel we should take the earliest opportunity to quit these quarters." He reached for his hat. "I take it you have a carriage waiting, Bedford."

The other man forced a smile. "Not in Hong Kong, Mr. Torrington. You will see why when we get ashore. There are sedan chairs to be had at the wave of a hand. Not the best mode of transport, I fear . . . and the midday heat is considerable. Perhaps Mrs. Torrington—" He broke off significantly.

Rupert jammed a tall hat onto his head and put a hand beneath Harriet's elbow. "My wife met with heat worse than this in Bombay and Singapore, Bedford, and I think it more important that she be conducted to a place of comfort where she can rest than remain within this stifling atmosphere with the odors you have already mentioned assailing her through the open windows."

The matter was settled, and Rupert had won his first polite skirmish with his manager. Harriet hoped it did not presage a conflict of personalities between the two men and ascribed it to Bedford's desire to dine in the owner's cabin and Rupert's equally strong desire to leave it. Bedford's easy conversation regarding company ships at the wharves, the great warehouses, and silent hoists that should be loading all met with cool disinterest, however, from Rupert. Knowing her husband all too well, she saw he did not like Bedford and had no intention of trying to be affable. It was a mystery to her why.

Sedan chairs had been called up to the ship, and it was with a feeling of embarking on an exploration into life at its most colorful that Harriet settled herself into the hooded chair, tucked down the skirt of her crinoline, and waited for the bearers to lift her for the swaying journey into the center of Victoria. With Rupert ahead, Valentine Bedford behind, and Bessie Porridge looking as apprehensive as a mouse on a cat's dinner plate bringing up the rear, they set off.

Harriet was glad Rupert had insisted on leaving the ship right away. It was good to be on land again, even if the motion of the chair that bounced on long pliant poles suggested that she was still at sea. Apart from getting away from the confines of the ship, she was anxious to see her new home—the house Aubrey had built on the lower slopes of Victoria Peak some ten years earlier, when he became owner of the company on his father's death. It was reputed to be one of the grandest on the island.

Once the waterfront was behind them, Harriet could see why Bedford had been amused at Rupert's mention of a carriage, for the streets were narrow, tortuous, and comprised of steps in several instances.

The sedan chairs were carried between rows of tiny cell-like shops with dim interiors that displayed goods of a mysterious nature to Harriet's Western eyes. Pigtailed men and women in dark trousers and tunics harangued each other over what looked like pieces of leather shaped like a fish, small bags of rice, jars and bottles of brown glass with strange vivid labels, bright gilt ornaments with scarlet tassels, small warbling birds in wooden cages hardly larger than themselves, small crimson envelopes, and little parcels of folded leaves hanging from loops of string around fingers.

Coolies in flapping clothes shuffled in a half-running gait, with flexible bamboo poles across their shoulders, from which dangled two baskets laden with fruit, vegetables, rice, or even live poultry thrust carelessly on top of each other, legs tied together and squawking their protest at such treatment. Women walked on tiny feet that had been bound since childhood, carrying babes on their backs by means of cloth slings. The black-haired infants slumped in their spread-eagled positions, heads lolling as their mothers climbed innumerable steps to reach the top of the street. Older children darted hither and thither, playing catch-as-catch-can or stood in groups like miniature adults as they watched beetle races and bet on the results. One or two were absorbed in a solo game that involved kicking a flighted weight up and up so that it was kept in the air for as long as possible with dexterous skill.

Fascinated and yet with a sense of revulsion, Harriet watched a half-wild dog chase and shake to death a rat that came from a hole it had been casually watching and, farther on, a street fishmonger take from his water trough a brown spiky fish, beat its head on a nearby stone, then tie it, still twitching, with a string around its tail for the customer to carry away. She was so absorbed by all this that it was not for some while that she noticed the smell of the East she would come to remember forever—indefinable, slightly menacing. She had only to smell it in distant years to be transported in spirit back to remembered places.

The terrible heat made her begin to wish they had already arrived at their destination. For the moment she had had her fill of indigenous peoples and their habitats. A shaded room and a tea tray seemed vastly more attractive. The regular rise and fall of the sedan chair were causing her to become queasy, and she longed for Bessie to loosen the strings of her corset, which was really too tight for her present condition.

Her sudden desire for peace and quiet made her intolerant of the noisy, pushing crowds of Chinese in the street that now seemed too narrow to contain them all. For a moment she thought she might swoon, but then her heart jolted with alarm as the haranguing they had heard earlier changed into a more menacing sound. No matter what the language in which it was voiced, it was always possible to detect fear and anger in the cry of a mob, and Harriet knew instinctively that danger had approached in an instant.

The throng at the top of the street of steps had changed its pattern. Some were turning in panic, others were trying to push on against a downward tide, and a few sought shelter in shallow doorways and tiny gaps between shops—anywhere they could cram themselves away from the screaming, brandishing tide forcing its way into the street.

The next minute the plodding bearers set her chair down with scant care and dived for safety, disappearing in moments, leaving her sitting in the path of the mob. In her sudden fear she noticed Rupert had been similarly abandoned just ahead of her and was on his feet and looking back. There was no time for further thought as a voice beside her said, "Quickly, Mrs. Torrington, you must come this way at once."

Dazed, Harriet rose awkwardly, fastening her gaze on Rupert as she allowed Valentine Bedford to lead her free of the chair poles.

"My husband," she murmured, but Rupert was already only a few feet from them and reaching for her.

The noise was deafening now. Those unable to escape the angry crowd had joined it, shouting the same chant, waving their arms in aggressive fashion. Somewhere in the center of the crowd lighted brands were held aloft—bright in the narrow crowding street—and the smell of smoke was added to that of sweat-laden fear.

The manager looked tense but confident as he spoke swiftly to Rupert. "We have to get away. Once they see us, it will be all up. The danger will be negligible if you follow me as speedily as possible."

"Where are you going?" asked Rupert sharply. "My wife cannot—"

"Mrs. Torrington will be safe and able to rest until the danger has passed," was the reassuring answer. "Please, come this way immediately."

He began moving quickly down the steps, and Rupert put his arm around Harriet to urge her in pursuit. Bessie, looking ready to faint, fell in beside her mistress, holding Harriet's crinoline skirt clear of the uneven footing and muttering to herself in her distress.

The pace was fast. Harriet felt the pull on her abdomen as she hurried down the seemingly endless shallow steps. Her heart thudded against her ribs and in her temples; perspiration stood out on her brow. The street seemed even narrower than before—sinister and incredibly dirty. All the children had vanished. The shops were empty. There seemed to be no other Europeans in sight. A cry louder than before went up, and the manager turned an anxious face.

"We must go faster; they have seen us."

He began running with great leaps, seizing Bessie's hand and dragging her behind him in a confusion of flying skirts and legs that were forced to run faster than they were able. Harriet hardly had time to take in the scene before Rupert picked her up in his arms and bore her downward in a pace that must have been punishing for him in such heat. She clung to his coat, biting her lips against the ache growing in her stomach with every jolting step he took. He looked strained, and yet she knew that he was afraid only for her. In the moment after the chairmen had abandoned them she had seen him reach automatically for the sword that was no longer there, ready to face the mob.

Lying in his arms, she saw the walls tilt as they turned into a tiny alley leading from the stepped street. It was even darker and smelled damp, as if the sun never penetrated here.

"We stand more chance here," grunted Rupert more to himself than anyone else. "They can follow only a few at a time. Much easier to pick off that way."

Follow they did, rushing into the narrow way. But at the end of the alley the manager had opened a door to a small wooden house reached by a few steps and standing alone in the clearing where several alleys converged.

"The woman knows me . . . you'll be safe . . ." he

panted as they went in. "I will be back as soon as I have drawn them away from this area."

Rupert swung around, Harriet still in his arms. "Bedford, are you—"

"Trust me," he said swiftly. "I have known this colony from its birth."

They remained, hardly daring to breathe as the savage noise of the rioters grew louder and then faded into the distance. Only then did Harriet become aware of her surroundings and of the woman standing silently in the simple room. She was young, dressed entirely in black brocaded silk, and remarkably beautiful in a dainty, fragile manner that made a mockery of the house's rough interior. She should have been in a place like Pagoda House.

The woman bowed low before Rupert and put out a graceful hand to indicate a doorway covered by a dangling curtain of wooden beads. When she went through it, Rupert followed without hesitation, and Harriet found herself set down on a couch covered in red silk in a small room lit only by pale daylight filtering through a window set in one of the walls. A mere six feet from the window an earthy bank rose up, preventing any view. The house was stifling, alien, and dingy, but it was clean and a haven at a time when Harriet was beginning to feel ill.

Her body ached alarmingly, and the spinning in her head brought on unwelcome nausea. Worst of all, she was ashamed to acknowledge an overwhelming desire to burst into tears. She, who had no patience with crying women, wanted only to cling to Rupert and weep into his shoulder while he cosseted her. There was little chance of that, however, for after an urgent inquiry to satisfy himself that she was all right he went back through the bead curtain and stood looking impatiently through the front window.

Bessie stood beside Harriet, cooling her mistress's brow with a long-handled raffia fan she had taken from the couch when they had entered. The sight of the girl's obvious terror put all thoughts of weakness from Harriet's mind. She even summoned up a smile.

"So much for our introduction to Hong Kong, Bessie."

"Yes, madam." The dark gleaming eyes turned toward the tall figure they could see through the bead curtain. "It might seem like excitement to some, but with you like this the best place is 'ome."

"Hong Kong is home now," Harriet reminded her faintly, caught in another wave of nausea.

The girl sniffed and wielded the fan with increased energy. "Hmph, good thing I took no notice when the captain dismissed me in Afreeka and at Singerpore. There'd be no one to see to you."

"I am all right," said Harriet with an effort, "just a little giddy from the heat. And how many times have I told you not to call your master the captain?"

Bessie shrugged. "There's no one won't persuade me he isn't still the captain in his mind. He talks of it all the time."

Unwilling to discuss it anymore, Harriet closed her eyes and concentrated on not being sick. It would be dreadful here in this woman's house! But her moment of peace was broken when a gentle touch on her arm brought her eyes open again. She saw an oval face of smooth olive perfection, black eyes slanted and luminous, a mouth tinted like an early blush rose. She was being offered a drink in a delicate china cup.

Grateful, Harriet raised herself slightly and reached for it, but the cup was sent flying from the Chinese woman's hand to smash on the floor. The contents formed an elongated pool on the beaten earth, and Harriet turned to her maid in shocked reaction.

Bessie's face was even whiter than before. "Oh, madam, that could've been poisoned. You know the captain told us all we wasn't to have anything apart from what was prepared in the house," she cried fiercely. "I couldn't let you drink that."

The woman was bowing and backing from the room, but Harriet's apology was cut off sharply. The flash of hostility in the slanting black eyes was no figment of Harriet's imagination; there was an unmistakable atmosphere of hatred in the room that banished any further signs of Harriet's indisposition in a flash.

Chapter Nine

In the strange manner of human nature Aubrey Torrington had built in the heart of Hong Kong a house that was as Western as his English home had been Oriental. Situated in a magnificent position overlooking the breathless beauty of the sea and the city of Victoria that grew almost as one watched, Sussex Hall was solid proof of wealth, good taste, and confidence in the future.

Square, colonnaded in gracious style, with a veranda running around it, the white-stoned mansion displayed a grandeur that was enhanced by the green, sloping heights of Victoria Peak rising up behind it into the morning mist that cleared to show the summit standing proudly against a sky as vivid as the sea. In front of the impressive canopied entrance, terraced gardens ran down to a rough track that was the only access to Sussex Hall and several other residences set into the lower slopes of the peak, which dominated the harbor.

The area was favored by the wealthy merchants and men of colonial importance—sometimes referred to by their Chinese name of Tai-Pan—and ambitious colonists coveted such eminence from their humbler homes in Victoria. Up there the greatest benefit of any breeze could be felt; up there it was possible to train a telescope upon the ships in the harbor and see a rival's clippers glide into open sea earlier than suggested or merchandise being smuggled into warehouses during the swift Oriental hour of dusk. Up there it was easy for a man to see unexpected visitors approaching and so quickly hustle away clients or dealers who were best unseen by others with sharp curiosity. Most of all, when a man lived up there, he had no need to speak of his own importance; the house did it for him.

But it was clear that those select domains would not remain isolated long. Hong Kong Island was small, and the harbor commanded maximum importance. Wherever one looked new buildings were going up under the efforts of armies of coolies who hauled stones manually from quarries some miles away. Trade was flourishing despite overtones of war. The infant colony was drawing men from all races and creeds, seeking adventure or to make their fortunes. Mercantile companies expanded with every season; banking corporations were attracting more business than their simple premises could manage; shipping lines brought in more and more passengers to demand hotel accommodations of the highest standard.

The waterfront was covered with warehouses, marine offices, storerooms, lading posts, agents' headquarters, and mustering points for seamen waiting to be signed on by ships' masters. Behind them were the banks, government establishments, civil departments, European shops and offices, restaurants, and clubs that were indispensable to Western men of culture and intellect.

Beyond those lay the homes of colonists and wealthy Chinese merchants who could not afford to build a house like Sussex Hall. But between those homes, all around the dignified portals of banking and commerce, squeezed into every yard of that bustling city, the Chinese population that increased with alarming rate lived a life of impoverishment and resignation that had been its lot for centuries past.

Somehow, in that narrow strip between hills and sea, they put up shacks, hovels, wooden terraces with cramped rooms, shops, temples, and markets. They swarmed everywhere—even into the sea, where boat colonies clung to the coast, with rotting walkways that ran on stilts all around the area to allow the water residents access to land. They produced children in large numbers, and despite deaths from disease and the deliberate drowning of many female infants at birth, their numbers posed problems of great gravity to the British administration. When others poured in from the mainland of China to escape brutal Manchu rule, the problems grew even more severe.

The city of Victoria would burst at the seams before long. What had been a pestilential island ceded to the British fifteen years before by Chinese who did not want it was now showing signs of becoming a place with a brilliant and prosperous future, and the only way to expand was to move up into the hills. The British were already consulting their nation's cleverest engineers and architects. Sussex Hall would doubtless be looked down upon by even more impressive mansions on the dizzy heights of Victoria Peak. Already one level above the Torrington house was an army barracks that served the various artillery emplacements on the peak and housed a detachment of reserve troops for the main barracks near the waterfront.

Harriet could not help disliking the close proximity of such a place, for Rupert had lost no time in making himself known to the officers and offering them hospitality. As a result, her house in the evening was frequently full of the laughter and voices of men with like interests as they drank together, played cards, and discussed military stategy. Harriet did not mind overmuch, for they all were entertaining company and treated her with great respect, but the lease of life Rupert gained from such company did nothing to help him settle into his role of silk merchant. Far too often his eyes strayed to study hillside barracks when they should have been checking figures in ledgers brought to him by Valentine Bedford when he came daily to the ground-floor study to discuss business with his new employer.

But if the army officers of the colony overlooked the recent scandal in the Torrington family, there were others who did not. They were treated coldly by the more aristocratic members of the administrative staff, the ringleader of whom must surely have been the cousin Caroline Dornacre had mentioned at the dinner table during Harriet's first visit to Pagoda House. While Harriet did not care a jot about such treatment, something told her that Rupert did.

That Hong Kong contained such a high proportion of mercantile and trading people meant the Torringtons were accepted with warmth and extended obvious friendship upon their arrival, even though Harriet's delicate condition made it impossible for them to begin a social life that would certainly follow after the birth of the child. Fellow merchants were also anxious to discuss with Aubrey Torrington's heir those things they felt he should know if he were not to be duped by Chinese authorities in Canton, who would, like all shrewd businessmen, take advantage of his inexperience.

Rupert always emerged from such meetings with a tight jaw and was quiet for the rest of the day. Harriet knew that he was able to grasp all he was told and that he remained resigned to what he must do. In Valentine Bedford he had a skilled and expert agent, who could have been a friend as well as a senior employee—he had virtually been running the company's affairs for several years—but Harriet could not change Rupert's attitude toward the man she found so charming.

She tackled the subject once more while they were taking breakfast six weeks after their arrival. The light meal was invariably served to them at a table on the veranda outside Harriet's bedroom. It was pleasant to sit in the early-morning cool and look out across the water toward Kowloon, on the mainland. They breakfasted early because the day began early in Hong Kong, and Harriet insisted on taking the meal in Rupert's company every day.

She saw little enough of him. Valentine Bedford arrived at nine every morning and claimed his employer's attention until there was a break for a light luncheon, which the agent ate with them ever since Harriet had asked him to join them on the first day of their arrival. It was not an arrangement Rupert cared for, but is seemed only natural, in Harriet's point of view.

In the afternoon she slept for a while during the hottest hours; by the time she awoke Rupert was down at the harbor, with his banker, or meeting with other merchants to discuss the continuing grave situation that gave no hope of their being allowed up to Canton when the trading season began in October. In the evenings he was discussing the problem with much greater enthusiasm with men from the barracks.

"I do enjoy our morning hour so much," she told him that day as she poured tea into fragile flowered cups. "I wish the time for your heir to be born would advance more quickly. I find the days of waiting to be full of boredom."

He glanced up quickly from the dish of eggs he had just uncovered. "You are not unhappy?"

"No, my dear, just a little weary of rest, taking care . . . and sleeping alone."

The glow of response in his eyes told her he hated it as much as she, but he attempted to tease her from her mood. "I have always understood women to find much pleasure in being cosseted and receiving the special attentions such a condition brings."

But she was not to be humored. "No doubt the women of whom you speak have no interest in what goes on around them and no affection for the man who coos at them the ridiculous words of praise for enduring what is, after all, a very commonplace condition." She put the teapot down with a sigh. "Rupert, there is so much I have yet to see. We have been in Hong Kong for six weeks, and I have visited Victoria only three times." She turned her head to gaze out over the veranda rail. "It is all down there to be seen, and I am trapped up here as surely as one of those little birds they sell in the marketplace."

Rupert's lips twitched. "I think all those birds are not *enceinte*, my love."

"I wish you would cease trying to be amusing," she snapped, feeling particularly dispirited.

He came around the table immediately, drew her to her feet, and kissed her gently. "I promise to show you all of Hong Kong you wish to see when you are able, but we cannot risk a repetition of the day we arrived now that you are so near the day. My wife . . . and my child . . . are too dear to me to put them in danger. In a month or so the cooler weather will be with us, and we shall have all the excitement you crave then, my dearest."

His nearness aroused her, and she cupped his face with hands that were tender, marveling once more at the change this man had wrought in her life. Two years ago she had faced a lifetime of spinsterhood and frustration. Tears formed in her eyes.

"Hold me tighter, Rupert, and kiss me as a lover," she whispered.

There on the veranda, in full view of anyone passing along the track, he did as she asked, and when they drew apart, desire had also flared in him. She knew him so well he could not hide it from her.

"Do you think me outrageously wanton to behave thus when I should be stitching tiny garments in tranquil contentment?" she asked breathlessly.

"Definitely," he murmured against her brow. "But I married a wanton, and if she ever grows tranquilly content, I swear I shall renounce the world and join the monks in their saffron robes over there on the hill."

She laughed shakily. "I love you madly, Rupert."

"Ah, in that case, the monks can do without my company."

He coaxed her back into her chair, stood beside her to pour tea into her cup, and then held it out to her. "In England most people have no notion how their morning beverage reaches them from the plant. You have seen the complicated activity and dare to leave it to grow cold. Shame on you!"

She drank her tea, restored to a happier frame of mind, and Rupert returned to his seat to enjoy his eggs and ham as she said, "Mr. Bedford was speaking at luncheon yesterday of the inevitability of tea prices rising. That will be a sad blow to Nanny, who dearly loves a cup at every opportunity."

Rupert sighed. "Half a season's trading has been lost, and prospects for October are thin. There must be a deficit in stocks before long."

"Will that apply to silk also?"

"I suppose so . . . and to any product shipped from China. Until we send an army up to open the port again, the situation will remain the same. It must be obvious to any man of sense, and I cannot understand the delay."

Hastily turning the conversation from the subject of war, Harriet used the warm intimacy of the moment to venture, "There is no doubt Mr. Bedford is a man of great worth to the company."

"Mmm," was the uncompromising reply.

"He seems to know all the right people and how best to approach them. How fortunate you are to have an agent like him."

"Most fortunate. In fact, the company does not need me at all with such a paragon at the helm."

With great care she smoothed the frilled and fluted sleeve of her pale green silk wrapper. "Rupert, what is it you so dislike about Mr. Bedford?"

"Everything."

Startled by his frankness, she repeated, "*Everything?*"

He nodded, the sun catching his blond head. "I have seldom felt such antipathy toward another man."

She was greatly dismayed. How could the business hope to prosper under such circumstances?

"But he is so capable—always here at the stroke of nine each morning. Fifteen years of faithful service cannot count for nothing surely?" She grew more forceful. "Rupert, he saved our lives on the day we arrived?"

"Possibly. That woman is his mistress."

His remark was so unexpected Harriet found it oddly disturbing. It had not occurred to her . . . but why should it have? The woman had been very lovely, and Valentine Bedford was a bachelor. Even so, she felt inordinately irritated that her husband should have said such a thing to her at this particular time.

"I should not have thought *you* would find objection in that."

His hand stilled in the midst of stirring his tea, and he raked her with a look that made her wish she had remained silent. "I had noticed you find him charming."

Her cheeks grew warmer. "Who could deny he is charming?"

The hand resumed stirring. "Certainly no woman who easily succumbs to flattery. My dear Harriet, on an island where Western ladies are scarce, there is hardly a man who will not try to charm them."

"Do you include yourself in that?" she flung at him.

His mouth tightened. "I have a wife who is about to produce my child. Your question is a little insulting."

The color in her cheeks deepened as her temper rose. "You have given the very reason why he keeps a Chinese mistress. What chance has he of finding a wife here when most of the European women are married? He cannot go back to England to seek one from the season's batch."

"Quite," he said with heavy emphasis.

"You cannot hold his past against him—it was fifteen years ago," she protested hotly. "You have not led the life of a saint yourself."

Rupert abandoned his breakfast to stare at her with grim contemplation. "Your defense of him grows a little too warm for my liking."

She flung down her napkin. "Now who is being insulting? I was merely shocked to discover that you condemned others for doing to you what you are now doing to him."

He rose, tipping his chair over as he did so. "The sins, may I remind you, were my father's and his father's before him. Bedford's are his own."

With his mouth set and angry he went along the veranda into his own room, leaving her as depressed as when she had first awakened that morning. How could their exchange have led to such words from her? All she had set out to do was improve relations between Rupert and the man he could not afford to dislike. As a novice merchant he needed all the help he could get. A break with Valentine Bedford would leave the company vulnerable, and with its owner spending all his spare time with the military its future would be shaky indeed.

When Rupert called his sedan chair and set off up the track that evening, he left Harriet about to retire. Their exchange of words over Bedford had left a slight constraint between them all day, which made Rupert dislike the fellow even more. He'd be damned if he let his agent come between him and his wife!

The night was particularly dark. Without the light from the lamps swinging on the poles jutting from the roof of the sedan chair it would be almost impossible to see the track at all as it wound its way up to the barracks. Fortunately it was wide enough to take the artillery guns and wagons, so there was no danger of his bearers going over the edge, but heavy rains had made the surface slippery and difficult for the bare-footed chairmen. The rain had ceased just before dinner, but Rupert could still smell it in the air. There was a heavy clamminess of atmosphere and far-distant murmurings that could be approaching thunder. Just six weeks in Hong Kong had told him the day's rain would not cease without first turning into a storm.

It was probably inadvisable to go up to the barracks on such a night, but he had no wish to remain in Sussex Hall. With the child due in three weeks' time Harriet found the need to rest more and more, so he had stopped inviting his military friends, who were often rowdy. With his wife gone to her bed at nine of an evening he faced lonely hours in which to contemplate all he had lost . . . and all he was now forced to accept. Too often during such times the words of his father beat in his brain. *You are ashamed of your inheritance. Not only have you no heart for trade, but you despise it. They will never totally accept you. The mark of trade is stamped on you forever.* With every day he spent as a silk merchant the brand grew deeper.

He hated the meetings he must attend to discuss market prices, renewed grading systems, shipping routes, port priorities. Among prosperous men with smooth tongues, wily minds, and the experience of years behind them he was out of his depth. Half their vocabulary he did not understand; that which they felt so passionately did not touch him in the slightest. They were mostly friendly, reasonable men who went out of their way to lay out in detail all they felt he would not easily understand, but they invariably turned matters over to his agent, whom he was obliged to take everywhere with him.

Day after day Rupert struggled with ledgers, figures, shipping costs, and load capacities, trying to absorb all Bedford told him and to make intelligent comment. But all the time there was a choking, agonizing protest within him that he had to fight to keep down. There in his memory, in his very blood, were the beat of drums, the roar of cannon, the cries of men rushing to defend their colors and the British flag. His pulse was as firm and steady as the tramp of regiments; his brain rang with the call of bugles. His whole being yearned for the glory of a misty morning when vague triangles of a tented camp drew near after a gallop across foreign fields. To sit and discuss tea, rice, and bales of raw silk with a parcel of men whose main endeavors were no greater than concocting ways of making more and more money for themselves was a supreme effort.

The strain of his new life was beginning to tell on him; without the solace of Harriet's invigorating personality or abandoned lovemaking he was feeling desperate. For her sake he pretended a contentment he did not have and strove to cope with the testiness her well-advanced pregnancy brought about. But it was not easy when her impatient mood led her to extol the virtues of a man upon whom he was forced to depend and yet whom he instinctively disliked and distrusted.

As the sedan chair made its slow way up to the barracks, he sat deep in thought. At the back of his mind was an awareness of sounds—the liquid slap made by the bearers' feet on the muddy rain-soaked track; the distant gurgle of water as small cascades sought their tortuous way down the slopes; the quiet murmur of the leading chairmen as they spoke their secret messages in a language incomprehensible to their master; and soft, savage cries from animals lying low in those areas of Victoria Peak still left to them. Rupert had a pistol with him, for there were boar, leopard, civet, wild dogs, and any amount of venomous snakes in the trees and the thick undergrowth.

Remembering Harriet's words that morning, Rupert impulsively likened Valentine Bedford to a snake—smooth, silently efficient, lying low but missing nothing, and liable to strike when a blow would be least expected but most effective. To a man like himself who had always been active, aggressively loyal to a cause, and fiercely defensive of his nationality and all it stood for, Bedford was a blackguard.

From his military experience Rupert could recognize in him the resentment of a captain who has his command cut short by the arrival of a colonel who is not only younger but completely inexperienced. That was natural enough, and Rupert would not hold it against any man; but whereas he had made it plain he had no intention of snatching the reins, Bedford had thrust them at him on every occasion and basked in the resultant attention when he was asked to take them back.

Aside from that, he was glib, a salon beau, a lady's man. Rupert had not needed Harriet's reminder that he was no saint himself, but it was to be hoped he did not cut a figure similar to Bedford, who glided from flattery among tiara'd society matrons to his Chinese mistress, Tzu-An. Yes, he had checked on that lady who had allowed them to shelter in her house. In Hong Kong under the current circumstances one could not be too careful.

If that were not enough to prevent him from liking the company's manager, there was an aspect of his character that would command Rupert's dislike forever. The fellow had been slung out of his regiment and also his country—forbidden to return. One could say on that evidence that he was a thoroughly undesirable and blackguardly fellow, and yet he lived in style in Hong Kong, was admitted anywhere, and did everything with arrogant confidence that suggested he did not give a damn about anyone or anything but himself. That same man patronized his employer. Oh, it was subtly done, but Bedford made Rupert continually aware that he himself was an aristocrat employed by an upstart merchant.

With great dexterity he avoided calling Rupert sir. It was always Mr. Torrington. He never opened a door for his employer, always nodded to a servant to do so, and never let slip an opportunity to refer to the old days when Garforth roistered his rascally way to eminence. As a soldier Rupert had to admire the man's stategy; recognizing it, however, he played a strong waiting game. Only in Harriet's presence did Bedford change his tune, and it was all too evident that he hoped to undermine his employer through his wife . . . and she, normally so perceptive and intolerant of façades, had fallen a victim.

By the time he stepped from his chair in front of the tiny officers' mess Rupert's thoughts had so lowered his spirits he had persuaded himself he was welcome there only because he had played generous host so many times to lonely men who welcomed any break from dull routine.

Ten minutes later he forgot his gloom in the company of men who greeted him with genuine warmth and pressed a drink into his hand. There was no chance of being depressed that evening, for a party of officers from the barracks below had been invited, together with their families. There were seven ladies, three of whom were the daughters of an aging major, and all determined to make full use of their popularity. The major's youngest daughter was a minx of no more than eighteen who set her cap at Rupert the moment he was presented, telling him she had lived among the military all her life and was delighted to meet one of the dashing traders who sailed before the mast and ventured into the barbaric interior of China.

Responding instinctively to her lively and breathless charms, Rupert began an outrageous flirtation in which he told exaggerated tales of piracy, villainous Chinese, and escape from near torture at their hands. He even satisfied her obvious desire to be kissed when they took the air on the balcony and then recklessly kissed her again for the sheer enjoyment of feeling her slender body in his arms.

The major soon came in search of his daughter and treated Rupert to close scrutiny, but the girl told her parent she had felt faint and Mr. Torrington had supported her until she had recovered. With such an accomplished liar Rupert knew the truth was safe, so when the major began a discussion on the mutiny in India and how it had affected the campaign in China, Rupert joined in with no feelings of conscience, while the girl slipped back inside, flushed with triumph.

The major had been in Hong Kong for several years and accepted Rupert's account of being obliged to sell his commission on the death of his father with no suggestion that he had ever heard the full story.

"Naturally I am watching events with a military eye. When I arrived in Hong Kong in July, I had expected the assault on Canton to be under way. The delay is particularly humiliating, as I see it, and hardly improves our reputation with the Americans, the Russians, and other Western nations," he concluded.

"Well, of course, Lord Elgin is on his way here from Calcutta. I suppose nothing can be done until he arrives with explicit instructions from London," said the other. "Cigar, Torrington?"

They took a moment to get their smoking satisfactorily started before Rupert went on. "Instructions from London are all very well, but the French are in on this and will have their own ideas on how best to deal with it. I will agree with any man that Elgin might be a very worthy plenipotentiary, but with our ships blockading the river below Canton and the Chinese causing murder and mayhem among the Western population, I would say it is a little late for an experienced diplomatic tongue."

The major smiled and exhaled smoke. "Spoken like a true firebrand." He turned and leaned back against a pillar, where a small lizard shot away in fright. "Guns should be used only as a last resort. There should always be verbal attempt to reach agreement whenever possible."

"Just so," was the firm reply, "and how long will it take us to acknowledge that verbal attempts are not possible when dealing with the Manchus? I have had no personal experience of them, but my father was always very vocal on the subject of our complete inability to communicate with them." He warmed to his theme. "Surely the well-known evidence of their contempt for existing treaties proves my point. What is the use of holding negotiations with men who nod and say yes, then go off and do exactly as they please?"

When the other offered no answer, he pressed his point further. "This colony is flourishing and will grow beyond anyone's wildest imaginings, I'll wager. Not only is it essential as a naval and military base, but it gives us a permanent foot in the Far East from which to preserve our trading interests, which are rich and invaluable to our nation."

He tapped the ash from his cigar. "But only a fool would ignore the slumbering implications of other nation's designs on China. The French are happy to ally with us for the furtherance of their own trading interests, but they have been our traditional enemy for too long to trust them overmuch. The Russians, whom we have both just fought for trying to enlarge their territorial power, are content to wait in the wings, taking advantage of treaties and concessions *we* pay for with British lives, but look covetously at China's northern borders. The Americans are extremely interested in gaining a firmer foothold in the East but are forbidden by Washington to do more than accept the benefits we have gained in battles." He grinned. "One cannot help admiring the United States commander who conveniently forgot such orders and seized the Chinese forts that fired on his ship not long ago. Like me, his opinion of orders given by someone on the other side of the globe is not very high. I believe he was chastised over the affair, but my sympathy goes to him. Was he to let his ship be bombarded and not retaliate?"

He shifted his position. "That is what *we* are doing in effect. The eyes of the world are upon us as we sit here undecided. We have begun a conflict and yet will not deliver the coup de grâce."

"*Cannot,* Mr. Torrington. Without extra troops we cannot hold Canton, even if we do take it."

"And the Chinese are laughing at us while our factories in the city remain deserted." He threw down the stub of his cigar and ground it out with his heel. "Dammit, we do not wish to conquer them, just trade freely."

"Ah, maybe, but they have no wish to trade with us."

"Do they not?" exploded Rupert. "They grab with eager hands the excessive taxes, port dues, and land rents they squeeze from us. Money, sir, is as attractive to the Chinese as to any man. Show me a Manchu official who is not greedy and corrupt, and I will be mightily surprised. The profit they make, my dear Major Greeves, does not go for the good of the Chinese they rule but into their own overflowing coffers. Each one is a law unto himself. They look upon us with contempt enough as it is. That we wait for orders from London must seem to them the height of idiocy and confirms their opinion that they are a vastly superior people. I tell you, I cannot wait to match them with troops and firepower. We shall soon discover which is the greater nation."

There was a short silence when he stopped speaking, and the major looked at him with interest. "I think you made a mistake when you sold out of the army, sir. Everything you have just said was spoken as a military man, not as a merchant."

Harriet spent a restless night. She was still bothered by the morning's argument between herself and Rupert, even though she had encouraged him to go up to the barracks, when he mentioned it, as one way of making amends. Once he had left, she perversely wished he had stayed. For some unaccountable reason the house seemed empty without him, mere fancy as the place was so vast she would not have heard him even if he had been at home in the library.

Weary, she lay for a long time, unable to calm her thoughts. There was an ache in her back that would not be eased, and the swell of her stomach made it difficult to get comfortable in any but one position. She fiercely punched pillows into rounded shapes and then stuffed them at first on one side of her and then the other, hoping to provide some support.

To blot out the savage sounds of the Oriental night and the thunder that grew nearer and nearer, she set her mind to thinking of the future. It did not seem likely that she would be one of those mothers who wished only to speak and think of babies, who cooed for hours on end of the virtues of her child with others who cooed of theirs. Being pregnant had been no joy to her—she had resented the bounds it had put upon her life—and the ending of it would be a great relief.

There was so much about Hong Kong that captured her interest. She must explore it and keep notes such as those Professor Deane had made. She had brought his work with her in her luggage, and she felt the book would benefit from her own personal experience of a foreign culture.

But it was not only the island colony that fired her interest and thirst for greater knowledge. Now that her life had become closely influenced by the shipping of silk, its production and history had become fascinating mysteries. She could hardly wait for an opportunity to study the subject. If she also hoped to alter Rupert's resigned attitude toward something that had forced itself upon him, it was not to be wondered at. He was so plainly unhappy in his new role she could only long to help him accept and enjoy what must be. *Face the inevitable and turn it to one's advantage.* She would tell him of her father's dictum and stand beside him, offering her support and understanding.

The storm broke soon after midnight—the worst she had ever experienced. Monsoon rain thundered for hour after hour without ceasing, bringing a sudden chill into the house. The trees outside swung and bent, visible from her bed when lightning put stuttering flashes of brilliance over the island. It did not frighten her, but when Bessie came hurrying into the room from her adjacent chamber, Harriet realized the girl was nervous and pretended she would be glad of her company.

When first light was breaking, Harriet woke with the sudden and certain knowledge that her child would be born that morning.

Bessie, who had slept curled up in a chair, was sent to fetch her master but came rushing back, muslin cap awry and eyes wide with concern to report that he had not been in all night.

"Fu-Wong says the captain's bed is as smooth as a christening cake, madam, and he's nowhere in the house. Here's a pretty state! He's more'n likely still up at them barracks."

Harriet tried not to show her true feelings at the thoughts of his not being near at such a milestone in their life together. Easing herself onto one elbow, she took a deep breath and said, "Send one of the servants into Victoria for the doctor; then take Fu-Wong with you up the track to the barracks. If Mr. Torrington *is* still there, he will wish to know of the child's early arrival."

The girl rushed off without waiting to say more, in a swirl of cotton nightgown and full-skirted linen wrapper, muttering to herself about the selfishness of gentlemen. When she had gone, Harriet struggled from the bed and went onto the veranda to watch the black-clad servant hurry down the track.

The ravages of the storm were apparent wherever she looked. Some trees were down; others, still standing and with their barks singed and curled away from the trunk by lightning, shed water as if it were still raining. The track was reduced to a winding path of reddish brown slime, and the distant view was obscured by a humid layer of air over the entire island. Looking upward, Harriet could not even see the barracks.

"Oh, Rupert," she said with a sigh, "why did I let you go up there last night when I needed you so much?"

Time passed in a series of dramas after that. Bessie returned to tell her mistress that she had been turned back no more than 200 yards from the house, where the track had disappeared into a landslide of mud and stones.

"There was soldiers on the far side already digging and heaving stones, madam, but it'll take till Barnaby's birthday before anyone can get up or down there." She sniffed loudly. "The soldiers said there's a whole lot of people stranded up there after a party last night . . . ladies included."

Harriet's stomach clenched with anger. No wonder he had made no effort to return at the beginning of the storm!

"I'm sorry, madam, reely I am," cried Bessie. "I told Fu-Wong to climb up through the trees, but he wouldn't not go—said there was bad *fung-shoy* and walked back quick as you like."

Still hurting from the evidence of Rupert's forced isolation from her in the company of ladies who would surely make his confinement pleasurable, she kept hold of herself sufficiently to explain that the local Chinese did, indeed, believe that the *fung-shui*—spiritual and elemental influences—of that part of the jungle were hostile. They believed the building of the barracks had displeased the resident dragons.

"There is nothing we can do until the track is repaired," she added, resigning herself to producing Rupert's child in his absence.

When, however, the servant returned from Victoria to say the doctor was not at his house, even Harriet's resourceful personality suffered a severe blow. She had had no experience of any other woman's childbirth to help her, and neither had Bessie. Holding her fears in check as best she could, she sent the servant back down the track to find another doctor—any doctor. She did not need experience to tell her the child was coming very quickly.

Two hours had passed since she had first awakened, and she was forced to take to her bed again. Bessie stood beside the bed, almost in tears.

"You know I'd do anything for you, madam, but I don't know what the *right* anything is in this case."

She wiped Harriet's brow with a cologne-scented towel. "He shouldn't ought to go off and leave you at a time like this, straight he shouldn't."

"That's quite enough," gasped Harriet. "I will not have you speaking that way of your master."

"He's not my master," muttered the girl, too beside herself to know or care what she was saying. "He dismissed me again yesterdee."

"Run onto the veranda and see if there is anyone coming up the track," begged Harriet. "There must be another doctor somewhere in Victoria."

She watched as the girl hurried outside and leaned over the balustrade, and she prayed that Rupert would miraculously arrive to take command of the situation. She did not know what he could do, but it would help just to have him beside her. But help was coming from another direction . . . and an unexpected one.

"Mr. Bedford is just coming up the steps. Oh, thank the Lord," cried Bessie, rushing through the room like a tornado.

Harriet lay alone in that room in a daze of increasing distress, summoning what fortitude she could. Then she became aware of raised voices outside her veranda doors before Valentine Bedford appeared to stand beside her bed with a reassuring smile.

"Forgive my intrusion at such a time, Mrs. Torrington, but emergencies sweep aside convention. I met your servant as I came up the track, and as soon as he told me the facts, I directed him to go to Tzu-An, the woman in whose house you sheltered on your arrival in Hong Kong. There is very little she does not know about bringing infants into the world, so I beg you to place yourself in her hands with confidence."

His mistress—he was bringing his mistress into Rupert's house!

Bessie was there like a termagant crying, "I won't let no stranger touch you, madam, never fear."

A surge of urgency shook Harriet at that moment, and she gasped, "I must accept any help if it arrives in time. Please, go now, Mr. Bedford."

He bowed. "Of course, ma'am. You will be quite safe, I promise."

The image of his swarthy good looks remained with her in the hour that followed. His punctual arrival at nine had been the answer to a prayer. The woman slipped in without Harriet's really registering the moment she came and the vocal hostility between Bessie and someone for whom she felt strong mistrust was muted by the imminent birth of the child.

Tzu-An's tranquillity immediately transferred itself to Harriet, who relaxed and gave herself up to the gentle hands of a woman whose face bore no expression as she delivered with ease a lusty, well-built baby. Through the realms of exhaustion, relief, and a surprising feeling of godliness, Harriet heard the child give a strong cry of life before she drifted off to sleep.

Later—much later, when the sun was streaming into the room—she opened her eyes at a sound and saw Rupert standing there looking down at her with eyes bruised by shock and painful gentleness. He was filthy, unshaved, covered with mud and pieces of foliage.

"We were cut off when the track collapsed," he told

her hoarsely. "I have just pushed my way down through the jungle."

She did not feel anything; emotion was too much of an effort. As she lay gazing at him, he fell to his knees beside her, kissing her hand with lips that seemed cold despite the outbreak of sweat on his face.

"How could I have guessed? I would have got here somehow, I swear."

None of his words mattered. He had come too late.

"I should like to call him Edward," she murmured, closing her eyes again.

For a moment his rough cheek rested against hers very gently. "Of course, we shall call him Edward. I always knew that."

Chapter Ten

The weather was as perfect as a Hong Kong December could produce: clear skies of endless blue beauty, sparkling jewel colors, sun on the sea to gild the wave crests, and the pleasant warmth Harriet associated with English summertime. It was good to be alive on such a day.

Inside the great warehouses beside the wharves belonging to the Battle Trading Company it was almost cool, and Harriett listened entranced as Valentine Bedford explained how the silk was produced from the minute silkworm grubs to rest on their racks packed into small bundles of skeins called books in the trade.

"It is a process so ancient, ma'am, its origins are lost in the realms of legend and folklore." He brought forward a chair, dusted it with a flourish of his silk handkerchief, and invited her to sit down. "If you truly wish to steep yourself in the subject of silk you must be prepared to imagine the China of ancient civilization, of deep and mystic inscrutability, of cruelty and incredible beauty. You must also be able to picture a vast land of walled cities, each a separate kingdom visited only by trading caravans and marauding armies, where brilliant unscrupulous men ruled their subjects with barbaric tyranny and amassed wealth beyond imagination."

Harriet smiled at him delightedly. "Mr. Bedford, you should be an author with such ability to conjure up vivid scenes. You make the past come alive." She looked up at Rupert. "Do you not agree, my dear?"

"It sounds very much like the China of today," he said. "It has changed little over the years."

He disappointed her. Nothing she did or said could persuade him to like his agent. Since the incident of Edward's birth Rupert seemed almost to dislike him more, despite the very real help he had given. She gave up her attempt and turned her attention back to the dark-haired man, who was so assured one might almost imagine *him* to be the owner of the company.

"Do continue, Mr. Bedford."

He smiled, a warm, provoking change of expression. "The full story would take a year and a day to tell, Mrs. Torrington. How much do you wish to hear?"

Her light laugh echoed somewhere in the pointed heights of the roof and vanished in the emptiness of a warehouse that should be full.

"I fear it must be only the first installment, sir."

Bedford leaned against an upright spar and folded his arms nonchalantly. "You are back in the century 2700 B.C., at the court of Emperor Huang Ti. The Imperial Palace is filled with gold and precious gems, the most beautiful artifacts, and wondrous inventions from the minds of wise men. There are blossoms of fragile rarity and perfume wherever one looks; crystal-clear pools are filled with shimmering gold and silver fish; musicians in pavilions play delicate melodies at the wave of a hand; fruits both luscious and sweet from many lands are piled high in golden bowls; tiny singing birds warble in cages with emerald-studded bars; handsome men and lovely women in embroidered robes and bejeweled headdresses stroll through shady paths.

"The empress has this all around her but is not content. She has been shown a length of cloth called silk and cannot be happy until she has a complete costume made from this material. To achieve this, she must have her own grove of mulberry trees, an army of silkworms, and weavers whose sole task would be to serve her requirements. Such manufacture must be a closely guarded secret disclosed only on pain of death.

"So it happened, but news of this wondrous cloth gradually reached the ears of princes and nobles throughout the land, who also acquired mulberry groves and silkworms. However, they too threatened torture to any person who betrayed the manufacturing secrets, and the Chinese kept the art of sericulture exclusively theirs for many centuries."

He broke off his narrative to return to the present with disturbing suddenness. "We must assume men like your grandfather were not to be found in those days, Mr. Torrington. Garforth would have taken the secret from them in no time at all."

Rupert's mouth began to tighten as it always did when the agent referred to the company's founder by his Christian name, and Harriet hastily intervened.

"Who finally risked torture, Mr. Bedford?"

"A lady, naturally, ma'am," was the amused reply. "According to legend, a beautiful young princess traveling to a province along the border with India in order to be married smuggled out silkworm eggs and the seeds of the mulberry in the lining of her elaborate headdress because she could not bear to continue life without the fabulous cloth she had grown accustomed to wearing. From her court, the secret leaked across the border, and it belonged to China no longer."

He straightened and raised a quizzical eyebrow at Harriet. "Will you agree with me, ma'am, that the lady most likely suffered the worst torture of all—that of seeing other ladies in her precious silk cloth?"

Harriet dragged her thoughts away from centuries of Eastern opulence and focused on him once more. "That supposition is not very kind, sir, but very probably true," she added with a rueful smile. "So vanity betrayed a nation."

"Does it not often do so?"

Strangely Harriet sensed deeper meaning lurking in his remark, as if their own natural rapport had some secret quality about it—like the silk—and her enjoyment of the morning was faintly overshadowed by something she could not identify.

Taking refuge in briskness, she said, "But the world still does not know how a man came to discover that a maggot could clothe the backs of the world." She looked up at her husband. "Do you not find that a perplexing mystery, Rupert?"

"Eh . . . oh, yes, perplexing, indeed," he agreed, dragging his gaze from a naval gunboat passing slowly through the harbor beyond the warehouse. "If you hope to visit your dressmaker before returning home, I suggest you make your way there very shortly, my dear."

The visit to the dressmaker was a delight because Harriet found she had returned to the slender proportions of earlier days. Edward was three months old already, and she needed dresses for the social whirl that would soon be part of her life. The cooler winter season always brought a round of balls and outdoor events such as garden parties, race meetings, and military reviews. Harriet was not at all sure that attending the latter would be advisable, but she knew with certainty they would not miss one.

After an hour she and Bessie entered their sedan chairs for the uphill return to Sussex Hall. Rupert had remained at the wharves to speak with the ships' masters about the possibility of leaving Hong Kong with empty vessels and finding cargoes en route. There were goods piling up in England with no ships to move them. With the start of the trading season come and gone and Canton still barred to the merchants, there seemed little prospect of shipping much from Hong Kong that year. Valentine Bedford had been advising his employer to take such action for most of the month, but Rupert had dug in his heels without offering reasons until he saw his rivals sending their clippers away. The agent had said dryly that it was probably too late to send their own out now because the best cargoes would have been taken from India ahead of them.

But the morning was too invigorating to spoil it by worries of that nature, and Harriet sat in her chair enjoying all that went on around her while looking forward to her precious after-luncheon hour with the child of her heart, who looked so like Rupert it was a painful joy to feel him pull at her breast.

Their progress was halted halfway by an exuberant street celebration in the form of the ever-popular lion dance. The chairmen set down their passengers side by side, at Harriet's request, and the two Englishwomen watched as the players performed to an accompaniment of gongs and cymbals. The performance itself was noisy, exaggerated, full of pantomime.

The lion looked like a grotesque mythical beast rather than the noble creature Harriet had seen at the menagerie with her brother Edward some years before. Its head was tremendous, luridly painted so that the features were exaggerated and comically threatening as the eyes rolled, the lids closed and opened, and the mouth and nostrils breathed fire. One man, wearing trousers of yellow shaggy fluff, bearing the great head and another, similarly dressed, forming the body, the pair pranced around, responding comically and aggressively to the two men baiting the creature and to the crowd gathering in growing delight and excitement.

Harriet watched with deep interest, reminded for a sad moment of Aubrey Torrington's having been accused by his villagers of pagan devilry. He had witnessed a few of the wonders of the world, rejoiced in them, and been condemned by those who were ignorant. There was little basic difference between peoples. The Chinese before her at that moment were happy and at ease with their dragons and fearsome beasts and yet were afraid of Westerners who wore strange clothes. It was widely believed that the women who wore huge bell-shaped skirts had only one leg and glided along like a snake; that European men were afraid of these female creatures and fussed around them in order not to incur their terrible wrath; and that Western missionaries took Chinese babies and cut them up to use their organs for religious rites. What would the villagers of Battle think of that? she wondered.

The performers were moving away, and Harriet had nodded to the men to continue when her idle gaze caught sight of one face she knew in the crowd. But it returned no sign of recognition despite the intensity of the gaze. Harriet's first feeling of puzzlement changed to one of disturbing chill as she realized that Tzu-An knew her well enough and yet remained unmoved, as if she had never performed that most intimate task of bringing her child into the world—surely the basis of a bond another woman could not dismiss?

As her sedan chair moved away, Harriet still felt disquieted. No matter what the woman's background and life-style, Tzu-An had aided them twice. After sheltering in her house, Harriet had tried to thank her, but Bedford had cut her short by explaining that the woman understood no English. His brief words in Cantonese had been met with a solemn bow as Tzu-An showed them out. At the birth of Edward Harriet had been in no state to express her gratitude but had afterward offered the agent money to take to the woman. He had refused, saying Tzu-An would be offended at the suggestion of payment. Chinese women were taught from childhood to serve others and expected no reward for doing what they regarded as their duty.

As the chairmen plodded up the increasing slope of the track, Harriet wondered if she had been right to believe the man who apparently kept the woman as his mistress. Whatever one was taught from childhood, an expresson of thanks was never out of place. There was hardly a race more concerned with polite manners than the Chinese. She knew Rupert must have made some kind of speech—and a difficult one it must have been after his own absence at a time when others should not have been asked to stand in his stead—but perhaps more effort should have been made on her own part. For someone who had just been deploring the lack of understanding between East and West, she had been as guilty as the rest.

Such matters were driven from her head when Rupert came in for luncheon soon after she and Bessie arrived back. When he came into her airy bedroom, which he had just begun sharing with her again, she turned with a finger to her lips lest he awake their son before she had eaten her meal.

"You must learn to move more quietly," she admonished in a whisper, moving into his arms eagerly.

His kisses were exciting—more so because they once again held the overtones of desire and demand—and she returned kiss for kiss with the hunger that was always shared by them when they were alone.

"Mm . . . wanton woman!" he accused softly against her ear. "Your cries of rapturous abandonment are more likely to awaken our son than my footsteps." His arm around her, he coaxed her toward the veranda. "Come, I have something of the greatest importance to tell you . . . and if we do not cease this delightful dalliance, there is no knowing where it might lead."

She smiled up into his face. "I am very willing to find out."

His light rejoinder hardly impressed itself on her, for she was completely taken by his air of contained but supreme elation. Gone was the shadow of all he had lost, the weight of his unwanted inheritance. Gone was the man she had seen earlier that morning, stiff-mannered, careless of his surroundings, lethargic, and resigned. His eyes were brilliant now with a fire that was more intense than what she saw when he took her in love and passion. She could even feel his vitality, that of a young man who had been slumbering far too long and was now spring-awakened.

Thrilled, unable to do more than gaze at him, she was in an emotional spin when he began speaking.

"We are off. Elgin has sent an ultimatum to Commissioner Yeh which has been refused. Troops are being embarked on transports as soon as the equipment is assembled. The French are already armed and standing by. We are attacking at last!"

The day seemed suddenly cooler than before. Harriet shivered as memories flitted through her mind of a November day when she had rushed downstairs to greet a brother who had been two months dead and unmourned.

"I see." It was the only rejoinder she could manage to utter, but Rupert was too tensed up to notice.

"This should have been done long ago. Until they are made to realize that entente means honorable recognition of it by *both* sides, the whole Eastern question will never be settled."

"Are guns the best way of doing it?" she asked through stiff lips, all her passion leaving her with nothing to replace it as she thought of the laughing simple people who had watched the lion dance so short awhile ago.

"They are the only way when innocent people are being attacked in the street, given bread that is poisoned, and driven from their homes by fire," he returned with heated emphasis. "We are not using force to take land from them or impose our rule in China. It will merely be the armed occupation of a port open to us by treaty but closed by the stubbornness of one man. It is in their best interests to follow the rest of the world in honoring peaceful treaties."

"Is it?" she asked tensely, aware that what had begun as a starburst of intimacy between them was turning into some kind of emotional confrontation, the reason for which was vague but frightening. "Is it in their best interests to follow the rest of the world? All they have ever wanted is to be left alone."

His hands dropped from her arms in the final loss of contact. "No one wishes to change his way of life or his culture—except missionaries who are driven to educate the heathen to Christianity. Even then, they use the spoken word, great courage, and infinite compassion in their work, not force. Do you believe they should also leave the Chinese alone—you, who believe in the one true God?"

Sick with something that was deeper than disappointment, more apprehensive than anger, she walked away from him to stand looking out over a city enhanced by winter clarity of atmosphere.

"You counter hatred with more hatred. It will not be dissolved but driven deeper into their souls. If you had read their history, as I have, you would know about their persistent fight to keep foreigners out.

Why do you think they built those great walls around their cities?"

He moved to stand beside her. "I cannot believe what I hear. You defend them?"

In a moment she was blazingly angry about the beautiful day he had spoiled with his words, the love unsatisfied within her, and the instinctive knowledge that it would be as easy to lose him as love him. Once again their power to destroy each other was evident to her.

"Defend them? Those are the only words you can use—defend and attack!" she flung at him. "I am speaking as my father's daughter, as a student anthropologist. As such I take no sides."

"No, indeed," he said grimly. "The student who reads his books in the comfort of his study reaches many conclusions, but he might be blind to realities. Do you know what your quaint and fascinating Chinese did to that French missionary? They took him from his peaceful preaching, flogged him until the skin had gone from his back, tied his wrists and ankles together behind his back, and left him in a cage to die in the blistering sun. When, by God's mercy, he did not, they dragged him out, cut off his head, and threw it to the dogs. Yes, ma'am," he added with growing heat, "it *should* make your eyes grow wide with horror . . . but I will spare your student ears the details of how they have used Catholic nuns."

In the distance Harriet heard her baby's first fretful hungry cries. But Rupert was in full flood, and nothing would now stop him.

"That is nothing compared with what they do to their own people. Have you also studied their methods of punishment, their cruel oppression of their subjects within those walled cities, the exploitation of their talents and skills for little reward—have you studied those alongside the artistic details of their ancient and marvelous culture? Do you not think the opening of their country to Western influence might be of benefit to the teeming population of China? Those who instructed walls to be built around the cities were anxious to preserve their personal positions of wealth and power; the men who quarried, hauled, and laid the stones might have seen the walls as those of a prison, shutting off all hope of salvation." He flung out a hand in angry impatience. "Oh, no, my dear student of anthropology, you see these people only as they are represented on a page. As a soldier I see them at their worst and best, their most human."

"But you are not a soldier, may I remind you once more," she cried, meaning to hurt him as she was now being hurt. But it barely touched the vital warrior he had become.

"I am arranging to take a lorcha upriver behind the attacking force. The company's factory and wharves there are in great danger of being destroyed, and it is important that I witness the progress of the battle. There should be—"

"Stop . . . *stop!*" she cried, knowing why she had been chilled and afraid, why he was at his most aggressively masculine at that moment. "It is not in the company's interests that you wish to go, but as a soldier—a soldier to whom no one will give a uniform." The growing cries of their son added fuel to the flames of her anger. "That is all you ever think of. You stare at ledgers and see only the regimental flag; your gaze passes over the graceful lines of the company's ships to fasten on the batteries perched upon the rocks. You stare at merchants who go out of their way to help you and deplore the fact that they do not wear scarlet coats. You hate the one man who holds the business together, yet you dare to stand there now and pretend to me you have your interests as a merchant so much at heart you must needs hold the coat-tails of the army as it sails off to war!" She put her hands to her temples in growing distress and inner pain. "My papa always told me to face the inevitable, but you never have, Rupert. Even while your son was coming into the world, you were living your pretense with those who are never from your mind."

At last she had struck where he was infinitely vulnerable. She marked her victory by the rigidness of his jaw and the narrowing of his eyes in swift pain. No word concerning his absence that morning had passed between them until now, and she knew it was a thrust beneath his guard. No man could have guessed his child would arrive three weeks early and with such speed . . . and no one could have pushed down through the jungle in such a storm.

"I do not expect you to understand everything I do," he said huskily.

"What of the ladies also cut off by the storm that night—did you persuade them to understand why you were there?" It was a flash of jealousy that had needed such as this to set it free.

"I imagine so, since I spent the greater part of the evening expounding my theories on the present situation in China." His face flushed angrily at her expression. "I see you do not choose to believe me. Shall I tell you that I pressed hot kisses on every bare shoulder in sight, despite the fathers and husbands present? Would you feel vindicated if I confessed I had bedded each and every one of them while you were producing my son alone and afraid?" He seized her arms in a fierce grip. "Do you think I have not regretted that night a hundred times or more? I do not need your jealousy to punish me; it is enough every time I look at Bedford's face."

Her passion swung the other way in a flash, and she caught at his coat lapels. "Rupert, forget this mad idea. You cannot go off to war."

"I have been to war before."

Heedless of the implacable note in his voice, she went on desperately. "You are no longer a soldier; you have no duty to obey. You know nothing about ships. What can you possibly do? A merchant lorcha will be in their way when it comes to battle. They will not want you there, needlessly hovering on the outskirts of something so deadly and vital."

His eyes had lost their luster of elation. "Is that how you see me—a man clinging desperately to an army like a small boy trying to join the ranks of an elder brother's enclave?"

"Isn't that what you are?" she cried bitterly. "In England they made it abundantly clear they did not want you. Has the lesson really not been learned?"

For a moment he stood immobilized by what she was doing to him, and then he said tonelessly, "I suppose not. Do you know me so little?"

The confession, the proof that he would lay himself open to such humiliation again, completed her rage against what he was and would always be.

"I do not know you at all," she said in a voice that shook. "That is the sound of your son crying in there—your son of three months. If it does not hurt you to desert me for the chance of bathing in the reflected glory of those who rejected you, do you feel no duty to him? You have described to me the horrors of war; I have read of them in the newspapers. My own dearest brother was killed in the prime of his youth. Will you expose yourself to death needlessly, risk making me a widow and your son an orphan for the sake of self-gratification, for that is all it is."

While she had been speaking, he had grown remote. He seemed defeated, but perversely her victory was no longer sweet in the face of what was written on his face. Only when he spoke did she realize it was no victory at all.

"If you cannot see the true reason, then I do not know you either. If I stay behind, it will be only because no crew is willing to man the lorcha. A man has to do what is in him, Harriet . . . and I have to go up to Canton with the army."

He was lost already; she could feel the pain of his death. She clutched the sides of her full skirt with fingers that ached. "If you go, I shall never forgive you . . . and neither will your son."

His jaw tightened until the skin was stretched tightly across it. "Don't ever blackmail me with your love, Harriet. It is a trick unworthy of you and all there has been between us. Can you really not see that my going up to Canton is, in some strange way, a dedication to you and Edward?"

She walked away into the bedroom, unable to face

him a moment longer. The baby was still sobbing when she picked him up and began rocking him with complete absorption. He was all she had left now.

"I am leaving at sundown."

The voice floated over and away from her. A few moments later heavy footsteps retreated along the veranda until a slamming door cut off the sound altogether. Somewhere below, a Chinese voice shouted an instruction, and out in the harbor a large junk was moving with clumsy tranquillity across her line of vision. It represented a culture she was striving in vain to understand.

The little creature in her arms was now whimpering fretfully. She bent to kiss the fair downy head, baptizing her son with her tears.

The master of the lorcha, an aging Irishman, was delighted to be taking his vessel to Canton to have at the Chinese. Rupert explained to him that it was merely a voyage to survey the situation, and in no way would they be involved in the Anglo-French attack. But he was treated to a knowing grin.

"No, sorr. It wouldn't be that a fine upstanding captain like yeself was thinking he'd be a useful man at the scene of a battle, now would it?"

Rupert grinned back. "If we appear to be getting the worst of it, it might be that help would be welcomed . . . but you are not to take the vessel within range of the shore guns. We have no means of returning fire apart from a rifle or two."

So they cut loose and followed in the wake of the army through the maze of islands at the mouth of the

Pearl River, then up toward Canton. Rupert stood at the flat prow, looking ahead to the fleet of transports being towed by small steamships. They made a fine picture in the dying day—a collection of gunboats, large-bellied transports with tall masts standing clear against the pearly blue sky, smaller and more modern steamships sending smoke straight up in the tranquil air, corvettes, and the squatter lorchas carrying supplies for the army.

To a man of the sea the sight would jerk the emotions; but Rupert was a soldier, and all his thoughts were with those packed between the decks of the troop transports, heading toward battle. He knew how they would be feeling, knew their fears and prayers, knew their longing for the moment to come, however terrible, that would end the agony of their wondering if they would prove cowards or heroes. He stood apart from them but was with them in thought, spirit, and thudding heart.

When night hid everything from view, he remained on deck, staring into the darkness. There had been no farewells of wife and son to recall now with sweet remembrance. Harriet was as passionate in anger as in love, and she did not easily forgive. Yet it was hard to believe she could not see that he *had* to be here. She had perceived the real reason behind his sailing to Hong Kong; why was she now so relentlessly opposed to his fulfilling that purpose? As a man who had once pledged his life to queen and country he had every need to be part of England's fight against people who seemed to insult and denigrate the nation and its representatives.

But there was another reason . . . and that could

not be explained to her even if she delayed forgiveness forcver. However often he told himself his dismissal from the regiment was unjustified, he found it impossible to shake off his feeling of failure, of unworthiness. Suppose he had faced their hostility, held his head high in the midst of their undeserved attack? But he had written out his resignation like a proclamation of guilt.

The merchants in Hong Kong were friendly enough, but they knew he was one of their number only because he had failed in his real profession . . . because the army would not have him. Harriet had gone to him only when she had seen him utterly defeated, but there was a burning need in him to prove himself in her eyes. From the moment she had accused him of taking the last penny from her dead brother he had done nothing to cause her to look at him with pride. Her love for him was deep—too deep perhaps—but it needed one more element to make it complete. Physically he knew it was all too easy to arouse her passion; tenderness welled within her to comfort and console him. But it was essential that she held him in honor also.

He knew he had no heart to learn what it had taken Valentine Bedford fifteen years to assimilate, and it did not help the situation that he was regarded as a failure by the man he disliked and distrusted. That it had been Bedford who had headed off the mob, while he had sheltered with the women on their day of arrival, and who had stepped into the breach when Harriet had been alone at Edward's birth seemed to emphasize his own sense of inadequacy. Harriet admired Bedford as a man of achievement and ability.

The only way he himself could earn her admiration was by doing what he knew how to do best. Bedford in a scarlet jacket had not made out so well, he thought grimly and not for the first time.

Now Rupert had a son—another person to whom he must dedicate all his endeavors. Would the boy look at his father later in life and see a man who had allowed himself to be spurned and had accepted second best? Garforth had been a rogue; Aubrey, a victim of his own passions. Hardly a proud legacy for Edward Torrington if his father died a complete nonentity!

With such thoughts as companions he slept little as the lorcha crept upriver, and he was on deck before dawn, anxious for his first sight of Canton, the city of which his father had spoken so often.

But hardly had his straining eyes made out the massive walls around the city than the silent morning shook with the roar of heavy guns. Excitement born of fear welled in him as the gray light was split by yellow flame-centered flashes from the gunboats when the bombardment of Canton got under way. The noise had aroused high feelings in other breasts to judge from the yells and battle cries that floated across the distance from the troop transports.

Rupert gripped the rail. He knew that sound, designed to intimidate the enemy and arouse one's own sense of aggression. Right now the soldiers would be standing to arms, staring across the water at the towering walls to be scaled; at the stone forts on the top where cannon peered wickedly from embrasures; at the pagoda rearing up with alien mystery within as the fast-lightening sky tinted it pinkish mauve; at the ancient gates built long ago to repel invaders down through the centuries. It was a formidable sight; but the Chinese soldiers were hopelessly equipped with out-of-date weapons, and a man's courage was often leavened by the power of his arms. Against the troops of England and France theirs could not compare.

It was not long before smoke billowed all around the ships anchored in the river and the air was filled with the smell of gunpowder that mingled with the odor of rotting matter drifting on the tide. It was no longer possible to see the fortifications except through a floating pall as the Chinese returned fire from cannons so ancient it was possible for the ships' guns to fire five times to their one. Most of the enemy shot fell short of the target and landed in the river, sending spouts of water high into the air.

The lowness of the tide had prevented the early landing of troops, and Rupert watched avidly as the level of the river crept higher and higher over the shoals and boats began to be lowered. He was not conscious of being a spectator, so lost had he become in the panorama of smoke, tall masts, ancient forts, and opaque water. The sight of the boats crammed with scarlet jackets inching their way through the churning froth that had been the river made him impatient for his own turn to come.

Up on the city walls small figures could be seen running back and forth in panic; the cannon on the walls had fallen silent. Rupert smiled; it should be easy enough to overrun an army that was moving in pandemonium. His ears had become accustomed to the roar of the ships' cannons, the scream of shells, and the echoing rumble as masonry crashed beneath the onslaught. Men's voices could be heard shouting;

bugles were stridently summoning soldiers and naval brigades to their places; winches and pulleys were squeaking as boats were lowered with a slap onto the river surface. From those scrambling ashore there was the lighter rattle of musketry fire as they darted from cover to cover in the extensive cemetery grounds beneath the walls.

Rupert could see British and French uniforms swarming all around a large temple, then moving to an outlying fort, which they soon held after a brief exchange of fire. Still the boats went from ship to shore until the beach was alive with uniformed men who pushed forward through the smoke hanging almost like a mist, shimmering in the sun's glare. With aching eyes he was straining to see how far forward the front line had advanced when a hand touched his arm and recalled his attention.

"Sorr, that blatherin' fool has run them aground, by all the saints!"

The ship's master was indicating a boat that had gone too far upstream and stuck on a sandbar a few hundred feet from the lorcha's port beam and in direct line of fire from the Cantonese guns, should they be fired again.

"Can we get them off?" asked Rupert.

He grinned. "Never you worry, sorr. O'Hare has towed an angel off a storm cloud before now, the divil he has! How good are you at throwing a line?"

"As good as any soldier," was the laughing reply. "What do we do with them once they're off?"

"Sure, and I know this river like Corrigan's elbow. I kin get them so close inshore they'll not even get their socks wet."

"I'll lay you ten to one on that," countered Rupert immediately. "Let's go to it, O'Hare."

"Aye, aye, sorr."

It was barely said when it seemed someone on the city walls had collected his senses and begun sending cannon shot toward the stranded boat. It became imperative to get under way, and O'Hare snapped orders at the Chinese crewmen that sounded to Rupert like a strange mixture of Irish, pidgin English, and Cantonese. The men understood it enough to leap into action, and the lorcha moved around toward the area that was being cannonaded from the fortressed walls.

Rupert was not aware of shouting orders or of sending down curses on the heads of a couple of soldiers who gave every sign of leaping from the boat into the water, and yet he heard his own voice above all the surrounding din.

"Stay where you are! I'll shoot the first man who jumps. Catch this line, lash it around the prow, and stay steady. We'll tow you in . . . sit *down*, damn you, or the boat will capsize when it comes off!"

Their own vessel was nearing the sandbar, and he watched anxiously, praying the Irishman was as good a seaman as he boasted. He could see the soldiers' faces clearly now, nothing with satisfaction that they were calmer and reacting to his authority in the midst of the regular explosion of shells that mercifully fell short of their target. He could feel the reverberations through the decks. One hit could sink the company vessel, and him with it.

Throwing the rope was easy. A corporal tied it quickly, and Rupert had turned to shout to O'Hare when a strange gusty roar filled his ears to the exclusion of all else. The sky burst into orange flame as the sails flew apart, leaving a broken mast to pelt down on him in a series of stinging blows, knocking him to the deck. It was a moment or two before sense returned to him.

A Chinese crewman was beside him, urging him up, but when Rupert gripped the spar, he felt no sensation in his hand or arm and remained where he was on the deck. Looking down, he saw his blood-soaked sleeve and realized he had been hit by a shell splinter. But the sky above him was passing fairly swiftly, by which phenomenon he guessed the lorcha was moving away from the danger area. Pulling himself up by his uninjured arm, he saw the smaller boat was now floating freely in tow and too close inshore for the trajectory of the cannon. The soldiers were cheering and smiling their thanks.

With a quick movement Rupert lurched along the deck toward O'Hare, who was maneuvering the vessel as easily as a baby carriage.

"Well done," he grunted.

"Ten to one, did you wager, sorr?" he asked with a grin.

"I should have known better than to put my money on an Irishman."

" 'Tis more than your money you've lost, I'm thinking . . . but you knew the stakes when you set off, I fancy. 'We're there to observe,' says himself, and didn't I know there was more than observin' on his mind now?" The man nodded at the bloody sleeve. "I've nothing on board to cope with that, so you'd best go ashore, sorr. There's medical officers with skill to treat wounds and the such."

So Rupert landed with the assault force that day and found himself in the midst of a scene he knew and had lived a thousand times in the quiet moments of those months since he had taken off his scarlet jacket for the last time. As at Sevastapol, he found it did not matter that he wore no coronet, that his coat was brown. Those men his ship had towed from danger crowded around him to praise his prompt action, and he was absorbed into the ordered melee of a military action without anyone's being aware that he had no right to be there. He ate a meal with a group of officers around a small fire after having his wound dressed, and they discussed the day's action as unrestrainedly as comrades-in-arms.

The force had settled for the night beneath the formidable north and east walls of the city, ready to storm it in the morning with scaling ladders. No one had any doubts as to the outcome, and Rupert lay with his friends beneath the stars that night, finding a kind of fulfillment in the throbbing pain of his arm. A night had never been so brilliant with stars, so velvety dark, so full of soft, harmonious sounds. Silk was forgotten as he fell into slumber with thoughts of the morning attack filling his mind. If a faint image of reproachful blue eyes and a miniature creature with his own fair coloring brushed across his dreams, it did no more than put a smile on his mouth in the midst of sleep. He had not let them down.

Chapter Eleven

The sound of crying was too insistent to ignore. It brought Harriet from her troubled sleep with the greatest reluctance of spirit, yet alarm crept in with wakefulness. Edward was not whimpering; it was clear he was in the greatest distress and screaming as only a small child can.

Feeling the disorientation of first rising, Harriet got up, threw a wrapper across her shoulders, and stumbled across the room to the small adjoining chamber. A quick glance at the clock told her it was long past the hour her baby amah usually awoke her to feed Edward. Puzzled and anxious, she went to the cradle to pick up her small son, who was scarlet-faced and kicking with a vigor that matched his vocal protest. There was no sign of the young Chinese girl employed as nursemaid.

Even his mother's arms and soft voice did not calm the baby, and as Harriet began to feed him, she tried to sort out her jumbled thoughts in the blessed silence. Her brain felt heavy, she was unrefreshed after sleep, and holding her child brought her none of the usual quiet joy. As a rule, the Chinese girl woke her with a bowl of tepid water to wash her face and hands, a silver-backed brush to sweep through her hair, and a ribbon to tie it neatly back. Now she sat on a chair feeling uncomfortably sluttish with tangled hair around a face that was hot and sticky from tossing all night. As for Edward, he smelled sour and burned with the heat his prolonged screaming had generated.

He was a large, lusty child, and her arms were soon aching from his weight. When she tried to shift to a more comfortable position, he set up renewed screaming that jangled her nerves. It all was gradually coming back to her: Rupert had gone off to a war that was not his, and she was alone again. There was no knowing if he would ever return. Her heart felt like lead.

They had quarreled again—very bitterly, this time—and she had let him leave without her giving him her blessing and love to sustain him. Small wonder she had been unable to find rest all night. He had said he was doing it for her and his son, but after a whole twelve hours of feverish searching she had found no support for his statement. His going needlessly and unwanted on an assault being launched by those who had thrown him out of their ranks could not possibly benefit her or the little creature in her arms. If he failed to return, she would be a widow, and his son an orphan. Of what use to her would be the Torrington millions if she lost her reason for living?

Her fingers went up to touch the creamy fair hair lying thickly on Edward's head. He was so helpless and dependent! Anger surged through her once more.

He was the product of a love she had thought so all-consuming, yet Rupert had cast it aside to chase a shadow.

The door flew open, and Bessie rushed in, her cap askew and her face white. "Oh, madam, I'm sorry if I have intruded," she cried.

"Yes, Bessie, what is it . . . and where is Ah Eng?" asked Harriet wearily and with slight irritation.

The girl came right up to her and bobbed a curtsy while her hands fiddled with the corners of her muslin apron. "She's gone—like the rest of them. We're the only ones in the house, madam. The Chinese have all disappeared overnight. There's no breakfast being cooked, the rooms haven't been swept, and there's no water on the boil. We're here all alone. What'er we going to do? If ever we needed the captain, it's now!"

"He is not the captain, Bessie. How many times do I have to tell you that?" cried Harriet sharply, feeling unable to accept the news that their servants had deserted them.

"Well, I'm sorry, madam, but he might just as well be," was the stubborn characteristic reply. "It's because he's gone off with the army that Fu-Wong and the others took off. I could see it in his face last night . . . but I never thought Fu-Wong would desert you, madam. You have always been so good to him—gave his daughter a lovely wedding present." She sniffed. "Just shows you can't trust anyone. All that you read me from the books is fantasy, if you asks me."

"I am not asking you, Bessie," snapped Harriet. "Is it to be wondered at that they leave the house when—" She broke off, realizing her anger was leading her into a betrayal of Rupert with the girl, who appeared to be showing her more loyalty than he at present.

For once Harriet found her brain a dullard. It was still grappling with the deeper implications of that morning and could not begin to consider the organization of the household. Conscious of her own unkempt state and Edward's need for attention, she forced a lighter tone into her voice.

"Let us show that we are not entirely dependent on those who have left us, Bessie. Bring up some water for my washing bowl; then make some tea. With a piece of bread and butter it will do nicely for our breakfast. Then we can give the baby his bath."

Bessie still looked doubtful. "It's not right, madam."

"Right or not, it is what we must do. We managed very well in England, if you remember."

"Ah," said Bessie darkly, "that was before you was married to the captain and became a grand lady. You can't never go back to that again . . . and the captain wouldn't like it."

"He is not here, so I cannot see that his wishes should be considered."

The words were out before she could stop them and indicated the extent to which her composure had been tried since the previous day.

She had cause to reflect on Bessie's words during the morning. Running a small house in an unfashionable part of London was vastly different from the management of a grand mansion such as Sussex Hall, and it brought home to her how completely she had become accustomed to all those things she had condemned during her first two months of marriage. The knowledge gave her a small pang of conscience as she bathed her small son and put him, contented now, into the basket cradle. Harriet Torrington had become a spoiled rich woman who was thrown into confusion without a team of servants at her beck and call . . . and lost without the man who plainly put his own interests before anything else!

But she was not so very far removed from the woman she had once been, and thirty minutes later she sallied down the stairs looking neat and business-like in a green-and-white-striped crinoline, ready to face the world—and herself—with a determination that could prove she needed no one, least of all a man who played at soldiers.

But she had forgotten one man who was unlikely to desert them, whatever happened. Valentine Bedford was standing in the hall looking up as she descended.

"Good morning, ma'am. You are well, I trust."

He looked so dependable standing in the center of the marble-floored hall she forgot the very slight restraint that had been her natural reaction to a man who had walked into her room in the midst of her labor and taken control of the situation, as a husband should.

"Oh, Mr. Bedford, you are always so punctual. What are we to do?" she asked, going forward to him as the right person to deal with the matter of staff. "The servants have all left us without a sign that they mean to return. Is it possible to engage others?"

A frown creased his brow. "I wondered why Fu-Wong did not greet me as I came in." He looked at her with meaning. "You guess why they have gone, of course. I doubt there will be anyone willing to come here just now. There will be many other families finding the same problem."

"Yes . . . I see." She now regretted her impulsive approach to him, for it seemed he was criticizing Rupert, and yet there was no way she could defend him, as she surely should. She forced a smile. "Then we must make the best of it. I will not keep you from your books any longer."

He smiled back, turning a handsome face into one that showed warmth and concern. "There is not another lady of my acquaintance who so well combines graciousness and competence, Mrs. Torrington. Certain though I am that you can weather any storm, please do not hesitate to call upon me for any assistance I can give. I shall be in the study all morning."

With a slight bow he went off, leaving her with a strange feeling of unease. She had expected more of him. Beyond saying that it was doubtful anyone would work for people who were presently fighting the Chinese, he seemed to wash his hands of the affair. In the past he had always shown great zeal in all aspects of his post as agent for the company. Today it was almost as if he wished her to be uncomfortable as a result of Rupert's going off. She made her way to the kitchen in a pensive mood.

At midday she sent Bessie to the study with a tray containing cold meat, bread and butter, and a flagon of wine, then sat down to a similar meal herself on the veranda of her room. It remained mostly untouched. The view was too full of yesterday when two people had discovered the truth about themselves.

She remembered his footsteps fading down the veranda and the sound of the door slamming. The hot temper with which she had been cursed had led her to say things that would be his last memory if he should be killed. Recalling her agony of mind upon learning of her beloved brother's death so far from the country and sister he loved, she knew this agony was far worse. How could she have let Rupert leave her with no kiss on lips that might now be cold, no word of love in a heart that could already have ceased to beat?

She had no way of discovering how the battle was going, and she knew in her heart that he would somehow be caught up in it. He had no weapons apart from the pistol he always carried, and no uniform to protect him if he should be captured. What was there in him that sent him into a situation most men would be glad to avoid? He had great courage—she knew that from the way he had faced the hostile villagers at his father's funeral—but it was not necessary to invite agony and possible death to prove it, surely?

For several minutes she sat back with eyes closed and all her senses fearfully throbbing as she succumbed to imagining his blood-covered body lying beneath the trampling feet of Chinese soldiers. If some scarlet-coated stranger came to her this time with such news, how would she ever withstand it?

Then she remembered her son and knew life would have to go on for his sake. Weakness turned to anger once more. Edward had two parents, and a father should consider his son, if not his wife. If Rupert had not been forced to leave his regiment, she would have accepted that his profession demanded too much from him, but this present gesture was unforgivable. Here in Hong Kong they had a good life, if he would only resign himself to it, and a business founded by his forebears that would be Edward's someday. Did he care nothing for his family name and heritage?

Unable to sit still any longer, she rose and walked the length of the veranda. It was so still and quiet without the chatter of the servants below. Way off in the distance she could see the rooftop of her nearest neighbors—a disagreeable family of bankers who plainly believed that the money passing through their hands each day was their personal fortune. There was no sign of life anywhere. The track was deserted, and even the birds of the jungle were silent that noon.

She felt as alone as she had been with Nanny in that little house after Rupert had given her a parcel of her brother's effects, then departed. The clear beauty of the day mocked her and whispered of love and passion now flown. Her hand pounded the wooden rail. If he came back, she would give him a lesson in loneliness. If he did not come back . . . *Oh, Rupert, God be with you!*

After feeding Edward once more, Harriet left Bessie watching over him and made her way downstairs with some purpose. Her present predicament had to be accepted, it would seem, but there was one aspect of it that must be resolved without delay, and she went straight to the study.

Bedford was sitting on the veranda in the shade, comfortably stretched in a cane chair while he studied a sheaf of papers with frowning absorption. Harriet was halfway across to him before he saw her, and she had time to notice his long, tapering fingers and thick lashes that lay against his cheeks as he looked down at his work. When he looked up and rose to his feet, she apologized for disturbing him.

"Not at all," he replied smoothly. "I was finding this report a trifle dull, and any diversion is welcome."

"Well, I do not intend to keep you long from it. You spoke with conviction this morning when you said it was unlikely that new servants could be found while this unfortunate war continues. I perfectly understand the situation, and I have Bessie who is most loyal and hardworking. Between us we can manage well enough until the situation improves. But there is one problem to which I have not yet seen a solution without your help."

"And that is?"

She walked out onto the veranda, which was at the back of the house, and looked at Victoria Peak rising jungle-clad a short distance away.

"It is isolated here, on this lonely track. The barracks are almost empty now." She turned back to meet the gaze of his dark green eyes. "I am afraid for Edward. Once darkness falls, there is no way of seeing possible intruders approaching, and there are no servants to discourage them." She took a deep breath. "I think I may have taken too naïve a view of the situation, Mr. Bedford. It is still hard to believe Fu-Wong could desert me at such a time. He even brought a present for Edward when he was born."

"Yes, to the Chinese a son is the greatest blessing on earth."

"One I cannot put in danger," she told him frankly. "For that reason I must ask you to provide some kind of watchman. I thought perhaps a man from our warehouses or the ships' crews—a brawny and knowing person who will come willingly and stay awake all night." She smiled faintly. "I daresay he will have a more comfortable time on my veranda than at the waterfront."

"Without a doubt," agreed the agent.

"Will you find me such a man before dark tonight?"

He threw the sheaf of papers into the chair and smiled. "You must know I would not allow you to be exposed to the distress of remaining here alone. I had already thought of your predicament."

"You have made some arrangement?"

He walked out to stand beside her on the veranda, looking up at the jungle the Chinese claimed held evil spirits. "It is a very lonely spot, isn't it?" Then he angled his head to gaze deeply into her eyes. "A rough seamen or warehouse keeper is hardly the right protector for you, I think."

Suddenly the word "protector" suggested quite another meaning to her when combined with the warmth of intimacy that had appeared in his eyes. She felt herself grow stiff. She had seen that look before—in the eyes of men at Rupert's regimental ball!

"Whom would you suggest, Mr. Bedford?"

His smile was lazy with that same charm she had previously thought attractive. "If a man goes off and leaves his wife all alone in Hong Kong, someone has to provide her with consolation. Do you think I do not know why you have just now sought me out?"

Gone was all her fear for Edward. In that moment she could have faced an entire savage horde and not felt afraid.

"My dear Mr. Bedford, I had not realized that among your many accomplishments was such an exquisite sense of humor. I assure you my spirits are not so low that you must needs think of ways to amuse me. All I ask of you, as my husband's employee, is to provide a reliable night watchman."

It was plain the rakish Bedford had never had his advances ridiculed, but his anger was cold and controlled.

"You are hardly in a position to afford levity, Mrs. Torrington. There is only that rodentlike creature in the house, and your nearest neighbor is too far along the track."

"You think I mean to cry for help, sir? How little you know me," she told him with icy sweetness. "I have dealt with greater men than you could hope to be and have sent them packing. If you imagine I am afraid, you have much yet to learn. I feel nothing but amused contempt for a man who slinks in the shadows until there is a clear field. Now I have seen why. Beside a man of my husband's caliber you are small indeed."

His eyes grew hard, and she saw the selfish calculation behind the shell of charm. "I advise you to beware, ma'am. If I should leave my position of command in the company, it will be finished. Garforth and Aubrey were full-blooded and as cunning as man can be, but the present Torrington is a shadow of a man, obsessed with ideals of honor and glory in a scarlet jacket. Without me at the helm he would be like a lamb to the slaughter. They would cut his throat and bleed him dry even while they shook his hand. The company would collapse, and with it the Torrington empire."

"On that we are agreed," she said. "But I am persuaded you would never let that happen. You have had things your way too long, and I have wits enough to believe now that you would lose almost as much as the Torringtons if the company failed. You will not leave our employ, for there is no other position that would give you as much power."

A smile touched his well-shaped mouth. "You should be in your husband's place, ma'am. There are the makings of the businessman's mind that will never become his." His hand reached out to lift her chin. "We understand each other, do we not? I have no wish to leave this profitable position, so it is to the advantage of us both to see that I remain. That is why, when the gallant warrior returns, you must keep this secret if he is not to ruin our plans with outraged nobility."

He was still smiling as he bent his head to kiss her, but his smile vanished when she moved a swift pace backward and laughed in his face.

"Well, I declare the female population of Hong Kong must all have turned against you if you have to resort to blackmail for your kisses. It is a sign of the greatest insecurity, I must tell you.

"I have already warned you to have a care," he snapped. "I can be a powerful enemy."

"And so, sir, can I." Letting him have the full force of her anger at last, she continued. "We have made our bargain, each for our own reasons, but let us have an end to these pathetic attempts at seduction, and a return to the work for which you are so handsomely paid." She walked past him and into the room before turning. "Do not overestimate your worth, however. The day is sure to come when even the raffish society of Hong Kong will turn against you . . . and your father's influential friends might not be on hand to help you slink from the country this time."

Going swiftly from the room on legs that were shaking, she felt a sensation of menace overtake her. The servants' desertion gave her a prickly feeling of vulnerability, of hidden eyes watching the house, of faces that had once smiled now being filled with hatred. The scene with Valentine Bedford had shattered her remaining trust. Was there no one on whom she could truly depend?

She was halfway across the airy hall when the front doorbell jingled. It was not until she had a foot on the first step that she remembered that there were no servants to admit visitors. To fetch Bessie from the distant bedroom would take too long. As she went to answer the summons herself, it was with the hope that the callers were friends who would ease her situation.

The man outside was a complete stranger, fairly tall and in his mid-forties.

"Madame Torrington?" he asked in a voice that was deep with Gallic attractiveness.

Harriet's glance took in the well-built figure in riding breeches, cream silk shirt fastened at the neck with dark red spotted cravet, green riding jacket, and soft hat. She noted brown hair, graying at the temples, that curled crisply against his neck and green eyes full of the echoes of experience. The word "handsome" could not be applied to him—any more than it could to Rupert—but he had that same indefinable air of compact strength that was more dangerous than good looks.

At her silence he took off his hat and bowed. "Forgive me, madame. To call upon a lady in such a manner is careless, but I come on an errand of rescue." He took a step toward her. "I understand you have been left without servants and are quite alone in the house."

If a man goes off and leaves his wife alone in Hong Kong, someone has to provide her with consolation. His remark was too much for her to bear after what she had just experienced. Her temper rose to alarming proportions.

"I do not know you, sir, and have no wish to do so," she told him in a voice that shook. "If I am alone, it is because that is the way I wish to be. Since it appears that gossip travels swiftly in Hong Kong, will you inform any other gentlemen who are thinking of calling that Mrs. Torrington is not at home to anyone—especially egotistical, disreputable roués! Good day to you."

The door was not quite slammed in his face, but she shut it with significant firmness. At the foot of the stairs Harriet had to stop and clutch the newel post. It was a long time since she had felt so humiliated. How could Rupert have left her exposed to such treatment . . . and how could the men of Hong Kong believe she would welcome their disgusting attentions?

"Madame, you are mistaken."

Spinning around, she saw the man standing in the doorway leading to the lower veranda. How foolish of her to have forgotten the open aspect of an Eastern house! Her quick rush of alarm faded slightly when he ventured several steps with his hands in the air in a gesture of surrender. It was absurd enough to appeal to her common sense.

"I have no weapons against the lash of your tongue, but I come in peace, I swear."

"Who are you, sir?" she asked suspiciously.

"Armand du Plessis, silk merchant from Lyons." He bowed. "Madame." Looking up from his bent position, he asked cautiously, "Do we have a flag of truce?"

His manner was irresistible and not unlike Aubrey Torrington's carelessly charming informality. Harriet sensed she had been wrong. There was humor rather than lust in his eyes as they continued to gaze up at her.

"The French and English are allies, so I accept your flag of truce, monsieur." She went across the marble floor toward him. "I was rude to you. I apologize."

He looked startled. "No, no, madame, it is I who must apologize for waiting this long to call upon you. I have been to Shanghai, where I have ships also. A week ago I returned, but this contretemps with Commissioner Yeh has had us all tied to out desks waiting for the outcome." He humped his shoulders in a Gallic gesture. "*Alors*, when I have the time to present myself, I find Mr. Torrington has shamed us all by going off to fight his own battles. But I can be of service to you in a way that will surely compensate for my delay in making myself known to you both."

"Oh?"

He smiled disarmingly. "You are still suspicious, madame, I see it on your face. If I tell you that the nephew of Fu-Wong is my head houseboy, you will understand why I have ridden across from my house to offer the services of my chef and two of my Chinese servants—a married couple I brought with me from Shanghai. They all are willing to remain with you until Mr. Torrington returns." He cast an eye around the lofty proportions of the house. "A lady would not wish to be here alone, I think. My chef is a most voluble and aggressive *artiste* from my own country who would not tolerate the intrusion of strangers, and the Chinese are from the North and do not care for their southern countrymen. That we are attacking Canton at present does not upset them."

While he was speaking, Harriet suffered a number of emotions that relaxed her tense muscles and banished the oppressive mood that had been with her all day. Armand du Plessis was a knight in shining armor as far as she was concerned, and she reacted with characteristic warmth to his offer of help.

"I cannot believe my good fortune, monsieur. I do not deserve it after the way I treated you." She smiled remorsefully. "I am not really the termagant I must appear, you know."

"On the contary, I find you refreshingly honest, madame." There was a twinkle hovering in his eyes that once again reminded her of Rupert's father. "Mr. Torrington is fortunate indeed."

She let that pass but asked, "Why did you say my husband had shamed you all?"

"Ah, I see him as a *commerçant extraordinaire*. While we all sit here waiting for the army to win us concessions, he goes off to get his own. When I was a young man, I also had such desires . . . but I regret I managed to resist them." He smiled again in rueful honesty. "When he returns, I would be honored if you would both dine with me. In business rivals should also be friends, *hein*?"

"Rivals?"

"But yes. I am Du Plessis of Companie Lascard."

Harriet was taken aback. One of the richest men in France, and she had shut the door in his face! Thank God he had stayed to explain. But at that moment she remembered something that overrode that.

"Monsieur du Plessis, one of your ships has just pirated a cargo from us at Bombay," she said accusingly.

"*Ah, oui,*" he agreed in mock tragedy. "Very regrettable . . . but one has to live."

She studied him for a moment. "Did you know Aubrey Torrington?"

"A man one found it difficult to outwit, madame."

"Mmm, just as I thought," was her musing reply. "Do not misjudge my husband, monsieur. He might be a novice as yet, but he can be very determined."

He half bowed. "A formidable partnership, I suspect. I look forward to our future acquaintance." He began to turn. "I will instruct my servants to come immediately."

She walked beside him to the door. "Your chef . . . how will you manage without him?"

"Miserably, I fear, but a Frenchman will always suffer gladly for the sake of a lady."

She laughed. "Said in the style of Aubrey Torrington, without a doubt."

He paused with his hand on the doorknob. "You were fond of him?"

"Yes," she told him wistfully. "He had flair and a zest for life that should never have been extinguished in such a way. I think all he craved was affection."

"As do we all."

He was leaving, and her ache of longing for Rupert returned in that moment. "Yes, monsieur, I suppose you are right. You have been very kind. I am grateful."

He took her hand and kissed her fingers lightly. "Please, set my mind at rest, madame. Do I really give the impression of a . . . how was it . . . an egotistical, disruputable roué?"

Her laugh was warm and honest. "No, monsieur, right now you give every appearance of being a true friend."

Canton was in the hands of the Anglo-French force. It had fallen at the first assault, and naval and military detachments manned the walls that entirely surrounded the city, holding those within as hostages and forcing the Cantonese to abandon the factory area. The forts rising all along the walls to provide defense against intruders from any direction were mined and blown up on an afternoon of roaring, shattering destruction. At the end, Oriental artistry lay in great piles of smoking ruins. Canton had had its claws drawn.

In the city itself the citizens went about their tasks with the centuries-old resignation of Eastern races. To coolies who hauled stones for building on poles balanced across their shoulders; to men who stood daily in the debilitating wetness of rice fields; to women who hobbled on tiny, stunted feet to market; to moneylenders, scribes, apothecaries; to tanka people living their whole lives on boats and witnessing every extreme of humanity; to infants poking iridescent beetles with sticks, it did not matter who controlled the city.

They had been living under Yeh's tyrannical rule;

would it be any worse under the red-faced foreign devils' control? Just hide one's children so they would not be dismembered by the barbarian holy men; just avert one's eyes when the women with pointed features and hair of strange hues flaunted their grotesquely shaped bodies in their indecent low-cut bell dresses; just bow and smile, as one always had done. A man could not be punished for what he kept secret to all but his soul.

But there were few who would keep secret the whereabouts of Yeh, the man who had brought about the storming of Canton through his shortsightedness and lack of honor. The little fat man was caught by two British naval officers who spotted him trying to escape from the back of the house in which they had been told he was hiding. For his refusal to honor promises and treaties, for his insults to Western traders who paid exorbitant taxes and duties at his demand and brought wealth to his personal account, for his high-handed treatment of Hong Kong Chinese legally under British jurisdiction he should have been sent the Silken Cord of Displeasure by his emperor, but he was spared the obligation of killing his unworthy self by being banished to India by his victors.

The Manchu governor of the district hated the British less and trusted them more than the crafty Yeh, so he bowed and smiled when they proposed governing the city itself until further notice. Faults the foreign devils might have, but Canton would undoubtedly be controlled with justice and a firm hand that would bring benefit to everyone living within the broken walls.

Canton was again an open port to traders of all

Western nations, who benefited equally under any agreement obtained through the loss of English and French lives. The Dragon Throne had been given a taste of Anglo-French might as an hors d'oeuvre to what could become a main dish, and all that remained was for Lord Elgin and his French counterpart to present their terms to the emperor's spokesmen. These were, as they had always been, that the five main trading ports were to be open to all Western traders; that such traders be allowed free movement in the city of Canton and the interior of China; that Western envoys from all the major powers be allowed representation in Peking. There was an additional clause, this time, that demanded compensation for the attacks against Europeans and the loss of valuable trade for a whole season.

Lord Elgin and Baron Gros, together with ambassadors from Russia and the United States, as interested neutrals, planned to sail north on the first stage of their journey to Peking.

For Rupert there was an acute sense of anticlimax. He had sailed from England anticipating this confrontation and had spent the five months leading up to it waiting with the certainty that it must eventually come. Canton had fallen in a day, and now the diplomats had taken over. There, staring him in the face, was the Battle Trading Company. Canton was open, and lorchas would be plying the river reaches with cargoes for the company's clippers and steamers. There was nothing to prevent his being a silk merchant now.

His return to Hong Kong had not been that of the conquering hero. Harriet had greeted him with distant reserve, and their relationship was almost back to what it had been during the first months of their marriage. Her icy tones as she had described how their servants had deserted and how a French merchant had lent three of his own in a noble offer to relieve her plight accused him more roundly than the hottest censure. Nothing was said of the assault on Canton—she behaved as if he had come in from a normal day's work in Hong Kong—and she ignored the bandages on his arm as if they were not there. Far from proving himself to her, his absence had seemed to diminish him even further in her eyes.

The desertion of the servants had shaken him. It had not occurred to him that they might regard his action so strongly that they would not work for his family any longer. He suffered considerably from the thought of Harriet's facing such a situation alone. When he asked why his agent had not engaged others immediately, she had been evasive, cutting him off short. He took it as a sign that she felt Bedford had stood proxy for her husband on too many occasions already.

He lost no time in dealing with the situation and returning Du Plessis's servants, calling on him briefly to offer his thanks and issue an invitation to dinner. He found the man pleasant and full of admiration for Harriet's calmness and capability. Rupert could detect no trace of censure in the manner of the Frenchman, who had even suggested that a few more merchants should have followed Rupert's example by sailing with the assault force.

Valentine Bedford had made no secret of his opinion on the matter. While careful not to put it into words, he nevertheless lost no opportunity to remind Rupert that such-and-such a thing had happened while he had been away or that so-and-so had had to be delayed until he was back to sign the authority.

Gritting his teeth, Rupert kept down the desire to rise to the bait but took the opportunity to end one habit he had never liked. Harriet had taken to eating her lunch in her room, so Rupert followed her example, leaving Bedford no alternative but to take a tray in the study. Those luncheons at which the agent had formed a third party were things of the past, which he would not reintroduce even if his wife should wish to do so at a later date. He had to work with the damned fellow in the months ahead; he need not eat with him!

So husband and wife were like strangers until the fourth evening after Rupert's return, when there were two guests to dinner: Armand du Plessis and a young captain who had transferred from Edward Deane's regiment at the end of the Crimean War and was now serving in the China Station. Giles Meredith was the impecunious fourth son of a West Country churchman, whose only hope of advancement was to fill dead men's shoes. With this in mind he changed regiments frequently and remained in the trouble spots of the world. It was not that he was a callous man, but with nothing in his pocket with which to buy promotion the only way of getting to the top of a profession he loved was by serving in battle areas or countries considered unhealthy for white men.

Rupert had come upon him during the assault on Canton, and both men had been delighted at renewing an acquaintance begun at Balaklava. With such similar interests and outlook it was inevitable that they should enjoy each other's company, and Rupert had lost no time in inviting him to meet Harriet, the sister of a man with whom Giles had served and been friendly.

That there were three men at her table and no other woman did not concern Harriet. She enjoyed masculine company more than that of many of her female acquaintances, and Rupert saw a spark of life in her for the first time since his return as she chatted to their guests about her father and the book she was hoping to finish soon. He watched her vivid expressions and the fluid movements of her hands and recalled a similar occasion when his father had commented, "It's plain she don't like you one bit." Was it apparent to Du Plessis and the young officer? he wondered gloomily.

Dinner was served in the dining room that had seen some extravagant banquets—and even more extravagant guests. The Frenchman spoke at some length on the parties Aubrey Torrington had thrown in his younger days.

"So the stories are true?" commented Harriet. "When he died so tragically, the newspapers were full of such things, but I believed most of them to be exaggerated."

Du Plessis smiled. "What is exaggerated to one man is perfectly ordinary to another, madame. Aubrey Torrington was the kind of man who needed superlatives in order to be happy." He turned to Rupert. "Your father was very much like his own father, but with a little more of the milk of human kindness. For all his friends and his extravagance I believe he was a lonely man."

Rupert shrugged. "Perhaps. I saw little of him. Because my two brothers died out here, he kept me in a school in England. It was only when I was at the university that I got to know him—as a friend rather than a father, I suppose."

The Frenchman studied him closely. "Then you must also have been lonely, *hein*?"

Rupert thought of those long school holidays when most of the boys had gone home, of empty, echoing corridors full of ghosts of term time, of the taunts of small boys called the Honorable Algernon Beetleworth; Hedley, third Viscount Meersford; and Charles, Lord Cornlythe. He thought of his escape from it all through his invented maps, military campaigns, and biographies of famous generals. He also thought of his determination to prove his worth by serving his country as they were destined to do. His loneliness had sprung from his knowing he did not really belong. He felt the same loneliness now.

He avoided answering by smiling faintly and asking, "Have you been out here long, Du Plessis?"

"Long enough to have regrets. There was a time when an honest man like yourself would not have lasted a week, but *diable*, Hong Kong is growing too respectable," he said with a laugh.

Rupert signaled for more wine and said, "Respectable or not, I still should not have lasted more than a week if it had not been for my father's having appointed such a knowledgeable agent. He placed a great deal of responsibility in Bedford's hands."

"Mmm, a mistake, yes? Whatever change has affected Hong Kong, men like Bedford do not change easily. Have a care, my friend. When a man has been *le capitaine* for so long, he does not welcome *le général.*"

It was an unnecessary warning, and Rupert changed the subject smoothly. "Your generals are at a loose end now, eh, Giles? A war that was merely a single battle."

The young officer grinned, turning a pleasant face into one of cheeky, lighthearted youth. "My dear fellow, that is not the last of it, as you said yourself. I doubt they have learned their lesson yet. We shall be at them with guns again before long, I'll wager."

Rupert smiled reminiscently. "My father once said to me that the army dashed in with guns and swords, then went off to do it all again somewhere else, leaving men like him trying to cope with the hatred left behind. After this I shall have seen both sides of the picture."

They finished their meal at that point and adjourned to the salon, where a fire was taking the evening chill from a late December evening. In two days it would be 1858, and as she handed tea to her guests, Harriet asked each what he hoped and believed the new year would bring. Not once had she met Rupert's gaze, and he knew her question did not include him. It was just as well, for he would need to be alone with her to give his answer.

"For me, madame, I should like fair winds, an exceptionally fine batch of silkworms . . . and adversity for my rivals," he added with a twinkle in his eye. "I do not wish them personal harm, you understand, just a wreck or two, a devious Chinese merchant, or a troublesome wife to take their minds from business matters."

Harriet laughed. "So, monsieur, you would make it the Year of the Snake rather than the Year of the Horse."

"*Non . . . non,*" he protested with mock drama. "Is a man a snake to wish such a thing? Captain Meredith has been telling us with great honesty that he will only become *la général* by advancing in the shoes of dead comrades. He does not wish these men to die but takes advantage of the fact if they do. So, Captain, your wish for 1858 is the battle you are certain will come?"

Giles nodded his curly head. "Of course." He smiled at Harriet. "You must make allowances for us, Mrs. Torrington. A man has to be what he must be. None of us is very virtuous."

"And you, monsieur?" asked Armand of Rupert.

Rupert was so busy watching Harriet's reaction to that last sentence of Giles's he had to pull himself back to full concentration.

"My wish for 1858?" He paused, searching his brain for an acceptable answer, but Giles, with his usual lack of tact, supplied one for him.

"It is the same as mine, Monsieur du Plessis. I have seldom seen a more natural warrior than Torrington. I fought beside him in the Crimea, and there was no one who kept a clearer head or straighter aim." He leaned forward in his enthusiasm. "As some men are gifted in music, poetry, painting, so this one was born with the gift of leadership."

"My husband is a merchant, Captain Meredith,"

said Harriet in a remote voice. "All that is behind him."

Earnest blue eyes turned to her, and the enthusiasm in his voice increased. "Then it is something of a tragedy, ma'am. Your own brother would have no man but your husband beside him while he lay dying. It takes great courage to face a close friend who has lost both arms and is in the greatest agony of body and spirit. But Rupert sat by Edward for three hours, sending him to his Maker in peace and reassurance, even though he was badly wounded himself. I am not certain I could have done it."

There was nothing Rupert could do. The words had been said before he even began to realize where they were leading. In the lamplight Harriet's face now looked as Edward's had done that night—cheeks bright with fever, tears of acknowledged weakness making blue eyes brilliant, and the terror of some unavoidable truth written across the features of youth. She got to her feet, swaying a little. Her mouth moved, but if she spoke, Rupert did not hear her words. The huge skirt of her sapphire-blue crinoline glided along the floor as she moved across the room, passed through the wide doorway, and continued across the checkered marble of the hall to mount the stairs.

Every step she took seemed to pound in his head. Her back was so straight and her body so rigid she hardly seemed human as she went up the curving stairway and vanished from his sight. Still with his gaze on the spot where he had last seen her, he murmured some kind of apology to the two men sitting like silent dummies on the chairs of his salon and walked out. He saw nothing on the way to her room except her face as it had looked a moment ago.

She was standing near the veranda door, which was closed against the winter chill and covered with heavy gold-colored curtains. The tears were coursing down her cheeks in a way he had never seen her cry before. It halted him just inside the door.

"You lied to me . . . that very first day you said he had felt no pain. You lied!" she accused with such passion her voice was hoarse.

He swallowed. "Yes."

"Oh, dear God!" Her clenched fists ground against her temples as she rocked in anguish.

"He died with great courage." The voice came from somewhere, but it was surely not his own. "His . . . his thoughts were all of you."

Suddenly she was rushing at him, gripping his coat with fevered hands while tears slid over cheeks already drenched with them.

"It could have happened to you. *It could have happened to you!* Have you *any* idea what I went through . . . how much I love you? Those bandages . . . how near . . . how near you must have come to—to. . . ." There was almost hysterical wildness in her eyes. "*Both his arms.* I cannot accept it, Rupert. It is inhumane . . . terrible. There was no way of knowing if you would come back like that . . . or at all. Just loneliness and nightmares." She gripped his sleeves in the full flood of shock. "You are my *life.* Don't . . . don't take it away from me."

He held her until his arms were full of her anguish, until the horror had left her mind, until she had made him swear never to go to battle again.

Chapter Twelve

It was a fool who imagined the assault and capture of Canton had been all that was necessary to bring about final recognition of something the Chinese had been opposing since history had been recorded. The English and French might have felt the corrupt and poverty-stricken nation would not risk an all-out war with the example of Canton before them; the Russians knew well that any suggestion of Chinese conflict with the major powers would result in a peace treaty that would increase its own coveted territories; the United States was shrewd enough to know the presence of American gunboats in Chinese waters was enough to tell the Eastern nation it would be easy to renounce neutrality and fight for trading rights and diplomatic recognition.

The diplomatic envoys sailed up to the mouth of the Pei-ho River and sent a message across to the emperor stating their mission and asking for representatives to be appointed by him. They suggested that negotiations should be conducted at Tientsin—a short way upriver—or in Peking itself. No one was unduly surprised to find the two men who presented themselves to the allies were lesser officials with no power to conduct the necessary negotiations. Elgin and Gros recognized immediately the age-old Chinese game of passing messages through endless channels of higher and higher authority until they became deliberately lost or were long out of date by the time they reached the Dragon Throne.

They ran out of patience when a second request brought no new officials, and the escorting gunboats were ordered to fire on the Taku forts guarding the mouth of the Pei-ho. As at Canton, the outmoded Chinese weapons were no match for those on the British ships, and the forts, the pride of Chinese defense, fell easily. When the force attempted to sail up the river to Tientsin, it found a boom of chains and wooden beams had been laid in expectation of such an event, but what effectively stopped the Chinese junk soon gave way beneath British steamers.

The emperor, seeing his ploy had failed, played the next step in his game and sent the required representatives to draw up the necessary treaty. Officially known as the Treaty of Tientsin, it was duly signed by all interested parties at the end of June. The Anglo-French plenipotentiaries returned to Hong Kong with the document, then sailed for home, leaving appointed envoys to organize their staff to sail up to Peking the following summer to ratify the treaty and begin setting up diplomatic missions at the imperial court.

But in his heart no man who knew the Chinese well believed it would be that simple. While admiring the dedication of people who would go to all lengths to resist integration with a world they had no wish to know, such men still believed China would be safer giving trade concessions to many nations than risking conquest by one—and its northern neighbor looked with greedy eyes across its borders.

But in October 1858 relations with China seemed, on the surface, to be happy for the merchants who had had two seasons drastically cut by hostilities, and they all moved with enthusiasm to Canton for the busy and competitive months until April. Most of them were bachelors, but those with wives and families decided to take advantage of the treaty terms by taking the women, children, and servants to the factories after several years of leaving them behind.

Canton still bore the marks of the December bombardment, Rupert noted as they approached the city he had first seen under gunfire. The great thirty-foot walls stretched away into the distance on all four sides; the North Gate, which had fallen first, looked sadly battered now, and the forts were much as they had been when he had left nine months before.

Those suburbs outside the city walls had sprung up again in a hodgepodge of patched roofs, makeshift hovels, lean-tos, and flapping calico walls hung from poles fixed in the ground. There was a pathetic bravado about the place at first sight, but the visitor's impression changed on his reaching the factories area, for the entire complexion of Canton was drastically altered by Western influence.

The port was its busiest and most cosmopolitan quarter. All along the waterfront were warehouses, shops, markets, and dealers of all kinds, anxious to trade with the merchants and foreign visitors. Steps ran down into the water at regular intervals, and around each flight was a bobbing, pressing jam of junks and sampans floating on the muddy, garbage-filled water that lapped against the steps, turning them green with slime.

The air was filled with the noise of winches, rattling chains, and the thud of crates; with loud Chinese bargaining, the crying of babies on the sampans, and the barking of half-wild dogs that guarded the holds of junks. Sedan chairmen called invitations to customers, roadside peddlers chorused a singsong repetition of the virtues of their goods, and every day there was a funeral procession with shrieking, wailing official mourners, crashing cymbals and gongs loud enough to scare away all devils.

Farther on, the waterfront took on a dignified aspect with gardens laid out neatly before a row of enormous buildings of European influence. Each of these factories was fronted by a shrubbery garden that had river steps and a flagstaff bearing the colors of the trading nation flying proudly. They were, of course, outside the city walls and strictly segregated—by the Chinese, not by the merchants, who yearned to be allowed into Canton proper.

The factories were, in fact, suites of offices, showrooms, storehouses, treasuries, living quarters, banqueting halls, reception salons, for they had to house the merchants for six months of the year. Because of the Chinese ban on women, all servants were male, and European wives had to remain in Macao or Hong Kong during the season. It had put a strain on the men. With their freedom restricted to just the factories and gardens they had had no means of relaxation in the midst of the testing business of acquiring the following year's profit.

In view of the defeat of Canton, the terms of the Tientsin Treaty, and permission from the British consul at Canton, who was virtually ruling the city with the approval of the governor, the merchants had this year brought their wives to the factories and walked freely about the city. But such arrogance on the part of the hated "barbarians" put fire in the breasts of many who bowed and smiled, and many a European would have felt distinctly uneasy if he had turned after passing and caught the malevolence in the dark eyes staring after him.

During those first weeks at Canton Rupert found his only pleasure in the company of his wife and son. Things had been good between himself and Harriet for some months—a passionate and giving relationship that had flourished in the social and environmental extravagance of Hong Kong—and they both found increasing delight in the growth of Edward, now just over a year old.

Remembering his own youth, Rupert was determined to see that his son had love and companionship from the start, and he set aside an hour each evening before the boy went to bed in which to exchange affection with the little blond creature. He was taking his first steps, and Rupert was puffed with pride, as if no child had ever done such a thing before.

But even his joy with Harriet and his delight in Edward did not diminish the dragging, endless monotony of silks, tariffs, cargoes, sailing times, and manifest sheets. Arrival in Canton had meant a new set of instructions and practices with which to become familiar, and Bedford had seen to it that he was presented with a welter of information no man could be expected to assimilate on one hearing. It was one of the ways in which the agent delighted in trying to humiliate his employer.

The silkworms were cultivated, to a great extent, in individual farmhouses scattered across the area and reeled off from the cocoons by entire families as their source of income. Since they had no means of selling directly to the merchants, they were obliged to work, for little reward, under the control of a central dealer, who, in turn, had access to the wealthy Cantonese merchants struggling against the crippling taxes imposed upon them by imperial decree.

The business of trading was a complicated one. First, the silk was brought into the city on mules, ox wagons, and other beasts of burden by intermediaries to the warehouses of Chinese merchants, who had once held their European counterparts in the palms of their hands. Still holding a monopoly of the trade from the Chinese side, they clung to the remnants of their old power, even more anxious to make money now that their coffers were fast-emptying. These hong merchants, as they were called, along with petty officials engaged in the mercantile activity mostly, had few scruples and little regard for the laws that were so rigorously forced upon the Westerners. Since the European merchants had hardly any more scruples and just as little regard for rules and regulations, it was inevitable that during those months between October and April there was played a sharp contest in which a man had to be at his most alert, conversant with the state of the crop and the yield that year, and ruthless in his determination to succeed over others.

The Battle Trading Company, in common with most, employed a Chinese comprador who acted as interpreter and go-between for his employer and the dealers. Such men could make or break the companies, if they so wished, but were usually too jealous of their own reputations to do anything other than their very best for their masters.

A great deal of jostling for preeminence took place in all quarters, and once one of the larger Western companies had won, bribed, or blackmailed a hong merchant to reserve all the best merchandise for it, the rivals were hard put to dislodge the favorite.

Where men like Garforth Torrington had shot to the top, and those like Aubrey had continued on the strength of what had gone before, Rupert was like a Christian slave in the lion's den. Each day he sat in the heavily carved chair beside Bedford in another, while their comprador, Sing-Chong, showed samples of silk, extolled the virtues of the cloth, invented a pack of lies to describe the pains he had been to to secure such excellent merchandise for his masters, and quoted prices he knew very well were nowhere near what would finally be paid.

During these sessions there was always a three-sided conversation with Rupert struggling to participate, despite the fact that he could only distinguish really bad quality and had no way of recognizing the finer differences between high-grade cloths. Sing-Chong knew it was really Bedford who made the decisions, but the agent went out of his way to emphasize his own importance and Rupert's dependence on his knowledge in a manner that somehow embarrassed the comprador, who did his best to show deference to the owner.

Rupert suffered it because the company needed Bedford, but deep inside he knew the day was not far distant when Bedford would push him too far and sabers would start rattling. But he was also deeply concerned. He knew Bedford's kind; he would overstretch himself and bring about his own downfall someday. He prayed the company would not be brought down with him.

The thought was in his mind one morning two months into the season when the usual bargaining session was taking place. They used the old bartering hall on the ground floor of the factory. It was large and low-ceilinged, with a floor of mellow polished wood that gleamed in the sunshine spilling through double doors that stood open. The owner and his agent were at one end, and down one of the long sides half a dozen Portuguese clerks sat at a heavy table ready to record details in the ledgers. It was a room full of the ghosts of past merchants, of Garforth and Aubrey Torrington—as Valentine Bedford had been quick to point out.

The ritual proceeded normally, at first, with Bedford competent bur rather brusquer than usual with the Chinaman. Then the elderly comprador in long black gown and round hat, from under which hung his pigtail, offered a sample of richly embroidered silk in a marvelous blue shade that immediately made Rupert think of how well Harriet would look in a gown made from it.

"That is excellent," he said enthusiastically. "I think I have never seen any quite like it before."

He put out a hand to take it from the smiling Sing-Chong, but Bedford said sharply, "No wonder you have seen none like it before, Mr. Torrington. We do not buy inferior goods." Then, to Sing-Chong: "You should know better than to bring such cloth here. It is very poor quality, and Ho T'sien will be hard put to sell it. If he does, it will be to the French, for I shall pass the word to the other English merchants."

The comprador looked upset and was taken aback.

Rupert was angry. "I can see nothing inferior in that cloth. It is every bit as rich in texture as the pink one we were shown a moment ago."

"You really think so? You will have to take my word for it that Ho T'sien is taking us for fools if he offers that and expects our approval."

The implication that he was a fool for being taken in by it was something Rupert could not let pass. After sending Sing-Chong away, he said in an undertone to the agent, "I have never pretended to be an expert, Bedford, but even I can tell top-quality merchandise when I see it. . . . And do not voice another of your sneering comments on my judgment," he added, seeing the agent's expression. "They are unnecessary in this case."

Bedford took a moment to digest the fact that his employer was standing his ground very determinedly and gave a thin-lipped smile. "I see I should have made known to you a few facts about Ho T'sien before putting on that performance before Sing-Chong. There is a score to be settled with that merchant, and I have awaited my chance. This is it. Everyone knows we have priority on Ho T'sien's silks, and once it gets around that we have turned down his merchandise, there is not a top-grade company that will touch it, believing we know it to be flawed in some way. All he will be able to do is offer it at well below its value to the small companies."

Rupert frowned, trying to see the sense in such reasoning. "So, we lose first-class silk, and a small company buys it cheaply to sell at great profit? That must be a very big score we have to settle. Give me the details."

Bedford looked back steadily. "It was a long time back. As I said, I have been awaiting my opportunity."

"That does not answer my question."

"It is *my* score, Mr. Torrington."

"And *my* company that is standing to lose."

Bedford flushed darkly with annoyance. "I have been with this company a long time. Aubrey devoted his life to it and heartily endorsed my method of handling this end of the business."

"I do not necessarily agree with him. A man is not always a copy of his father, Bedford," Rupert pointed out forcefully.

"No, that is true enough. You have been used to settling scores with guns. A very easy method."

"It is methods like yours that make guns necessary, but there is nothing *easy* about fighting other people's battles."

"I know. I have been doing it for you ever since you arrived in Hong Kong."

It was an open declaration of war, and Rupert entered into the first stages glad that he could now fight instead of having to stand back. Despite the curiosity on the faces of the Portuguese clerks turned in their direction, he said steadily, "One of the first things I learned in the army, Bedford, was that one should always bow to the superior knowledge of the man on the spot—hence the reason why I have put up with your insufferable manner for so long. But I also learned that it is often necessary to temper his age-old methods with a little of one's own wisdom." He shifted in his chair and nodded in the direction of the comprador, who was still holding the silk. "There is nothing wrong with that cloth, and we shall buy it. Since you claim the score with the merchant is personal, you will settle it in a way that does not affect my company. You will do well to remember this new rule. The owner has the last word on what his company will or will not do."

A muscle in Bedford's jaw jumped, making his handsome features hard. "Too many new rules and the company might have to do without me."

Rupert looked back at him with saber drawn. "Break them, and the company might find it does not want you. You are good, Bedford . . . not God!"

The owner's quarters were on the second floor of the factory and as luxurious as Garforth had determined to make them. They comprised a whole suite of living rooms furnished as fully as a man confined within their walls for six months at a time could wish. The salons and dining room were designed for entertaining on the grand scale—even if all the guests were male—and the study and bedrooms followed suit to make it as well appointed a place of residence as any house in

Hong Kong. The ground-floor treasury held silver, glassware, fine china and linen, wines of antique vintage, cigars and liquors—all the necessary requirements for gentlemen of wealth and consequence.

The Battle Trading Company's agent had used the owner's suite, in the past but was relegated to his own now that the Torringtons were in residence. Ever since that incident in Hong Kong Harriet had avoided Bedford as much as possible, and Rupert had never asked why. She knew the situation between the two men was worsening, and although she sympathized with Rupert, she dreaded a confrontation that might lead to the agent's leaving them. The company would not survive long without him—Armand du Plessis had told her that, if she had not seen it for herself. Until Rupert finally put away his dreams and concentrated on his new life, Valentine Bedford was necessary and had to be tolerated.

Harriet was thinking about the problem one afternoon while watching the scene from the large window overlooking the garden and distant view of the river. Between the two was an area known as Respondentia Walk, which provided a place of exercise for the merchants, but it was invariably full of peddlers, hawkers, and beggars who crowded around the Europeans to press their claims for money on those they hated and tried to banish from the country.

That afternoon there was the usual press of pigtailed figures with their accompanying paraphernalia, filling the air with shouts and invitations to those Westerners taking the air. Just for a moment Harriet felt sad that her father had seen it all not through his own eyes but rather through those of others.

It was all there outside her window, from the tall masts of junks to the azalea blooms in the cultivated shrubbery; from the row of colorful national flags streaming out in the breeze to the little black-clad hawker of nuts from a wooden box hung around his neck on a wide cloth strip; from the fretful half-naked infants on sampans to the cases of champagne being unloaded from European-owned lorchas at the water steps. It was there in the tailors who sat cross-legged on pieces of cloth spread on the ground and sewed anything from an exquisite handkerchief to a gentleman's suit and in the soothsayers and professional letterwriters with their entire business premises contained in portable wooden boxes. The roadside cobblers, sellers of ointments, and owners of birds trained to sing for a coin; the magic of the gulli-gulli man; the cunning of the traveling peep-show men with their "scene on a stick" were all part of the substance of life that Harriet was now privileged to see because of Rupert.

She sighed. Little Edward was a beautiful child—the pride of her own and Rupert's hearts—and there was only one thing throwing a shadow on her happiness. Despite the promise she had forced from him, she knew Rupert still yearned for the life of a soldier even as he struggled to learn a trade Fate had decreed should be his. What was in him that kept alive a flame that ought, by now, to be quenched? Would she ever understand it? The savage pain that stabbed her every time she thought of the truth of how her brother had died attacked her again then. *Dear God, please keep him from such terrible things.*

A knock on the door heralded Bessie, holding Edward by the hand. She walked across, guiding the small boy on his chubby, unsteady legs, until she reached her mistress.

Her smile was very fond as she indicated her charge. "There was no peace to be had until he had come to Mama, madam. I'll say one thing, and that's my opinion that he'll be as determined as the captain when he grows up." She winced. "Well, I'm sorry, madam, reely I am . . . but I can't never seem to call him anything but that. He runs this whole household like it's the army, and Master Edward has got one of them soldiers to show you again."

Harriet was annoyed. "I told you to lock them away, Bessie," she scolded as she took her son onto her lap.

The pointed nose twitched. "So I did. The captain comes in, grabs me by the apron strings, and demands to know where I put them. You know what he's like, madam, when he puts on his Friday face. When I told him they was locked away, he was cross as mustard and he straightaway gets the key. Next minute him and Master Edward was on the floor, marching them up and down."

"Oh, Bessie!" cried Harriet in exasperation.

"He dismissed me on the spot, of course. That's the fifth time since we came to this awful place." She tightened her lips. "I don't like it here in Canton, not at all, I don't. It's too full of strangers. There's even one of them outside, hoping to come in here. He won't not go away. Just stands there, like they're fond of doing, and seems set to wait until kingdom come."

"Has he said what he wants?" persisted Harriet, curious to know why a Chinese should be so anxious to patrol her corridors.

"I arst him. He just says a lot of words I don't understand and points at this door. I'm carrying on as if he isn't not there." She smiled slyly. "The captain'll be in any minute. He'll soon get *him* lined up and marched out of here, or I'm a Dutchman."

"The captain has—" She broke off in irritation. "*Mr. Torrington* has enough to do without being bothered by little matters, Bessie. The man must be there for a good reason. The Chinese might be mysterious in many ways, but they never call at the house of an Englishman just to stand and stare. I had best see if I can discover what he wants."

"Oh, no, madam! The captain says you aren't to have anything to do with the locals in this place unless he's with you. There's all kinds in Canton—worse than in Hong Kong. He'll like as not drop me in the river if he knows I've so much as told you about that stranger outside."

Harriet laughed. "If you truly believe he'd do such a thing, you are very brave to ignore the number of times he dismisses you."

"Not reely. You see, I know you'll never turn me out, madam . . . and he'd do anything to keep you happy. He dismisses me as a matter of habit . . . and because we can't seem nohow to keep from rubbing each other up the wrong way. Funny that, because I think he's a gentleman in a million, most of the time."

Hiding her amusement, Harriet put Edward on the settee beside her and stood up, smoothing the skirt of her crinoline. "What possible danger can there be from one Chinaman in this factory surrounded by Europeans? I wonder how he got right up here to the private apartments without being seen and stopped?"

To the accompaniment of Bessie's dire warnings and fears of what Rupert would say when he found out, she went to the door and looked out. The man stood a short distance along the corridor. He turned at the sound of a door opening. He was old in the way that many Chinese seemed ancient after the age of forty, the lines on his broad face folding his eyes into even narrower slits. He wore a long gray silken robe and a small round hat of black embroidered with red and orange dragons on the stand-up brim. His pigtail and thin, drooping mustache were gray. He might have been standing there for centuries rather than minutes.

Harriet approached, and he bowed, holding out a paper. She ignored it and asked what he wanted in words spoken clearly and slowly. He bowed again and held out the paper. Suspecting that he did not wish to speak to a female "barbarian," she took it. The thick black Chinese characters meant nothing to her, of course, so she looked at the man's calm wrinkled face and asked, "Who is this for?"

He bowed once more. "Much honored Sing-Li is pleased to send servant."

"Yes?" she said encouragingly when he appeared to have nothing more to say. "Have you come to see Mr. Torrington?"

"No Mr. Tollington. Mr. Bedford," was the dignified response. He indicated the paper. "Much honored Sing-Li is pleased to send servant."

It seemed that a Cantonese had sent this Chinaman

as a prospective servant, and what she held was some kind of letter of introduction. She knew that Valentine Bedford spoke enough of one Chinese dialect to make himself understood and that he was ultimately responsible for all company staff. Who had sent the man to the owner's quarters and what kind of servant such an ancient could possibly make were thoughts occupying her mind when a shout from farther along the corridor made all her nerves jump.

But it made the Chinaman jump even more. Bedford had just turned into the corridor that led in the opposite direction to his own rooms and was standing at the junction, bellowing in Chinese at the old man. At first Harriet accepted it as his natural annoyance that such a person had wandered up onto the private floor of the factory, and then she was an astonished witness to his anger. As she watched the old man hurry down the corridor, the agent's rage increased until she saw what she had suspected but never seen: Valentine Bedford could be a cruel and savage man.

As the Chinaman reached him, he seized him by the pigtail, tugging it so the man's head was painfully tipped back, at the same time twisting his arm behind him. For a moment Harriet thought he was going to strike the gray-clad figure; instead, he flung him forward down the corridor toward his own quarters, castigating him in rapid Chinese as they went.

She turned back into her room, lost in thought and somewhat shaken. Unfamiliar though she was with violence, she sensed there was a sinister implication in the scene just played out, and it made her uneasy.

It was with even greater unease that she opened the door shortly afterward when a knock heralded Bedford, and she was glad of Bessie's presence with young Edward. Somehow the sight and sound of their game of pat-a-cake gave an air of normality to an afternoon grown strangely chill.

The agent was wearing a strained smile. He was not invited in, and he gave no indication that he wished to be.

"I apologize for that disturbance, Mrs. Torrington. Why you were pestered by him I cannot think. But they are creatures of habit, and he has been used to finding me occupying this end of the corridor for several years now and naturally came here again."

She said nothing, and her silence seemed to bother him. His glance flicked to the maid so opportunely in the room behind her before returning to study her with narrowed eyes.

"What did he say to you?"

"He had little time to say anything before you began shouting."

There could have been a shadow of relief flitting across his face. "I see. It was a matter of some shoes I sent to the cobbler. The wretched man mislaid them and sent his messenger to tell me he will supply me with two new pairs to compensate for my inconvenience. He is afraid for his good name, of course." He gave a strained smile again and waited for her to comment. After several moments he realized she was not going to do so and said with crisp annoyance, "I understand he gave you a letter."

Harriet looked at his outstretched hand and closed her own over the piece of paper she still held. "Is this cobbler called Sing-Li, Mr. Bedford?"

He looked shaken. "Ye-es . . . yes, he is. A common enough name out here."

"And a careless man, it would seem. Does he always lose the shoes you give him to mend?"

Eyes narrowed further. "Why do you ask that?"

"You said the messenger was used to finding you here and came again this time out of habit. I am surprised you still deal with him."

"May I have the letter, ma'am?"

"There was no letter."

"He said he handed it to you."

"I cannot think why."

Each knew the other was lying, but with the servant girl and baby playing within sight and earshot of the open door Bedford could do nothing about the situation.

Lowering his voice, he said. "He gave you something—a piece of paper, a note. It was addressed to me, and you have no right to retain it."

"Are you saying you believe the word of an old Chinese messenger instead of that of a lady?" she replied with a provoking challenge meant for his ears alone.

In a moment she knew she was playing a dangerous game by facing him with equal determination, for his expression grew savage.

"I warned you once before that I can be a dangerous enemy," he breathed.

"So, Mr. Bedford, can I," she replied softly. "Please return to those quarters that are allocated to the company's agent."

When she closed the door in his face, she realized

that she had just done the very thing she had previously made every effort to avoid—jeopardizing the future of the company by crossing the one man on whom they depended so strongly. The remainder of the afternoon spent with Edward passed slowly. All she could think of was what Bedford would do next. She could not give the note to him without losing her own dignity, yet she could not believe he would let the situation rest as it was. What if he should go to Rupert?

As time passed, she grew more and more certain there was a great deal more to the incident than a cobbler's mislaying a pair of shoes. He would hardly have been so insistent about a letter concerning such a trivial matter. But what could he possibly be doing with an old Chinaman as an assistant—something that had been going on for some time since the man had appeared at the owner's suite of rooms from force of habit? If she was lost for ideas on that question, on another she was full of them. Trouble was certain to develop from her impulsive decision to hold onto the letter—a letter she could not read—and there was every chance Rupert would come out of it the loser.

With such things on her mind she was quiet during dinner that evening, when Armand du Plessis was a guest at the table. But it did not much matter that the hostess had little to say, for the two men were full of conversation on trading matters and soon fell to arguing.

"I was under the impression that we were in command in Canton," Rupert was saying, "but this fellow Sing-Li seems to wield as much power here as before.

I have heard of men like him, but this is the first time I have been obliged to deal with one. The fellow is corrupt through and through."

Armand smiled at him across the table. "*Mon ami*, of course he is corrupt. He has the perfect opportunity for villainy. At a word from him any merchant would find it impossible to trade. His moorings would be blocked by sampans; his coolies would be unbelievably careless with the merchandise; the winches would jam, chains break, and nets split; the dealers who supplied him would find other customers. Sing-Li can increase taxes and duties at a whim and so penalize any merchant who displeases him, and can force a factory to close, if he so wishes. *Mon Dieu*, if I had half the power that man wields!"

Rupert grew angry. "You take a damned light-hearted view of it."

"What other attitude would serve any purpose? We are all at his mercy, and he knows it."

Harriet felt the unease inside her increase. *Sing-Li!* There could be two men with the same name in Canton, of course, but the agent of a merchant would have every access to a port official, and if he were engaged in something that aroused tension of the kind she had seen in Valentine Bedford that afternoon, it could hardly be straightforward business.

"I am astonished you accept such treatment in the face of our successful assault last year. It was designed to put an end to such insults."

"Oh, la, la," said Armand in laughing tones, leaning back in his chair and fingering the stem of his glass. "When a man has reached my age, he understands the wisdom of compromise. He sees life in softer hues than in his youth."

Rupert had the bit between his teeth, and Harriet wondered for a fleeting moment whether their friend was deliberately baiting him. If so, he would be sorry for it very soon.

"It is because of our willingness to compromise that we are no further advanced in our relations with China than in Garforth's day," cried Rupert. "These people are inexhaustibly patient. They take us on leading strings and draw us around in a circle. We set off with demands and propositions and end up just where we began. Men like Sing-Li are laughing at us, and one cannot blame them when they see a parcel of European merchants accepting tyranny with *compromise.* How are we to impress upon the Chinese the advantages of our Western freedom if they see us kowtowing to minor officials instead of making a stand?"

Armand tut-tutted, still with amused tolerance. "No, Rupert, not kowtowing. Why, it was one of your own country's very dignified envoys who said he would kneel before the queen of England and no one else." He continued eating his duck with relish. "When you have been in this country as long as I, *mon ami,* you will temper some of your fiery ideas. As you said, these people are inexhaustibly patient, but they can also be corrupt. *Bien.* While one of them may demand this-and-that to suit his own ends, another will happily help you deceive him. That way every man is content, *hein?*"

Rupert stared at him, caught up in overwhelming anger. "What of the poor devils who put their lives at risk and lost them in order to gain the respect and recognition our countrymen deserve? Is that how you treat their sacrifice—match the unscrupulousness that you encounter with your own?"

Armand's expression hardened, and he looked his full forty-eight years. "It is a great pity you cannot ask your father and grandfather that question."

It was the wrong thing to say at any time. In that context Harriet knew nothing could more inflame her husband.

"I am not my father, or my grandfather," he roared. "Too many people make that mistake—put their thoughts into my head and their impulses into my body. No one will ever persuade me that the way to deal with a man like Sing-Li is to beat him at his own game." He leaned across the table, his eyes alight with passions not easily quenched. "I have seen men die for a cause—my wife's brother did so in the most agonizing manner—so do not expect me to admire behavior that is designed to ensure that the flow of money into already overflowing pockets does not cease."

Armand was quite as full of anger as Harriet had ever seen in their eight-month friendship. "As to overflowing pockets, yours still manage to hold that which you win at the card tables. Did you know Van der Westhuizen is finished if he does not have a good season?"

Rupert flushed darkly and threw Harriet a vivid glance before attacking Armand again. "There was nothing to mark his coin as his last as it lay on the table. It is a fool who plays with money he does not have."

"*Peute-être,* but he was hoping to redeem himself in that game."

"The cards were against him. I cannot be blamed for that."

"No one is suggesting . . . I mention it only as an example of why Sing-Li has to be tolerated. Van der Westhuizen is trying to recover from the misfortune of having two wrecked ships and their entire cargoes lost as well as the curtailment of the past two seasons. A disastous year this time could finish him off completely, you know. Would you wish that upon him?"

Harriet saw the muscles in Rupert's jaw tense. "It is a risk of the business."

"*Sacre-bleu,* that is cold," said Armand sharply.

"I have been in a profession where what is risked is more than mere wealth—it is a man's life," was the equally sharp reply.

"But you are not in that profession now."

"No. I wish to God I were." He got to his feet. "The issues were straightforward then. Now, it is a matter of deceit, lies, pretense, and opportunism—yes, even among those one thinks of as friends."

"That is the only way a merchant survives," Armand told him, taking a draft of wine as he looked up at a man twenty years his junior who could not quell his anger as quickly. "If you do not conform, you will be swallowed up."

"I find it an unpalatable charade."

Armand sighed and gave a slight smile. "Then you must leave it, *mon ami.*"

"To that rogue Bedford? It is not that easy. I now have a son, who is entitled to the best in life that I can give him. But I'm damned if I will force on him a heritage he neither wants nor admires when he comes of age."

Harriet felt herself melt inside at the desperate note in her husband's voice. It was two years since he had been forced to leave the army, yet his pain was as strong now as it had been on that day, it was all too evident.

"Your son is already making his wishes known," she said with forced brightness. "This afternoon I truly believe he asked for Papa."

Rupert's eyes told her he knew very well what she was doing, and he sounded unutterably weary when he said, "It is a wise mother who pretends her son's first words are for his papa. You are quite wonderful, my dear."

Armand nodded at Rupert's vacated chair. "Come, finish your meal, my hot-blooded young friend, while I use my aging charm upon the most lovely creature in Canton."

She made herself laugh. "No, that is too much, Armand. I will accept a *little* flattery, but I have seen some of the exquisite Manchu ladies of this city and know I could not possibly compare. Why, my own husband has cast his eyes in their direction all too often, and I am loath to admit, theirs are also to be seen looking in his."

Armand patted her hand. "*Ma chère*, let his wicked youthful eyes stray to those ornamental ladies. Disreputable roué that I am, I will remain faithful to one. You may always count on me for consolation."

Harriet found herself doing just that later in the evening, although not in the way Armand had intended. Rupert had gone off to fetch another bottle of wine, and so, on impulse, she handed their French friend the piece of paper Bedford had been so anxious to recover. Knowing Armand understood enough of the Chinese language to read the characters, she explained to him what had happened and how she had acquired the mysterious note.

"He was quite desperate for me to give it to him," she continued, "and I cannot help feeling he will not let the matter rest. To tell the truth, Armand, the whole incident has made me distinctly uneasy. As things are, I could not go to Rupert with it . . . and you are the only other person I would trust with something like this."

Armand studied it, frowning, for a few minutes, then looked up at her with eyebrows slightly raised. "Your agent, *ma chère*, is an opportunist. He has used his unique position of authority here to indulge in opium smuggling. This is a note of authority from Sing-Li to the Bank of Canton to transfer money to Bedford's account."

Harriet was appalled. "Opium! But that is illegal. How do you know it is opium?"

He gave a rueful smile. "No other commodity would command such a price and be easy to hide. *Bien,* Monsieur Bedford is a bigger fox than I thought."

"Fox is not the animal I think of in connection with that man," she said vigorously. "This means he has been using the company to bring in illegal merchandise. If he had been discovered! How dared he put us all at such risk?"

Armand seemed to be taking a lighthearted view of the matter, and his next words increased her anger. "What risk? His buyer is plainly Sing-Li himself . . .

and what is safer than breaking the law in company with the upholder of it? In any case, *ma chère*, Bedford is probably only continuing something begun by Aubrey Torrington."

"Aubrey? He would not—" She could not finish the sentence because it suddenly did not hold her conviction. Had she read too much into the charm of Rupert's father and overlooked the real nature of the man?

Armand patted her hand—something he did quite often—and clucked. "As that young man Giles Meredith once said to you, we are none of us very virtuous. Can you not accept us as we are?"

"Us?"

"I, too, have traded heavily in opium in the past. There is still a great deal of money to be made from it." When she still looked at him with a set expression, he added, "It is not so terrible."

"Rupert would not do it."

The words were out before she knew it, and in a tone that put him above all those who had committed the crime of making money from a commodity that brought ecstasy and then agony to so many. She heard the sound of returning footsteps and grew anxious.

"What am I to do? If he knew of this, it would be disastrous. I must stop it without his knowledge."

"In that one thing I agree." He slipped the paper into his pocket as Rupert reentered. "I shall return this to Sing-Li first. Then it will be possible to think what must be done about Bedford."

"Whatever you do, be certain Rupert does not suspect," she begged.

He smiled. "That is what friends are for—to help deceive the husband."

It was said in his usual roguish manner, but Harriet did not like his choice of words for once.

Chapter Thirteen

"You are finished, Bedford," said Rupert. "The responsibility given you by my father was a great compliment, but I knew the first day we met that you did not deserve it."

The two men were facing each other across the bartering hall just after midnight. They both were in a state of partial undress. Bedford was disheveled and pale; Rupert held a pistol. Beside the long table used by the clerks stood the cases of opium. The Chinese who had tried to take them from the agent at knifepoint had left empty-handed.

"How dare you use the company's ships for your own illicit trading?" spat Rupert, still trying to recover from the shock of his nocturnal discovery.

Bedford, panting heavily from the struggle, gave a short laugh. "That's really amusing, coming from the son of one of the biggest opium smugglers in the East. I had an unspoken agreement with Aubrey that I should continue and take a percentage of the profits. After he died, I took it all." He wiped his bloody mouth with the back of his hand. "Dammit, I was doing the owner's job for an agent's salary and deserved the profit—every damn penny of it." In the pale light the sneer on his face made him look ugly. "If you had done your filial duty instead of trying to cut a dash in a scarlet jacket, Aubrey could have kept it in the family."

"You are no man to speak of filial duty," snapped Rupert. "I hear your father died a broken man."

"Much the same as yours, Torrington . . . except that mine is buried in a churchyard, not in his own back garden."

The barrel of the pistol cracked against Bedford's jaw, sending him staggering back to fall across the table. Rupert stood over him, enraged and quickly losing his self-control altogether.

"I want you gone from this factory by dawn," he told the sagging man. "I want every piece of evidence that you have ever been connected with this company removed from Canton and Hong Kong immediately."

Bedford looked up at him and wiped his mouth, now oozing blood. His eyes were glittering with malice. "A fine speech—typical of the officer and gentleman you try so hard to be. It emphasizes your immaturity, that is all. I am eight years older than you, and a lifetime older in experience. I hold this company in the palm of my hand, and you know it. You can't dismiss me, or your fortune, along with the company, would vanish overnight." His lips curled. "You are behaving hysterically."

Rupert gripped his pistol hard, longing to strike the man again. "I don't become hysterical, Bedford. Several thousand men in the infantry alone could vouch for that. It is you, is it not, who became hysterical—on losing a race to a better rider. And because of it, those you chose to ridicule threw you out."

"They threw you out also."

"For my father's sins, not my own," he cried, as he had done so often before.

Bedford had recovered his composure somewhat and now perched on the edge of the table, still breathing heavily. "You don't really believe that, surely?" he asked insultingly. "I tell you, my father could have ravished a dozen married whores, then taken the coward's way out . . . but they would have turned a blind eye. You see, Torrington, I have a pedigree. It was the smell of trade you exude that they could not tolerate. Some fool accepted you into their ranks in a moment's aberration, and they seized on the first chance to kick you out. Money does not compensate for not making the grade, you know. The world will not tolerate a commoner dressing as a noble—it never has!"

With tremendous self-control Rupert replied, "And I will not tolerate a rogue, noble or not. I have told you on many occasions not to make the mistake of believing I am like my forebears. I do not need to make money from selling obnoxious merchandise beneath the law. I will not profit from the misery of others."

Bedford applauded. "Bravo! Spoken like a jumped-up gentleman."

"*Get out!*" roared Rupert, at the end of his patience. "Just thank your lucky stars I heard the fracas and came down to investigate, or you might now be lying dead with a blade between your shoulders."

"*You* thank your stars I am not—you and the company. Without me you would not last another day," was the assured reply. "You cannot tell silk from spiders' yarn. The hong merchants would bleed you dry, and the other Europeans would watch you go down without a trace of regret or sympathy." He thrust his face closer. "Where are the best return cargoes to be found? What merchandise will combust within two months in a hold? What must never be put in the proximity of raw silk? Which of our ships must never be fully laden on the outward run when the Cape drift is strong?" He got slowly to his feet. "Do you know any of the answers?"

After turning around, he began to walk the length of the tables as he consolidated what he believed was his moment of triumph. "You have played your little scene—the gallant captain speaking to his villainous cutthroat of a trooper. Now let's get back to reality. You are full of noble ideals, but you have to accept that you are descended from a blackguardly eel fisherman, whether you like it or not. The odor of fish will follow you wherever you go."

He turned and walked back toward Rupert to emphasize his next words. "Being the owner of a vast mercantile empire is not enough for you . . . but by God, I would be satisfied with it and have every intention of getting it. I carried this company on my shoulders for four years before you arrived out here. Since then I have also been carrying you. Only a fool could believe he could order me off like a gamekeeper caught poaching on the side. You need me, Torrington, and don't you forget it. That clever wife of yours knows it only too well, and it is time you did. I even had to substitute for you when your son was born . . . and again when all the servants left because you had sailed off in the wake of the soldier boys. Good thing I was on hand to protect Mrs. Torrington then . . . from men like Du Plessis. She is a very vital woman, and he is a free man." He smiled contemptuously. "Ah, caught you on the raw, did it? A merchant has no friends among other merchants. Competition is tight—even with the wife of a rival."

Stunned and angered by the implications of his remarks, Rupert grabbed him by the shirtfront. "Get out, Bedford . . . *now!* Your country decided it could do without you. So have I and my company."

The agent pulled the hand from his shirt. "You fool . . . *you fool.* No man makes an enemy of me and survives," he panted. "I'll go, believe me, but you'll be more sorry than ever before in your life. Sing-Li has paid for that opium and will not rest until he gets it."

"A man who deals with the devil must settle his debts the best way he can. If you feel you cannot slide out of this country as easily as you left your own, I suggest you give Sing-Li his money back." Rupert told him, indicating with a wave of the pistol that Bedford should return to his quarters upstairs.

"I haven't got it," was the silky answer. "Mrs. Torrington holds Sing-Li's banker's draft. She refused to hand it over when I demanded it, but I think she has no idea what she has done by keeping it secret. You saw what happened with those men tonight. When Sing-Li hears the truth, he will turn his attention from me to Mrs. Torrington. I think you'll lose some of your bloody nobility then. The mandarins are devious at the best of times, and with a novice like you, he will play merry hell before he has finished!"

* * *

Harriet awoke immediately, gazing at him with eyes dark with hovering sleep. He felt her disloyalty like a needle within his soul as she smiled from her pillow and whispered, "I was but slumbering until you came. Quickly . . . ease my longing with your own."

As she put her soft arms up to twine around his neck, the bedclothes fell away to reveal her naked body. Her sweet-scented skin mocked him, turning all their past hours of rapture into Delilah nights.

Pulling her into a sitting position with hands that dug into her flesh, he rasped, "Where is the paper the Chinaman brought?" He shook her fiercely. "The banker's draft, where is it?"

Shock increased the dark luminosity of her eyes, and she could have been only lightly asleep, for awareness returned immediately. "With Armand. He has undertaken to return it to Sing-Li. Rupert . . . how do you know of it . . . and now, at this hour?"

She made to move, but he held her where she was, sickened by her words. "*Armand!* By God, I found it impossible to believe you knew about this and kept it from me. Now . . . now you admit to me that you have turned to a man who is no more of a friend than his way of life will allow him to be."

Into his mind came Bedford's words, and a vision of a face of mature attraction and eyes that deepened with warm lights when they looked across the table at Harriet. Something exploded in his brain.

"Or is he more than a friend?" he cried in hot, bitter suspicion.

She pulled free of him and flung herself from the bed, taking the coverlet to wrap around her nakedness. She had awakened a wanton; now she was a virago.

"You dare say such words to me! Dear heaven, you should look to your own morals and ask whether you do not tar me with your own brush."

"You have not answered," he countered in a fury.

She walked past the end of the bed to face him.

"Very well, I will answer your insulting question. Armand is to me as my father was—as your father could have been. He helped me at a time when there was no one else. He came when I was in need—*when you were away playing at soldiers.*"

She knew where to hurt him, but he was beyond further wounding. "But you still turn to him when I *am* beside you," he said savagely. "You entrust him with *my* affairs, *my* problems, and turn a face of innocence to me while you do so. He is not your father or mine. Du Plessis is an experienced mature bachelor who is not the slightest jot paternal in his approach to any woman. You have known him a mere eight months and yet place my affairs in his hands." He gripped her wrist and pulled her so close it was possible to feel the heaving of her bosom. "Where does your loyalty lie? Have you any notion of what you have done by his deceit? You have made me out a weak fool before Du Plessis and that blackguard Bedford. You have placed me in the hands of a vicious mandarin—me and the company." He tossed her wrist aside in a gesture of bitter rejection. "You have shown me, and the rest of the world, that I count for nothing with you except as a stud stallion."

His deliberately shocking words held her rigid and

silent for a moment in that room lit only by moonlight flooding across the great four-poster. The pale beams caught and silvered the tears at the corners of her eyes.

"If you are trying to destroy me tonight, you are succeeding," she whispered. "That was unforgivable."

"So was your destruction of me before the eyes of a rival and a man who has done his best to humiliate me. A wife should be true, but what is the world to think when *she* handles her husband's affairs, keeps from him, as from a child, anything unpleasant, goes behind his back to another man in order to keep secret the knowledge of treachery against him; when she protects the villain and dupes the man to whom she has promised loyalty and devotion?"

"I did it to protect you, Rupert," she said flatly.

Incensed further, he gripped the bedpost to stop himself from striking her. "Only a weak man needs protection. Is that how you see me? *Is it?*"

"*No!*" she cried immediately. "But you are vulnerable until you have learned the business, you have to acknowledge that. I did it to protect you from a confrontation with the man who governs your survival. You cannot afford to lose Bedford."

"I have just told him to go," he told her coldly.

There was a prolonged silence as they faced each other across that moon-striped room. Then she burst into bitter accusation. "So it is finished! All Garforth and your father achieved has counted for nothing! The inglorious end to years of endeavor, adventure, and desperate gambles. Our son's inheritance thrown away in a moment."

He could not believe what he heard and gripped her arms again in his passion. "Garforth was a rogue—a pirate filled with greed and the desire for self-advancement at the cost of anyone who got in his way. My father's loss was hardly deep enough to cause loneliness—my mother gave him so little affection he had many women to console him—and he was quite as ruthless as his own father, as I have discovered tonight. Those two succeeded by discounting morals, honor, and humanity. Is that how you wish me to be?" he demanded in awful tones.

She had become a stranger in a white coverlet. "They *succeeded,*" she cried. "They created something against all odds. If you appear to others as a weakling, then it is by your own choice. No one would expect you to learn in twelve months what it took your agent fifteen years to know, but you have devoted no part of yourself to the company since you arrived here. Instead of accepting the inevitable, you have spent the whole time looking over your shoulder at a faded dream. I could have done more with this company in two months than you have done in twelve," she finished passionately. "Captain Torrington is gone forever, Rupert. Now you are about to destroy this—to fail yet again."

"You are telling me I have been mistaken in you all this time," he began. "You are saying that you believe my values to be worthless. You are scorning my principles, my integrity, all the things I hold dear. You are saying that the love and respect I believed in were false—simply a desire for success at any price. You are calling me a failure because I stand by my own convictions. That is what you are saying, isn't it?"

When she made no answer, he felt violent anger surge up in him again. "In that case, there is nothing more between us than physical lust, and I can buy pleasure in any back street. You will return to Hong Kong immediately, and I will arrange passage for you to England on the first available ship."

It took a moment for her to absorb what he had said; then she replied coldly, "I shall take Edward with me."

He drew in a painful breath. "Very well. It is later that he will look to his father instead of you . . . but I swear to you now, my son will never suffer from any deed of mine."

He went out, left the building, and headed through the darkness for the factory housing Companie Lascard and Armand du Plessis. Deep within him was flowering an emotion akin to that he had felt when he saw the life drain from Edward Deane's broken body. He had vowed then to do so much with his own life.

The streets of Canton were busy with a press of Chinese who might have been immortal. The scene around each corner reminded Rupert of the magical machines which, for a penny, set moving tiny Oriental figures against a backdrop of pagodas. So colorful, so unchanging was it one could easily imagine that a lever had set it all in motion as one approached and that it had all been there twenty-five centuries before.

The peddlers sat in the shade thrown by buildings to sell eggs, fruit, fish, and live poultry; others took their wares door to door in baskets or shallow pans hanging from poles across their shoulders. Those with shop premises sat perched on wooden stools in the dim interiors, looking at the passing scene with faces that had witnessed everything and been touched by nothing.

Canton was a city that watched the world go by. In contrast with Hong Kong, everyone moved slowly. Manchu ladies in long colorful robes and silken sashes walked with elegance and grace, their elaborate bejeweled headdresses glittering in the sunshine. Their Chinese sisters in plainer colors and full smocks picked their way along on their stunted tiny feet.

The buildings were wooden, with much carving and colorful embellishment on balconies, façades, and lintels. The roofs mostly flew out in upward curves, intricately carved and often decorated with dragons or beasts of mythical origin. Windows were shuttered with brightly painted wood. Here and there a Manchu beauty could be seen in an upstairs room sitting near the window to survey the scene her ancestors had witnessed. The Chinese women were too busy for such idle pleasures.

The system had been in existence for so long that it was easy to forget that the Chinese people were oppressed by foreign conquerors. There was no sign of change. In central China the Taiping rebellion was refusing to die despite its unsuccessful bid to capture Tientsin, but the movement begun eight years before was now adulterated by personal greed and desire for power. When such elements entered a crusade against oppression, its defenders lost their strength.

Sing-Li was one of the hated Manchus, and Rupert sat in the official's sedan chair being carried to his house through the busiest part of Canton. He had had no personal contact with Sing-Li but knew him by repute and edicts he issued in his official capacity. What he knew of the man he did not like. The summons had arrived first thing that morning, and Rupert was thankful he had visited Armand du Plessis during the night. He would meet the mandarin on equal footing.

The sedan chair took him to one of the small landing stages along the banks of the tributary running north; there a Chinese boat painted in vivid green and red with dragon's eyes decorating the prow was waiting to take him across to a house that gave him cause for surprise. It was smaller, certainly, but he could have been looking at Pagoda House. There was the same complication of levels and pseudobalconies, of color and ornamentation, of upswept roofs and carved pillars. The lake at Aubrey's home had been separated from the house by a sweeping drive; here a canopied entrance projected over the water on stilts.

The boatman in cone-shaped hat, blue smock, and trousers propelled the boat by means of agitating an oar at the stern, and Rupert felt the river coolness against his cheeks as they glided beneath overhanging branches to where a servant in bright robes and round black hat awaited him on the platformed entrance. As usual with the people of the East Rupert found himself towering over the servant when he climbed from the boat, and he felt an absurd instinct that he should tiptoe across the high stone-floored hall that echoed his heavy tread in contrast with the silent passage of the servant wearing black slippers. So still and undisturbed was the atmosphere it was like marching through a tomb.

If the house was overly ornate outside, inside it was

austerely cool. Floors were all stone, furniture heavily carved of dark wood and fashioned without comfort in mind. Window apertures were covered in wooden gratings in octagonal shapes, and ceilings were so high the huge red-tasseled lanterns dangled from lengthy chains. Rooms were large, divided by exquisite mother-of-pearl screens. Leafy ferns and plants stood in gigantic porcelain jars, and the dry, slightly sinister scent of burning joss sticks hung everywhere, rising above that of the dank insinuation from the river beneath.

Sing-Li might also have been there a thousand years or more. He sat in a chair covered in bright material with his feet resting on an elaborate tablet of dark green stone, carved and with a luster that made it extremely beautiful. He was a fat man—even the flowing embroidered silk robes did not hide his obesity—with a smooth, full face above the stiff-winged cape collar of rich blue edged with scarlet. The round black hat had the mandarin's button of distinction on the crown in a matching blue. He looked like a permanent and immovable part of that somber room.

"Ah, Mr. Torrington, the morning is much honored by your presence," he said in a ridiculously high-pitched, childlike voice for such a man. He waved a pudgy hand that had fingernails several inches long—a sign that he was a privileged noble who did not toil. "You are allowed to sit here."

A carved chair shaped like a curved letter *X* stood before and a little to the side of the mandarin, and Rupert realized immediately that it was low enough to ensure that his head would be below the level of his host's. Between the chairs was a lacquered table bearing a tray containing cups and all the utensils necessary for the ritual making of tea. On another table lay a comprehensive selection of tempting tidbits which Rupert knew were merely visual evidence of a man's ability to provide lavish hospitality; he would not be expected to eat any of them.

"Your father was a man of much wisdom and clearness of eye," said Sing-Li when Rupert was seated, and he went on to describe the occasions on which he and Aubrey had met.

There was no doubt that the Manchu had felt a malevolent tolerance toward someone he had regarded as an inferior and decadent barbarian, but he spoke in such tones of flowery civility against the background flamboyance of a servant preparing tea that Rupert stopped listening and studied the bland face before him.

Its smooth contours belied the cruelty of the fleshy lower lip showing mostly red through a mustache that was thick on the upper lip and then grew into a thin line that drooped until the ends almost met across one of the fat folds beneath his chin. Sing-Li's eyebrows grew parallel to his slanted eyes, giving him an expression of constant surprise, but the darting black irises missed nothing and had seen those things that made a man unsurprised at the depths and heights of humanity.

Rupert felt a faint prickling at the back of his neck. He thought of those things that had been done to European missionaries and Westerners who had ventured into the heart of China. Then he thought of Harriet's romantic notions of the Oriental character. It did not do to be charmed by one trait and forget the other.

Tea was offered with due ceremony while Sing-Li boasted of its quality at great length. Rupert said nothing. He was not expected to make any comment; that was just as well, for he was in no mood for social chitchat after the events of the night. He had approached this meeting with every intention of coming out best in the exchange. But he did not yet know this man.

Dismissing the servant with a languid hand, Sing-Li went straight from a description of a blossom tree in his garden to a challenge without noticeable change of tone.

"The flowers are of a beautiful crimson. So where is the merchandise, Mr. Torrington?"

Taken unawares, Rupert did not immediately answer, so the mandarin went on. "Your wife has my banker's draft; you have the merchandise. A little one-sided, do you not agree?"

"Certainly," he said. After taking the banker's draft from his pocket, Rupert placed it on the table among the dishes of little rice cakes, pastry balls, and savory dumplings.

Sing-Li pretended uninterest, but his eyes assumed a brighter gleam as he sat on his throne like a monarch. "But the merchandise, Mr. Torrington."

"It is in my factory, where it will remain."

The mandarin gave a simpering smile. "Arrangements can be made. It is our understanding that a regrettable mistake was made by our servant. We did not know that the son of his father was in Canton."

"I find that very hard to believe. But this son is not the son of his father, as it happens," said Rupert firmly. "I have no intention of selling that opium."

Sing-Li showed no surprise, and Rupert knew in that instant that Bedford had been there before him that morning. It increased his determination.

"But it is our understanding that this merchandise was brought from India by *Mr. Bedford.* It therefore belongs to him, does it not?"

"No. He brought it as part of the cargo on my ships. Everything carried by them belongs to the company, and I am the company. Bedford holds no claim to that opium. Neither is he any longer in my employ."

The mandarin nodded and folded his hands within the width of his sleeves. "Then it is my regrettable duty to charge you with breaking the mercantile laws of China. You are required to surrender the opium," he said, referring to the merchandise correctly for the first time, "and pay a heavy fine for bringing into Canton an offensive substance." His face broadened into a smile. "It is a most grave offense. One I trust you will not repeat?" The remark ended on a high questioning note.

Rupert exchanged smiles with his host, even though he was churning inside at the skillful way he had been led into claiming full responsibility for the opium and exonerating Bedford. Something concocted between the agent and the mandarin, no doubt.

"May I remind you that by the Treaty of Tientsin, signed in June of last year, it is no longer an offense to sell opium in China."

The smile froze along with the rest of his fat person. "Treaty? I know of no treaty."

"But it is our understanding that you are an official of some importance," said Rupert. "How can it be that you are ignorant of revised laws?"

The smile loosened but contained an element of calculation. "If I do not know of it, it cannot exist. The opium must be handed over to me."

Rupert saw it all clearly then. Bedford, knowing there was no way his ex-employer would sell Sing-Li the opium, had suggested to the mandarin a way of getting the drug for nothing, along with a heavy fine—a percentage of which would be paid to Bedford for his trouble, no doubt. They both took him for a fool, but they would see their mistake.

He stood and considered the mandarin from his advantage of height. "I am protected by a treaty this city was conquered to obtain. I came up on one of my ships. I saw the walls crumble beneath our guns, saw your soldiers run from us. Englishmen died that day to protect the rights of merchants, and I have no intention of letting this treaty be ignored, as all the others have been." He took up the bank draft and dropped it into the silk-covered lap. "You have been buying opium for years while your own laws forbade it. Now you seek to get it for nothing. The law is still against you by the lifting of that ban on opium. You no longer have the power to demand my merchandise or to extract a fine for its presence in my factory. Unless you wish to receive the Silken Cord of Displeasure from the emperor, I suggest you remember the existence of that treaty." He gave a small bow. "May I also respectfully suggest that you do not make the mistake of thinking the son is always like the father?"

As he walked with ringing steps across the room, the mandarin's voice floated after him. "You have women at your factory. That is also against the laws of China. They must go. You all must go."

Rupert walked on, unheeding, thankful Sing-Li's apprehension over the treaty had allowed him to escape so easily from the presence of a man not used to being thwarted. But he was uneasy. Something told him the confrontation had not ended but had only just begun.

By midday the factory was surrounded by Sing-Li's personal troops and virtually besieged. The mandarin demanded the surrender of illegal merchandise, payment of a fine for breaking the laws of China, and the immediate departure of the women. Rupert met the last demand for reasons of his own, but his adamant refusal to comply with the other two precipitated a situation so serious it soon brought to the scene a member of the staff of the British consul in Canton.

Nugent Goddard was a man with a fine diplomatic brain, but he was very much like Rupert in that he was incorrigibly patriotic, abhorred any kind of double-dealing, and dug in his heels over anything about which he felt strongly. However, present relations between China and the trading nations were bruised and tender. If they were to heal successfully, confrontations such as the present one were to be avoided at all costs—as Goddard explained to Rupert in the second-floor drawing room.

"You know he is wrong, I know he is wrong, even he knows he is wrong, Torrington, but the fact remains that until that damned treaty is ratified this summer, we cannot insist on the terms it contains."

"All right, all right, it is the same with all peace treaties," conceded Rupert angrily. "But the two sides stop all the slaughter meanwhile."

"Quite," agreed Goddard. "It is a gentleman's agreement, but that is not the case here."

Goddard turned from the window, where he had been studying the cordon of troops around the building. He sat on the windowsill, the skirt of his frock coat falling clear of his beautifully tailored fawn trousers as he crossed one leg over the other. "When you have dealt with these people as closely as I have, a glimmer of understanding comes through. Only a glimmer, mind, but the Chinese are as complex and surprising a race as any in the world. First, it must be remembered that the majority of the people in this country are under foreign rule. Secondly, the vastness of the interior plus the strong resistance that has always been put up against Western penetration of it means that the majority of Chinese people have no notion that China does not constitute the entire world. They know nothing of life outside their own walled cities; they know no other rule than tyranny."

He shifted his uncomfortable seat on the windowsill and went on. "Yes, they are cruel because that is all they see around them. Arrogant, you said . . . but is it arrogance to believe in one's superiority only because there is no true knowledge of other races? As for being rogues, you will also find they are hardworking, happy to share what they have with their friends, and too afraid of demons and devils to chance their arm too far with roguery." He tilted his head toward the window. "Those soldiers out there have no idea why they are guarding this place. For centuries their ancestors simply did as they were told, and so do they. To them, we are two of the strange devils that arrive in ships from the watery outer regions of the

Celestial Kingdom, with red faces and tight clothes that allow us to leap and prance about like animals. Oh, yes," he assured Rupert, "some really do believe we are some kind of half human/half beast. If we realize their obsession with dragons, sea serpents, and other mythical creatures, it is easy to see how they can be persuaded that we are malevolent and have to be driven from their shores."

"But that still does not account for men like Sing-Li," said Rupert, irritated by a lesson on anthropology that reminded him too painfully of Harriet and her imminent departure from his life.

"Ah, Sing-Li *is* a cruel, corrupt, arrogant rogue," Goddard told him, "and all the more despicable because he knows all the facts that he and men like him keep from the native Chinese."

"Right then you have just given the very reasons why I will not hand over that opium."

The consulate man frowned. "You might have to, Torrington."

"Who is going to make me—you?" challenged Rupert. "You will not succeed. Sing-Li can beleaguer me as long as he wishes, but I still will not give it up."

To his surprise the other man began to chuckle. "If we did but have a free hand, between us, we might make Sing-Li recognize the might of Britain and the Empire, eh?"

"We don't have a free hand. That is what you have come to tell me, isn't it?"

Goddard sobered. "It is an unfortunate fact that our troops are back in Hong Kong, and Sing-Li's are right on your doorstep. Aside from that we have envoys going up to Peking in four months' time to ratify that treaty and establish embassies to the court. We cannot possibly have a military skirmish *after* the peace terms have been drawn up; neither can we endanger the position of all the other nations involved."

"To hell with the other nations," swore Rupert. "Aside from France they have done nothing but sit around waiting for the benefits we won for them in battle. Oh, no, sir, pray do not give me the interests of the other nations such as Russia, Portugal, Holland, Prussia, and the United States as reasons why I should bow to injustice."

Goddard rose and went across to him. "I will pretend I did not hear that. I heartily agree with you, but my sensitive diplomatic ear would be offended." He sighed heavily. "Let me approach you from another direction. British impregnability in this situation might result in penalties being imposed on all merchants at present in Canton. They have suffered disastrously for two seasons already."

Such an argument left Rupert unmoved. "Because the Chinese have been allowed to dictate on such occasions for too long. You must agree that nothing will ever be achieved here until a stand is made. How much longer are we all going to allow ourselves to be duped, insulted, and betrayed by these people? By God, I was here when this city was conquered by our army. This situation touches on farce, whichever way one looks at it."

"That, my dear Torrington, is an apt description of diplomatic practices on many occasions. But I have to consider those others who might suffer from your stand."

Rupert became implacable. "Nothing is ever gained without some kind of suffering. Consider those men who died storming these walls and those who are now maimed. Is their suffering to be made ridiculous by an obese, sadistic criminal who makes us jump at his command?" He tried to hold onto his overriding anger. "He bought illegal opium from Bedford and, before that, from my own father," he continued with emotion. "Now all he is interested in is getting the drug at no cost to himself. Whether opium dealing is legal or not is immaterial to him. Whether the treaty stands or not makes no difference. This is a point of principle, as far as I am concerned, and no one will make me hand that opium over to him."

Goddard studied him for a moment and then sighed. "By God, there speaks a man after my own heart! It saddens me that I might have to bring pressure to bear against you." He picked up his tall hat and prepared to leave. "I'm sorry about your wife, but I think it best if she leaves under my protection now. I understand Du Plessis has undertaken to see Mrs. Torrington safely to Hong Kong."

"Yes," he replied heavily, almost viciously.

"Yes . . . well, I'll take my leave. Trust in me to do what I can within the restrictions of my office."

Rupert shook his hand. "Thank you. I am sure you will."

After the visitor had gone out of the room, Rupert stood at the window looking at the blue-clad private warriors of the mandarin, who were enduring the height of the day's temperature with only the padded cone-shaped hats as protection against the beating sun. Perhaps they did not understand why they were doing it, but they would go on doing it with the inbred patience and obedience of centuries. His hands clenched into fists. Sing-Li could put ten times as many there, but he would not get what he wanted. All they could do was break him, and he did not break easily.

There was a sound from the doorway, and he turned to find that belief was false. Harriet looked pale in a traveling gown of brown cambric, and when he looked into her eyes, he was broken by her going. She held Edward by the hand. Rupert walked slowly toward the boy, squatted before him, and ruffled his hair. It was suddenly almost impossible to speak with those big blue eyes staring at him from a face of sweet, soft immaturity.

"Good-bye . . . old fellow," he said with difficulty, remembering his own father's going off and leaving him uncomprehending at an early age. For a brief moment he held the child's other hand with fragile strength between his own, then stood up to face other blue eyes even more dear to him.

They said nothing; it had all been said the night before. But as he looked at her, he knew they loved each other too well. It was a love that gave them no peace. When it did not drive them with passion, it led to pain such as that which they both felt at that moment. For some moments they tried to conquer it, and then, when he felt he would crush her against his chest and weep, she turned away and left him.

He watched from the window as they walked safely between the armed soldiers, a slender woman in brown, a little boy with sunshine in his hair, and a skinny maid—all in the company of the consulate official. Harriet did not turn to look back. Edward gave no little wave for Papa.

He stayed watching until they disappeared from sight. She had accused him of being incapable of running the company. Perhaps . . . but he knew very well how to defend it.

Chapter Fourteen

The lorcha had been prepared to sail with all haste. As they moved away from Canton, Harriet deliberately kept her back to the city. She was not one to indulge in long, heartrending farewells, and she had found this one almost more than she could bear. Her mind had to be forcibly closed to the memory of how Rupert had looked as he said good-bye to Edward. Despite his brave words about a son's not needing his father yet, she knew he had felt the tug of separation as strongly as she would.

The majestic junks with dragon-painted prows rode past her unnoticed; the cries of the tanka people on their bobbing homes went unheard. She stood looking south toward Hong Kong, down the winding Pearl River.

"That was the very place where himself pulled the boat free," said a voice beside her, and she turned to see a small man with grinning pointed features. "O'Hare, ma'am. It was meself who had the privilege of bringing your husband up for the shenanigan. Rarin' to go, he was, an' all. I niver see a man so much like a hare in a basket as he was on that day. I swear he was inside every man's coat as they clambered onto the shore." He wiped his brow with a dirty rag, making his face even dirtier. "And if he had been, the city would have fallen even quicker, 'tis my belief. Cool as you like, he throws that rope, yellin' and wavin' his arms at the fools tryin' to get out." He shook his head admiringly. "Ha . . . and when we gets to the shore, he stands up as covered in blood as a battling turkey cock and grins like that young shaver of his."

Harriet followed the direction of the man's nod and saw Edward, in Armand's arms, grinning in childish delight at a tiny monkey on a chain held by one of the crew.

"Bejasus, that's a fine limb of a fine man, ma'am. You'll forgive me for sayin' so, but all me prayers are up there with himself facing them divils, and me not bein' a godly man, as you might say, that's as great a service as I can do. Don't you be aworryin', ma'am. Himself is not a man to be easily beaten."

He meant it in a kindly way, but Harriet found herself giving a sharp retort. "No, indeed. Mr. Torrington is never happier than when fighting a battle."

The house had to be opened up and the servants set to coping with Harriet's unexpected arrival. In many ways it was good to be back in Hong Kong with its cosmopolitan atmosphere, the freedom view across to the harbor, the large, airy house, and the feeling of being British and *belonging*. Compared with Canton, it might be a brash and uncertain community, not yet having decided whether to be European or Oriental, but here there was an air of enlightenment, of room to breathe, of hope for the future that was missing within the crumbling antiquity of the Chinese port.

Yet her own future seemed to be hanging in the balance. Rupert had once said to her they could destroy each other very easily, and they were on the brink of doing so now. Or he might destroy himself. God knew, he seemed to be set on it.

The company had taken some damaging knocks in the past two years. With Valentine Bedford gone—a man with powerful friends and nursing a grudge—the Battle Trading Company would lose both financially and in goodwill. The Torrington millions were well known, but Rupert had shored up the company heavily after his father's suicide and ever since. He had invested thousands in the building of a mansion to replace Pagoda House and apparently owned a Sussex mill and a forge in Norfolk, which he ran as experimental centers for disabled ex-soldiers and soldiers' widows. He vowed they would be self-sufficient, in time, but had to subsidize them now. Two broken trading seasons had penalized him, as they had all other companies, and now he was beset by problems in his own factory with no agent, no chance of buying from the hong merchants, and no knowledge of how to survive in a highly ruthless, competitive trade. When he emerged from this present situation he himself had brought about, the company might be finished.

Armand did what he could to see her comfortably settled in that evening and then left, promising to return in the morning to say good-bye before sailing back to Canton. Business had to go on even if a fellow merchant was being held prisoner in his own premises.

When he had gone, loneliness descended, keeping

sleep at bay and tormenting her by a procession of memories: nights of unbearable passion; others of sweet tenderness that became drenched in tears; still others of longing that clawed at her stomach, of times when they had quarreled or when he was away at the barracks tied to the gaming table and lost in the ranks of the army.

Tossing and turning, Harriet tried to plan what she would do back in England and burned with the certainty that it would be impossible to be away from him. He said she must go back, but nothing would be helped by her departure. Someone had to try to save their future, and she could not do it on the other side of the world.

Yet again she asked herself why Rupert was so set on self-destruction. After Aubrey's death he had been broken and defeated. Here they had had the chance to begin again, yet he rejected success and prosperity to chase a shadow. With dedication he could have been riding high on the mercantile wave. He was young; few men were given the opportunity of a second chance at a time when brain and body were at their peak. Did he give no thought to his wife and son? This present stubborn resistance would only take them all down.

The thought was insistent enough to make her rise and wander into the adjoining room to gaze at her sleeping son. Rupert loved the child with deep pride, she knew that. Why, then, was he endangering Edward's future? The answer had not occurred to her even by the time that dawn broke.

Bessie brought in her breakfast, and Harriet remonstrated with her, saying it was the task of the Chinese girl.

"I know that, madam, but this is different. Before we left, the captain took me to one side and told me to look after you, so that's what I'm doing. Master Edward's had his and is jumping about like a moggy on hot coals." She plonked the tray on Harriet's bedside table and promptly burst into tears. "I'm sorry, madam, reely I am," she blurted out thickly, "but I can't help thinking of all the foreigners with guns. So many against one. It's not right . . . and little Master Edward not knowing what his papa is doing for his sake."

Harriet grew still. "What do you mean, Bessie?"

The great tear-filled eyes looked at her from a face that seemed even more pinched and pointed than ever. "I know it's not my place to say this, madam, but old Mr. Torrington doing for himself like he did gave the captain a terrible time of it. Took all the fight out of him. It stands to reason he wants young Master Edward to be proud of his papa . . . never to go through it like he did." She gave a great sniff. "I'm not saying the captain isn't unreasonable, at times, but—but he's up there all alone and no one seems to be on his side. It was like that in the orphanage—everyone for himself and no one on your side." Tears rolled down her cheeks. "If they . . . if they go and chop off his head—"

The rest of the sentence was smothered by the long white apron she threw up over her face and held there with trembling hands.

Harriet was filled with sudden cold fear and, in her emotion, spoke sharply to the girl, using the military rank she could not be persuaded to forget.

"You are speaking nonsense. No one is going to chop off the captain's head. Mr. Parkes, and consul, would not allow it."

"But that's what the Chinese do to people," wailed Bessie.

"Not to Englishmen protected by our consul. Besides, it would never come to that. We have just fought a war to prevent such things."

The apron was lowered enough to show dormouse eyes that had acquired a sudden fierceness. "Then it was all a waste of time, if you arsks me. The Chinese don't take no notice of wars, or anything else . . . or they wouldn't be doing that to the captain. And we wouldn't be letting them," she added for extra measure.

The fear stayed with Harriet, and when Armand arrived soon after breakfast, she confronted him with it.

"I thought it was merely a case of Mr. Parkes's reading the book at Sing-Li and persuading Rupert to hand over the opium," she told him. "There is surely no question of physical danger to Rupert, is there?"

Armand put his hat on the table and turned to take her hands. "*Ma chère*, what is all this? You are too clever not to have known the answer all along." He stared hard at her face, which had gone still and cold. "*Mon Dieu*, but you surely knew the risk he is taking? Why else did Goddard whisk you away so immediately?"

Afraid in a way that tore at her lungs, she heard herself confess, "We . . . quarreled . . . over the piece of paper I gave you. He said I must return to Hong Kong. I . . . I thought that was why I . . .

dear God, I should have stayed with him. If ever he needed me, it is now."

"*Doucement*," he chided gently. "Rupert is a man well able to fight his own battles. It is your small son who needs you."

"But I did not dream . . . I believed he was just being stubborn. . . . Real danger did not enter my mind." She gripped his arm. "Armand, what will they do to him?"

"Nothing . . . if he keeps his head and gives up that opium."

"If he does not? Armand, you are French. Did not our combined armies conquer Canton a little over a year ago? How, then, can Rupert be in danger? How can this be happening?"

By way of answer he drew her over to the veranda and swept the panoramic view with his hand. "That, *ma chère*, is a colony of mainly Chinese people created and run by your own countrymen. It has been in existence under twenty years." He turned to give her a reproving smile. "Does an ignorant French merchant have to tell the daughter of Professor Deane that Canton is older than antiquity and utterly Chinese in character? Have you not yet learned that nothing changes these people or their way of life? We did not conquer them—merely swarmed into their city for a few weeks. Now our soldiers have gone, and things go on as they were. The occupations of Canton was but as a heartbeat in the life of an ancient civilization. It counts as nothing."

"And we just shrug our shoulders and dismiss it?"

"Tsh!" he exclaimed impatiently. "What can we possibly do?"

"What Rupert is doing!"

"A foolish gesture that will only anger them further. It will get him nowhere. The Chinese have infinite patience and will wait as long as they must to get what they want."

"They do not know Rupert," she cried with fire. "He can be iron-firm in determination. I have seen him in such a mood."

Armand shook his head. "Let us hope he is not in such a mood now. No good will come of it, and we all shall pay the penalty for his *geste grandiose*."

It took her a moment to assess what he was saying. "So, you are a merchant first and a friend after. You disappoint me, Armand."

He smiled with the rueful charm that so reminded her of Aubrey. "It is a sign of youth to demand the sacrifice of one's all on the cross of friendship. With the years will come the wisdom of fallibility. I am a merchant. For how long do you consider I will succeed if I bow to friendship?" Patting her hand with gentle apology, he said, "For Rupert, it is a matter of *honneur . . . intégrité* . . . but this action could mean the end for small merchants if the season is again curtailed."

Harriet pulled her hand away in sharp anger. "But you are not a small merchant."

"Because I am a businessman first and not a man with too much nobility in his soul. *Ma chère*, do not look at me that way. What do you want of your Rupert, *hein*, tell me that? He cannot be the great merchant you visualize and yet remain the crusading knight. Trade is not only in the head but in the soul."

She turned away, finding his words too disturbing,

and gazed out over Hong Kong with her senses in a turmoil.

"It is a fine view, is it not?" said Armand softly. "Hong Kong was dangerous in the early days, so a man protected himself and his interests in any way he could. Aubrey Torrington sited this house so that it overlooked something he had worked hard to help build. Garforth had endowed his son with many of the necessary qualities, but Aubrey also had style. There was a great longing within him to be accepted, to receive affection and approval. Unfortunately the woman he married was cold and without understanding, so he filled this house with those whose affection he could buy. But it was not love, *ma chère*."

Caught by the alien tone in his voice, Harriet looked up to catch a startling warmth in his eyes.

"You are a lady of quality; it shows in everything you do. This house is more right for you than for Aubrey's friends who never gave him what he sought. With a woman like you at his side he could have reached the heights of achievement. Any man could." His voice deepened. "Your Rupert is an *imbécile* to throw it all away."

It shocked her, the realization that while she had seen in him a father, he was, in fact, a man in the prime of his life and still capable of harboring impossible dreams. The fabric of their relationship rent in two. Was there nothing upon which she could rely, no one person who would not show a sudden disconcerting face in the midst of peace?

After walking past him into the room, she went to the table and took up his hat in hands that were unsteady. "I must keep you no longer. You have already been more than kind in escorting me and my son to safty. I trust your business has not suffered because of it."

He winced as he came toward her. "Ah, madame, do not be cruel, I beg of you."

"But you, monsieur, would not be hurt if I were. Your heart belongs to silk, does it not? You do not believe in *honneur, intégrité*."

He reached her and stood looking down at her with the regret of middle age that has only just discovered its youth. "Perhaps he is right in throwing away his future when there is still time to build another one. For me it is too late." He took her fingers to his lips. "*Au revoir, ma chère*. I must go and do what I can for your noble young man, or you will never again speak to me. That I could not endure."

He walked across to his sedan chair and departed without another glance. When he was almost around the corner, Harriet picked up her skirts and ran down the steps after him, calling, "Armand, tell him . . . tell him . . ." But it was too late. The Frenchman had gone.

By the end of a week a certain king of routine had settled on the factory. The Chinese servants had gone on the first day of the siege, pressured by Sing-Li on pain of punishment. The Portuguese clerks had been obliged to cook for themselves, but Sing-Chong, the comprador, had loyally remained in the building and offered to provide meals for Rupert and the other Englishmen, numbering about twelve. When Rupert had questioned the wisdom of the Chinaman's decision, the old man had said he had no relatives to suffer from his actions since they all had died at the hands of Commissioner Yeh some years before and his hatred of the Manchus would remain with him beyond the grave. If his time had now come to join them, he would be very happy defying another of the mandarins.

After three days provision were no longer allowed into the factory, but vast stores ensured that the victims of the siege would not go hungry, even if their diet were somewhat unusual and monotonous. On the sixth day the water carriers were stopped by the soldiers, and Rupert grimly arranged for buckets of river water to be brought up through the garden. When it was boiled and strained, it served for washing and cooking purposes, but for drinking it was most unpleasant.

Nugent Goddard had been allowed in daily to see Rupert, and the two men had formed a warm respect for each other during their discussions. Even so, he was obliged to warn Rupert that the longer the incident remained unresolved, the greater was the danger that it would blow up into a diplomatic row that would endanger the chances of the treaties being ratified that summer.

"Mr. Parkes has been in touch with the governor of Hong Kong, but the question of sending a gunboat or two upriver cannot be considered," he told Rupert at the end of the week. "It would constitute an act of aggression."

Rupert gave a short laugh. "While this siege does not?"

Goddard shook his head. "We are foreigners on Chinese soil. If Sing-Li insists that you have transgressed against Chinese laws, there is nothing we can do except protest and negotiate." He smiled ruefully. "That was straight from the horse's mouth, Torrington, but how do I negotiate in this case? It all boils down to personalities. He hates you, my dear fellow, because you displayed a disrespectful attitude toward him. The hatred will last a lifetime. A Manchu never forgives and forgets, in my experience . . . and he wants that opium just as badly as an addict."

"He won't get it," Rupert told him smartly.

"Yes, yes, so you have said all along . . . but I may have to order you to hand it over."

"By God, whose side is our government on?"

Goddard sighed. "Let's not go into that. What about all these other people in the factory—your employees. Damme, it can't be very pleasant in this abominable heat."

"It isn't." He tipped the bottle over his guest's glass once more. "This wine will have run out by the end of next week, and things will be even more unpleasant. Look, none of my men has complained or suggested that I should surrender. It is the same with any siege. The captain of the fort has to hold out as long as he can, even though people might suffer."

Goddard looked up with furrowed brow. "This is not a military operation, and your factory is not a strategic stronghold, Torrington."

Suddenly Rupert felt unutterably weary. His loneliness without Harriet and Edward was beginning to tell on him, and this man had just reminded him of something that brought him down whenever he thought about it. He got to his feet and walked to the window. The soldiers were still there; their fighting prowess might be doubtful, but their patience was indisputable.

"Perhaps I have been acting like a military commander over this, as you suggest, and have no right to put my employees through a harrowing experience." He turned to his guest who had also risen. "But a principle is not unlike a strategic stronghold, surely? Once it is smashed down, the whole cause is lost."

The diplomat came across and put his hand on Rupert's shoulder. "It is not lost yet, but unless we can see a way out of this in a few days, it might well be."

Rupert looked the man in the eye. "I sat beside a good friend while he died in agony after defending the rights of his country. I made a vow then that I would do my utmost to support him in that sacrifice. This might seem like a foolish display of stubbornness to some I know—it does to Du Plessis, he has been trying to talk me out of it—but it is my way of—" He shrugged. "How can I expect you to understand?"

"I do. In my own way, I understand what you are trying to do. But I am a diplomat and have been trained to compromise if it is for the larger good. The damnable thing is that once that treaty is ratified, Sing-Li won't have a leg to stand on. It will be quite legal for you to bring opium onto Chinese soil."

Rupert gave a short laugh and turned back to look at the soldiers again. "I didn't bring it this time. It was Bedford." He watched the scene outside for a moment or two. "I wonder what they would do if I simply walked out of the gate?" he mused half to himself. "I once went clean through an enemy picket in the Crimea when I came upon them by accident. They were so astonished they did nothing whatsoever. Mind you, they probably imagined I was leading an entire company. By the time they discovered their mistake I was clean away."

He was so lost in memory of the incident his nerves jumped when a hand came down on his shoulder.

"By George, you have given me a possible solution to this impasse, Torrington. This may well turn into a military operation, after all."

After Nugent Goddard had left, full of mysterious enthusiasm, a sense of futility descended on Rupert once more. What was he hoping to gain by winning the battle with Sing-Li? Personal satisfaction, perhaps, but what use would that be when all else was lost? Harriet had given her opinion of him that night he had dismissed Bedford. There was no doubt that she loved him, but if she did not respect him, their relationship was doomed.

In his heart he knew she had been right when she said she could have learned more in two months than he had in a year. Harriet found the details of the silk trade fascinating; she had a head for accounts and business management. She saw the charm of old Chinese legend in the conduct of this business—a bringing to life of all her father had studied with her. Her frugal days of household economy before marriage had taught her a certain delight in balancing books. Dammit, she had even tried to curb his extravagance in furnishing the house when they first married.

He thought of those weeks of wanting her and knowing nothing would make him take the first step toward physical union. He had that now—had discovered a passion beyond any he had experienced with other women—but of what joy could it be when he was dominant only in sexual unity? Harriet set her values high, and he had not yet managed to live up to them. His one attempt during the assault on Canton had not impressed her. But, God, he knew he could never do it as a silk merchant.

He poured another glass of the fast-dwindling wine and stared with unseeing eyes at the speedy onset of night outside his window. Nugent Goddard's conversation had precipitated it, and now, with no one to pretend to, no one across the table to watch his every expression, no one to spur him on, he admitted the truth. This defiant stance had been undertaken under the pretense of his being what he once had been . . . because he could not face the person he now was. If Harriet had no respect for him, he no longer had any more for himself.

He leaned forward with his head in his hands. Was there any peace for a man in doubling his fortune, throwing away all scruples for money's sake, holding friendship only as dear as it suited his ends, when he still remembered the faces of those who died beside him, believing it was for the freedom of those who still lived?

One thing was certain: The days of the company's prime were over. Since his father had killed himself, the Torrington millions had diminished by half. With himself in charge of the company they were certain to drop further. He could do one of two things: employ another agent as knowledgeable but less of a rogue than Bedford and struggle on in a business he loathed, or he could sell out.

If he did the first, he would be turning his back on

the vow made at Edward's deathbed. If the second, he would be denying his son his inheritance—the son he promised Aubrey would continue the business in his stead. For a long while he sat considering all the complexities facing him and acknowledged that whichever course he took, he would do it alone. He had told Harriet she must go back to England. Without her and his beloved son would it really matter what he did?

Fired by such thoughts, he went back to the window and looked at the soldiers standing outside his gates, illuminated by the flickering flambeaux. A frown creased his brow, and he conjured up a vision of a fat, sadistic villian with a girlish voice and the cruelty of centuries in his eyes. Oh, no, nothing would make him hand over the opium even if it meant taking the biggest chance of his life.

He frowned even more as his brain began working on something he understood. What if he did simply walk out those gates? Would any of those men take it upon himself to shoot? His eyes narrowed as he studied the position of the armed troops in relation to the gates. Once he was outside, those presently besieged with him would be free. If he walked to the safety of the consulate, Harry Parkes and Goddard would have greater bargaining power and could hold out indefinitely—at least until the treaty had been ratified and the case against him dissolved.

The possibilities grew, and so did his determination. The soldiers had no idea what Rupert Torrington looked like. If he strolled casually to the gates, opened them, and passed through, as if he had every right to do so, would those men challenge him? There was a strong chance they might not. Nugent Goddard and Armand du Plessis had come and gone frequently during the past week, and he could easily be taken for another mediator by those guarding the premises. They had probably been sent with orders to surround the place, no one dreaming the principal prisoner would attempt to leave openly. He knew something about irresolute soldiers with no firm orders on what to do in an unexpected situation and no NCOs to tell them. Unless someone ordered the soldiers to open fire on him, they would most likely remain right where they were, guarding the building.

His heart began to pump with excitement. Action was much more preferable than waiting. Siege tactics demanded that every attempt should be made to break it, even at the risk of failure . . . and loss of life. He had only a momentary feeling of hesitation as he thought of Harriet, and then he admitted that, alive or dead, once he was outside the factory, those inside would be freed . . . and if the opium were still demanded by Sing-Li, a dead man could not reveal its whereabouts!

His thoughts were broken by the sight of a hurrying figure coming through the gates, and the light of the flambeaux revealed it to be Nugent Goddard, moving in great haste. Still half-absorbed in his own plans, Rupert went to meet the man as he came up the stairs to the second floor. The only thing that could have sent him back at that hour was a new development, and the grin on Goddard's face seemed to uphold that opinion.

"Well, my dear fellow, it worked. I have you to thank for putting the notion into my head."

"Oh?" said Rupert, perplexed.

They reached the spacious drawing room, and Goddard refused a chair or a glass of wine. "No time for that, I fear. You have to leave right away for Hong Kong."

"Leave?"

"One of the terms for the cease-fire. But you have won your main battle. The opium stays with you."

"Now just a moment. What is this all about?"

Goddard grinned. "Sorry. Success must have gone to my head." He leaned against the back of a chair. "When you told me that anecdote about walking through an enemy picket, you said, 'They probably imagined I was leading an entire company.' It struck me then that if I could use that ploy on our friend Sing-Li, it might be to our advantage."

In his excitement Goddard rose and paced the room. "God knows what Mr. Parkes would say about my methods if he knew. I told the mandarin that troops were being assembled in Hong Kong to sail up here within the next couple of days and that there would be the devil to pay if they had to be used. With the Treaty of Tientsin about to be ratified the emperor would frown on any of his officials who endangered the cordial relations between the nations, and unless he wished to be sent the Silken Cord of Displeasure, he would be well advised to reconsider the situation."

Rupert grinned. "The devil you did . . . and . . .?"

"And he believed me. I trust you realize my career hung in the balance for a few moments for using such tactics without the knowledge of the consul, but if a man does not take a risk now and again in this business, he might as well be out of it. Besides, you have been taking a hell of a risk yourself for a good cause, and I felt someone should support you. Your fellow merchants do not seem inclined to do so."

"Thank you for that," said Rupert warmly, feeling life showed promise again.

"The promptness with which Sing-Li responded made me feel he was only too thankful to see a way out of a nightmare you had created." He made a face. "But there are penalties, Torrington. I think he knows you would not hand over that opium even under torture, and my reminder that it was not you who brought the stuff in, but Bedford, persuaded him to surrender it. However, he stipulates that you must leave tonight for Hong Kong and not return this season. All your present cargoes of silk must also be forfeited."

"But that will cripple the company," he protested hotly.

"It's a choice between that and the entire port's being closed. He has the power to force the hong merchants to cease trading with any foreign merchant at the drop of a hat. I'm sorry, Torrington, but you have no word in this. Mr. Parkes is empowered to force your compliance for the sake of trading interests in general, and he will, if need be."

Having given Rupert time to absorb that, he went on. "To be seen letting you leave would make Sing-Li lose face, which would be deep and utter humiliation. Therefore, you are to go under cover of darkness in the pretense that your Western guile and deceit have led you to escape punishment. That way trouble is averted, the situation resolved, and his reputation stays unsmirched."

Rupert stared at him in disbelief, and Goddard put a hand out to grip his shoulder. "Look, Torrington, you have made your stand, and he has yielded. The people of Canton will not know it, but we do. He has had a lesson in British determination he will not quickly forget. For the sake of the other merchants—and your own safety—you must leave here immediately. This could turn into a nasty diplomatic affair in a flash, and you could be in the greatest danger. You realize that your refusal to give in has made you Sing-Li's enemy for life, I suppose? If he does not get you this time, he will await his opportunity in the future."

"Yes . . . of course," murmured Rupert, trying to see a victory in something that appeared remarkably like defeat to him. His sneaking out under cover of darkness to be banished for the remaining three months of the season suggested the mandarin held all the trump cards.

The taste of defeat was still in his mouth as he said good-bye to Goddard at the gangplank of his lorcha after being allowed through by two soldiers on production of an order in writing from Sing-Li. Even so, he tried to express his gratitude for the one man who had supported him when his so-called friends told him he was a stiff-necked fool.

Shaking Goddard's hand, he said, "My heartiest thanks for your help and for your staunch support. I hope this will not mean the end of our acquaintance."

"I hope so also . . . but I was just doing my job, you know, in the same way you felt you were doing yours. Keep your gratitude for those two poor devils who have just let us through."

Rupert frowned. "Oh, why?"

"They'll lose their heads tomorrow."

Rupert's stomach heaved. "They'll *what*?" he shouted.

"They will be beheaded by Sing-Li for allowing you to escape. He cannot let it be known that he ordered them to let you go. An example must be made of them to deter further disobedience and show the mandarin's displeasure to Canton at large." He caught Rupert's arm in a steel grip as he made to walk back onto the jetty. "Torrington, you cannot change China in a day. Life is cheap here, and heads roll at the slightest thing. The only reason you are free now is that Sing-Li is afraid for his own."

Rupert fought against the restraint, feeling sick with anger. "Those men faithfully obeyed their orders. Is that how they are to be rewarded for loyalty? I will not let any man suffer death for my sake. My God, what kind of humanity do they uphold?"

"The same that has been keeping them going for centuries."

Goddard nodded at someone behind him, and Rupert felt himself grabbed by two of the seamen and persuaded up the gangplank.

"Nothing you now do will change it, believe me," called the diplomat after him. "Just be thankful it is not your head or those of your fellows that will be lost tomorrow. With these people you can never be sure who might be next."

Manhandled onto the deck, Rupert watched impotently as the last link with the jetty was hauled up and the ship got under weigh. It was like a voyage into desperation. Two innocent men were to be killed in a few hours as a result of his obstinacy and another man's pride. He had fought for a principle, believing it to be important, but others were to be made to pay the price. Never mind that they were strangers, completely unknown to him. They were soldiers doing their duty.

All through the journey down the Pearl River that fellowship stayed with him. Standing by the bulwark, he stared down into the silvery black water gliding past, seeing in the shattering patches of light on dark the pattern of his life. Nothing was constant. Love, fellowship, career . . . everything swung from the brilliance of success to the darkness of failure. In that moment he knew it could go on that way no longer. His gaze traveled from the water to the moon that was putting the silvery light upon it. It shone on his face with a brilliance that made everything suddenly clear. Those two men would be barbarously killed a few hours hence because of his quixotic defense of that which was his despite his unwillingness to have it. They would die in vain if he did not make use of what their deaths had left free for him.

It was more than Harriet's wanting it, more than his son's deserving his inheritance. It was a tribute to two innocent soldiers who would suffer in his stead. He would become a dedicated silk merchant and trade freely in Canton . . . and if his gaze began to stray to scarlet jackets and gun emplacements, he would drag it firmly back from something he must finally surrender.

* * *

It was still an hour before dawn when the lorcha crept alongside the company's wharves at Hong Kong. The January chill reached Rupert's bones as he stood, weary, yawning, and bleary-eyed from the all-night voyage, and looked at the darkened colony.

Hong Kong never slept. Pale, flickering flames of the saucer lights used by the Chinese could be seen through the gloom, and the soft shuffle of feet plus somnolent chatter betrayed the presence of those always on the move through the rubbish-strewn alleyways. Along the waterfront were the bobbing lanterns of the sampan colonies, where the noises never changed night or day. Babies complained fretfully; dogs savaged imaginary intruders; poultry squabbled sharply; neighbors cursed or blessed each other in tones guaranteed to travel over the surrounding square mile. Over everything hung the smell of burning joss sticks, fried rice, and sewage.

Yet here there was an aura of freedom that was missing in Canton. Rupert stepped ashore with a surprising burst of understanding of his father, who had spoken of these places so often in the past. Aubrey's feet had trodden the very planks on which he now walked. Had he really been so lonely? Had he ever given thought to a lonely child in school in England? Suddenly Rupert longed to see his son and put his gentle touch on the cloud of pale hair on the little head.

He threw back his head and breathed deeply. In Hong Kong there was an overtone of sanity that made nonsense of dawn executions and the barbarism of mandarins. In Hong Kong there was Western humanity to temper Eastern fatefulness. For a fleeting moment he thought again of a sharp sword slicing through a man's neck, and then he swallowed his feelings of guilt and climbed gratefully into the sedan chair called for him by one of the crew.

The journey took a little longer than usual because the bearers had to tread warily. It was common for night-returning Europeans to be set upon by robbers, and their passenger was particularly vulnerable because, for once, he carried no weapon. But all was peaceable that night, and they reached Sussex Hall just as the blackness was lifting. Dawn came quickly in Hong Kong. Within half an hour there would be full daylight.

The night watchman rose from his squatting doze against the front door and muttered a greeting as he bowed to his master. He showed no surprise at Rupert's arrival; such things happened in life that he no longer wondered at anything. Inside the house all was silent except for the scuttle of cockroaches as he passed through the orangery to reach the rear staircase leading to the rooms he used when not sharing his wife's bed. With the abstraction that follows deep emotional stress he told himself he would not live at Sussex Hall alone. It was too big and full of memories. He would find a small place in Victoria when Harriet had sailed.

By the time he reached the upper floor there was enough lifting of the darkness to make out the blacker shapes of pedestals and tallboys bearing Oriental treasure along the corridors. He walked with weary carelessness and almost knocked over a table bearing a great brass urn from India. Bending to steady it, he realized he was beside Edward's door, and the desire to go in overcame him.

The room smelled of a child's warm sleeping sweetness and of soothing ointments and honey. It touched his senses with unbearable tenderness mingled with pride because that was the essence of his own son, whom he must soon surrender. It was absurd to tiptoe, for the boy, in common with most toddlers, fell into sleep so total there was almost nothing that would awaken him before he was ready.

But Rupert never reached the cradle. Several feet from it his attention was caught by a strange fancy that could have been real. In the blotchy light of half dawn it seemed to him that a swift, silent figure had passed the open window onto the veranda. Blinking his bloodshot eyes to clear the possibility of fantasy, he moved across the room to look out. His scalp crawled. Someone had just entered Harriet's room farther along the veranda, filling him with fear.

He began to run. The sound of his footsteps was smothered by the pounding in his head. It was only a matter of twenty yards, but it seemed to stretch ahead of him like the road to forever. The door had been left open, and he crashed through it to hurl himself at the figure in Chinese dress poised in a crouching position over his sleeping wife.

His momentum carried them both off-balance to fetchup against the wall by the head of the bed. The figure was light and slender—a woman. She recovered from the fall first and sprang away, but it was possible to recognize her in that moment as Valentine Bedford's mistress, Tzu-An. Rupert staggered to his feet and lunged at her just as she reached the door, but she was ready for him. He gave a yell as she used the small dagger with fierce but misjudged aim, and his grasping hand went instinctively to the base of his neck just above his shoulder where blood was already spurting.

It could have been no longer than a second or two, but when he managed to push through the door onto the veranda, there was no sign of movement. She had vanished into the grayness to mingle with the shadows of dawn. He stumbled to the edge of the veranda, but the garden was too shadowy and revealed nothing.

With the breath rasping in his chest he grappled with the appalling facts. That woman had come to avenge her lover. Seeing in Harriet the cause of Bedford's downfall, she had used her knowledge of the house and bedroom to reach her. Tzu-An had meant to kill Harriet. If he had not returned so unexpectedly at that moment . . . if he had not gone into his son's room on impulse . . . !

There was movement and sound behind him, and sudden flooding light. Still half-caught up in the macabre drama, he turned to look through the doorway into the room. The lamp had been lit, throwing a yellow glow over the bed and ceiling. Harriet was sitting as still as death with her hair flowing in tangled disorder over her shoulders, looking out at him.

He found himself walking toward her, conscious of the overturned table beside the bed and the scattered hairpins across the floor. The warm trickle of blood ran down inside the neck of his shirt, and the stinging pain of the wound made him long to increase it, rip himself open and bleed even more. The nearer he grew to her, the greater the longing grew.

When he was but a few feet from her, it became reality. His whole body was open to agony as he saw what was in her face. All her pride and indomitable spirit had melted into dark-eyed weakness in the shock of noncomprehension. With her mouth slightly parted she gazed at the wound in his neck, which was making a dark crimson stain on his shirt and coat, then up to meet his eyes in a swift sharing of pain. He read the suffering of the past week in her face and the relief of his presence . . . but overriding it all was the emotion that exposed his soul to the daggers of her love.

The loneliness of his boyhood, the sly insults on his background, the casting away of his scarlet coat, and the death of two distant soldiers all were swirling around in his mind as he reached out and touched her hair with a hand that shook. Its softness broke him.

After dragging her up against him, he forced her head back to kiss her with a mouth that wanted only to take reprisal for all he had seen and heard that week. Her pliant softness drove him further into something that took possession of him completely, and as he pressed her farther and farther back, he became aware that she was rushing headlong into those same realms.

It began as a battle, with her attack as fierce as his, each seeking and taking punishment as if their need would never be quenched. She began to cry, to plead with him, but they both knew it had to be a fight to the finish. The blood from his wound found its way onto the pillows and across the white pureness of the coverlet, even onto her soft skin, but he felt no pain. There was more pain in the glistening blue depths of her eyes as she gradually surrendered and acknowledged the lies she had believed of him; there was more agony in the words he forced from her by his desperate mastery.

Never had he been so brutal; never had she challenged him so wildly. Finally, she lay with her hair spread over the wreck of the bed, her face tearstained and with the joy of ecstasy upon it. In her eyes was all he wanted to see, had ever wanted to see. His head swam; his body felt leaden with conquest. The past was over. The future would be different, and she had just ceded it to him to do with as he wished.

"Thank God," he murmured in exhausted relief as he drifted away from reality, sprawled beside her. He had no more thoughts of the headman's ax in Canton.

Chapter Fifteen

Her fingers caressed his neck, gently massaging the stiffness from it as she stood behind his chair.

"Mmm," he grunted appreciatively, but he was so lost in his reading she might not have been there. Looking down on his bent head, she felt a rush of love and touched the creamy fair hair lightly with her lips, as she often did with little Edward. But her fingers continued their massage.

Rupert was a changed man. In the four months since the siege of his factory he had bent all his energies to learning his trade. Sometimes she felt he was driving himself too hard; but her husband was the kind of man who did all or nothing, and the only thing she could do was help lessen his burden.

In that way they had faced the crisis threatening the company. The loss of four months' trading when other merchants were continuing theirs was more severe than the effect of the two whole seasons which had affected everyone, and it had been impossible to find another agent in midseason. Rupert had promoted a senior assistant temporarily; but he had none of the flair and expertise of Bedford, and so it was a case of owner and employee struggling together.

There had been small quarrels between Harriet and Rupert, but nothing that had disturbed the ecstatic happiness they had found. He had been stubbornly firm about refusing to allow her to work on the accounts, but she was doing them daily right under his nose. When he went to the warehouses or shipping office and arrived back at an hour when luncheon was quite spoiled, she was often in a fighting mood. But she found, to her eventual delight, that he was in even more of a fighting mood than she. They were both occupied and fulfilled. What more could they wish for when they also had a son born of their love?

Their whole life had taken on a new perspective. When Rupert was not talking to the masters of his ships about the availability and merits of various cargoes or consulting warehousemen on the art of storing goods, he was at the headquarters of the Trade Council, consulting books, mercantile charts, and legislative documents. Then he came back to Sussex Hall to study the history of the company, the assets and liabilities, and how best to compensate for the damaging losses of the last two years. Together he and Harriet pored over the accounts, she explaining the entries and making suggestions for economies. He teased her, saying she was more of a housekeeper and mistress than a respectable wife. She retaliated by saying he had all three in one for once.

They both faced the fact that the company was not the premier organization it once was, but with hard work and the right agent the next season could do a lot toward building up its reputation again. The latest of their schemes had been to start learning the official Chinese language—a skill Rupert was convinced would be invaluable when dealing with the hong merchants in Canton.

Harriet struggled with the complicated signs that seemed to mean several conflicting phrases at one and the same time and all but gave up. Rupert manfully struggled on, and it was this that he was studying as she began to massage his neck. Her fingers touched the scar he would always have, and she remembered the night she had awakened to find him standing blood-spattered, unshaved, and shaking beside her bed when she believed him to be in Canton. It was only later that she discovered the truth about that wound.

The police had failed to trace Tzu-An. Her house had been abandoned, and no one would admit knowledge of her whereabouts. She could have left the island or could be down in the sampan colonies amid the thousands crammed onto the small boats. Rupert had hired extra night watchmen, and the veranda doors and windows were all securely locked at night now. Their combined fears for Edward had led to the fitting of extra bolts on his doors and windows and securing a new amah who was more efficient and less doting. Rupert had also bought three large guard dogs, who set up a rumpus at the slightest noise. They were barking at that moment—probably at someone going along the track toward the barracks.

"Damned infernal row!" muttered Rupert absently as he tried to copy a row of Chinese characters onto a sheet of paper.

She smiled. "That is the reason you bought them, dearest."

"Mmm? Yes . . . I suppose so," he replied, more intent on his calligraphy. "There, what do you think of that?"

She rested her chin on the top of his head and peered down at the little drawings. "Splendid, my love . . . but if that is one of the sayings of Confucius, he would surely wish it unsaid if he could see your interpretation of it."

Quick as a flash he pulled her around and across his lap. "Baggage!" he cried. "I will no longer have you as my wife and housekeeper." Then he kissed her. "You make a far better mistress than either. What do you say to my proposal?"

She laughed up into his face. "As a mistress I shall demand presents."

"Shall you, indeed?"

"You gave all your other mistresses presents, I'll wager."

His next kiss was insistent and aroused her quick passion. "Yes, I gave them presents . . . but only if they pleased me. What do you propose to do for yours?"

She pulled his head down and said fiercely against his mouth, "Leave your silly books and I will soon show you. No other mistress will have pleased you the way I shall." She could not quite keep the ring of jealousy from her voice, and he took advantage of it to tease her further.

"That is quite an undertaking, my sweet wanton. Shall I be able to withstand such exquisite delight?"

She bit his ear sharply, then whispered closely against it, "Dare you put it to the test?"

She was struggling in his arms when the knock of a servant broke the delightful moment. When he entered, it was to announce that Monsieur du Plessis had called to see them both. Rupert cursed the interruption and told Harriet she must entertain the visitor while he went upstairs to make himself tidy.

"Nonsense, my dearest, you look quite well enough to greet Armand," she told him, smoothing down the collar of his shirt. "With your hair in disarray from my fingers and the width of your manly chest visible through your open shirt, you possess a panache, a certain *élégance,* that will have his Gallic vanity instantly ruffled."

His swift kiss promised later ravishment. "I was right . . . you are a baggage." He turned her around and sent her in the direction of the withdrawing room with an instruction to be charming, but not too charming, until he returned properly dressed.

Crossing the hall, Harriet felt a certain reluctance to come face-to-face with Armand once more. They had not met since he had escorted her to Hong Kong in January, and she now felt that her easy acceptance of him as a friend of another generation could not be maintained. How was she to treat him?

Her fears were groundless. Armand greeted her as he had always done.

"*Ma chère,* you look radiant," he told her, kissing her fingers. "I am glad to see it. My excuse for such bad manners in calling uninvited is because I have just now learned of the attack upon you by the Chinese woman. *Mon Dieu,* if Rupert had not that night returned . . ." He shook his head. "The East is no place for *les femmes.*"

"Is that why you have never married, Armand?" she asked pointedly.

"*Peut-être*. I have seen too many people become unhappy. The husbands must go to Canton and leave the wives and children for half the year. It is not good for men . . . or for their women, such loneliness."

"But that will no longer happen once this treaty is formally accepted, surely? Rupert says I shall go with him to Canton in October."

Armand frowned. "He will continue without an agent? It is madness."

Sinking gracefully onto the couch, Harriet took a great delight in saying, "You will not think so when you speak to him. He has become a silk merchant. His days of indecision are over . . . and we are both so happy," she added impulsively. "Armand, he has worked so hard he cannot fail to succeed. Once he finds another agent, the company will become what it once was. Now that the merchants are all back in Hong Kong, it should be easy to find a man with experience whose personality will blend with Rupert's."

Armand laughed. "*Ma chère*, I think you know your husband better than that. He is strong-willed, restless for action, and stubborn. Your new agent's personality will not blend with Rupert's; it must bow to it."

As she thought of the night Rupert had returned from Canton and made hers bow to his will, the color in her cheeks deepened. Hastily she asked if there was any news of Valentine Bedford, hoping Armand would not notice the blush.

"He is certainly not in Canton. Several merchants are after his services and cannot find him."

"But surely . . . after what happened." She looked

at him in disbelief. "He was using our ships to smuggle opium, and Rupert suffered the consequences. Is that any recommendation for his character?"

The Frenchman put his foot on the marble fireside curb and rested his arm lightly along the mantelpiece as he looked down at her. "There is much you still do not understand, I see. When one is a trader, one *trades*. It is of no use to consider ethics. Opium fetches high prices in China. It is forbidden, *hein*, but there is little difficulty in selling it. When there are buyers anxious for merchandise and the means of supplying what they want, it is only a fool who thinks of laws. If he does not provide it, someone else will." He shook his head and tut-tutted. "Ah, do not look at me with big eyes, madame. A true merchant would have made money from Bedford's opium, not stood as one against a nation only to lose half his season's trade."

"But Rupert kept his self-respect," she cried hotly, her new role leading her to forget her own attitude at the time.

"Pouf! What use is self-respect when one is beggared? There is always another to step into one's shoes."

"Is that why you stepped into mine and took all the silk from my regular dealers?" asked Rupert as he came into the room respectably dressed in a coat over his shirt and a cravat knotted at his neck. His neatly brushed hair gleamed in the lamp glow as he went across to shake Armand by the hand. "I understand you did rather well out of my banishment."

"*Ah, oui,* I heard of your overnight departure before

it was generally known, so my agent was there to intercept your dealers and lead them to my factory before they were offered other temptations." He laughed. "Both Roland and Marshfield were sick over their lost chance, *mon ami.*"

"Yes, I daresay," commented Rupert in such equable tones Harriet began to think she had misunderstood.

"Rupert . . . Armand . . . I cannot believe this. You are not saying that Companie Lascard has stolen our dealers, that silk we were unable to buy has found its way into its warehouses." She looked from one face to the other and saw their hesitation. "Well, is that what you are saying?" she challenged Rupert. "Did Armand take our silk?"

He looked steadily back at her. "It was not our silk. I was not there to buy it. Naturally the dealers would sell elsewhere."

From deep inside her rose the old protective anger. "You knew about this and deliberately did not tell me?"

"Yes. I heard about it at the Trade Council."

"Why did you keep it from me?"

"Becuase I knew you would be angry."

"Any you did not feel angry?" she cried. "Betrayed by a friend." She swung around to confront Armand as she rose to her feet. "How do you excuse your action?"

He playfully put his hands up to shield himself from her attack, but she was past humoring.

"So that is why you were so anxious to get back to Canton when you brought me here—so that you could be in at the kill!"

"Harriet, I think you have gone too far," said Rupert sharply. "Armand is in our house."

"Then I do not understand how he can enter it after what he has done."

Armand shook his head quickly at Rupert, then moved toward her. "You defend your man, and that is natural, *ma chère*. But you must let him fight his own battles, *hein*? He knows if I had not taken his trade from him, someone else would have done so." He spread his hands. "If I ever fall upon misfortune, it is my sincere hope that Rupert will benefit rather than another of my rivals."

She tossed her head. "Rupert would not treat a friend in such manner. Am I not right, dearest?"

"No, you are wrong," was the staggering answer. "I would put the company before friendship, or I would not deserve the name Torrington."

She stared at him in the disturbing knowledge that their recent happiness had been a pool of stillness in the midst of troubled waters. At that moment there was a ruthless quality in his eyes that had always been hot with emotion, whether anger or joy. Now the deep brown had grown a little stony. Had that cynical twist to his smile been there before; had there always been lines tugging down the corners of his mouth?

"I . . . do not understand you, Rupert."

"I have become a merchant, my dear."

"But you are also a man of principle," she protested.

The cynical smile again. "My principles lost two men their lives and the company a great deal of money. I find I cannot be both."

Angry with Armand but more so with Rupert for disconcerting her before their guest, she said coldly,

"Then I must tell you I do not like the merchant Torrington."

"It is what *you* wished me to be."

Armand was forgotten as she looked across at a man who had just shown her the extent of what had happened to him in the past four months. It was not merely a question of learning from books but forcing his whole personality into a different mold. Inexplicably something inside her cried out against it.

A month later, at the end of June, the Western community was stunned to learn that the envoys who had sailed up to obtain ratification of the Treaty of Tientsin had found rebuilt the Taku forts captured by them the previous year and the mouth of the Pei-ho River reblocked to prevent their entry. This time an army of 50,000 Chinese was awaiting the British and French storming parties, and the resultant slaughter plus the sinking of four British gunboats had forced the small flotilla to abandon all hope of reaching Peking. Their return to Hong Kong gave rise to Chinese jubilation and the bitterest feelings of animosity in the Western nations. There was not the slightest doubt in any man's mind now that the Chinese must be given a lesson so hard they would never forget it. The rest of the world had had enough of imperial prevarication.

The news had a devastating effect on Rupert, who felt the defeat almost personally. All his old heated ideas on showing the Chinese they could not play fast and loose with the British burned on his tongue again. Remembering Sing-Li, he grew restless with the desire for action. God, what he would give to see them forced to honor their promises.

It was by chance that he met Giles Meredith in Victoria as he was leaving the waterfront a week after the news broke. The two men had not seen much of each other after the fatal evening Giles had unthinkingly betrayed the truth about the manner of Edward Deane's death. But it had not been due to that. The season had taken the Torringtons up to Canton, and since Rupert had been back, he had deliberately avoided contact with military men. They greeted each other warmly on that morning and immediately fell into a discussion on the prospect of a full-scale war against the Chinese as retaliation.

It was only a short conversation because Giles was due back at the barracks, but he clapped Rupert on the shoulder and suggested he might like to visit the officers' mess that evening. He was on loan to the battery on the peak above Sussex Hall, and that evening they had as guests several marine officers who had gone up with the envoys on the disastrous mission.

"We are all avid to hear the details," he said with enthusiasm. "We have heard the Chinese fire was murderous. After Canton it seems remarkable, but these men were well trained under the leadership of a talented Chinese general. If we are ordered to go up after them, there might be a stiffer battle than we had last year, eh?"

It was not until he came to the point of telling Harriet that Rupert realized he had agreed to visit the barracks without hesitation. He had forgotten about being a silk merchant in an instant. He found himself trying to sound nonchalant as he told her of the meeting with Giles and the invitation for that evening.

"You are going?" she asked quickly.

"Er . . . yes . . . probably."

"Very well."

He sighed. "My dear one, please take off that disapproving face. You cannot accuse me of deserting you. For the last six evenings we have been delightfully alone together, have we not?"

"While we tried to learn Chinese!"

He put his hand gently under her chin. "And did I not also teach you other things?"

She covered his hand with her own and took it up to lay against her cheek. But her eyes looked apprehensive. "I love you to distraction, Rupert."

"And I you, *baggage*," he murmured, kissing her hard. "I swear to you no ladies are invited."

She tried to rally. "Then I cannot think why you are going."

"Giles says some of the men who went up–" He broke off, realizing what she had nearly led him to admit. "I have rather neglected him, and he is such a pleasant fellow. Earned himself a medal in the Crimea, you know."

"You are going up there to talk about the coming war," she said. "Did you think to deceive me with that airy nonsense?"

Wanting to leave the subject, he said rather misguidedly, "If there *is* to be a war, I must know the consequences for the mercantile companies. We cannot afford another lost season."

More alarmed over his lie than the truth, she was instantly suspicious. "Rupert, you gave your word. You swore to me that you would never go to battle again. There is Edward to–"

"Wait . . . wait," he protested. "When have I said anything about going to battle? I am going to discuss a situation that concerns the entire colony, that is all. Besides, I could hardly take a lorcha up to Peking, for that is where the battle will be this time." He said the last almost to himself and missed the speculative look that entered his wife's eye at the tone of his voice.

When he finally made his way up the track in the sedan chair, it was with a faint lethargy of mind and limbs. While he had been dressing, Harriet had made such a seductive attack on him he had been unable to resist her. Only afterward, when she lay whispering endearments against his throat, had it floated into his mind that she might have hoped to keep him at home that evening. But he dismissed the thought as nonsense when she insisted on perfecting the arrangement of his cravat and pulling his coat smoothly into place. She even smiled and sent her kind regards to Giles Meredith, telling Rupert to be sure to invite the young captain to dinner soon.

All thoughts of Harriet left him when he stepped into the officers' mess and saw the familiar sight of scarlet coats and the uniforms of the marines. A great rush of homecoming swept over him as he was greeted warmly, given a drink and immediately absorbed into the hearty, strictly masculine world of the military.

There was little social chitchat in that high, airy room furnished with such tradition they could have been at Woolwich or Brighton. The only indication of its Eastern location was the large steam-powered fan some ingenious man had invented to give some relief from the cloying heat of a tropical night as they launched straight into the sizzling topic of the moment.

"They have signed their own death warrant," declared one of the visiting marines. "Believe me, every one of us who was there will not rest until we are back at them again. Old Hope"—as he affectionately referred to his admiral—"went ashore in a boat to demand clear passage for envoys to the emperor, but there were no officials or anyone with connections at court. All he saw was a rabble claiming to be the local militia. They threatened him, shouted abuse, and danced around to prevent the boat from being beached. Damned insulting, to say the least."

"Still," said another, anxious to break into the telling of the story, "he didn't let that go as the last word. Our envoy instructed him to take the men an ultimatum to clear the river or stand by while *we* did it."

"So I should think," was Giles's indignant comment. "Blocking the river was an deliberate act of aggression. They dashed well knew our people were going up to ratify that treaty. We subdued Canton to create it. What did they think we were going to do—turn around and go home like whipped pups?"

"It's what we did do," said a gloomy subaltern with more fire than sense.

He was promptly sat upon by a large marine with a fighting light in his eyes.

"That threat soon brought a message from the emperor, who said we were forbidden to use the river and must go farther north to Pehtang, where other arrangements would be made on arrival." He laughed.

"If he thought two of the greatest nations in the world would meekly shuffle off to some godforsaken Chinese town to await instructions that would never be sent, he must be totally ignorant of world affairs."

"He is," said Rupert with force. "Or he knows and dismisses the knowledge as immaterial. His own country is so vast and ungovernable he had enough to do trying to deal with internal problems. As it is, his mandarins are vicious, corrupt, and sycophantic to the point of keeping anything unpleasant from reaching his ears. It suits their own ends to encourage the belief that he is a god incarnate. How can such a man ever discover the true state of affairs? He will know only when we have ambassadors at Peking—and they are going to get there only behind guns. It has been obvious for years."

"Well said." A major applauded. "So far all we have done is mount punitive attacks on Canton. What we have to do is march up to Peking in force and give them a taste of our might. All they have yet seen of us is a small scratch force with nothing to get its teeth into. By George, I would immediately confront them with numbers of our crack regiments. They would not then tell us to run away and play."

The marines looked at each other in the face of this military fire, and the senior of them said with commendable reserve, "We hardly went away to play, sir. We lost over four hundred killed and wounded."

The major realized his error and apologized. "Got carried away, you know. We have all heard of the magnificent display you put up against overwhelming odds. Admiral Hope himself was twice wounded, I believe."

The man smiled proudly. "The old boy rushed in with a gunboat and then, when it was finished off, had himself carried to another to lead the attack. He was hit again and collapsed."

Another marine leaned forward enthusiastically. "Then the most extraordinary thing occurred. The commander of the American ship that took up the United States envoy threw his neutrality to the winds and pitched into the battle as hard as he could, his sailors replacing our dead and wounded at the guns, and his two ships towing in our reserves. We heard he was reprimanded for it, but being a man of obvious red blood, he staunchly replied that no man of any worth could be expected to stand by and watch other Westerners butchered. I think nothing more will be said to him."

"If I ever come across him, I shall be proud to shake his hand," said the senior officer present. "Could we invite him to join us in our coming war, do you suppose?"

A laugh greeted that, but Rupert was quick to say, "Have you heard anything definite, sir?"

He shook his head. "Only rumors."

"Such as?"

"Such as half a dozen regiments from India, field artillery from England, infantry from the Cape. All conjecture, of course; but I dined with a fellow in the administration last night, and we estimated the probable moves. It's not difficult if you consider availability and accessibility. The Indian Mutiny is over, and we can now have the reinforcements that were diverted from Hong Kong two years back."

"Your friend in the administration—is he certain they will be called?" Rupert persisted eagerly.

"Oh, yes, this time the Chinese have gone too far. Of course, we can't do anything until next year. We have to get the troops here and go up in the summer, but I would wager we'll be on the march by this time next year."

The trading season will be over, thought Rupert, and I shall be free . . . to watch them all depart. A stab of pain he thought quite forgotten hit him in the chest. When the transports had filled with troops, when the gunboats nosed their way from the harbor, he would be left standing on the jetty alone.

The little rows of Chinese characters on scattered sheets of paper across Rupert's desk touched Harriet with loving tenderness. She picked them up and felt, in some absurd way, that she was touching him, drawing him closer. In that room his presence was so strong. For four months he had spent so much time with books, at study. They had been together in a manner new to their marriage. There had been a peaceful joy, a partnership, a complete blending and complementing of personalities. They had captured each other and lived together in what the Chinese would call the inner temple of heavenly tranquillity.

Tonight Rupert had gone. From the moment he first mentioned Giles Meredith she knew their tranquillity had ended. Feminine instinct had rung the warning bells and urged her to use the lures of love to avert his departure. But he had gone, and she had been forced to fall back on the other instinct known to women the world over—put on a bright face and never let him know what lay deep inside her heart.

On the surface nothing could possibly change. Rupert had pledged himself to the company; the army was still as lost to him as before. He had said himself that he could not possibly take a lorcha up to Peking to watch this battle. Yet she was restless and desperately uneasy.

A glance at the clock told her it was late. He had said, "An hour or two, I promise." She had retired once, then wandered downstairs again, too restless to sleep, wanting to watch and listen for his return. The house was still—too still for her present unease. Why did he not come?

Sitting in his leather chair, she made herself go through all the good reasons why her apprehension was foolish. Then she picked up the book they both were studying in order to learn something of the Chinese language. It was an effort, but she bent her mind until the little drawings blurred and she could resist the pull of her eyelids no longer.

The dogs were barking, barking, barking. "*Damned infernal row*," said Rupert again, only it was not Rupert but she herself speaking, through a layer of cotton wool. There was a loud banging and a roaring noise. Voices were shouting—angry voices of men who were also afraid. Struggling up from sleep, her brain tried to understand why the dream noises still continued and grew louder instead of fading away. Her eyes opened slowly, and she gazed at the rows of books on the shelves and the heavy desk in front of her. Books . . . desk . . . where was she?

A crash . . . running feet. Two men were there, seizing her arms, shouting her name, saying she must go immediately. Their faces were red and shiny with sweat. They smelled of fear.

She resisted. "No!"

"You must come . . . no time to lose . . . don't panic . . . come quickly."

They were afraid. Something terrible had happened! As they dragged her to her feet she cried, "Rupert . . . is it my husband?"

"Is he in the house?" roared one man at her face.

"No . . . no, he has not come back. Where is he? What is happening?"

The men looked at each other as another crash shook the floor.

"Let's get going."

Holding her, they led her across to the door. There was a terrible smell. She began to cough, and so did they. The roaring sound became deafening as they opened the door. There was a vivid yellow light everywhere, and tremendous heat. Across the great hall and up the curving staircase was the entrance to hell.

Fire!

Across the hall and up the stairs! *"Edward,"* she screamed. *"My son is up there."*

Already the landing walls were blackened, the expensive wall coverings shriveling into brown sticky masses. The tallboys were pillars of flames; priceless china jars were exploding into fragments.

They held her tighter. "No, everything is all right."

She knew by their faces . . . knew it was a lie.

They could not hold her. As she ran, her hands tore off the clinging wrapper that hampered movement, and she lifted the wide skirt of her nightgown. They were after her, but they would not stop her. Nothing, nobody would stop her.

He was toddling toward her on unsteady, chubby legs, holding up a velvet ball in childish triumph.

"Edward," she sobbed.

Up the staircase the air was full of flying ash. A trickle of some obscene substance was oozing down the top three steps, and the polished wood was shimmery yellow. There was no noise other than the roar of flames racing through the airy upper corridors, seizing on each object, surrounding it and moving on the minute it had become an integral part of the inferno. The corridor leading to the nursery was a sheet of flame that dropped with a slow, agonizing tearing apart of wood into the hall as she reached the upper floor.

She was ice that even the satanic heat could not melt.

Edward was sitting in her lap, pointing to a picture in his favorite rag book. He smelled warm and innocently precious. His little fair head drooped against her in an infant's sudden sleep.

The men caught at her again, but she was soon away. Their shouts were lost in the symphony of fire. Along the other corridor on the west side, to the veranda! Smoke swirled thickly, shutting off the lurid brightness as she sped along the carpet, and then, just as she reached the opposite corridor, a licking orange tongue reached up from below to blacken the banisters beside her.

After tugging at the door of a guest room, she slammed the door back against the wall as she threw herself at the shuttered doors across the room that led to the veranda. They were locked. As her hands fumbled with the key, one of the men seized her arm.

Stronger than anyone in the world in that moment, she threw him off and cried through the hair plastered to her cheeks, "Keep away or may God never forgive you."

She was through and into a night full of stars and the heavy scent of oleanders. It was terrible and cruel in its beauty. The veranda was a road to eternity that she must spend her whole life endeavoring to reach. Rounding a corner, she crashed into the rail and almost fell, but her pursuers did not catch her.

Along that wooden corridor stretching away into the open night a little boy was marching soldiers up and down with absorption and encouraging, "Boom, boom, boom."

"Edward," she moaned through icy lips.

Around another corner, and there was his window. It was yellow with brilliant light from within. Wild prayers rose in her throat as she hurled herself at the shuttered windows. Blow after blow with her fists failed to move them. The men were there beside her, hammering, hammering at the windows and doors double-locked to keep the child safe from intruders. No one, not even his mother, was meant to get in there!

Through the slatted shutters smoke poured out, and tiny fingers of flame began poking through into the darkness in which she stood. Blinding brilliance of light accompanied a sudden creaking, tearing crash from within. The men were taking her away, and they were now stronger than she.

Her screams hurt her throat, but their red, shiny faces were expressionless. She fought, kicked, struggled. She begged to go back. She appealed to their humanity. Her sobs racked her body, but their iron clamp on her did not weaken. As she threw her head to the left in the anguish of looking back, her mind broke. In a voice that was terrible to hear she put upon their heads the curse of eternal torment and cried aloud to God to uphold her words.

Then they were away from the house and standing beneath some trees. Life had ended.

In the officers' mess they all had grown voluble with wine. As each man gave his opinion on how he would show the Chinese who was boss, their bravado grew. The gloom of defeat had turned into a gleeful advance victory. Rupert was sprawled in a chair, blissfully encouraging the boasts of an ensign who had not yet seen battle, when a voice broke across the general conviviality of the evening.

"My God, it looks as though the Chinese have started a fresh campaign of arson. There are several large fires down below."

The statement was arresting enough to break up the conversation, and several men crowded to the window. Rupert went with them and peered around the curtains.

"The bastards!" exclaimed one.

Giles, standing close to Rupert said, "One of them looks damned close to your house."

His own voice echoed through the room like a visiting spirit at a séance. "*It is my house.*"

There was brilliant moonlight, but the air was full of the smell of charred wood and smoke. Down the steps in a great leap, past the sedan chairs—they were too slow. The track was steep, full of pitfalls. Branches tore at his face and clothes as if to prevent him from getting to where he must be. He fell and struggled to his feet in running, scrambling steps. He fell again on a bend that overhung a sheer drop. His mouth was full of earth and saliva; his lungs struggled to pump out the smoke. Had the track ever been as long before?

Around a final bend, and it was all there before him. A fire so tremendous, so awesome, it overhung the whole colony. Black figures stood against the sheet of orange-yellow. He cannoned into someone who caught his arm. Two men, three men held him steady.

"*My wife,*" he cried hoarsely.

"She is safe, Torrington."

"Edward . . . my son?"

There was a pause. "I'm sorry. We did all we could."

He lunged.

"No, it is too late . . . too late . . . too late."

The words went around and around in his head in a never-ending echo as they held him against a tree until he stopped fighting.

He looked at the circle of faces that were blackened and full of shock. Their eyes were red and could not see what he held inside him in that moment.

"Harriet . . . I must go to her." His chest and throat were so raw it made him bleed even to speak.

"We will take you to her."

They led him across grass littered with fine black ash that disintegrated beneath his feet. A little way on Bessie Porridge was sitting on the grass, propped up by a man he recognized as a neighbor. Her face was blackened, and she was in a blessed state of shock.

Then he saw Harriet, held by several men, in her nightgown with a man's coat wrapped around her shoulders. She was an old woman. The smooth contours of her face had become concave and emphasized the huge black-shadowed eyes. Her hair was streaked gray by the ash, and her skin had taken on the yellow pallor of death.

They stared at each other like two people who had never met and yet had never parted. They were two, yet one. Just for a moment they were like that. Then she began to back away from him further and further in a shrinking crouching movement.

"Where *were* you?" she said accusingly in a voice so terrible he knew the sound would never leave his ears.

They took her away. One by one they all went until he was left alone, sitting under a tree where they had held him back from reaching Edward. The blinding yellow light gradually dimmed into deep dark red that glowed fitfully in the blackness. Then there was blackness alone. It was like that for a long time. After that the blinding yellow grew again. It was low at first, then grew higher and higher until it shone into his face. It was hot and like the fires of hell.

He got to his feet very slowly and stared at it. Then he was running toward the pile of blackened rubble in front of him. He was back at the foot of the defenses at Sevastapol. At the top lay something terrible, but he had to go up there.

Bricks, sharp charred pieces of wood, jagged chunks of china and glass, sticky unrecognizable lengths of cloth that all went flying in his frenzied attack. The palms of his hands grew blistered and burned, but the red-hot pain was nothing to the pain inside him. On and on he went, tugging and heaving, until his blood ran onto the blackened debris and his tears mingled with it.

Part Three

Chapter Sixteen

The sweat stood on his brow and trickled down his face; his shirt stuck to his back. Even the adoption of the broad linen hat favored by colonials did not much mitigate the driving force of a sun that glared from a cloudless sky, and Rupert's head thudded with every upward step he took.

The track was bone-dry and brittle beneath his boots, the stones breaking easily from their resting place in the crumbly earth to rattle away down the slope, betraying his approach. But there was no one to heed the sound except a still, silent figure on the track ahead, and another beneath the shade of the trees, who watched him with large, apprehensive eyes.

He went straight across to Bessie. "How long has she been here?"

"Most all the morning, Captain. It was only by chance I saw her leave." She looked very upset. "It don't not do any good to keep coming back, as I keeps telling her. This place is . . . well, I'm sorry, Captain, but it fair gives me the shakes, her standing here day after day."

Her words faded in his ears as he looked at the blackened wreck of Sussex Hall and the fire-scarred trees all around. The slopes of Victoria Peak looked wilder and more awesome without the elegant white colonnaded house to temper it with the evidence of civilization. Birds now flew to perch on charred spars sticking out at angles; wild animals scavenged among the tumble of debris and scampered away when disturbed.

Moving out into the blaze of mid-August once more, Rupert went across to the thin figure wrapped in a shawl on such a day. She did not heed his approach.

"It is time to go home," he said gently, putting his hand on her arm with infinite care.

Her head turned slowly. So desperately ill did she look he wondered how she could even stand. Whereas she had always been slender, her body was now wasted and bony. The skin stretched across her face was yellow, like that of a person who has spent her life in unhealthy Asian climes.

"It is time to go home, Harriet," he repeated hoarsely, trying to lead her away, but she shrank from his touch, moved back and away as if from something evil. The sweat broke more freely on his body, and he nodded to Bessie, who came across to lead her mistress away from the spot she haunted day after day.

Rupert fell in behind the two women and looked no more at the scene of devastation, but Harriet's head turned yearningly as she walked away. The sedan chairs were waiting in the usual place to take them all back to the house Rupert now rented in the heart of the city. As they were carried down the track, he thought back to the doctor's words.

"Tragedy affects people in different ways, Mr. Torrington. You must realize that a mother has a relationship with her child that a man will never fully understand. I think it would do more harm to prevent your wife from visiting the scene of the tragedy than to allow it. Her present state of shock will pass, believe me."

But ten weeks later Harriet was still haunting the ruins where the little boy had been snatched from their lives. There was hardly a day when Rupert did not return to find that he had to go up that track after her. Bessie loyally dogged her mistress's footsteps, but she did not have the courage or persuasive power to bring her away from the scene. Strangely Harriet always left with Rupert when he appeared, not letting him touch her but moving away immediately she knew he was there. It was not for some time that he realized it was she who was leading him away: that his presence in that place was something she would not tolerate. Harriet's love had died that night with Edward. She would never forgive him.

In five weeks the trading season would begin again, and Rupert was at his wits' end over the situation. In the first days following the tragedy his own overwhelming need had been to get away from the scene and especially from those people who had done so much to him . . . to them both. In the blackness of grief he had suffered a frightening aggression that had him so hating every foreign face he saw around him that he had to fight the urge to fly at them and fasten his hands around their throats. He thought of the maddened mob on the day of their arrival, of the servants who had deserted them, of the Chinese woman who had tried to knife Harriet, of Sing-Li and his cruel arrogance, and those who had burned down his house and everything in it, killing his precious son and taking his wife away from him.

The hatred and desire for vengeance so ruled him he was almost afraid to stay and face it; the great blackened scar on the side of the peak broke him apart. But Harriet, whose hatred and desire for vengeance was centered on him, refused to leave Hong Kong, and any suggestion that she should do so made her wild with distress. In her anguished mind she believed the child's spirit to be in that tragic place, and nothing would make her leave it.

While Harriet still remained in that state, Rupert had come to terms with the driving need within him. But he could not even begin to reach her, for she spoke no word to him and retreated whenever he drew near. Eventually he had to discuss the problem with Armand, who was the only person able to approach Harriet since the tragedy. Rupert suspected she had somehow found a father in their friend and turned to him when she rejected her husband. It was a shattering experience to hear of her feelings and wishes through another man and be compelled to ask Armand to say and do that which he now could not.

But it was soon clear to both men that it would be cruel to order her departure from Hong Kong even if there were any way it could be enforced. In her present state Harriet would fight tooth and claw to remain in spiritual proximity to her child.

"I cannot go up to Canton leaving her like this," Rupert said in desperation. "Bessie is like a dog in her devotion, but one cannot expect a young, uneducated girl to take on such responsibility."

Armand frowned. "I agree." There was slight hesitancy in his voice as he went on. "*Mon ami*, I am not certain you fully realize the dangerous fineness of balance in which Harriet's mind hangs."

"Oh, I think I do," he replied stonily. "Even though she prefers not to give me firsthand evidence of it. Do you think it does not trouble me night and day that the slightest false move now might be fatal? Why else do you think I am so anxious about leaving her?"

Armand leaned back in his elegant chair covered with rich gold French brocade and lit a cigar. "The solution stares you in the face, *hein*?" He let out smoke through his nostrils. "You must remain with her."

"I can't do that. The company is rocking, and I cannot afford another lost season."

Armand stared at him, the cigar halfway to his mouth. "It would not be a lost season. You have a new agent—young but competent. He would conduct the business in Canton at your directions."

"I am a merchant and must be there to supervise him. You, of all people, should understand that," said Rupert.

"But . . . under the circumstances—"

"The circumstances are that I am Torrington and the company is my responsibility," Rupert told him with as much conviction as he could muster. "I have my shareholders to consider. The company must come first."

"*Mon Dieu*, that is cold!" Armand got to his feet in an unusual explosion of emotion. "Harriet is your *wife*."

Rupert drank deeply of his wine, then held out his

glass to be refilled. "I think you know that is no longer true. Our marriage is broken." At Armand's darkening expression he added savagely, "Come, she confides all else to you, why not that? She will be glad to see me go."

"No . . . no, *mon ami*," was the overeffusive protest.

"She regards me as Edward's murderer." As he said it, Rupert felt an echo of that flame-filled night in his ears and mind.

A hand fell on his shoulder and gripped it hard. "It is the shock . . . only the shock. It will pass. Give her time—a short while to accept what she cannot find it in herself to admit. How could you have known such a thing would happen? *Alors*, you both could have been away at a dinner party . . . a ball—"

"But we weren't," cried Rupert with savage force, sending his glass crashing to the ground with the need to rise. "I was in the one place I should never have been. That condemns me forever in her eyes." He swung around to Armand. "Do you think I cannot see it each time she turns from me, each time she shrinks from my touch? By God, she does not have to condemn me with words—each day of our lives since that night she has expressed it in everything she does."

Armand regarded him with embarrassed gravity. "And for this you will leave her?"

The savagery went from him, and he felt drained of energy. "I . . . my presence distresses her further."

"You will not stay to vindicate yourself?"

He pushed his hand through his hair and sighed deeply. "When the battle is lost in one area, it is essential to take up arms elsewhere. I intend to go to Canton for the trading season, and nothing will alter my decision."

"So, you intend to desert her!"

He turned away and leaned on the mantelpiece. "Is it desertion when my departure is best for her?" When there was no answer to the question, he turned back to surprise something in the Frenchman's eyes. "You are in love with her."

There was a momentary pause. "*Oui* . . . not as you, with the fire of youth, but in my own way."

It was the final defeat. "I suppose I should have guessed before. Well, what would you do in my place?"

Armand had no hesitation. "What my conscience dictated."

"That is why I am going to Canton."

It was a small sound, but it broke the stillness and Harriet's intensity of concentration. It must not be Rupert so soon! She dragged her gaze away from the great blackened mound of stone and wood, expecting to feel the touch of his hand that filled her with such loathing.

The woman stood a few feet away, looking at Harriet with such an expression of peace on her face it held her attention completely. Her age was difficult to guess because of the smooth broadness of her features and the loose tunic and trousers that concealed her shape, but something about her mouth and eyes suggested that she had seen a large slice of life go by and had come to terms with it.

She gave a little bow. "Wah-Lin, mother of Wei-Li."

While part of her cried out against the disturbance

of her vigil, Harriet was drawn to the woman who had appeared as if from nowhere. Why she had come was not clear, but there was a definite purpose in her approach, and it did not suggest anything evil.

The woman drew closer and smiled. "Wah-Lin, mother of Wei-Li."

Suddenly a fierce figure in a dark blue cotton dress came between them, waving her arms at the Chinese woman and attempting to protect Harriet. "Go away! We've got no money for you. Go away, or I'll fetch the pleece."

At that moment Harriet realized what the woman had been telling her, and she put a hand on Bessie's arms. "No . . . wait. She does not want money. Listen to what she has to say."

The woman smiled again and nodded. "Yes. No want money. Wah-Lin, mother of Wei-Li."

Harriet went to her, ignoring Bessie's pleas to go back to where there were others around, where it would be safe. "Your daughter died in the fire with my son," she said, throbbing with fellowship, remembering the petal-smooth face of the young amah engaged to look after Edward. "Why have you sought me out?"

Still smiling, Wah-Lin began to move away. "You come." After a few steps she looked back and beckoned gently. "You come."

In Harriet's mind there was just one thought. This woman was a mother who had lost her child, as she had done, yet she was smiling, wanting to share the secret of her tranquillity with the one person who had shared her loss that night. Harriet began to follow.

"*No*, madam," cried Bessie, seizing her arm. "You can't not go off with her. It's a trap. There's no knowing what she is going to do. You know what the captain said."

Harriet brushed the girl aside and began walking faster after the black-clad figure hurrying ahead, then turning to beckon before hurrying on again. Nothing must make her lose sight of Wah-Lin.

"Oh, dear, oh, dear," wailed Bessie, stumbling along behind and talking aloud to herself. "What am I to do? If I goes back for the captain, there's no knowing where she'll be taken, and we shan't not know where to look. If only he'd come right now . . . this minute. Oh, Lord, please make him come right now."

Wah-Lin turned off the track onto a narrow path between the trees. Harriet had seen Chinese people go along there as her sedan chair had carried her up to Sussex Hall and assumed that it led to some kind of community. But the path grew ever more narrow, and the trees denser. If there was a village ahead, it was certainly isolated and well hidden. Twigs and thorns caught at her clothes, but she hardly noticed them. The shawl slipped from her shoulders without causing her to stop. It was sweltering amid the dank humidity of semijungle, and the eternal coldness within her bones was easing with every step.

Edward is not dead. He was taken to the safety of a Chinese village with the amah and has been kept there until his identity was known. I am being led to him. Oh, dear God, he is there waiting for me.

Her heart was bursting with renewed hope, with returning feeling. Her lips silently mouthed the name she had been unable to speak. Already she could feel the soft, sweet warmth of her child in her arms; see the tear-filled, desperate blue eyes gazing at her, those of a lost child seeing his beloved parent again.

The sun dappling through the trees partially obscured her vision of the woman hurrying with such sense of purpose ahead. Harriet began to push faster through the undergrowth, almost running. To lose sight of Wah-Lin now would be disastrous. The path wound and twisted as it penetrated deeper into the dark green world. Birds no longer sang, but creatures stirred in the dense tangle of greenery as they passed—creatures that lived their life in hiding until they struck swiftly and silently.

Soon . . . soon she must be there. She would see his sturdy figure coming toward her in unsteady, fumbling steps . . . would hear him call "*Mama!*" Her throat grew agonizingly tight; her breast ached with all she had suffered. Breathing became a labored agony of gasps as she threw herself forward into the solid mass of foliage that now blotted the path from sight.

Edward!

Light broke into the emerald depth; growth fell away on all sides. The clearing was a magical place from the pages of folklore. A great shaft of sunlight beamed down to silver the tumbling cascade of a stream while turning the rearing curved trees into the vaulted nave of a great jade cathedral.

Harriet gazed around wildly. Wah-Lin had disappeared with unbelievable swiftness. Where was the village? The woman who had cared for Edward? Where was the hovel in which he had been kept until she should come? Where was the tiny, stumbling figure coming to greet her?

"Edward," she whispered in trembling tones, spinning around in a frenzied attempt to look in every direction at once. Then louder: "Edward." It was impossible to swallow, for her chest and throat seemed paralyzed. *"Edward!"* she cried in a great moaning sob as she ran about the clearing, feeling a return of the nightmare moments when they had dragged her from the blazing house. The interior of his room had been brilliant with yellow light, and she now saw that same brilliance in the sunshaft, heard the crackling flames in the sound of water tumbling from the waterfall.

Madness took her by the throat as she realized it had all been a delusion. Edward was truly gone—consumed by the flames that had consumed her own soul that night. This was some terrible macabre trick, a torment of hell. She had been led along the path to purgatory, and she must enter.

It was blacker than she realized and her body suffered blow after blow as she twisted and writhed. Terrible sounds echoed in her head; cries that came from her own throat put the curse of everlasting anguish upon the head of him who had given her Edward and taken him from her again. Around and around she spun; then she began falling in a ghastly travesty of motion that repeated the fall over and over without her ever hitting the bottom of the chasm.

When she finally felt the solid layer beneath her, the curses had stopped pouring from her lips, the sounds of the roaring inferno had softened into the splashing of water, and the freezing chill of her bones had melted to leave her bathed in perspiration.

There was moss beneath her spread fingers, vivid green and with an iridescent beetle clambering across its uneven surface. It was hard going, and the creature was being showered with fine spray, but it struggled on toward its destination. Harriet watched it through eyes drenched with tears, unwilling to pull her exhausted body from the ground. The demons had escaped from her, and there was a warm lassitude in limbs that had been icy for three months.

The beetle dropped out of sight, and she lifted her gaze to discover that she was not alone.

His hair and beard hung long and gray and wispy, merging with the gray gown he wore. His frame was so slight it was amazing that he was alive, but a glance at the vitality apparent in his face told her it was the spirit, not the body, that was the true essence of the man. She knew immediately that he was what the Chinese called a holy man: a soothsayer. It became clear then why she had been led to this place by another sorrowing mother. Such men were reputed to be in touch with the spirits of those who had passed from this life into the next.

There was no smile on his face, just a gentle tranquillity that dispensed with such transitory moods as happiness, sorrow, or anger, yet Harriet knew he was well aware of why she was there and he welcomed her. There was some kind of opening in the bank beside the waterfall—hardly a cave, more of a shallow displacement of rocks—that must be his place of contemplation. The Chinese had said this jungle was a place of bad *fung-shui*, but the presence of such a man surely disproved that.

She approached him slowly. His nod was encouraging, but she needed no reassurances. This man would be her salvation. When she reached him, he turned into the hermitage, plainly expecting her to follow. It smelled particularly Oriental inside with the inevitable burning joss sticks and rice, but her full attention was caught by a rocky shelf like a natural altar, upon which was a wooden carving of a twisted dragon painted in the lurid colors beloved by the Chinese and with features exaggerated to awesome proportions. It was the soothsayer's talisman, and some arrangement of the rocks above allowed a pale gray-green light to filter through a gap onto the figure to illumine it, giving it a spectral aura.

The old man indicated the wooden beast. "Shu-Lung knows many things."

Harriet was surprised. "You speak English?"

He shook his head. "I speak many tongues and no tongue. When Shu-Lung speaks, I speak."

His voice had an echoing quality in that small cell-like area that suggested it was separate from the man, coming from some presence above. Some strange mystic peace descended on her.

"You know of my son?" she asked on a breath.

Black tranquil eyes gazed deeply into hers. "The spirit wanders and cries aloud at the place of fire. Here it is at rest."

"Edward's spirit is here?"

She needed to hear him confirm the fact.

"Shu-Lung has captured the wandering spirit. It ran from the place of fire. It could not reach you there.

All is now possible. In this place the spirit may rest before moving on."

"Moving on," she cried sharply. "Where . . . when?"

He put an aged hand on hers with the lightest of touches. "It will not move on until you release it. Shu-Lung controls the ways to further life."

Caught up in a passion of relieved emotion, she clung to his hand with a beseeching clasp. "Does . . . does he forgive me?"

In a calm smile that made her anxiety seem foolish, he nodded. "The spirit is happy that you have come at last."

She stayed in that clearing, finding peace and a return to sanity against the gentle sounds of falling water and the rustle of foliage in the faint breeze. The old man sat on a stone, lost in contemplation, but his silent, withdrawn presence soothed her beyond belief until she was able to leave.

It seemed necessary to make some kind of offering—as one did in church—but the soothsayer shook his head.

"Shu-Lung needs only a bowl of rice. When the spirit calls again, it will be sufficient."

"When may I come again?" she asked softly.

He turned his head away as if to end the communion. "The wind carries the voice into the soul. Then is the time."

A certain knowledge of the way back sent her off across the clearing, pausing only to smile at a girl in dark blue whose face was terrified and streaked with tears.

"It's all right, Bessie, we are going home now."

* * *

"She went off straightaway, and I couldn't not stop her, Captain. I tried, reely I did, but it was like she had gone away somewhere."

Bessie was almost beside herself, clutching her apron and crying as shc tried to tell him of the afternoon's events. He listened with a growing sense of impotence.

"She went through them trees like someone possessed, crying out Master Edward's name like he was in there somewhere. And when we reached this clearing it was like she suddenly went mad—right out of her mind." The enormous eyes gazed up at him with a hint of what she had felt at the time. "Round and round she went as if she couldn't see anything—bumping into trees and moaning out loud. Then she fell in a heap on the ground. I . . . I thought she was dead, Captain. I never see anyone go on like that before, nor never do I want to again."

Rupert swallowed hard. "What happened then, Bessie?"

The girl tried to take a hold on herself. "This funny old man come right out of the rocks. It was like he was a ghost."

"What kind of man."

"A Chinese man—old and gray—but not like them you see walking about. He looked like . . . well, he didn't not seem real somehow. They went off between the rocks, talking together as if they already knew each other; then they come back and just sat there, saying nothing." She resorted to tears again. "I waited and waited, wondering what I ought to do. Then the mistress got up and came home. When we got back on the track, she didn't not even look back to where it happened—like she had forgotten all about it." Her tears increased. "Oh, Captain, did I do aright?"

Rupert patted her shoulder absently, caught up in a great surge of hope. "You have always been most loyal, Bessie. No one could ask more of you than that."

It seemed to cheer the girl, for she wiped her eyes and tried to smile. "One bit of good come out of it, I will say. The mistress ate everything on her dinner tray tonight."

When the girl had gone, Rupert sat for a long time looking out at the stars. The doctor had promised him that the state of shock would pass, and it seemed that the events Bessie described had broken Harriet's pattern of grieving—the pattern that had shut him completely out of her life. For three months he had endured her silence, her shrinking away whenever he drew near, her refusal to share with him their combined grief and, by sharing, making it less. For three months he had told himself it was the reaction of shock; had tried to banish from his ears the sound of that terrible anguished accusation. "Where *were* you?"; had hidden from others his fear that she would hold him forever in her heart as the real cause of Edward's death.

Now it appeared she had returned to normality, and he was afraid. Whereas it would have been the most natural thing to do to go to his wife's room on hearing Bessie's story, he held back, knowing the truth would be there in Harriet's face the minute he saw her. His courage was missing now, when he needed it most. He sat on as the evening lengthened into night, lowering the bottle of port steadily until he had lost enough command of himself to dare face what he had earlier shunned.

The house was small in comparison with Sussex Hall, and he arrived at Harriet's door quicker than he wished. Hesitating for a moment, he almost turned away, but the knowledge that he must face her eventually led him to knock. Bessie answered and slipped past him into the corridor, leaving him to enter. The lighting was dim. Harriet turned her head toward him as she sat in the chair, and he was reminded of that occasion when he had approached her with his heart in his hands, unaware of what awaited him.

They looked at each other for a long time, neither moving, the flow of love going only in one direction. Powerless to turn and walk away, he said hoarsely, "I shall be leaving for Canton at the end of the week."

She turned back to her book.

"Since I shall be away for six months, I shall leave instructions with Chalmers at the bank. If there is anything you want, he will be happy to be of service . . . and if you should need to reach me, he will ensure that a message is sent."

She looked up at that. "I shall not need you—*ever*."

He left and went back to open another bottle of port. The decision had been made for him.

It was plain from the start that Nugent Goddard had been right when he warned Rupert that Sing-Li would bear a grudge for life. Even as he approached Canton, the normal formalities required by Chinese mercantile officials were mysteriously delayed when the company's ships passed upriver. The ritual of "measuring the ship" took twice as long as usual and had to be done with great care several times before the men were satisfied. The necessary clearing documents were then lost and took up to a week to find, obliging the ships to stay at anchor in the river during that period. The crews grew angry and restless, but Rupert knew there was nothing he could do.

When he eventually reached Canton and took up residence in the factory, the persecution continued there. Sing-Chong, the old comprador who had been so loyal during the siege of the factory, had been imprisoned and no one knew his eventual fate. The reputation of Chinese prisons suggested he would most likely die in there, as he had wished, still defying a Manchu official.

Hardly a day passed without some minor official's presenting himself at the factory to demand fines and taxes, issue complaints against the company, or present trumped-up cases of misbehavior by Rupert's employees. In addition, the eagle eyes of Sing-Li's officers missed none of the articles brought in on the ships as Rupert's personal items of trade and not listed on the manifest. Knowing the Chinese fascination with clocks and "singsongs," as they called music boxes, Rupert was not surprised when they demanded the handing over of all such articles as payment of fictitious fines and levies or as bribes to withdraw charges against sailors who had been seized and held prisoner on suspicion of offensive behavior in the streets of Canton.

Greed was a major vice of most mandarins, and the working models so cleverly made by English and French artisans delighted them beyond measure. Dancing ladies, singing birds, and tumbling clowns that performed at the turn of a key were a source of absorbed wonderment to men like Sing-Li.

The ships of the Battle Trading Company brought in an endless supply of these delights; no sooner had the officials set eyes on them in the course of their normal inspection of the cargo than a messenger came from the mandarin to enact a ridiculous scene that ended with Rupert's reluctant surrender of the toys. The new young agent employed by the company protested to his employer time and again at his meek acquiescence to the mandarin's demands, but Rupert sharply silenced him with a reminder that all the articles were his personal property and had nothing to do with normal company trade.

But normal trade was not going well. The Chinese merchants seemed loath to deal with the young man who had replaced Valentine Bedford or with Rupert, who now spoke enough of their language to read into their words the fact that they were acting under orders. The regular dealers who had gone to Companie Lascard on Rupert's banishment the previous season remained with Armand. New ones were reluctant to come forward.

It was of the difficulties facing Rupert that Nugent Goddard spoke one evening early in January, when he was dining privately with the man who had become a friend.

"We at the consulate appreciate that the situation is most definitely vindictive, but sadly there is very little we can do to ease it. The Chinese system of communications is guaranteed to frustrate all attempts at protest or discussion, and any request by Mr. Parkes or myself for a meeting can be lost, delayed, or just ignored if the mood takes them."

Rupert clapped him on the shoulder. "Don't distress yourself on my account. I knew before I set off for Canton that something like this would probably occur. After that affair last year it was inevitable."

The diplomat regarded him with a frown. "I must say you are taking it all damned lightly."

"What other way would be sensible?"

"But you were so full of fire last year, so hell-bent on maintaining a principle that you defied Sing-Li to the extent of personal risk."

"That was last year. A lot has happened since then."

"Yes . . . yes . . . but I would expect the tragedy to heighten your feelings against these people."

"Would you?" Rupert said it with careful nonchalance and spoke of something else that told his friend he wished to leave the subject, but it did not remove the frown on Goddard's brow.

Over dinner they chatted of England, of steeplechasing, and of rowing regattas, and it was not until both were comfortably settled with a decanter between them that Goddard brought up the subject of the forthcoming war.

"We have received an indication that our troops are embarked and setting out from England. Those coming from the Cape will set out next month, and the main bulk of the force is assembling from various stations in India ready to take ship immediately."

Rupert leaned forward. "How many men?"

"Nothing official, of course, but I have heard the figure of ten thousand mentioned—that is, excluding those already garrisoned here. The French are sending slightly less." He smiled. "It is already being said that General Hope Grant, who has been nominated to lead our troops, wishes we had the expedition to ourselves. He apparently has a dislike of combined operations—particularly with the French."

Rupert raised his eyebrows. "Clash of personalities?"

"Let us hope not, for the sake of the men beneath their command."

"Well said! We had such a situation in the Crimea—with our own commanders, as you know. There are those who blame the loss of the Light Brigade on that, but I think that is going too far." He was away in thought to those foreign fields. "It takes a very special kind of man to lead an army. He has to make instant decisions under the most terrible stress and discomfort. Mostly it is instinct that magically comes to his aid, but all men are human and make mistakes. When a military leader makes a misjudgment or error, he does not deprive himself of part of his fortune or the top dealers in silk—he sacrifices the lives of other men. He has to stand and watch helplessly as scarlet-coated figures fall one after the other and acknowledge that he has ordered the execution of several hundred men who will leave widows and orphans in England. Whatever a man's private character, it is his judgment and behavior in the field that matter to those whose lives he holds in his hand."

There was a short pause, and then Nugent Goddard said, "That was a speech from the heart, if ever I heard one. Whose defense were you conducting?"

Rupert rose restlessly and turned to face his friend.

"I think I shall never stop until someone listens and applauds."

"The plight of the diplomat is even worse, my friend. A wrong word or action at the wrong time can set nation against nation and thousands battling in a bloodbath in which he cannot even make his feeble contribution. Your officers witness the tragedy of their mistakes; we sit comfortable and well fed to read of ours in impersonal reports." He sighed. "I sometimes wish I could serve my country in a more sacrificial way."

"I think you do well enough as it is. To live out here in the East and uphold the dignity of British sovereignty against all the provocations and insults dealt you by these people is sacrifice indeed. I think I could not do it."

"But you are doing it, old fellow."

"Eh?"

"I had not expected such meek acceptance of Sing-Li's persecution."

His smile was a little strained. "Perhaps you do not yet know me well enough."

"Obviously not." He sat back then with the air of a man about to surprise another. "As it happens, my daily grind *is* shortly to take a more adventurous turn. Harry Parkes is to go with the army to assist with negotiations, and I am to accompany him as one of his staff."

"You are? That is splendid," cried Rupert with enthusiasm he could not hold back.

Goddard looked at him curiously. "That was said as if you expected to be there yourself," he said with quiet accusation.

Chapter Seventeen

Christmas and New Year's passed unnoticed by Harriet. This year the season had been neglected because Harriet was caught up in the salvation of her meetings with the Rice Dragon, as Harriet called Shu-Lung.

On her frequent visits to the soothsayer she always took the required bowl of rice as an offering, and in return, the old man gave her the reassurance that allowed her to live again. During those hours she spent bathed in the peace of that glade beside the stream many truths were revealed to her, and she wandered in the realms of her father's studies like an explorer in the volumes of time.

They spoke of inner thoughts and realities—some of which had been hidden from her until the old man made them plain. He used the language of ancient China, in riddles and mystic phrases that were difficult to unravel, but whether they were in English or Chinese, she found herself able to understand him and reply. As time went by, she understood more and more of the lore and wisdom of centuries past . . . and of centuries to come.

Time sped. Left in peace by friends and neighbors, and with the devoted Bessie as her companion, Harriet took up work again on her father's book, going back to its opening pages and embellishing the text with her wider knowledge and adding a spark of passionate understanding that all his learning had not given him. But overlying it all was her communion with Edward's spirit made through the Rice Dragon. Shu-Lung would not send it on its way until she released it . . . and that she could not yet do.

Bessie still grumbled and protested that "it wasn't not right," but the girl accompanied her mistress without the fear of that first day and waited silently until she was ready to leave again. Harriet had regained her strength and health; she managed her household affairs with her old competence; she went shopping and spoke with gracious charm to those she met. But her mind remained closed to one aspect of her life, and everyone was aware of it.

It was on a day at the end of January that she returned to the house to find a surprise visitor awaiting her in the salon.

"Armand, whatever are you doing in Hong Kong?" she exclaimed, going to meet him with hands outstretched.

"Combining business with pleasure, *ma chère*." He kissed her fingers, then kept her hands clasped in his own. "*Bien*, how much better you look! Already, in six weeks, I see a difference."

She smiled at him warmly. "Six weeks! Is it really that long since you were last here?"

"Ah, now I am devastated. You have not missed me."

Drawing her hands away, she turned to ring the bell for tea. "How could I help missing such a good friend?" Sinking into a chair and waving an invitation to him to take another beside her, she went on. "But I had resigned myself to your absence during the trading season. You will take tea with me?"

"Of course." He flicked out the skirts of his dark green coat and sat with the grace of a sophisticated Frenchman.

"So what is your errand of business this time?" she asked, suspecting that he had done as on the last occasion and invented a flimsy excuse in order to keep an eye on her.

"Companie Lascard, as you know, also has interests in Shanghai, and I have things to discuss with my agent up there. We agreed to meet in Hong Kong as a convenient halfway place."

"How long shall you be staying?" she asked, concentrating on the tea tray brought in by a soft-shoed houseboy.

"A week, at least. May I hope we can meet frequently?"

"Of course. I should feel extremely ill-served if you neglected me." Pouring tea, she added, "But, Armand, I do not need to be watched, like an invalid. I am quite well now."

"So I may see for myself, *ma chère*." He put out a hand to take the cup from her. "But cannot a friend be allowed the privilege of calling whenever he is in Hong Kong?"

She smiled warmly. "You have proved yourself more than a friend over these past months. I have depended upon you." With her head to one side she teased him. "How do you vindicate your protestation of being a merchant first and foremost?"

His returning smile was a little sad. "I once said to you that with the years came the wisdom of fallibility that put success before friendship. *Peut-être* . . . but I have found that the foolishness of youth returns when one is fifty. It may be that I understand Aubrey Torrington after all. Age and loneliness do not make good partners."

She set her cup carefully into the shell-thin saucer. "Neither you nor Aubrey need have chosen to remain alone. There were many ladies, I am persuaded, who would have been glad to join you in matrimony." A smile forced its way through to belie the severity of her next words. "You do not pull at my heartstrings, Armand, or earn the slightest sympathy for your lonely plight. I fancy you did not wish for the restrictions of marriage when younger, so you cannot bewail the absence of its advantages now." Offering him an almond biscuit, she asked, "Is it a good year for silk? How is trade?"

He leaned back and sipped his tea. "The silk is *magnifique*. It is my hope to recoup the losses of two broken seasons in this one." Taking a bite from the biscuit, he said conversationally, "Rupert is in severe straits, I fear. Sing-Li could easily break him."

Slipped in so quietly, the reference to Rupert took her unawares, and her anger was the greater because of it.

"You need not call again if you intend to speak to me of him. You are well aware of my feelings. Is it your intention to hurt me?"

"Do you think he is not so hurt that he does not care whether Sing-Li breaks him or not? Is that *your* intention?"

She got to her feet in a passion that set her shaking. "Did he send you? I am contemptuous of him!"

Armand also rose. "He would not send anyone to you. He has given up hope . . . of everything. *Ma chère,* he is my friend also. Is it not my duty to tell you of his condition?"

"Your duty is done." Turning her back on him, she added icily, "Reaching the age of fifty has brought you more than a return of youthful foolishness. Suddenly you have acquired those virtues you previously held to be incompatible with trade. I prefer the Armand I first knew."

"And I the Harriet I first knew."

She swung around at that. "Then I shall understand why you visit me no longer." With bosom heaving she exclaimed, "I do not need friends. I do not need anyone."

"*Oui,* so I understand from the society of Hong Kong." He approached and stood searching her face with eyes grown wary. "There is one you need, *hein*? Do you not seek him out nearly every day."

Taken unawares again, she could only reply, "How do you know of that?"

He shrugged in Gallic fashion. "In Hong Kong there is little that is not known." He frowned. "It distresses me . . . yes, more than your hatred for Rupert."

Tightening up, she snapped. "It should not concern you at all."

"*Ah, oui,* it concerns me, as it concerns the Christian community. You are turning your back on the church, Harriet. This ritual . . . this communion you have . . . it is *pagan.*"

"Pagan? What is pagan?" she cried hotly. "It is no more pagan than the idols you have in your Church of Rome, Armand. It is no more pagan than praying to the unseen God for my dead child. It is no more pagan to offer Shu-Lung a bowl of rice than it is to put a wreath of flowers beneath the headstone bearing Edward's name. Of course I go there. His spirit is in that glade."

Armand seized her arms. "His spirit is in the church where his soul was entrusted to the Christian Lord."

In an anguish of memory she shook her head violently. "No, Armand, there is nothing in that churchyard but a headstone," she cried. "You know it as well as I do. Edward vanished that night up on that hill, and his spirit is still there. I *know* it is there."

He gripped her arms tightly. "No. His spirit was put to rest at his funeral. Go to the church, Harriet. Forget this dangerous ritual."

Growing still, she told him with all her heart in her words, "In the churchyard I feel nothing. Up there, with the Rice Dragon, he is close to me. Do not ask me to abandon him, for I cannot do it." Her eyes began to blur. "*I cannot do it.*"

A change came over him. The fierce grip softened into a hold full of caring. "*Ma chère*, you are wrong. You *do* need friends."

"Then be my friend," she implored. "Understand; don't condemn. The Rice Dragon has made me understand more things in life than I could hope to know. There is no right and wrong, black and white, fear and courage. All things are outside us, yet within us.

We do not live now but a thousand years ago—or a thousand years hence. Can you not see that this is not life but a plane of existence in a series of before and after?"

For a long time Armand looked at her, and she knew he was unable to step into the realms in which she could now wander with her eyes fully open.

"You say Edward's spirit is in that place?"

"Yes . . . until I am ready to let it move on."

"You will never give it up."

"Yes . . . yes," she cried, wanting to believe. "Soon I shall give the word."

He shook his head with heavy unhappiness. "That man has put a dangerous temptation within you. Can you not see it is like opium? The Rice Dragon has drawn you into a false happiness from which you will never dare escape."

Rupert was in the cabin with O'Hare when Sing-Li's officials walked in at the precise moment that he was demonstrating to the Irish captain the performance of the latest clockwork toy he had bought. It showed a marvelous combination of ingenuity and mechanical skill. An orchestra of monkeys clad in prerevolution French costume and white wigs played their instruments with graceful accomplishment, at the turn of a key that also set in motion the music box beneath their podium. It was the most colorful and intricate piece of sophisticated nonsense Rupert had yet brought into Canton on his ships, and the eyes of the Chinese officers grew bright with wonderment and avarice as they watched.

Although he was conscious of their entry, he made no attempt to turn to them, letting the clockwork run its full course and pointing out the clever movements of the monkey musicians to O'Hare, who exclaimed long and enthusiastically. When the mechanism stopped, Rupert was prepared to devote the next hour or so to his unwelcome visitors but for once, they found no fault with either cargo or documents and hurried away within a matter of minutes.

"Mmm, I wonder what has precipitated such urgency," he murmured to O'Hare.

"Aye, sorr, 'tis full of wonder I am." The man's grin was broad and joyful. "Am I to be puttin' this away now?"

Rupert looked at the elaborate music box and nodded. "Be very careful. It is highly valuable."

Just how valuable was soon demonstrated when a summons to appear before the mandarin arrived at the factory within the hour. Rupert's mouth tightened. What excuse would Sing-Li use to steal his property this time?

He kept the sedan chair waiting for half an hour while he finished some paper work. During the journey he reflected on the other time he had visited the man and the result of that meeting. Two men had lost their lives because of it, and the feeling of guilt still remained inside him.

It could have been that other time. The boat awaited him, as before, the boatman in loose blue clothes and cone-shaped hat giving the impression that he had done nothing since last taking Rupert across in his boat guided by the long pliant pole. His heavy tread once again echoed in the silence of the high, austere chambers of the outer sanctum, and the great porcelain griffins standing about the room stared at him with eyes and bodies dulled by condensation.

The audience room was almost chilly when Rupert entered, but his body burned with a fever that had begun on receipt of the summons. There were no tidbits this time, no teamaking utensils, no chair. It was clear Sing-Li had no intention of treating Rupert as a business associate. He held the advantage and was prepared to state his demands.

There was no sign of it on his face—it remained smooth and placid—but his eyes were deep and devious. The back of Rupert's neck prickled again.

"You are allowed to stand *there*," cried the mandarin, pointing swiftly with his hand elongated by the grotesque fingernails.

Rupert stopped at the spot indicated—far enough away from the ornate chair to obviate any suggestion that his head was higher than Sing-Li's.

"It is possible to see now that you will never be the son of your father," said the high, piping voice. "It is my regrettable observation that you bring dishonor and disgrace to your ancestors. A man of my race would not wish to live under such circumstances."

Rupert said nothing.

"I have been a patient man, but my patience now runs out. You were ordered to pay a fine for bringing into Canton a forbidden substance. You did not pay it. What is more, you left this place with guile and deceit in the dead of night. You have broken all the laws of China and must be punished. The bars of our prisons are strong, the darkness of the cells everlasting."

Still Rupert remained quiet, but his hands tightened into fists at his sides.

"I see you have learned the wisdom of dumbness. It is a thousand pities you did not know such signs of respect last time you were here." With no change of tone he went on. "You have a wondrous singsong on your ship *Cork*. I will accept it in settlement of the fine. You must prepare it in a box for my messengers. They will come to your factory tonight."

Rupert shook his head, "Regrettably it cannot be done. The singsong goes to Shanghai when *Cork* sails."

"Shanghai. *Shanghai!* It cannot go to Shanghai. I have ordered you to surrender it in payment of your fine. It will be easy for me to add to it the number of taels you should have paid, if you do not obey me."

Rupert found it difficult to sound unemotional. "I cannot pay the taels. Already this season I have lost too much money."

Sing-Li smiled in triumph. "Then I must have the singsong."

"The singsong must be taken to Shanghai," repeated Rupert firmly. "It is already promised to a mandarin in Sinho." He delayed long enough to note that Sing-Li was as shattered by the news as he had expected, then added, "In one month I have another ship arriving from England. There will be singsongs on it."

"As wondrous as this one?"

"I shall not know until it arrives."

"I am told there are animals dressed as barbarian musicians, making music with pieces of wood. I am told that these animals smile and nod and their feet tap on the floor. I am told that they make sounds that have never been heard before—so beautiful it is like the almond blossom brushing against the gates of the Celestial Kingdom. Am I told the truth?"

So great was Sing-Li's anxiety his hands beat on the arms of his chair, his long fingernails clicking together with the vibration.

"That is only half the truth," said Rupert with deliberation. "The eyes of the animals open and shut, as do their mouths. They are of exquisite design, and the music they play is sweeter than any singsong ever made. It is my opinion that the mandarin who owns this will be much envied—a man of lesser eminence than yourself, I understand."

Sing-Li's eyes seemed to sink further into his full face and take on a blackness that suggested they were looking into his own devilish soul.

"When is the singsong to go to Shanghai—to this unworthy mandarin?"

Keeping his voice steady, Rupert said, "*Cork* sails at first light on the day after tomorrow. When she returns, she will have on board a selection of merchandise in which there might well be something of equal value to the singsong."

"Then let that thing be sent to Shanghai, and I will have the singsong. A man of lesser eminence will bow to my wishes."

Rupert made plain his unease. "If I do not send what I have promised, it will go badly for my trade in Shanghai. I am already in debt and cannot afford to lose any more cargoes this year or my company will be finished." He thought for a moment. "I will give you *two* singsongs instead of this one I must take to Shanghai."

Sing-Li leaned back, well satisfied. "*Three* sing-songs!"

Heaving an audible sigh, Rupert reluctantly agreed. "Very well."

There were several moments of silence. Then Sing-Li waved a languid hand. "You are allowed to leave."

He turned and was nearly across the room when the mandarin stopped him. "Mr. Torrington."

Rupert turned back. "Yes?"

"We understand you have not brought your women with you this year. That is good. You are learning to obey the laws of China."

Choking with the desire to attack then, Rupert forced himself to stay silent as he left the room he would remember all his life.

The following morning a letter arrived from Rupert's banker, asking him to return to Hong Kong immediately as the health of Mrs. Torrington had grown worse again. Hurried arrangements to sail were made, and Rupert made it known to his fellow merchants and to Nugent Goddard that he was called away to his sick wife and was leaving immediately. The young agent was given powers of discretion, and Rupert paid a last visit to one of his lorchas.

O'Hare was awaiting him and grinned as he approached. "The plan is laid, sorr?"

"Yes," Rupert told him grimly. "The rest depends entirely on you. Don't fail me."

"Have I done so yet, sorr?" He pointed to the corner of the cabin. "There's itself, large as life and very easy to see in the dark."

Rupert nodded. "Good. I believe they will leave it until the last minute before they come. Now, remember what I say. Make no sign that you know they are aboard, or there might be the devil to pay for you and the crew. Make no attempt to stop them . . . and once they have gone, weigh anchor and get as far from Canton as you can. Oh, and for God's sake, don't let anyone wind that thing up."

The little Irishman studied him for a moment. "I'll not ask why it's so anxious ye are for the Chinese to steal the band o' monkeys, for I've a feeling I'd be better off not knowing. But I'd like to tell ye at this minute, sorr, that I niver did believe you'd lost all the fight in ye. Wait, says I to them all, and ye'll see the captain is playing a deep game. And so I believe ye are."

Rupert gave a strained smile. "I'm grateful for your loyalty, O'Hare. I had men like you in my company, and I have never forgotten them." He held out his hand. "Good-bye."

O'Hare wiped his hand on a rag tied to his belt. "Good-bye, sorr . . . and may the angels smile on ye up there."

"Up where?"

He grinned. "It isn't hard to guess where ye're going, Captain. Sure, and if I wasn't a seafaring man, I'd be right there beside you like O'Donnighan's twin."

Rupert took a long last look at Canton as the lorcha made its way downriver. He would never return. The first part of his plan had worked splendidly. Chalmers of the bank in Hong Kong had followed out his instructions to the letter with that lie about Harriet's health. Now all that remained was the second part. O'Hare would not set a foot wrong, he was sure, and

Sing-Li had fallen into the trap as easily as Rupert had known he would. Last year the mandarin had sent his henchmen to steal the opium under cover of darkness and been foiled by his arrival with a pistol; this time they would be sent aboard *Cork* to secure the music box at all costs.

After three months of viewing Rupert's apparent weakness Sing-Li was filled with confidence, and the beautiful toy was more than he could resist. The suggestion that a mandarin junior in station to him was to receive that which he coveted was the last pretense in a waiting game designed for deadly revenge. Rupert had no doubts that his careful plan would succeed.

He fell into a reverie as the masts of other ships passed unnoticed. The armed Chinese would steal aboard *Cork* under cover of darkness and, meeting with nothing more than apparently sleeping watchmen, would carry off their prize. Sing-Li would wait impatiently on his thronelike chair until the box was carried in and placed before him. Then he would descend, eyes gleaming and breathing fast with pure excitement. He would take hold of the key and wind the mechanism to the full. The monkey musicians would begin thier complicated pattern of movements, and Sing-Li's smooth, round, sadistic face would press closer as he thrilled to the wonders of Western ingenuity. But three-quarters through the complete program . . . !

Rupert's hands gripped the rail along the top of the bulwark. It might be four years since he cast off his scarlet coat, but he had not forgotten his knowledge of explosives.

* * *

It was intolerable! How dare they come to her house and say such things? Harriet was still trembling with anger half an hour after they had left and could not settle to her work. Bessie should never have admitted them. If only she had been out when they called! But they would have come again. Those people always did.

Pillars of the church and do-gooders. The latter a clutch of pale, straight-faced women in modest gowns, who sat as Nanny had done all that time ago on first entering Pagoda House, as if they were in a den of iniquity. The two men with them, ministers of the Protestant Church, had merely looked saintly and embarrassed.

They had come to offer help and brotherhood, they said, to someone who seemed to have "Lost the way." There had been some little excuse for the ministers; it was the duty of their calling to see that their flock was complete. But the busybody women had been spinsters or childless wives who had turned to the church in their loneliness. What did any one of them know of that bond between mother and child?

Their disapproving faces, their pinched, condemning features had sent Harriet's temper soaring. They reminded her of those women in England who had looked down their noses at her spirited conversation with gentlemen at parties on subjects they considered unsuitable for women to discuss. If any one of them had truly suffered, she would have come with sympathy and understanding, reaching out in compassion. Not in frigid piety!

But she had seen very clearly it was useless trying to impart anything of her new dimension of understanding to such people. Armand had refused to listen, even to allow her an explanation of her actions—Armand, her closest friend, had warned her of danger ahead if she continued to visit the Rice Dragon. Now these people had felt it their duty to rescue her from the path of sin.

There was only one person who would have known there was no sin in understanding the wisdom of another culture. Professor Deane would have applauded her new vision. Her father would have known it was not necessary to abandon one principle to accept another. He always said blessed was the mind that was open to receive all knowledge, yet kept the strands from a tangle of incomprehension.

Suddenly she missed him more than at any time since his death. Her sympathy with ethnic cultures had been sown in her by him; how cruel that he was not able to share with her the experience of all that combined study. He would have stood beside her to counter the narrow-minded conceptions of right and wrong that had been flung at her that afternoon.

Going to the desk, she toyed with the pages scattered upon it. The book had been going well, yet she now felt restless and unable to pick up the thread she had left the day before. From the window she could see between the white dignity of banking premises and the half-constructed walls of a hotel the deep blue of a bay that never failed to astonish even those who saw it day after day. How unchanging the ocean, yet beneath the surface many things remained hidden.

Because she had brought her own hidden aspects to the surface, people threw up their hands in horror. A great sigh escaped her. Of course, she had known what was being said about her in Hong Kong. It was impossible not to miss the strange glances as she passed, the cool nods of those who had once been friendly. Some had even gone so far as to draw their children closer at her approach. Many times she recalled the hostility of the villagers to Aubrey Torrington, and she felt his sadness with her own. But she would not bow beneath it. If she discontinued her visits to the Rice Dragon, there would be nothing left. Not all the pious spinsters and meek churchmen could give her what she found during those times of communion with an old Chinese soothsayer.

Fighting down the feelings of rage and impotence their visit had aroused in her, she sat at the desk and tried to concentrate on the work awaiting her. Yet her gaze kept rising to fasten on the waters of the harbor just visible through a narrow gap between buildings. It made her uneasy. It suggested that her life consisted only of that narrow blue strip, and yet, if she only knew where to look, the whole wonderful ocean would be visible, as it had been from Sussex Hall.

She must have sat day dreaming for some while, for when a slight sound made her turn into the room, it was as if she had traveled back in time. He stood just inside the door. The scarlet jacket was vivid in the changing light of late afternoon; the dark blue overalls made him look taller than ever. Soft across his brow was a fall of creamy fair hair that contrasted strikingly with dark, dark eyes. Bemused, she stared in incomprehension as he moved toward her.

"If I startled you, I'm sorry," said Rupert.

She turned away, rose, and made for the door.

"There is no need. I have come just to say good-bye."

The words halted her. The shock of seeing the one person in the world she could not bear to look at had set her heart thudding and put a sudden feeling of sickness in her stomach. Why was he not in Canton? Why the scarlet—*Good-bye?* She spun around to face him, guessing everything in that moment. It made her more contemptuous of him than ever.

"I know you wish never to speak to me again, but I ask you just to listen—stay and listen," he said in a voice that was surprisingly husky.

When he moved several paces nearer, she did not retreat—just stiffened.

"I know that you are suffering—*what* you are suffering. I know that you will hold me responsible for as long as you live. I also know you have found your salvation in rejecting me and turning to that which has always fascinated you."

She saw his throat move as he swallowed.

"But Edward was also my son, and I can find my salvation only in taking revenge on those who murdered him. As you hate me with burning intensity, so I hate those who put the burning torch to the house that night—all those who have treated me and mine with such aggression since we first set foot here. The first act of vengeance has been successful. But that was only the beginning."

He waited as if he expected her to speak, but all she could do was stare at the rough serge jacket bare of gold embellishments and insignia, at the thick, shapeless overalls, at the heavy black boots.

"I enlisted in Giles Meredith's regiment this morning—took the queen's shilling. I am off to war, and every enemy who falls at my hands will die because of Edward, that is my vow."

He waited again, but she still could not bring herself to speak to him.

"I have instructed Chalmers at the bank to dispose of my shares in the company—I know of several men who will snap them up—and the money will be all yours to use as you wish. He will advise you on anything you want to know."

Then she spoke; *then* she put all her contempt and rejection into her words. "That is all it has ever been—the army. It is all you have ever cared for, all that fills your heart and mind. You abandoned your son that night to play soldiers. He died because you were not there to save him." She struggled to control her voice. "Now you have abandoned your true heritage to join a company of rough, uncouth cutthroats and lick the boots of those who threw you out. How can a man so demean himself?"

If she expected him to flinch, to see in his eyes the kind of pain that had been there on other occasions, she was wrong. This was a different man before her in the trappings of a shilling-a-day soldier.

"Why have you always condemned in me what you uphold so fiercely yourself?" he asked quietly. "When I first met you, it was those qualities that I loved—honesty, courage, loyalty to a cause, and the determination to follow a chosen path against all odds. I still love you, Harriet, even though those qualities have led you away from me and onto a course that brings censure from those around you. But because of that, I am free to follow my chosen course; I am released from my promise never again to go to war." He swallowed again. "If I return and you are gone, I shall know you have made the irreparable break between us. If I do not return . . . your decision will be made for you."

He took a long, long look at her, then turned away and left. She went back to her desk and recommenced work on her book as if she had not been interrupted. Her gaze did not stray once to the blue ocean beyond.

Chapter Eighteen

To young hot-blooded men the war was getting off to a slow start. The British grew increasingly aggravated over the delay in preparations by the French, who seemed, to them, inefficient and reluctant to start fighting. In truth, it was difficult for forces straight from France who had not the British advantage of bases in India, Singapore, and Hong Kong to supply their needs. They found themselves hopelessly short of baggage ponies and mules, not having understood the kind of terrain across which they had to pass, and plans were halted while supply officers went to Japan only to find the British from Hong Kong had already bought the best.

Relations were not improved between the allies when it was learned that the two forces were to establish separate camps along the China coast from which to launch their attacks completely independently. The British muttered darkly about wishing they had never agreed to the French's joining in on something they would handle much better alone; the French threw up their hands emotionally and declared that the arrogant British wanted to lay first claim to Peking and add it to their Empire. Hardly an auspicious opening to a combined desire to show Western strength to the treacherous Chinese!

On one thing the allies were agreed, however: They felt an aggressive resentment at the presence of American and Russian envoys, who explained their interest was that of "Neutral observers." As more than one soldier said, "They've come along to watch us die for the concessions they're going to get for nothing."

The British troops landed to establish a base at Talienwan, and the French encamped at Chefoo, across the Gulf of Pechili, to prepare for the start of their march on Peking. To reach the imperial city, there was really only one way for a foreign army on the march, and that was to follow the Pei-ho River through Tientsin straight up to that city of fable and corruption, of superlatives and atrocities, of beauty and evil. By this method the troops and animals were within reach of water all the way, and the supporting naval force could follow them with supplies and take off wounded back to the base camps.

But first, the rivers must be entered, and guarding its mouth were the Taku forts that had bombarded the British so mercilessly the previous summer and driven the envoys back to Hong Kong. And there were the formidable lines of chains and spars beneath the water to prevent ships from passing through. The memory of the humiliating defeat of those trying to ratify the Treaty of Tientsin made every man in that army anxious to teach the Chinese a lesson that would make their pigtails curl with fright.

At last the French were ready, having further delayed the assault by discovering that the landing place designated to them was so shallow they would be able to sail only within two miles of the shore and would have to struggle through the mud for the remaining distance. Much disgruntled, the British general agreed to let his allies join his own landing at Pehtang. One English wag, on hearing this, declared that the French were not so much afraid of two miles of mud as facing the Chinese with no one to hold their hands. That this opinion was taken up by the troops hardly helped.

As it turned out, they all had to struggle through mud to land at Pehtang, for the river was down and there was half a mile of stinking ooze on the foreshore. Rupert, fighting his way through it, reflected that even in the Crimea the mud had never smelled quite as bad, nor had he been laden down with fifty-six rounds of ammunition, a rolled greatcoat, three days' rations, eating utensils, two full water bottles, a haversack, and a pair of heavy boots slung around his neck to keep them dry.

The farther he advanced, the harder it was to pull each leg from the mud, for it caked on his coarse trousers to weight him down all the more. The cotton smock he had been issued for the campaign was plastered to his body by the August rains that beat down upon them all as they struggled in disorganized ranks across the foreshore. They had been given wicker helmets instead of shakos to protect them from heat stroke, but at that moment the wide brims were protecting their faces from the blinding rain.

But Rupert had seen enough of heat stroke along with fever and dysentery since he had enlisted. Until now he had been sleeping each night in a bell tent with thirteen other soldiers, feet together and fanned out into a circle, with rifles piled in the center. As a tall man he barely fitted into the radius of the tent and quickly realized how insanitary the system was. With so many crammed beneath an airless cone-shaped tent in temperatures of stifling proportions, sickness spread very rapidly. After the first night he had slipped beneath the canvas to sleep in the open and had been caught by an NCO, who ordered him back inside with a kick to help him on his way. Since then he had been content to stick only his head out . . . until it rained with tropical ferocity!

He preferrred to forget how he had slept on the ship from Hong Kong, jammed belowdesks amid the stench of vomit, urine, and tar for hour after hour, listening to the coarse ribaldry of his companions, their grumbles and sudden maudlin fears for wives and children left abandoned in England when they had sailed off four years before.

Earlier, in the barracks at Hong Kong, Rupert had established his relationship with his fellows, who had recognized a "toff" at once and ganged up defensively against someone unlike themselves. Rupert emerged somewhat scathed, but they were prepared to acknowledge that he had survived the initiation with admirable defense and treated him with distant respect after that. They also recognized that he was an experienced soldier who was only too willing to impart his knowledge to any man who needed help, and it was not long before he was nicknamed the General. It was plain they took him for a gentleman's son who had been disowned for some scandal, and he let them think it.

Another person quick to recognize that he was a misfit was his sergeant. Rupert said a prayer of thankfulness that the man was worthy of his rank, for he could have made life hell by sadistic use of his authority. Sergeant Spence was a true soldier and used to the full what he saw as the talents of his "gentleman private." Any task that required intelligence rather than brute strength was given to Rupert, and a strange kind of understanding grew up between the two men. When Rupert let slip a comment about the Crimea, Sergeant Spence admitted he had never been to war and added roughly that he would be expecting Private Torrington to know all the answers when the time came for action.

As for Rupert's officers, they hardly knew whom they had beneath their command. There was one ensign who was zealous but painfully shy, who always blushed when hearing one of his men answer in an assured and cultured voice, but the campany commander was a captain who delegated most duties to his subalterns and kept as far from the troops' lines as possible. That suited Private Torrington very well. He did not want to be discussed in the mess, have questions asked of him, or have Giles Meredith see and recognize him.

But riding above all considerations was the need for revenge that had never left him since he had torn at that pile of smoldering rubble that had been Sussex Hall. The initial, almost uncontrollable desire to choke to death those responsible had hardened into cold dedication to a plan! He had gone to Canton to kill a man who had held himself and his country in contempt. Sing-Li was now dead, and there remained only the need to kill as many more as he could to avenge the life of that little boy who had been so dear to him—and so dear to Harriet that she had departed from his life as surely as Edward had on that terrible night.

When he said good-bye to her, she had despised him for following his passion by taking the shilling and mixing with common soldiers after what he had been. She had not understood that this time he was not driven by his passion for the army, but it was only in the army he would have a chance to make China safe for the English. As a soldier he had a right to kill, and the more who fell at his hand, the greater would be the acclamation.

Fighting his way through the mud that day, he dismissed all the discomforts and humiliations in anticipation of running his bayonet through Chinese bodies and quieting the cry of his son that echoed in his ears day and night.

"Get a move on, fer Gawd's sake," yelled an NCO beside him. "We ain't 'ere fer a bloody picnic, Torrington."

Rupert hardly heard him. The shoreline was only 100 yards ahead, and he could see the distant walls of the town through the drenching rain. On the horizon a large body of cavalry appeared to be watching the landing, and Rupert longed to come to grips with them.

But his day had not yet come. The Tartar cavalry rode away as the landing proceeded, and after a night spent on the mudflats without food or water, the troops were ordered to enter and occupy the town.

Harry Parkes, the consul from Canton, had gone ahead to negotiate the surrender of Pehtang, and the inhabitants were fleeing to the safety of Taku, many of the women having to be carried because their stunted feet would not allow them to move fast enough. Even so, many were still present when the armies moved in, and Rupert watched passively the rape and plunder going on around him. He had no desire to spoil women or to ransack the houses for tawdry souvenirs. He wanted to kill and waited for the trumpet call of battle.

Pehtang was filthy, closely confined, and much too small to quarter the two allied armies. Rupert found himself occupying, with a dozen others, a thatched mud-brick hovel that was running with water from the storm rains, moving with lice, and plagued by rats the moment darkness fell. Across the very narrow lane of liquid mud were stabled the cavalry mounts, which added to the overwhelming stench of the surroundings.

A fire was lit to cook their rations, and he shared a box with an excitable thin-faced man who claimed he had bought a young girl for sixpence.

"Where is she then . . . where is she?" inquired an amused ex-farm boy. "Bring she in and share she with you'm mates."

"Har!" guffawed the other. "I knows better'n that. She waitin' fer me at a special place, don't you worry."

"That's if they Frenchies don' find she first. She'll wish she'm stayed with mother then, I'll wager."

"Ar, bloody French," muttered another. "They goes arf-mad when they enters a place. I mean, a bit o' fun's orl right, but they goes on like bloody savages."

"That's what the Chinese are—a lot of savages," declared a sage from the corner. "I ask you, would you live in a place like this?"

Rupert had had enough of their company. After taking a pice of bread in his hand and scratching at his lice-bitten side, he wandered outside into the gathering darkness, squelching through the mud in the hopes of finding a spot open enough to allow him to breathe. When he did, he munched abstractedly on the piece of bread as he watched the frenzied activities of the commissariat department as it assembled the mass of stores considered necessary for the operation. Men were landed within a couple of hours; stores could take up to a couple of weeks.

For some while he kept his gaze on the growing pile of chests, the strings of ponies and mules that were being brought ashore across the mud that had the poor beasts struggling up to their hocks, and the testy altercations between British and French supply officers who had no intention of trying to work together. He had seen it all before, in the Crimea, when he had been infuriated by it. Now he viewed it dispassionately. It would make no difference to his actions in the coming days.

"My God, I can hardly believe what I see," said a voice beside him, and Rupert turned to find a man he knew.

"*Bedford!*" He stared in disbelief. "What in hell's name are you doing here?"

The good-looking face broke into an incredulous smile as he took in Rupert's mud-caked, stinking uniform and the dry bread in his hand.

"It is all too plain what you are doing here. By all the saints, I never thought to be so amused. I knew the company would crash when I left, but not so quickly . . . not half so quickly." He threw back his head and laughed. "Ha! How does it feel to go to the wall, Torrington?"

Gritting his teeth, Rupert said again, "What are you doing here?"

Valentine Bedford gave a smile that was full of charm. "I am employed by the French as a civilian contractor for their supplies. My knowledge of the language and the personal relationships I had with the right people are invaluable to them and I have been able to buy for them things they would otherwise have been unable to get. I am on my way to Peking with the French army in a most lucrative position, believe me. It smacks of adventure after all those dull trading seasons in Canton and promises all kinds of rewards in being the man-on-the-spot in Peking when the embassies are established."

"You hold no military rank?"

He smiled again. "I am above that kind of thing, Torrington."

"That is all I wished to know," murmured Rupert, and launched himself at the man in blood-red fury.

Unprepared, Bedford went down on his back in the mud, and Rupert was on top of him with his hands around the throat that felt too soft beneath his fingers. In fact, his whole body was too soft, a life of pleasure and ease having taken its toll. The two rolled in the mud, the one struggling for his life, the other telling him savagely that his kept woman had tried to kill his wife.

The rain beat down, plastering the hair to Rupert's face and his clothes to his body, but the shock of seeing Bedford again blotted out all sane thought. Then he felt himself seized from behind by men who knew him and knew the penalty he would pay if seen by an officer. Breathing hard, almost sobbing, he was dragged back to the stinking quarters and dumped in a corner with explicit instructions to stay there if he did not want to get himself shot at dawn.

He sat with his head hanging down between his bent knees, fighting down his rage. No, he must not get himself killed yet . . . not until he had truly avenged Edwards death. Then it would not matter anymore!

During the ten-day halt at Pehtang the allied commanders argued over the next move but finally agreed on the wisdom of attacking the Taku forts from the landward side, where they were more vulnerable. Small contingents were ordered to blow up the approach forts, and his was successfully achieved within several days without much loss of life. Confident, and anxious to shed as little blood as possible, the commanders sent Harry Parkes as an envoy to the defenders of the great northern forts—the most formidable of them all—inviting their surrender. But the offer was refused in the most insulting manner . . . and the battle was on in earnest.

Having stayed in reserve until then, Rupert's regiment was selected as one of those to take part in the battle for the forts and the town of Taku at the rear of them. He heard the news with a leap of his pulse and a sense of release for the pent-up anger of not being engaged in the earlier exchanges. But this would be a more bitter battle, a harder road to victory, and it could not have suited him better.

At first sight it was a discouraging target. Having moved up in the predawn across marshland made difficult to cross by the pounding heat after storm rains, the troops stood armed and waiting for the artillery bombardment that would be a prelude to their assault. Rupert stood in their midst, weighed down by his equipment and armed with the unfamiliar bayonet-tipped rifle instead of the sword to which he felt more accustomed. The morning promised to be sweltering. He was sweating profusely already as he gazed out across the terrain they were to cross.

The fort rose on the horizon, its great gray crenellated walls stark against the pearl sky that was as yet untouched by the cruel, brassy brilliance of full daylight. The ancient fortification was heavily endowed with turrets and embrasures where guns could be swung around, elevated, or lowered to command ground in every direction, and all around it were two water-filled ditches similar to the moats encircling medieval castles. Between the moats and the towering walls the ground was thickly studded with knife-sharp bamboo spikes to impale any man unfortunate enough to fall there.

As it grew lighter, the full immensity of their task was made clear to those watching. Any man lucky enough to avoid being blown to pieces, drowned while trying to cross the ditches, or staked by the bamboo spikes would then have to scramble up scaling ladders that could be pushed away by the defenders to send him crashing down onto the bayonets of his own comrades. Many a face looked pale and set as it gazed out, waiting for the great boom of artillery fire to announce the moment to move forward and face it.

Rupert was as pale and silent as those around him, but for a different reason. His moment had come at last. All he wanted was to get inside the fort, where they were waiting for his avenging hand. For the first time he did not feel any of the usual tense, nauseating anticipation of battle, and he realized it was because he no longer held any value on his own life.

Something told him that morning would be his last, yet he did not care. He felt none of the soldier's fears of possible agony or death, nothing of the strange sudden certainty that there was an almighty being who would stage-manage the entire battle according to his will, none of the longing to see a loved one once more—a regret for things said or left unsaid at their last meeting.

On that morning Rupert faced the fact that he did not really wish to live. Harriet was irrevocably lost, and without her, there was no future. He would bear her censure for the rest of his days, and no matter what he did or how far he traveled from her those words. "Where *were* you?" would hound him to the grave. All he prayed in those moments of waiting was that he would not fall before reaching the inside of the fort.

The crash of heavy artillery close beside him set his nerves jangling. The attack had begun! The guns were directing a murderous bombardment on the fort, but the Chinese guns retaliated almost as fiercely, making it hellish for those advancing across the open ground.

Rupert moved forward on Sergeant Spence's command, not liking the sensation of being surrounded by others. He was used to being out front on his own, where he could see the entire situation. Now he was stumbling forward in the midst of sweating, cursing soldiers who took him at their pace and shut off all vision of what lay ahead or at each side. Already the smoke from the guns on both sides was making it almost impossible to see.

But the problem was being cruelly relieved every time the grayness was broken by a vivid yellow flash, and earth and men flew into the air, leaving behind a great crater filled with pieces of bloody flesh. But whereas others recoiled, changed direction or swore in excited bloodlust, Rupert walked on, untouched by any of it. *He must get into the fort!*

The next minute he was running on the barked orders of the sergeant, advancing at the double through smoke that made his eyes stream with tears. The ground had become semimarshy. His boots squelched into it, leaving behind a sucking noise as he ran, crouching low and holding the unfamiliar rifle across his chest. The ditches could not be far away. *He must get into the fort!*

"Take the other end of this, fer Gawd's sake. Robson's dead," panted a voice beside him.

He returned to see a pale youngster left with a pontoon to carry on his own now that his partner was spread on the ground in a mass of blood. The boy looked no more than a child, white and frightened.

"Go on," he implored.

Rupert ran on, ignoring him and fixing his gaze on the walls that were again visible through the thinning smoke. They were much nearer. Only twenty-five yards away was the first ditch—much too wide for the pontoons, as everyone could now see.

The advancing sweep of men was now piling up in red ranks along the edges of the ditch, temporarily halted by the expanse of water. Several officers were trying to decide on the easiest crossing place. Marines floated their pontoons in an attempt to ferry across small numbers of men. Farther along some enterprising Frenchmen were crossing on their scaling ladders held on the shoulders of some of the Chinese Coolie Corps, who had found a stretch shallow enough to allow them to stand in it up to their necks. But all this frenzied activity was within reach of the rifle fire from the fort's defenders on top of the walls, and men were falling all around them. Rupert could not risk delay in such a death trap. *He must get into the fort!*

Without checking he plunged into the water, holding his rifle high and striking out with one arm for the opposite side. It was no easy task, accoutered as he was, but his example was quickly followed by others. The ditch was soon a threshing, moving mass of human endeavor as the allied armies struggled across it in one way or another, cursing, swearing, or yelling the battle cries of their regiments to intimidate the enemy. Through it all a hail of bullets rained down on them from the towering gray-stone walls.

Up the bank on the far side, staggering, nearly falling, then regaining his footing, Rupert kept his gaze on those walls and dashed across the boggy stretch before the second ditch. He did not notice the stinking wetness of his clothes, the heat of the risen sun, or the bullets kicking up tufts of grass all around him. None of it mattered. He could see them now—the faces that peered down from the heights of the walls.

Raising his rifle, he fired, loaded, and fired again, still at the run. He wanted to go on firing, but the width of the water was there before him. He plunged in once more, the nearness of his goal putting extra strength into his arms so that he swam with speed. He had to get into that fort before they killed him. He must avenge Edward or die a broken man.

On dry land once more he was faced with the incredible spread of bamboo stakes, as closely spaced as the tufts of a hairbrush. There was now no question of running. He was forced to pick his way carefully, presenting an easy target for the marksmen above. Worse, the English and French artilleries were misjudging their target now and again, the shells falling in that area to send metal splinters flying in every direction and filling the air with choking smoke once more.

On each side of him men were struggling through the forest of spikes, some falling dead from bullets, others being knocked over by explosions that threw them onto the deadly spikes to impale them in agony while their comrades pushed forward, slowly forward. Rupert moved as quickly as he could, loading, firing, loading again. At the back of his mind he registered that his captain had lain dead at the edge of the second ditch, and the boy ensign who blushed too frequently was skewered through the chest several feet from him, blue eyes still registering the agony he had felt at his last breath. It did not touch him. He was his own commander in this battle between himself and the murderers of his son.

At the foot of the walls! Where were the ladders? Why did no one bring them forward? A glance behind him showed the main body of the force still contemplating the bamboos, hampered by matchlock fire and the length of the scaling ladders. Smoke was making it extremely hazardous to cross that bamboo pincushion, and the bodies already stuck on those wicked spikes could be seen writhing as they waited for medical teams to rush forward under fire and pull them free. Those few, like himself, who had arrived beneath the walls of the forts were powerless to do anything but fire up at any sight of the enemy. His temples began to pound with the madness that was in him, and his body shook with battle fever. He must get inside that fort. *Oh, God, he must get inside there somehow!*

It was then that he spotted through the wispy smoke a breach in the walls made by the allied artillery. At the same time he saw an officer of another regiment rush forward, followed by several of his men with the colors, and enter the fort through the small breach. He did not hesitate. After running along the foot of the wall, he too entered.

Inside, all was confusion. Rupert did not care about the whereabouts of the others who had entered. The dust-smoke atmosphere, the gray dinginess, the smell of occupation of that place swirled around in his head until it had become the smoldering pile of his home, macabre against a blood-red sunrise, beneath which lay the body of his son.

The enemy fell one after another in his orgy of killing. He thrust with the bayonet, fired at point-blank range, clubbed them with the butt, pushed them to death over the walls. The blood ran over his hands until the rifle slipped and slithered in his grip. It soaked into his cotton smock to mingle with his sweat—hot against the coolness of ditchwater wetness. Throughout, he remembered tearing at the red-hot bricks of his home, searching for something he knew was not there. The tears coursed down his face, and his throat grew hoarse with profanities that accompanied their destruction.

Finally, there was no one left near him, and he slipped to the ground in a stupor. Where was he? *Who* was he? The shaking increased until his teeth chattered and the barrel of his rifle clattered on the stone beneath him.

It was this rattling sound that made him aware of noise once more, and when his ears heard that, they heard the full din of battle. Thundering, shuddering roar of cannon, the crack of rifles. Men's voices shouting oaths, screaming with pain and sudden death, calling for mercy or for a loved one in their last breaths. He frowned through the daze in his brain. He had heard it all somewhere before. A man had died—young and full of fear. He had vowed to live that man's life in his own.

Slowly the memory of Sevastapol filtered through his numbed senses, and sanity returned. The wall against which he was leaning became a wall once more; the smoke-filled abyss of revenge became the inner courtyard of some stronghold; the mottled pattern around him focused into an array of Chinese spread in dying attitudes around him that had him swallowing the bile that arose in his throat at the sight. The shaking stopped. He got clumsily to his feet, taking in the spectacle around him.

Below and to his left crouched a small contingent of men, led by Sergeant Spence, who were trapped in a breach in the wall by the accuracy of a small gun on a firing platform farther along the wall. In various parts of the inner fortress hand-to-hand fighting was going on in a bitter struggle for possession, and the entry of reinforcements was being held up by the gun trained on the gap.

Even as he watched, Sergeant Spence made a dash forward; he was felled when he was halfway across the open stretch, giving a great cry and rolling onto his back, his face a mass of blood. Rupert felt a surge of compassion for the man he had come to admire. But such emotions had no place in the midst of battle, and he hesitated no longer.

From his position on the walls he could see the situation at a glance and acted intuitively. He began to run with great strides along the ledge used as a firing level toward the gun that so easily bombarded that breach in the wall. With speed rather than stealth the essential virtue, it was inevitable that the gunners would spot his headlong dash, and they were ready for him with their long knives when he launched his fierce attack.

But it was a repetition of Sevastapol when he had reached that Russian redoubt and fought alone, miraculously remaining unhurt. Two Chinese had fallen dead or dying when he spotted the sword of a dead enemy officer lying near his feet, and he seized it, shouting at the top of his voice to those below to take advantage of the lull to advance. With the sword in his hand he knew why he was there, who he was.

He battled on, with strengthened arm and sharpened sight and wits. They were merely "the enemy" now; no more did he see the murderers of his son before him. Holding his own with the remaining two Chinese guards, he soon struck down one of them, leaving him to match his sword with the knife of his skillful opponent. The noise below him doubled. There must be hundreds within the fortress now! In the distance he was aware of scarlet-clad men clambering over the top from ladders, and he knew the day was theirs.

His personal tussle might have gone on until both fell exhausted, for his enemy fought with great courage, but just as Rupert felt his arm tiring, there was a great roar from the bowels of the earth, a brilliant yellow light, and something thumped into him with tremendous force. The world turned black.

The fall of the fort was the first in a chain of victories in which all the strongholds protecting the mouth of the Pei-ho River were stormed and captured. The Chinese general who had inflicted defeat on the envoys and their escort the previous July retreated upriver with his Tartar army. The naval force lost no time in removing the spikes and chain booms from across the river and entered with appropriate jubilation at avenging their comrades of thirteen months before.

Envoys were sent to the governor-general of the province that included Tientsin in its territory, with demands that he surrender and avoid further bloodshed. But true to form, the demand was met with a series of letters, each superseding the other on details of a meeting and terms, and was so plainly a tactic to avoid the issue and delay the allied forces until the onset of winter made it impossible for them to march north. Lord Elgin and Baron Gros, once again the diplomatic ambassadors on the mission, decided nothing would be achieved until they reached Tientsin and informed their military commanders of their decision.

When the news of the advance was heard in the troops' lines, a great cheer went up. They had set their hearts on seeing Peking and had no intention of being fobbed off with a few forts while the diplomatic boys did all the sight-seeing.

Rupert was greatly cheered at the thought of a further push north. After five days he was almost back to full fitness. He had been slightly concussed after being caught in the blast from the exploding magazine, and his face was discolored by bruising. The first two days following the assault passed in a haze, but the regimental doctor had that morning agreed to pass him fit enough to see further action, after Rupert had pleaded strongly to be allowed to do so. All that remained was a faint wooliness of hearing that should clear in time . . . and it might be a blessing in the tumult of battle.

Packing his gear on the evening before the advance, he experienced a feeling of achievement such as he had not felt for a very long time. Some kind of madness had sent him to China, and it had governed him in all he had done during that day, until the blood mist had cleared from his eyes and he had seen as a soldier once more. There was a vast difference, he had discovered, between killing for oneself and killing for a cause. The former made a man sick almost beyond recall. Thank God he had stopped before it was too late!

His soul was empty of revenge. He had faced his son squarely in that orgy of slaughter, and the boy's cries had at last gone from his ears. There was thankfulness in freedom, rising hope in being back where he belonged. It did not matter that his uniform lacked insignia and gold embellishments or that he lived cheek by jowl with some of the roughest creatures on earth. He was doing that in which he excelled . . . and no man could surely ask more of himself. The past must be forgotten, Harriet put from his heart (oh, God, could he ever do so?), his mind and body truly fulfilled through his military skill. His life was once more his alone, to do with as he wished. If he surrendered it during this war, he would have done something toward redeeming his father's and grandfather's exploitation of society; he would have dedicated some little worthiness to the memory of his son. *And if he surrendered his life during this war, he would never know if Harriet had made the final break and left Hong Kong.*

"Torrington, you're wanted."

"Eh?" He turned, hearing his name but not the words.

"Wash out yer ears, fer Gawd's sake," bawled the NCO. "You're wanted by the adjutant."

"What, now?" he asked in surprise.

" 'Course, *now*!" was the snide imitation of his cultured tone.

"Get darn there double quick, cloth ears, or Captain 'inks will've gorn ter bed."

Captain Hinks was nowhere near retiring by the look of all the maps and papers on his table. He looked up at Rupert's entry and eyed him comprehensively.

"Are you Torrington . . . Rupert Garforth Montague?"

Rupert gave a faint grin. "I'm afraid so, sir."

"Does your family reside in Sussex?"

"I have no family . . . but yes, they had a place at Battle. Why, sir?"

The adjutant smiled. "Just checking that I had the right Torrington here. Feeling better now?"

"Yes, thank you. It was only a touch of concussion, sir."

"Good." He rose. "I'll tell the colonel that you are here."

"The colonel?" repeated Rupert sharply, suddenly remembering another occasion when he had walked in to see his commanding officer and been given a copy of *The Times*. What had gone wrong? *Harriet?* His heart turned over.

"He wants a word with you. Don't look so worried, man. He's a capital fellow."

Bewildered, uneasy, Rupert blustered, "I'm hardly in a fit condition. I was told to drop everything and come . . . I–I am in a pretty filthy state."

The man smiled again. "Yes, you are rather . . .

but I don't think the old man will give a damn about that."

Before Rupert had time to ponder on the adjutant's calling Colonel Crackthorne the old man before a private, he was told to go into the stone house that had been chosen as a temporary headquarters. Bending his head beneath the low lintel, he went in to face a man he had seen only several times at a distance. He had no idea what the man was like, except from a casual word or two from Giles Meredith in the past, and he was astonished and extremely dismayed to see that young officer also with the colonel. There was no way of avoiding recognition, and he felt the dirty state of his uniform even more keenly.

The elderly, grizzled man looked sternly at Giles after Rupert had saluted and announced himself. "I believe you are well acquainted with this man, Captain Meredith."

"Yes, sir."

"Then I suggest you greet him."

Giles turned to Rupert with a slightly anxious expression. "Hallo, Rupert."

He swallowed. "Good evening, sir."

The colonel frowned. "Are you quite recovered from your injuries sustained during the assault on the fort?"

"I wasn't injured, sir, just concussed. I was too close to the magazine when it went up," said Rupert through stiff lips.

"Mmm, so I understand." He studied his soldier for a moment. "What were you doing in the vicinity of the magazine?"

"Trying to spike a gun, sir."

"Did it not occur to you to stay with your section? Why did you not wait for orders?"

Feeling angry at such an approach in front of a man who had been his friend, Rupert reacted with some heat. "The officers were both dead, sir."

"What about the NCOs?"

"Sergeant Spence was killed by that very gun. But that had very little to do with it. I was the only man in a position to reach the gun with any speed."

"So you took it upon yourself to rush at a gun manned by four of the enemy without waiting to consult with your superiors, whom apparently you had already left behind when entering the fort?"

Conscious of Giles's watching him, he grew angrier. "There was a breach in the walls which, when I arrived at the fort, was the only way of entering. The ladders had not been brought up, and the men trying to traverse the spiked area were being shot at by marksmen on top of the walls. It was imperative for someone to get inside and stop them. Once inside I was on my own. There was nobody to consult even if I had wanted to." He took a deep breath. "Look, sir, it was mayhem in that courtyard. A man must act as the situation demands."

Colonel Crackthorne nodded. "I understand you used the same philosophy in the Crimea and were twice decorated for it." He saw Rupert flash a swift look of incomprehension at Giles and added, "Yes, your friend has spoken of it to me."

"I . . . see."

"This will be the third recommendation for gallantry to your name, for I intend to send in a report on your courageous attempt to put that gun out of action." He frowned again. "It seems a great pity that I have to recommend *Private* Torrington, in this case. When you were with The Fishers, you were a captain, I believe?"

"Yes . . . yes, I was," he said in a daze.

"Then I take it as a damned affront that you skulk in the ranks of *my* regiment as a shilling-a-day man. I will not tolerate officers trying to shirk their responsibilities," he said in blustery fashion. "Because of this engagement, we are short of several junior officers, and there is a lieutenancy up for purchase. See that you buy it and get out of that filthy suit. The next time I see you I want a gentleman who looks like a gentleman—not a bloody ruffian."

Rupert was not certain he had heard aright. The other man was speaking rather fast, and his hearing was still not good.

"Are you offering me a commission in the regiment, sir?" he ventured.

"I am not proposing marriage, Mr. Torrington," he said gruffly.

The world seemed to stand still. Giles was grinning at him for all the world like Satan offering temptation.

"Do you . . . ?" He had to clear his throat. "Do you know about my background?"

"Damn your background, man. If you are going to fight this war like an officer, it will be best for all concerned if you are dressed like one." He gave a soft smile. "And if you are going to continue with your damfool habit of spiking guns against all odds, your background will be of no odds to anyone but yourself." He held out his hand. "Welcome to the regiment, Lieutenant Torrington."

Rupert shook hands in a state of rosy disbelief.

Then Giles stepped forward. "Come on, I'll find you some quarters. Then we'll drink to old times."

They saluted and went out together. Once outside the door Giles clapped him on the back and shook him by the hand. "Well done. Welcome home, you old fraud."

"Thanks," he said thickly. "Thanks very much."

Chapter Nineteen

Hong Kong in that August was attacked by great heat. Europeans found it insupportable during the afternoon and retired behind shuttered windows until the sun went down. Businesses closed from noon until 4:00 P.M., when they reopened for two hours; government offices naturally remained open all day, but the employees sat with their feet up and handkerchiefs over their faces after luncheon until afternoon tea was brought. Work on new buildings slowed, even the coolies finding they could not ignore the merciless sun.

In the narrow alleys Chinese sat listless in their doorways, their incessant chatter stilled for a while. Children lolled against walls, poking fretfully at beetles with sticks to relieve their irritation over the state of things. The poultry abandoned their eternal scratching for tidbits and collapsed in piles of ruffled feathers, breathing through open beaks. The usual smells were heightened; new ones were added as water evaporated, leaving rubbish to putrefy. The tempers of everyone rose as the barometer climbed higher and higher.

But Harriet still made her pilgrimages to the Rice Dragon, taking with her the obligatory bowl of rice as thanks for his communion. The sedan chair took longer, and the walk through the jungle left her clothes sticking to her body; but it was cool in the glade by the stream. It was the only place she visited now. Her refusal to abandon her connection with the soothsayer had completely alienated her from the Christian Europeans, who saw her actions as a going over to the devil.

At first such severing of ties did not worry her, for she saw those people as unenlightened and bigoted, but as the weeks passed, her sense of isolation had insinuated itself into her every waking hour. People ignored her in the street; European shopkeepers tried not to serve her by pretending she was not there and hoping she would go away. It had happened so often she now did not attempt to go shopping at all. Those same men were only too pleased to take Torrington money, however, and delivered anything she wanted to the house, thereby not being *seen* by other valued customers to supply her.

Even Chalmers, the bank manager, was undisguisedly embarrassed in her presence, so she conducted all business with him through letters. Her old astuteness with accounts had led her to instruct him to invest the money Rupert had left in her name; with Hong Kong expanding at the rate it was, it was important to buy and sell at the right time. With nothing else to do, financial juggling became an obsessive occupation with which to while away her hours.

It did not help that she had finished all work on her father's book and sent the manuscript back to England at the start of the month. To help fill the gap left by it, she had tried to resume her study of Chinese, but it reminded her so vividly of the night she had awakened to find her home ablaze she had to abandon it.

Bessie, dear loyal Bessie, remained with her, but the only other European she saw was Armand—and he continued to oppose what she was doing. She knew he risked the good opinions of others by continuing to visit her, and was grateful, but not all his pleading would make her give up what had sustained her throughout the past year. There was nothing with which to replace it, and without it she would then be completely lost.

When he called early one evening in the last week of that month, she welcomed him warmly, for the day had seemed endless and that narrow strip of blue ocean visible from her window had tormented her with its symbolic implications. Armand, with his overtones of paternity, was just the company she needed at that moment.

"How good of you to call when to move at all is such an effort," she told him with sincerity, giving both hands into his and smiling up at him. "I shall reward you with a cool drink on the instant." Turning to pull the bell sash, she continued, "To brave this excessive heat as well as the pagan evils of this house smacks of friendship indeed." Swinging back to face him, she added in heartfelt tones, "What would I do without you, my dear friend?"

"That will be entirely up to you very shortly, Harriet."

His face was unusually grave; the silvering at his temples that gave him a debonair attraction merely emphasized his years tonight. In evening clothes and with merry eyes sobered by something unknown, he suddenly presented an almost sinister figure. Apprehension rushed into her.

"You have not come tonight as a friend?"

He hesitated before replying and then did not answer her question. "I have to go back to France. My father is dying, and as head of the family I must be there."

She was stunned. "Of course. I . . . I am sorry about your father."

"He is well over eighty. A good life fully lived, he would say." Then, almost without a pause: "I have come to ask you to go to Lyons with me."

It made her sink into a chair very abruptly. The Chinese boy who was sent for drinks in an abstracted tone closed the door softly, and she sat trying to believe she had heard aright. Neither spoke until glasses of iced tea had been set on the tables before them and the servant had gone out once more.

"Armand, I think too highly of you to have heard what you just now said to me," she told him at last.

He sipped from his glass, quite unperturbed by her words. "*Ma chère*, you have chosen the wrong moment for one of your rare conventional moods. I think you heard only too well what I said, and I think you attempt to avoid it because there is only one answer, *hein*?"

It angered her immediately. "It is out of the question—of course, it is out of the question. I am disappointed that you should ask such a thing. Please say no more on the matter or I shall be obliged to ask you to leave."

Armand grew still and wary. "So it is *not* over?"

"Over?" she repeated sharply.

"Your marriage."

Pain pierced her. "Marriage . . . what is marriage? It does not exist except in the vocabulary of society. What has never been cannot be over. People come together like the wind bending almond buds so that they touch for a moment, then spring apart again. It means nothing and is forgotten in the aeons of time."

He was before her on the instant, half kneeling on a footstool and looking at her like a man in shock. "You begin to speak like him . . . of vast and incalculable thoughts. He has bewitched you. You will never leave Hong Kong."

Her anger bubbled higher. "Not you also, my friend—not you!"

He took her hand and spoke urgently. "I think you already know that I am not only your friend but a man deeply attached to you. I beg you now with the concern of one and the love of the other to listen to my words. It is six months since the day I came to you from Canton and you told me you would soon give up the spirit of Edward and go to that place no more. Six months! *Mon Dieu,* you are no nearer to letting your son rest in peace than before. It is wrong. It is against your beliefs and the ways of your own people. It has become something that will swallow you up."

Pulling her hand away, she got up and moved across the room as if his nearness burned her. "You know nothing. You are like the rest, and they are like the ignorant creatures who drove Aubrey to his death." Blazing with emotion, she turned on him. "Does your mind never stretch? In all your fifty years have you never strayed from the path of your own people?"

He stood up slowly and shook his head. "So defensive, so fiery! My years that double yours have taught me that I cannot spread myself across the world, however much I might wish it. Aubrey knew this, I suspect, and gave up trying some years before his death. It was not ignorance that led him to kill himself but the realization of his own isolation. Do not wait for that, Harriet. Do not let this destroy you."

"Destroy . . ." She almost choked in her anger. "It has *saved* me. Dear heaven, I was so near to permanent darkness . . . you cannot know."

"The Rice Dragon is a piece of carved wood," he said in careful emphasis.

"The Rice Dragon is a talisman—a symbol," she cried. "The wisdom comes from the man who sees in it the personification of hope. That same hope made me sane when madness hovered near."

He came across and put gentle hands on her arms. "For that, heaven be praised. But now it is time to let go, or it will be too late."

The blood drained from her face at the prospect. "Armand, how can I? If I give that up, I shall have nothing."

"You will have me," he told her gently. "Come to Lyons, and forget all that has happened here. It is the only way. In Hong Kong there is no person who will care what happens to an Englishwoman who has taken the pagan path once I am gone. You will be quite alone. Europeans will shun you; the Chinese will not accept you." Drawing in his breath, he turned her to face an ornate mirror over the mantelpiece. "There . . . do you see what you have become? Do you see those eyes that know too many secrets, that face grown thin and haunted by truths that are better not revealed? I grieve each time I see the woman you have become."

He turned her back to face him, and she saw the glint of moisture in his eyes. "You are but eight-and-twenty, and yet I see more than my father's life-span written there before me now. Come away, before you are lost forever. I shall ask nothing more of you than that, I swear."

The world was tilting again, threatening to slide her off into an unknown complexity. For three days Harriet had struggled with herself and a decision she could not make. Armand was leaving at the end of September on one of his own ships, giving her three weeks in which to make a decision about her future.

Catching her at her lowest ebb, his words that night had held too many barbs to pierce her isolation—an isolation that had turned into an aching loneliness before she had been aware of it. Initially drawn by the immense comfort of the soothsayer's wisdom, she was now almost engulfed in her relationship with him. What had, at first, seemed to offer her a new enlightenment now threatened to fix her in an emotional limbo. Standards and values fell away; time was meaningless; she was nothing in the vast complex of life and afterlife.

Struggling to understand, she now translated his earlier comforting statements into a philosophy that almost suggested she did not truly exist—had never existed—and that Edward was merely a thought-dream from another life. Rather than comfort, she felt unease, bordering on fear. Coming to accept that Edward was finally lost to her, she rejected the suggestion that he had never been hers in the first place. Yet the old man was suggesting in his grave, otherworldly way that it was so.

Has she traveled too far into philosophy and lost her way? Had she reached her point of no return? Vastness and centuries swallowed her up until she was beginning to lose all sense of identity. Were her visits prompted only by a desperation to rediscover the peace she had once felt in that place? It seemed that the Rice Dragon no longer smiled upon her but might devour her completely.

Armand was her last link with herself. He was like the bag of sand that kept the hot-air balloon from rising up into the sky to float away and vanish forever.

He intended to engage an agent in Hong Kong to run his company for several years. He wanted a rest from the East, he had told her. Together they could live in his family home in Lyons and indulge in the quiet pleasures of country life, patronize the arts, and put the past years from their minds. He would demand no more from her than her companionship and her return to being the woman she had once been. In the sylvan surroundings of the Château du Plessis she could rest and learn to laugh again. It was a tempting prospect, yet something inside her cried out at the prospect of leaving Hong Kong. Not yet, she told herself; I cannot leave yet.

Indecision tormented her until she began to feel feverish. Armand called upon her every day, talking in rational but desperate words, which increased her dread. The terrible heat sapped her strength, and her brain pounded. Finally, a week later, she sat brushing her long brown hair prior to retiring and put the facts to Bessie.

The girl was sitting by the window, mending a frill on a camisole, but she dropped her work and rose to her feet in a tremble of protest.

"You can't not do that, madam. What about the captain?" she cried.

"I think it does not concern him, Bessie," she replied wearily. "That is over."

"Not for him, it isn't." The girl was pale and extremely moved. "He's brokenhearted, that's what he is. I've heard of such things, and now I've seen it for meself. Madam, you *can't*. Oh, no, you can't do this to him. If you had seen him like I did, you'd never think of such a thing. He says to me before he goes that I'm to stay and look after you, whatever happens to him." She began to tremble again, and tears broke on her eyelids. "But I shan't go with you to France. No, that I will not do. I'll wait here for the captain to come back from that war, that's what I'll do." Crying openly now, she went on. "I'm sorry, madam, reely I am, but if you go off with Musher Dooplessee, I can't stay with you."

"Bessie!" she exclaimed. "You can't mean that. Not after all these years."

The girl nodded miserably. "I've tried to understand what you're doing, madam, reely I have. I loved little Master Edward, too, and know what it must be like for you. I've been up to that place that gives me the shivers and told myself I'm too ignorant to understand all that mumbo jumbo—which I am. But one thing I understands is feelings, even though I'm only a servant girl. You've never looked at the captain since that night, but I have. I've never seen anyone so broken up as he is—not even you, madam. You've got your Rice Dragon; he's got nothing and no one." Working herself up to a frenzy, she blurted out, "Might jest as well blame me as him. I didn't get the little boy out—*no one* could've, with all those bolts on the door. Now he's gone up to fight because it was *them* to blame and no one else." She began to edge backward toward the door, still crying freely. "If the poor captain comes back—*if* he comes back—and finds you gone off with his friend, I shall be here still. We might not always see eye to eye, but . . . he's worth two of that Frenchie."

She fled, sobbing, slamming the door behind her. Harriet was left in shocked disbelief at the outburst, but not for long. The reminder of things she had tried to forget, the uncertainty of her own mind, and the oppressive heat all wore her down until she found tears trembling on her own lashes . . . she, who despised women who sobbed!

The spasm of weeping brought on a headache, which in turn led to retching. By morning it was apparent that she was suffering from more than low spirits, for she was desperately ill. Unbearable stomach cramps racked her body as the strength poured out of her, and repeated vomiting left her breathless and bathed in sweat. She lost count of time and became beset with the certainty of her own death. The doctor did not attempt to hide from her the nature of her illness. Cholera was too virulent in Hong Kong for Harriet not to know its symptoms . . . and its seriousness.

For five days she lay in the grips of the agonizing fever while demons danced in her brain. The thought of death was not unwelcome; it would solve her uncertainties, and she would be reunited with all those she had loved—her father, brother, and son.

The images of those three swam in her feverish thoughts, distant at first and then growing nearer and more distinct until an image terrible and threatening superimposed itself upon them. She recognized Rupert at once, but . . . oh, dear God . . . he had no arms and was covered in blood. She cried out, ordering him away, and strove to recall those other three, but they faded, leaving only the war-torn body that had become a faceless stranger. The nightmare set her screaming, but her fear only brought forth a great, vividly colored dragon who seized her with wrenching claws into her stomach and flung her up into the sky so that she floated there forever, disoriented and alone. Even when she was about to be drawn down into a garden surrounding a great gray château, the dragon breathed fire that sent her spiraling upward once more until the fire of the dragon turned into the raging furnace that consumed everything. "*Edward,*" she screamed again and again; but hands were laid on her to hold her down, and the vomiting began once more.

On the sixth day she saw Bessie's face clearly and understood the things she spoke to her. But there was no gladness at the doctor's words that she had fought the battle and won. There was no sense of victory within her, just a deep, intolerable weariness at the thought of having to go on. Bessie felt more emotion, standing by the bedside with tears of relief sliding down her cheeks.

"It was wicked of me to say what I did, madam," she told her with remorse. "The captain said I was to look after you, so that's what I'll do—wherever you go."

The weather broke in mid-September; it rained, and Hong Kong breathed again. Harriet sat by her window day after day in the welcome lethargy of convalescence. Armand could not expect her to make a decision yet. She watched the world go by and forgot the cholera demons.

Bessie fussed around her, not letting the Chinese girl tend her mistress. But she made no mention of going to France. The girl was subdued but polite enough when Armand called, although she looked tense, pale, and exhausted. It occurred to Harriet that in her limited way Bessie was facing the decision of a lifetime also, that even her simple straightforward intelligence had become complex with the demands of loyalty.

Harriet watched her with compassion. For all her spirit and bluster little Bessie Porridge was full of sentiment, which now tore her in opposite directions. The loyalty and gratitude she felt toward her mistress were arguing against the hero worship inspired by the man she had confronted on many occasions. Bessie had a fellow feeling for the underdog, whoever he might be, and she could see no such tendencies in Armand du Plessis.

But the cholera had not finished with that household. The vile germs crept back ten days later and took Bessie in a matter of a few hours. Worn-out and distressed, she had no resistance to the disease; she died at midnight, when the rain was lashing down on Hong Kong, as it had done on the night Edward was born.

To Harriet, it was the final blow. She sat in the darkness haunted by the ghost of a little dormouse girl who had become so much part of her life that her death had left Harriet with nothing at all. They had all left her—her father, her brother, Edward, Aubrey, her darling son . . . now Bessie. Through the remainder of the night she relived all those times when the girl had given her sly smile and confessed to annoying Cook or putting the valet's shoes beneath the tap to make them squeak; her half-brave, half-fearful defiance of Rupert before being hurried from the room by his firm hand on the bow of her apron strings. She thought of her fierce defense of those she served—her knocking of the cup from Tzu-An's hand on the day of their arrival and her attempt to stop her own first visit to the Rice Dragon. And she remembered the heated championship of a man besieged in his own factory by Chinese.

Bessie had been with her for ten years. It was not a servant who had been lost but someone somewhere between a friend, a younger sister, and a foster child.

Harriet mourned Bessie with such tremendous sense of loss and despair that when the Chinese girl came into her room to open the shutters onto daylight and revealed Armand waiting in her dressing room, she stumbled from her chair and ran to him in desperation.

"Armand, take me with you," she moaned. "For pity's sake, take me away from this place."

The allied armies encamped around Tientsin while diplomatic negotiations took place between their own ambassadors and three Chinese mandarins, who presented themselves as envoys of the emperor. All concerned were anxious to halt the army that was causing havoc as it advanced alongside the river, rendering homeless many poor inhabitants of villages as it went. The British deplored the ruthless plundering and killing of animals by their French allies, who had not the plentiful rations they themselves were issued. The French retaliated by blaming much of the despoliation on Indian troops brought from that country by their British officers. There were scuffles in the lines, and officers were hard pressed to keep the peace between two nations that were supposed to be fighting the Chinese, not each other.

As August moved into September, the heat continued to plague troops from temperate lands, and the desire for adventure slackened into a desire for home. Inaction took the gilt from the gingerbread; Peking was not worth the effort of marching there. The military grew restless while letters passed between the mandarins and Elgin and Gros. If there were no more fighting to be done, they might as well be back in comfortable barracks in Hong Kong or newly leased Kowloon on the mainland. Better still, they could be sailing back to England!

When it was learned that the terms had at last been agreed to by the three mandarins, who had no authority from the emperor or an official seal to legalize the treaty, the troops were furious. That distinguished diplomats should have fallen for so obvious a Chinese trick disgusted them, and long were the curses put on the heads of those who had given the enemy the delay for which they had been conniving.

"It is *we* who will have to march up to Peking in the bloody snow—and I mean that in both senses of the word," said Rupert to Giles and to Nugent Goddard, whom he had reencountered in Tientsin.

They were sitting in Rupert's tent, drinking wine, late that evening, and he was as angry as the rest of the army.

"My God, have they really not had enough examples of their treachery? While we have all been sitting here like sweltering fools, they have been reassembling their forces for attack the moment we advance. When I think of the glee in which they must have prepared their campaign, I swear I could explode with anger. We should have marched straight on to Peking. Any man with sense must see we shall achieve nothing until the emperor sees us at his gates. It has been as plain as a pikestaff for years."

"You diplomatic boys are afraid of upsetting Anglo-Chinese relations too much, that's your trouble," added Giles with heartfelt accusation at Nugent. "I tell you, it is impossible to fight a war without upsetting the enemy's feelings."

The diplomat put up his hands in protest. "I have no intention of taking your censure upon my shoulders. It was Parkes who discovered these men were lying rogues, or we might have been here until Christmas. My senior and I are doing all we can do to expedite matters, believe me. *We* have no desire to be in Peking during winter—or have all of you imitating Napoleon retreating from Moscow!"

Rupert smiled with sudden warmth. "Apologies, old fellow. It is always tempting to blame the one person who is present."

"Yes," said Nugent throughtfully, giving him a straight look. "It was a good thing you had already left Canton when Sing-Li was killed or you might have been blamed for that."

"So I might," he replied, giving back an equally straight look. "Have they yet discovered who did do it?"

"No. There was an explosion of some kind, which left very little evidence. It could have been done by any number of people. That man made enemies by the hour."

"I suppose we couldn't put some explosives beneath these three mandarins, could we?" suggested Giles. "Not to kill them, of course, but just to move them a bit."

They all laughed, but Nugent, sobering first, said, "I envy you fellows. Everything is cut-and-dried where you are concerned. Attack and defense, advance or retreat, kill or be killed. You are given the chance to express your feelings in the most satisfactory way possible. You, Rupert, hate them for personal as well as professional reasons and can get out there in vengeance. We have to smile and pretend, sit and wait, try again and again to reach agreement, while in our hearts there is a great desire to wring their treacherous necks. You have no idea what it has been like these past two weeks, talking endlessly with smiling men who mean nothing of what they say."

"Couldn't stand it myself," said Giles, helping himself to more of Rupert's wine, then waving the empty bottle at him. "Sorry, old chap. Senior officer's privilege to take the last drink."

Reaching under his bed for another bottle, Rupert asked, "Is that right you are taking Wainwright's majority?"

"Yes, isn't it splendid! Major Meredith! Of course, I'm damned sorry about Wainwright . . . but if it weren't for accidents and fever, none of us would ever get promotions, would we?"

"The story I heard was that he accidentally shot himself while cleaning his pistol."

"Ah, yes, Rupert, but you haven't been with us long enough to know your fellow officers. Wainwright's wife had found separation rather too lonely and found a cozy baronet to console her back in England. The poor devil had a letter from a well-meaning friend two days ago." He squared his shoulders and tossed back the drink. "I suppose I should thank *Mrs.* Wainwright for my promotion—or the aging baronet who stole her away," he added reflectively.

Rupert's thoughts immediately took him back to Hong Kong. It was painfully ironical that Harriet, who had always been so fearful of his own fidelity, should now have an aging admirer ready to become her lover the moment she gave the word. He felt it was only a matter of time before that happened, even if she now only looked upon him as a father. Armand was patient and worldly-wise. Such an alliance would probably be Harriet's salvation. The love she had felt for himself had been too all-consuming, as was his own for her. They had destroyed each other, and yet . . . and yet without her he was nothing but a fighting machine.

"Your outlook on life and your fellows is bloody dispassionate, to say the least," Nugent was saying.

"No worse than yours," was the inebriated reply. "I hope for promotion as a result of the natural hazards of my profession; you find advancement in toadying to a host of Chinese and keeping Parliament happy."

"Not always . . . not always," was the sharp reply as Nugent accepted another drink from his host. "Don't forget it was Parkes who rode into Pehtang to demand surrender with only a flag of truce to protect him . . . and Parkes who went forward into Taku to discover if the place was mined."

"Then he was a bloody fool," was the ungracious comment. "He should have left it to sappers who know what they are doing."

"Stow it, Giles," warned Rupert, who was beginning to find his head spinning from the wine and the heat beneath canvas. "We all do what we have to do within the demands of our professions. I have personal experience of Nugent's comprehensive talents. It's not all talk, you know. There are risks involved, and diplomatic men can be broken, like us, if anything goes wrong."

Giles looked suitably chastened. "No offense," he said to Nugent, and then raised his glass. "To the diplomatic boys."

"I'll drink to that," said Rupert.

Nugent smiled wistfully. "Well, I'll drink to adventure . . . and the chance of some of it for me."

They all found that toast far more exciting and drank to it so enthusiastically they ended up dead drunk, sprawled beneath the canvas of Lieutenant Torrington's tent.

The "diplomatic boys" were not fools, and they decided to take their next step without delay—that of advancing the armies to within firing distance of Peking. The troops cheered and decided the imperial city *was* worth seeing after all.

But the delay in Tientsin had been advantageous to the Chinese. Their army had gathered before Peking in force, small portions of cavalry had been posted all along the route to report progress of the allied advance, and the continuing heat had caused the Pei-ho River to run dangerously low. Even so, the forward march of the Anglo-French force brought a spate of letters from mandarins and other Chinese officials, each promising different things but each urging the halt of their enemy. Lord Elgin replied that he would listen to nothing more until his forces were established at Tungchow, twelve miles from Peking. Once there, he would be prepared to consider negotiations once more.

So the long, lumbering column of men and beasts moved off during the second week in September, finding little relief from the brassy heat as they moved farther north. Because of the need for a large commissariat, only half the force advanced to the outskirts of Tungchow, while the remainder stayed at Tientsin until the supplies had been brought upriver from the base camps.

Rupert's regiment formed part of the advance guard, and he was glad of it. Inaction left him with too much time to think, and that was something he tried to avoid. It was bad enough lying awake night after night, haunted by what had once been. To counteract it, he had taken to drinking himself insensible, but he could not use such methods during the day. On the move he had duties, discomforts, and hazards to keep his mind alert, so he rejoiced in the advance.

Yet there were long hours in the saddle when thoughts of Harriet pounded in his head, and he was tormented by physical longing for the temptress she had once been. Now that revenge had been purged from his soul, softer but equally savage emotions took its place, and he thought more and more of Major Wainwright, who had received a letter from a well-meaning friend. Would it be better for both Harriet and himself if he did not return from this war? He would not take his own life, as Wainwright had done—his heart thudded; *as his own father had done*—but it was ridiculously easy for a man to ensure that he was cut down in battle.

Day after day, as he rode beside the column of marching men, the obsession stayed with him. The weather cooled, but he still stayed awake at night, sweating with the fever of decision until finally driven to the bottle as a means of banishing the ghosts. He grew haggard and short-tempered, speaking sharply to Nugent or Giles when they attempted to shake him from his mood. He took to gaming again, staking huge sums on the turn of a card, and winning . . . always winning. It only turned the knife inside him. He could not win the only prize he wanted! Even the small skirmishes, the landscape of China passing before his eyes, the demanding duties gave him no relief from his jealousy of Armand du Plessis, who stood to win a woman who had shut him so completely from her heart and life.

The armies swarmed through northern China like locusts, lowering the level of rivers, stripping the land of grass for fodder, looting villages, and terrifying the inhabitants. This time, it was members of the Chinese Coolie Corps and those Chinese among the camp followers who mainly oppressed the villagers. Having no love for their northern compatriots and the usual lack of conscience, they ransacked the primitive dwellings for all they could lay hands on and in such a way that fear rode ahead of them to result in panic evacuation of houses and even to the suicide of young girls who could not face the possible shame of rape.

Allied officers did what they could to prevent brutality from their own men, but when it came to Chinese against Chinese, they found it no simple matter. There had been too much national and personal injury to their own countrymen to feel much compassion for *any* Chinese.

Still the letters flowed back and forth between mandarins and the allied diplomats in a spate of useless wordage. Sick of delays, of duplicity, and of personal affront, the invaders would now be stopped only by a development so full of concession there would be no need to threaten Peking. As it happened, when something shattering did occur, it had quite the reverse effect and sealed the fate of the Celestial City in a manner that crushed the Chinese and had the whole world agog for years afterward.

Neither Lord Elgin nor Baron Gros wished to take a whole army into Peking, feeling that outright conquest would damage future relations with China rather than improve them. What was more, the Anglo-French leaders had no desire to establish a conqueror's military garrison in the imperial city that would require a permanent strong force to maintain it, and there seemed little advantage in marching in only to march out again, as they had done in Canton two years earlier. The tactical plan was to threaten the city with a huge army *outside* the city walls until the emperor, fearing the destruction of his picturesque and ancient buildings, agreed to receive the European ambassadors and allow them to set up legations within Peking—something for which they had been struggling for years. At the first sign of such capitulation the plenipotentiaries would be only too willing to halt what was proving to be a costly campaign. Then there could be negotiations.

Such an opportunity presented itself just short of their destination at a place called Chanchaiwan when a message arrived from the commissioner of that district asking for envoys to be sent forward for discussions. Harry Parkes, with members of his staff and an armed escort, rode forward under a flag of truce to investigate the sincerity of this latest approach, and he returned with optimistic news. As the allies had hoped, fears for Peking were so great the emperor had sent his own envoys to arrange for the invading army to encamp in a much-favored spot and be provisioned by the Chinese while the Anglo-French ambassadors proceeded to Peking with a large handpicked escort to be received at the Dragon Throne.

Although the size of the escort still remained to be settled, in general the proposal was a sound one and acceptable to the diplomats, if not to the military. Parkes had returned to report to his leaders and, receiving their agreement to conduct further talks on the details, returned the following day with an acceptance of the proposed cease-fire while negotiations went ahead. He took with him, in addition to his own staff, an escort of the finest cavalry and representatives from the commissariat and medical branches who wished to inspect the site of the encampment that had been provided by the Chinese. As an observer, a jounalist attached himself to the group, anxious not to miss any of the story attached to the campaign.

Meanwhile, the regiments prepared to move off in the direction of Chanchiawan to set up their tents, cookhouses, field hospitals, canteens, and messes—all essential to an army in the field.

Rupert and Giles were riding together while exchanging details of the position the regiment would be allotted in the new camp when the sound of firing ahead took all their attention.

"What the . . . !" exclaimed Rupert sharply, standing in his stirrups to look over the heads of the front ranks in the direction in which they were traveling.

Nothing stirred; all looked peaceful across the fields and orchards. Yet there was the insistent and determined exchange of fire somewhere ahead. A general murmur went up. Some officers requested a halt while scouts went forward to investigate; others were all for rushing ahead to join in the battle—if such it was.

"Trouble?" suggested Giles with querying eyebrows.

"By God, if there is . . . if this is a trap . . . they can hope for no quarter from us ever again," breathed Rupert through set lips. "Goddard is with them under that flag of truce. If they—"

"A *flag of truce,* old fellow," emphasized Giles. "They would not dare violate it."

Three years' experience of what the enemy would dare rushed through Rupert in a second. He saw again the maddened faces of the mob on the day of his arrival in Hong Kong; the figure of Tzu-An bending over Harriet with a knife; the bland expressions of servants who had deserted them; *the inferno of Sussex Hall*! It left him shaking and cold.

"They would do *anything*. Believe me, I know!"

A shout went up, telescopes were raised, and rumors flew through the column wending its way along the dusty road. They were many and varied, but there was no doubt about one report, for a cloud of dust and the thud of hooves heralded part of the cavalry escort that had gone with the envoys that morning. Several carried bullets in their bodies; one had gaping wounds in his back; all looked white-faced and shocked.

The story they told was appalling. Arriving at the proposed site, they had found the area surrounded by Chinese troops and artillery lying in wait. When it was evident the hidden troops had been spotted, a body of Tartar cavalry had galloped from the trees to encircle them, attacking and killing a French officer, then falling upon the others. Harry Parkes and his diplomatic party had been set upon, dragged from their mounts, bound with wrists and ankles tightly drawn together behind them, and thrown into a cart that had rattled off toward Peking. The Indian soldiers in the escort had been dragged off to be tortured, together with several British and French officers, along with the journalist. Those who had escaped had done so by charging with drawn steel through their captors' ranks and riding hell-for-leather. The white flag of truce had been trampled underfoot; the proposed cease-fire had been no more than a trap to draw the allies into certain annihilation by the hidden cannon and troops around the campsite.

There was no time to contemplate the full implications of this violation of one of the international rules of warfare and the barbarous treatment of unarmed men invited to go forward and negotiate. Later the news was to shock Western civilization, but the army had barely accepted the truth when it was called upon to attack on all fronts.

With half their number still in Tientsin, the allies were overwhelmed numerically, but outrage and vengeance give men stronger sword arms and keener eyes, even when iron discipline still controls them into some of the best warriors in the world. Gradually the enemy ranks thinned, allied cavalry charged again and again, infantry moved relentlessly forward at bayonet point, and the Battle of Chanchiawan turned from a brave attack into a complete rout of the enemy.

All through it Rupert pressed his men as hard as he pressed himself, and they backed him all the way, especially when he remained at their head fighting to take a vital bridge after a bullet had grazed his temple and sent blood running to blind one eye. Without pausing even to tie a handkerchief over the wound he seized his chance to rush the enemy and personally accounted for two stragglers with his sword. There was none of the maddened killer instinct in him now; he fought with the skill, intelligence, devotion to duty, and instinctive qualities of leadership he had discovered in himself at Sevastapol.

What insanity had led to his thoughts of suicide in battle because of Harriet? He still had that obligation to compensate for lives that had ended too soon. So far he had done little to indemnify Edward Deane or his own son taken tragically early. That was a double debt he must still honor. Now, there was a third, for Nugent Goddard had been betrayed in the most appalling manner. Rupert remembered them drinking to adventure so short a time ago and prayed his friend was already dead—that all the prisoners were dead. It did not do to think of the alternative.

Chapter Twenty

With defeat staring him in the face the emperor of China sent an envoy, under a flag of truce (proving conclusively that the Chinese perfectly understood the meaning of such a flag), who informed Elgin and Gros that the Son of Heaven was prepared to end hostilities on condition that the enemy barbarians restore the Taku forts and leave his country immediately.

The allied reply was terse and to the point. Unless the prisoners taken from under a flag of truce were returned on the instant, Peking would be bombarded and captured. The enemy's reply to that was equally terse and to the point. If the allies fired one shot at Peking, the prisoners would be massacred to a man.

Lord Elgin was faced with a decision that would affect the future of East-West relations and the lives of thirty-seven prisoners—if they were still alive. As often happens in such cases, another element stepped in to control it, and this time it was the allied military commanders, who informed their diplomatic leaders that they had no intention of attacking Peking until their heavy siege guns had reached them from the road leading up from Tientsin.

The delay might have saved Elgin from making a difficult decision, but it meant further suffering for the prisoners, whom the Chinese refused to return. That some, at least, were alive was proved when letters arrived from Harry Parkes begging the army to accede to the Chinese demands or their lives would be forfeit. That the letters were dictated by the Chinese was never in doubt, but to impress the fact upon his leaders, the envoy had added a postscript in Hindustani—a language unknown to his jailors.

But the greatest fears were still felt for the lives of those held hostage since the Chinese refused any neutral or medical contact with them and reiterated that the first shot at the walls of Peking would signal the execution of every captive.

It was mere bravado, as it turned out. That, or a lack of faith in the belief that having marched all the way to the gates of Peking, a mighty army would meekly turn back to save the lives of a mere thirty-seven prisoners who might already be dead. No Chinese general would do it, so there was little hope the "foreign devils" would. By the time the great siege guns were dragged up to the waiting army and the reinforcements marched in, the emperor had fled to safety, leaving one of his mandarins to take command of the situation.

It was a vain hope. With the wicked great barrels of allied siege guns trained on the gates of the city and the Chinese army filtering away hour by hour, having lost faith in beating back the allied, defeat was certain. Then, and only because they feared reprisals in defeat, the Chinese sent back the hostages. Twenty were dead!

Those still alive told a dreadful story of their torture, the cruelty of their captors toward themselves and their own countrymen, and the prisons in which they had been incarcerated. The Indians had suffered worst because of their race or perhaps because there was less fear of reprisals from non-Europeans. Many had died while being tortured; those who returned were broken and starving. The Westerners had fared little better. Some, mercifully, were beheaded at the outset; others had only coffins bearing mutilated remains to tell their story. The rest could still recount their ordeal, and what they reported decided a course of action that would never otherwise have been taken.

Deep and red was the rage within the breast of every man in the invading army as they filed past the coffins of their comrades and imagined their sufferings. Rupert stood a long time before the one marked with Nugent's name—the remains identifiable only by papers that were found in a pocket—feeling a coldness that froze even the marrow in his bones as he remembered the man that had once been. Recollections of his friend filled his mind and blurred his vision. All of Nugent's years of tact and patience with smiling, nodding men had been rewarded with agony. Those he had treated with courtesy, dignity, and a genuine wish to communicate had torn him apart like an animal.

Staring at that coffin, Rupert suddenly saw nothing degrading in his friend's death. He saw instead the true justification for what he himself now was—what he had always wanted to be. Flooding into him came a rebirth of assurance, an absolute and eternal certainty of his destiny. Failure dropped away from him. It did not matter that he had never achieved mercantile success; the company was inanimate, intangible, and of no importance in his life. It was what he was to himself that really mattered, and that fact had become lost somewhere in the scandal over his father's suicide.

While some men were born to be traders, Rupert Torrington had been born to wear a scarlet jacket. He should not have abandoned his rightful path; when they had rejected him, he should have taken the shilling then. Nugent's sacrifice had highlighted once more all his old principles. The coffin before him made them shine with genuine worth and pushed aside the false values he had tried to adopt in his endeavor to become a man he could never be. Burning inside him again was the need to uphold all he held dear—all Nugent, and those who had suffered with him, had held dear—and he knew in that moment that there was a future, a hope still inside him that would stand firm.

He saluted and turned away, remembering one evening at the factory in Canton when Nugent had said wistfully, "I sometimes wish I could serve my country in a more sacrificial way."

He had done so now, and Rupert would ensure that it was not in vain.

She went alone, taking the bowl of rice as her last offering. There remained in the house only her personal maid, a cook, and the houseboy. The other servants had been paid off. White covers decked the furniture in the majority of the rooms; large cabin trunks stood ready in the hall to be collected by men from the ship later that afternoon. Tonight she would sleep aboard, ready for the dawn sailing.

The Chinese girl would have come with her on this last quixotic visit, but Harriet wanted to make it in the sole company of a little pinch-faced ghost, for in a way it was a dedication to Bessie, who had waited so patiently in the glade on so many occasions . . . without understanding why.

She found herself speaking softly to the girl as she left the sedan chair at the usual place and began walking up the track toward a spot in the jungle where a path led to the cave of the Rice Dragon. It helped Harriet to know that Bessie would be on Hong Kong Island with little Edward; her son would not be abandoned by all who had loved him when she left tomorrow.

Each step of the way brought memories that told her it was right to say good-bye to something that had held her in thrall so long. Wah-Lin, mother of the amah who had perished with Edward, had found comfort in her simple belief in the symbolism of the Rice Dragon, but Harriet had gone beyond and into realms suitable only for philosophers, who could abandon all for the sake of wisdom. For the very simple and the very wise, the Rice Dragon was comprehensible. To someone like herself with emotion that tended to override intelligence, it was dangerous. All the same, she had been unable to deny herself one last visit.

She had said nothing to Armand of her intention and waited until the eleventh hour to release that spirit which she had kept hovering so long in that place. She accepted that pagan beliefs could not exist alongside her own, and yet they still held enough of her mind for her to be unable to leave Hong Kong without performing the ritual farewell to that which she had believed to be in that place.

The terrible heat had softened into a gentler combination of sunshine and warm breezes, and she felt tendrils of her hair stir at her temples. The sensation put within her a sudden fierce longing to feel the summer zephyrs of England, to smell sweet hay newly cut, and to hear ducks quacking around a pond that mirrored oaks and a thatched Tudor farmhouse. It stunned her, her longing for home after so long. Numbness appeared to be melting away with every step.

The bowl in her hands was smooth to the touch; the rice inside it, fluffy and white. It was pleasant to look at. Somewhere in the distance a bird was filling the air with vivid liquid song. *In a forest that had previously been so silent?* The lizard spread-eagled against a nearby tree shone a beautiful iridescent green against the rough darkness of the bark. She walked through dappled paths, green yet brilliant with sparkling sunlight on rain-sheened foliage. There were blossoms high and out of reach but sending fresh perfumes to wash over her. Like a butterfly emerging from the cocoon, she felt life stirring within her—a second more beautiful life than the first caterpillar existence. When she turned her face up to the warmth, the shimmering blue of the sky held her attention. It no longer threatened her with its endless eternity . . . and somewhere along the path the little accompanying ghost had left her!

The glade looked superbly beautiful as if Nature had excelled herself in everything from crystal waterfall to velvety verdure, and Harriet stood for a moment, moved by such perfection. Then she saw him, sitting on the stone and looking at her gravely. He spoke across the width of the glade in the language she always managed to understand, yet his voice sounded as if it echoed across a chasm rather than a ribbon of water.

"It is better that you do not approach. Shu-Lung is angry. He will not accept your bowl of rice."

With hands that were suddenly shaking she set the bowl on the grass at her feet. He knew she was leaving; in his mysterious way, he already knew!

"What is it that makes him angry?" she asked testingly.

"You ask that which is already revealed in your heart but will not see with the eyes of clarity."

Not attempting to approach, she said quietly, "I come only to release that spirit which I have kept here too long. Such a mission should not make him angry."

There was a silence—so long Harriet began to believe the man had gone into one of his moods of deep meditation. Then his voice came again like the whisper of a wind that blows across a barren plain.

"In the multitude of ways to Serene Understanding there is for each man only one true path. You have wandered in the Star Palaces within the Season of Fire and found a serpent of evil who has twisted his coils around you. There he has held you for too long and your fire has risen up to consume you."

He appeared to go away once more on a mental journey, then continued speaking as if there had been no pause. "The wider significance of eternal understanding has blinded you and led you to one who lives in the Season of Water. But this water will extinguish the fire, so that no flame remains to light others when you are gone."

How could he have known this was her last visit, that tomorrow she would place her future in the hands of Armand? She understood only too well that he was telling her the union would be disastrous for one born during the Season of Fire and one in the Season of Water.

"But this cannot always be so," she protested desperately.

He shook his head. "The Inner Temple of Heavenly Tranquillity must be eternally sought. The spirit must conquer much to attain it. Your path lies through the Season of Earth."

Her heart thudded violently, forcing her to cry out, "*No!*"

"The Season of Earth," he repeated calmly. "The fire will burn fitfully but will never be extinguished. Finally, the earth will glow with the fire, and the flames will be borne by the unyielding strength of the earth."

Trembling from head to toe, she put her face in her hands. Rupert had been born in the Season of Earth—the steady beacon that guides those who are lost or frightened; the one who remains true to ideals and dedication; the one who never wavers.

"The Rice Dragon is wrong," she whispered. "There is no Heavenly Tranquillity that way."

"Shu-Lung breathes smoke and flames. Your rice must be taken and fed to the serpents of eternal darkness."

It was sharp and final. The soothsayer had risen and was turning away.

Cold again, heavy with the return of ghosts and fears, she cried out, "I came only to release the spirit of my son so that it may rest."

The reply floated over his shoulder as he entered the cave, so that it could have come from within the cave itself. "The spirit will never rest when Fire and Earth are separated. It will wander forever searching for him who lies at the gates of the Celestial City."

He vanished, and it was as if he had never been there, even though she could hear his movements at the shrine of Shu-Lung, the Rice Dragon. A great wave of desolation swept over her to set her running from that place, which now seemed sinister and hostile. The sun must have been shining still, the bird singing, the lizard basking on the trunk—but she saw none of those things that had formed a mirage of happiness. Rushing headlong through the jungle, she tried to escape the words that threatened to keep her from escape on the morrow. It was as if she would never run far enough from that glade.

Yet, when she finally collapsed in thankfulness, she discovered it had been no distance at all. The shimmery mist disappeared from her eyes as she gazed down at the blackened rubble of Sussex Hall. Since that first visit to the old soothsayer she had not once been up the track to this place, and yet her feet had carried her there without hesitation. Trembling even more violently, she rose as if the stones were still red-hot, but when she turned, poised for flight once more, the instinct to run was slammed from her mind and limbs by an instantaneous revelation. Before her lay an uninterrupted view of the whole width of an ocean so blue it caught her breath. Up here there were no narrow gaps between buildings that grudgingly gave her glimpses of freedom; up here the whole magnificent, earth-shattering spectrum was hers.

Mesmerized by the magnificence of that cobalt expanse, she slowly crossed the track to where the slope fell away to Victoria and the waterfront. Leaning against a tree trunk, she gazed at the panorama and saw what her eyes had been closed against for so long. The confines around her fell away as she followed the wake of boats drifting across, their sails graceful in the sunlight, heading for anywhere in the world. The terrors that had held her disappeared as she lifted her gaze to the gently rising hills on the distant mainland, so green between sea and sky, stretching away as far as the eye could see across the vastness of China.

From Sussex Hall she had witnessed this whole panorama; with Rupert she had known the fullness of life and freedom. Since then walls had blocked her view of the ocean; grief had turned him into a monster.

Clutching the rough bark of the tree trunk, she was filled with a renewal of sweet anguish. With Rupert there was no peace, but without him there was no hope. Seeing those ships, the undulating hills, she knew there would never be an escape from what she was now, never be a chance for happiness no matter how far she traveled, or who traveled with her, if Rupert were left behind.

Having sunk to the grass beneath the tree, she leaned back against it, keeping her eyes on the distant horizon as a startling recollection of a day six months ago returned with a clarity she had not experienced when it actually happened. The uniform had been rough serge, ill-fitting, unadorned with insignia of rank. It should have humbled him and yet had not. He was a young man, yet youth had gone from his face. Life had bruised him—shadowed his eyes and hollowed his cheeks. Strange that she should see so clearly now what had made no impression on her at the time; painful that she should now hear his words with ears that had been closed to his voice then.

"Why have you always condemned in me what you uphold so fiercely yourself?"

Her lashes grew wet; the distance blurred. The charge had been true. *Face the inevitable and turn it to one's own advantage.* So strongly had she upheld that maxim, so determined had she been to instill the belief in him, it had not occurred to her that there were two ways to interpret it. While she had believed it was Fate's design that he should be a merchant, he had acknowledged that soldiering was in his blood and fought to return to it against all odds. Their tug-of-war struggle had eventually destroyed them.

Yet . . . was it irreparable? Was the fire completely extinguished by earth? Her pulse thudded with sudden rapid energy that sent waves of giddiness over her. "The Inner Temple of Heavenly Tranquillity must be eternally sought," she had just been told. "The spirit must conquer much to attain it."

Closing her eyes against the brilliant light of hope,

she nevertheless told herself there was time. Armand's ship did not sail until dawn. Her baggage could be taken off; the lease on the house could be extended, servants reengaged. There was time. *There was time!*

Urgency filled limbs and senses. She was on the point of running down the hill when the remainder of the old soothsayer's words rooted her to the spot.

". . . him who lies at the gates of the Celestial City." What had he meant? For once there was no certainty of comprehension; the words remained enigmatic. The Celestial City! Had he referred to Peking or . . . or . . . heaven? Was it too late after all? Putting her head back against the tree, she gazed up into the serene glory of the sky for a long, long time.

"Oh, dear Lord," she prayed to her one God, "send him back to me. Please send him back."

Since the jealousy and unease between the allies were never far below the surface, it was not surprising the French and British wished to mount separate assaults on Peking when the time came. But both sides had to be aware of what each was planning to do, and the British suggested a rendezvous at the imperial Summer Palace just six miles to the north of the fabled city where plans could be discussed. The French immediately marched to the spot, but the British force was held up by a body of Tartar cavalry that offered some resistance before being routed. The weary troops were obliged to bivouac for the night some distance from the Summer Palace.

Rupert spent an uneasy night beneath the stars, haunted by shadows of regret and sadness, even though his heart now beat with assured serenity. He rose at dawn with the stiff muscles that come of open-air sleeping and was in the middle of shaving when Giles approached at a run, through a regiment waking up and instilling order in the midst of chaos. He leaped over the small fire which was cooking Rupert's breakfast and came up to his friend, puffing and panting, and with his face alive with news.

"*Major* Meredith, I beg you to remember your dignity and stop leaping about like a junior officer," admonished Rupert with a grin. "What has conspired to send you rushing at me in such haste? Don't tell me Fredericks has had an accident and you are now a lieutenant colonel!"

Giles was too full of wrath to cope with humor, so he ignored it. "Those damned French!" he exploded, mopping his brow. "Didn't I say at the outset we should have done better without them?"

Rupert was immediately interested. "What is the latest?"

Fighting for breath, Giles told him. "There's no chance of an assault on Peking yet. Those plundering bastards no sooner set eyes on the Summer Palace last night than they were over the walls and helping themselves. Our scouts have just ridden in and say they have never seen the like of what is contained in that treasure trove: jewels, gold and silver, jade, furs, and silks such as you never saw in your days as a merchant, I'll wager." He paused for a quick breath, then panted, "The damned frogs are taking the lot in an orgy of looting that could go on for days. The officers can't stop them because they are too busy securing the best for themselves. The war has been forgotten in this frenzy of plunder."

"Good God . . . to get so near to taking Peking, then turn aside for the spoils of war," cried Rupert in disgust. "We shall have to attack on our own."

"Eh?" Giles looked startled.

"Peking will have to be stormed by our troops alone," said Rupert, thinking fast of the implications of such a move.

"Not a hope in hell of that," was the swift reply. "Our officers are already setting off for the Summer Palace."

"To try to halt the French?" asked Rupert incredulously.

"No . . . to secure their share of the spoils. If we don't saddle up right away, there'll be nothing left when we get there."

When the British force led by precious few of its officers arrived at the rendezvous, the scene that met their eyes was one they would never forget.

The imperial Summer Palace was, in reality, a great park of more than eighty square miles containing several hundred buildings designed to house the incredible treasures only before seen by a succession of emperors and members of their courts. The park presented a breathtaking panorama of lakes, ornamental bridges of marble or lacquered wood, tiered gardens of stunted trees and heavily blossomed bushes, fantastic designs of rock and carved pagodas rising into miniature cities of some legendary time, great halls with red and yellow upturned roofs, one upon the other, open-sided pavilions tiled with gold that gleamed in the bars of sunlight, fountains, courtyards, summer houses, waterfalls, orchards, temples, and shrines. Surrounding the whole was a wall with gates, and through these was a never-ending line in both directions of soldiers, civilians, and pack animals, scrambling, pushing, and shouting in the grand endeavor of greed.

The noise was unbelievable; the ground from the gates to the tents of the French encampment was littered with scraps of brocades, broken china, springs from clockwork toys, ribbons, dead flowers, lacquered boxes emptied of their rich contents, ladies' hair ornaments, and a thousand beautiful things broken, hacked, or crushed for the one jewel inlaid upon them. In the orgy or plunder exquisite workmanship, gorgeous materials, and rare design counted for nothing against ignorance blinded by flashing stones and gold ornamentation.

The British troops stood silently watching for no more than ten minutes, until someone spotted members of the Coolie Corps along with local Chinese villagers sneaking over the walls on the scaling ladders, carrying armfuls of booty in a kind of inscrutable daze at their wondrous *joss*.

Up went a cry. "The divils are taking a share of it, an' all!"

Discipline vanished; order broke. The British descended on the gates in waves of scarlet and blue, and no man dared try to stop them. Left with no men to command, those few officers, including Rupert, who had not galloped off early that morning decided they might as well go into the park and see the wonders within before the whole place was laid flat.

In all that teeming crowd Rupert must have been the only person who wanted none of the treasure. Excessive wealth had never given him happiness; he had known the true source of that blessing and lost it. Oriental treasures had never appealed to him—he had sold all those in Pagoda House—and there had been enough piracy and plunder from earlier Torringtons. But there was no wish in him to protect the property of the emperor from destruction. He knew that the other emotion besides greed that had instigated this despoliation was rage. They were destroying all the emperor held dear as vengeance for men cruelly murdered.

Rupert walked through those gates as much an approving spectator as anything else, and for as long as an hour or two he wandered detachedly through an incredible moving crush of authorized thieving. After traversing great ornamental lakes containing gold and silver fish, after crossing innumerable bridges to pavilions and grottos, he eventually entered some of the larger halls and palaces, staggered by what he saw piled within.

There were carved chests crammed with jade, enamel, and gold ornaments; lengths of priceless silk, furs from the North, and robes of satin and brocade embroidered with gold thread and studded with jewels. In one pagoda that had plainly been used by ladies of the court were exquisite robes thick with pearls and precious stones, jeweled hair ornaments, ropes of pearls, enameled boxes with lids covered in rubies and sapphires, silver brushes and pin dishes, ebony screens inlaid with mother-of-pearl, jade ear ornaments and rings, enamel finger nail shields, gold-rimmed mirrors, and sweetmeat dishes.

Rupert did not cross the threshold, for inside, men were ripping and tearing at the dresses, hacking at jewel-encrusted lids with their bayonets, gouging rubies from tortoiseshell combs, quarreling over ropes of pearls.

He moved on across a courtyard surrounded by ebony pillars, in the center of which was a fountain shooting up between great gilded dragons on six sides, and passed between two of the giant porcelain jars that lined the cloisters. A long pathway bordered by blossom trees of matched height led him to a small palace crammed with men of all nationalities all with one intent. The noise was deafening; the smell, predominantly of sweat. There were French uniforms, the scarlet of the British and Indians, vivid yellow of Zouaves, and the blue of the Coolie Corps . . . and these were in the greatest number, for it was a room of toys. There must have been an example of every type of clock and singsong ever made. The Europeans were grabbing clocks, little knowing or caring if they were Louis XV or ormolu, some merely to hack out the jeweled hands or figures upon the faces, but the Chinese were lost in the wonder of the toys they had set in motion in a cacophony of bells, trumpets, and chimes.

Rabbits were drumming as they marched along the shelf; tiny birds in jeweled cages sang and twittered with mechanical piping notes; monkey musicians played trumpets over and over again; clowns turned somersaults to the rat-a-tatting of a drum roll; dancing couples waltzed with slowing frenzy to a tune from Vienna; tiny ballerinas spun endlessly to peals of tinkling bells; a brass band of black-faced weasels blew strident notes on their instruments while their legs swung back and forth as if marching; windmills whirled; tightrope walkers crossed and recrossed their thread; hens pecked at corn; maidens drew up water from a well, then let down the bucket again, all to the tinkling tones of well-loved classics or folk tunes of Europe.

Rupert was held by the sight for a few minutes, until another sound broke across the fairy tunes of the singsongs. He turned sharply. Two soldiers were quarreling over a broken clock, and the situation had grown ugly. A Scotsman and a Frenchman—not the best combination—both uncouth fellows, who had smashed a marble clock for the gold pendulum, were determined to carry off the prize. Their voices rose in vicious confrontation against the deafening din of the music boxes as the Frenchman punched the other in the stomach. In a flash the Scot brought up his bayonet and slashed at his adversary's face. The Frenchman brought out a knife.

Rupert moved quickly, drawing his sword as he ordered them to stand apart. For an instant it seemed they could not or wished not to hear, so he sent the sword whistling through the narrow space between them. It was a sound they instinctively knew, and they gazed at him sullenly as he demanded the pendulum. Hatred in darks eyes turned to astonishment when he tossed the gold shape through the open archway into the lake beyond.

"If you have wives," he said in both languages, "I suggest they will be better pleased to have you back than any piece of gold."

He walked out, thanking his stars there was no liquor in the Summer Palace, as there had been in Sevastapol. If those two had been drinking, he would never have stood a chance!

The incident seemed to be reflected in a new general mood of aggression outside in the park. As he walked on, Rupert discovered that men who had returned for a second or third time were smashing, breaking, and tearing for destruction's sake. The pillars of little delicate pavilions were being kicked away; the silk-draped walls, scored by bayonets. Gold tiles were being hacked off roofs with scant regard for the interiors, but wooden pagodas were being accorded the same treatment. The imperial Summer Palace was being methodically torn apart.

Doing what he could to stop actual bloody violence, he saw other officers becoming conscious of their duty and attempting to call a halt to the last desperate bid for booty. Bugles were ringing out the recall to camp at the onset of night, and soldiers were grabbing such mountains of silks, jewels, furniture, cushions, and boxes they were hard put to carry them. Staggering along, dropping rubies, priceless gold plates, and coins like so much litter as they went, still they could not resist stopping to seize a jade egg or ivory ball that had been dropped by the man ahead.

Most of the officers had found themselves some kind of pack animal for their more discerning prizes, but one man in the caravan of laden beasts put a sudden blaze of anger in Rupert's breast, and he was off after him with instinctive reaction. It was a short sprint, for Valentine Bedford had halted to pick up a jade buffalo dropped unnoticed from the pile of another's spoils. He spun around quickly at the sound of a voice.

"Put that down, Bedford!" Rupert yelled, sword drawn.

Bedford looked him up and down with no more than insolent surprise. "Well, well . . . so you found yourself a pretty uniform with gold braid after all. Dead men's shoes, no doubt." He continued his study. "And not a mark on you to boast of the hero. What will your dear lady think of that . . . or has she also gone over to the French?"

With expert judgment Rupert flashed his sword and left a gash down Bedford's cheek that would mar his good looks for years to come. Bedford's insolence turned to violent anger as his hand went up to cover the wound.

"I cannot run you through, as every instinct dictates, but some man will do it for me one day. But I can see that you are deprived of any share of these spoils of war," grated Rupert, all his loathing of the man and what he represented coming to the fore in that moment. "I do not consider that you, of all people, are entitled to any of this treasure. You are an opportunist. It takes one rogue to recognize another, and my grandfather saw you from a great distance. You have suffered no hardship on this march, faced no danger, fought no war . . . but men like Goddard died in agony for you and your kind, and I'm damned if you are going to make money from his sacrifice."

The point of his sword pricked the rump of the mule, and it shot off, braying, right into the waiting arms of two gleeful troopers who had just been robbed of their own booty by a party of armed Zouaves.

With the sword back to threaten Bedford, Rupert was just taking possession of the jade buffalo when something thudded into his back. Giving a great cry, he pitched forward, but the piercing agony remained with him, increasing until his entire body throbbed, and he could not hold back the moans that pushed through his lips. Grasping convulsively at the grass at each side of his head, he saw through the blur of moisture across his eyes a pigtailed figure swiftly stoop to snatch up the buffalo that had fallen a few feet from him. It was done so quickly the Chinese was away around the side of a wrecked grotto within seconds.

Knowing then that he had been knifed for possession of the treasure, Rupert twisted his head with a great effort of will until he could turn his eyes up to Bedford. The man was smiling.

"By God, there goes an opportunist if ever I saw one. A useful man to have around."

Rupert would not believe Bedford could watch a man die and do nothing. As he tried to raise his head, the movement brought further torture, plus the knowledge that the knife was still in his back. Collapsing onto the grass once more, he heard his own voice, harsh with pain, croak, "Bedford . . . for God's sake . . ."

The shoes two feet from Rupert's face began moving away. "I always told you nobility would get you nowhere," came a calculating voice. "See how right I was."

The shoes moved farther away, faster and faster,

until Rupert could no longer see them through the glaze over his eyes. Still unbelieving, he lifted his head to call after the man, but the action was more than he could endure, and darkness descended.

There was noise all around him—noise which he recognized and which had given his unconscious mind a message it could not ignore. Yet his body would not obey. It was no longer the mountain of pain it had been, but he had no control over it. All he could do was lie helplessly on his stomach, looking around as far as his field of vision would allow. He was numb—like a spirit outside a body. But it was a spirit that had risen above anguish.

The scene had changed drastically. Approaching night hung over the distant sky like storm clouds, turning the wreckage of a once-beautiful park into a scene from Hades. But it was not only the broken buildings that suggested that. There were strident bugle calls summoning everyone to return to camp, carrying on the evening air like the Last Trump. There was an enactment of panic and chaos wherever he looked. Men were scrambling, pushing, shouting in urgent voices; animals were braying or neighing as they were urged ever faster. As the great exodus continued, the ground became strewn with the debris of centuries of cruelty and extortion. Heirlooms were trampled underfoot—gifts received by a line of emperors who laid their hands on anything of value by means of threat, demand, or death. The greatest skills and talents that had gone to fashioning objects of beauty and wealth were counted as nothing as the frantic horde of foreign invaders fought to reach the gates of that park.

In another moment Rupert knew why. Above the shrill terrified screams of animals, the urgent shouts in all languages, the din of clocks and music boxes that would not stop was another that froze him and yet, at the same time, brought sweat springing up on his face. It was a sound he would never lose from the darker recesses of his mind, and with it always came another—a woman's voice, low and terrible. "Where *were* you?"

Slowly, inch by inch, he forced his head around and saw the great yellow flames that had turned the sky of fading day into one of sunshine morning. Leaping from pavilion to pavilion, from pagoda to audience chamber, from quaint arching bridge to lacquered teahouse, the great conflagration rushed forward, devouring everything within its path.

Carved outswept roofs collapsed in a pile of charred wood; rich brocade paneling shriveled into sticky messes; idols and gods toppled in flaming pillars to the grass, which flared fitfully before becoming stinking spirals of smoke. The blossom trees looked like flambeaux in rows so straight they could have been part of a fireworks display; pagodas burned like giant colored candles. Lakes became great shimmering pools of reflected leaping lights in red, orange, and yellow. But behind the advance guard of flames, black billowing smoke began to turn dusk into deepest night. As the ultimate reprisal for all those done to death through the treachery of the mandarins, the allies were burning the imperial Summer Palace to the ground.

Rupert relived a nightmare of a year ago as he lay helpless in the path of the fire and prayed aloud for the soul of his son and for his own. The plunderers had fled; they had not seen him lying beside a small pavilion as they rushed for the gates and their encampments . . .

Vengeance is mine . . . saith the Lord. Was this the exquisite vengeance for a man who had not been there when his son had died by fire? He lay with his face in the grass while tears flowed as they had at the sight of Sussex Hall in ruins. God knew he could not be blamed for what had happened. Harriet had abandoned her faith in the face of something she could not accept, but he had remained sane only because of the belief that Edward Torrington had been taken, as had Edward Deane, as part of some divine purpose. Only now did he have his first doubts—now, when the fires of hell had come for him.

The noise of fire was all around him, crackling, sucking, roaring. The heat fanned his cheeks; air being pushed forward by its advance stirred the hair against his forehead. But he could not move. His body had become a separate nerveless entity, even though his brain registered approaching death. He lay helpless as little tongues of flame ran across the grass toward his outstretched hands. The whole world had grown scarlet-yellow; the air was impossible to breathe.

There was a flurry; two small black slippers appeared beside him. A heaving, tearing sensation in his back; then agony returned to make him cry out. Beneath his jacket was a rush of warm, sticky blood, and then he was aware of being dragged, stretched on the rack, broken on the wheel. Through eyes nearly blinded by flames he made out the vicious face of a Chinese man who held a bloody dagger between his teeth. The man was one of the Coolie Corps, who had helped fight their northern brethren but had no love for "foreign devils."

As he was dragged into a great wall of flames that had once been a pavilion for music, Rupert closed his eyes and prayed the flames would kill him before the man could begin using the knife on his body. Then a sudden tranquillity descended on him as he had a vivid recollection of sitting in a tent beside a dying armless man. He would be in good company . . . and his would be quicker than Nugent Goddard's ordeal by torrture.

The last thing he did as flames began to snatch at his clothes and hair was pray that Harriet would one day forgive him.

Epilogue

Peking was surrendered several days after the destruction of the Summer Palace, such devastation hastening the capitulation of the emperor. The city gates were thrown open, and the victorious allies marched in without firing a shot. Through the absent emperor's envoys the European plenipotentiaries finally achieved what it had taken three small wars and years of frustration to establish.

The Treaty of Tientsin was formally ratified, and sites were chosen for the legations that were to be built for the foreign powers. This representation at the imperial court of China was to herald long years of peace and understanding between Britain and China, but until the ambassadors took residence the following summer, a garrison of allied troops was set up at Tientsin as a safeguard against further treachery. The remainder of the force was hurriedly shipped down the Pei-ho, which was already beginning to freeze over.

The soldiers returned with stories of the wonders they had seen and the hardships they had suffered. From those wounded or with comrades who were now gone there was also some small bitterness at the other nations that had gained all the benefits and done none of the fighting. But victorious troops do not bear grudges for long, and many were seen handing out food and souvenirs to those they had robbed on the way up, accepting also in their philosophical way that their own success would be beneficial to any others who found it impossible to deal with the Chinese.

Apart from the garrison at Tientsin, one was retained at Shanghai, at Canton, and at newly acquired Kowloon, across the water from Hong Kong. The Indian regiments that had fought so well were to return to their home stations; four British regiments were listed for England. Among them was that one in which Rupert had enlisted as a shilling-a-day man and signed away the bulk of his life.

Harriet listened to all the gossip that traveled down through China to a now-peaceful Hong Kong and prayed that he would return. At first she was overwhelmed with fears and nightmares that he would have no arms or bear an unrecognizable face on the body she knew and loved so well. Then she accepted that every woman in love with a soldier had to live with fear and conquer it for the sake of their men.

While waiting for news of the final outcome, she found her returning vigor and restlessness needing an outlet. Since she could not accept or forgive those who had cold-shouldered her, time hung heavily and reminded her of those days before Rupert had come into her life. She missed Bessie desperately—that little character who had served her so devotedly. Armand had written to her from Singapore that should she find herself a widow, there was always a place for her at Lyons. She would not go. If Rupert should be killed, she would never leave the East. All she loved best were here.

Face the inevitable. How often that phrase had been with her in the past two years; how often she had had to do so. While thinking of it one afternoon, Harriet admitted she might have to face Hong Kong alone for the rest of her life and resolved to prepare herself. She could never marry again if she lost the one man who had ever meant anything to her, so she would have to engage herself in some kind of employment. The obvious answer was to continue in her father's footsteps, but she determined she would never become a penniless eccentric, as he had been.

To this end, the minor dabbling in investments she had been conducting through Rupert's banker now became the subject of her serious attention. Hong Kong was expanding daily. Gas and transport companies were being formed; building land was being snapped up; trading routes were being shortened. In anticipation of the successful outcome of the war, prospects in the East were dazzling. A man with insight and flair could make a fortune almost overnight. Why, then, could not a woman with the same talents?

Harriet began studying the newspapers and haunted the office of Rupert's banker with such fevered determination he began to get caught up in it. Yet what had begun as a need to fulfill some part of her character that had long been crying for recognition gradually became a desperate dedication to a man who might never return. She was tormented by that time she had accused him of greed to the extent of taking from her brother that which had been left owing after his death. Memories of how she had ignored his presents, refused to wear dresses he bought her, lived frugally amid plenty, dogged her waking hours. Even worse, she had done a complete *volte-face* when accusing him of throwing away his wealth and inheritance for a mere principle over the opium. When the Torrington millions had been offered her, she had turned her back on them, yet she had been bitter in her condemnation when Rupert risked them for something he regarded as more important than money. How could he have understood her when her values had appeared so inconsistent? Yet she knew he would take her back with joy if he returned, knew it without any shred of doubt.

The days went by, and Harriet grew more and more successful. It was not long before gentlemen passing her in the street doffed their hats to a respected business associate as well as a gracious female. She might conduct all her business through the banker, but it was a foolish man who did not recognize the brain behind the machinations. The Torrington name began to resound in trade and commerce circles with a new dignity. In the hallowed halls of financiers' establishments the smell of eels began to fade, driven away by the sweeter scent of perfume and the sight of a lively face beneath a bonnet.

Torrington money was invested in government projects; Torrington hundreds bought building land, then doubled when demand for it reached a premium. A piece of land in Kowloon bought very astutely by "an unknown investor" was sold at five times the price when a merchant hankered to extend his business to the mainland.

Such activities needed a clear head, sharp business acumen, and a determined personality. Harriet, released from the frightening realms in which she had been traveling, found these qualities that had always existed in her gratifyingly highlighted. But she also needed the devoted support of a male colleague who could enter portals forbidden to females, conduct negotiations in places of business run by men, and provide the necessary liquid conviviality needed to persuade reluctant financiers. In this, Rupert's banker soon found himself a bewitched and ardent accomplice.

The driving force within Harriet seemed to ensure that every calculted risk, every prudent investment, every farsighted purchase could not fail. But her frenzied activity and gratifying success did not completely blot the fear from her aching heart. *Let it not be too late!*

At last the great troopships began to come in, returning from a victorious campaign that would settle the trade question for good. Harriet went every day to the place where Sussex Hall had once stood. It no longer held any fears for her, and she could see the vessels as they inched toward the jetties. For once she was uncertain. Would a shilling-a-day soldier be allowed to visit his wife, or must she go down to the barracks gates to join those Eurasian and Chinese women who clustered there, looking for a particular man? Her future as the wife of a common soldier could not be guessed at, but if Rupert could take it, so could she.

The ships continued to sail in, but no one came to the house. Still, Harriet hesitated to go down to the barracks. Fear of hearing the words she dreaded, unwillingness to see pity in the eyes of those who had once turned their backs on him kept her in the house, where hope still remained until someone called to dash it.

It was three days later that she heard sounds of a visitor arriving late in the afternoon and ran to look from her window onto the street below. A sedan chair had halted outside, and she could glimpse a scarlet sleeve within the little cabin. Her heart leaped, then was stilled. There was the insignia of an officer on the sleeve. Another day, another war sprang to mind, and she leaned against the side of the window in sudden weakness. The visitor was Giles Meredith. She saw him alight and glance up at the house before turning back to the bearers.

Trembling, she turned away, knowing she had to face the inevitable with more courage than ever before. It was natural that Rupert's friend should be sent with the news, yet she wished it had been anyone but Giles. He was such an ingenuous and cheery young man this mission would be ill-handled by him, she felt sure.

When the knock came, she went forward to meet her visitor with surprising calm, thinking only of sparing him as much awkwardness as possible. At the top of the stairs her heart stood still once more, but this time it was with the shock of joyous disbelief. She gripped the banister rail as she looked for a long long time at the figure in the hall below, unable to move another step forward. He wore the uniform of a lieutenant and leaned heavily on a stick as he called a farewell to Giles at the door.

He was pale and strained, as if he were emerging from a long period of pain. One side of his face was puckered and discolored; his creamy fair hair was yellow-brown at the ends. He was thinner than when she had let him walk away with only the sound of her contempt ringing in his ears.

She must have made some movement, for he turned sharply, a spasm of pain crossing his face as he looked up to where she still stood. It was a moment that destroyed all the barriers with crushing speed and kept them apart with its promise of unbearable pleasure-pain. The tears welled up in her eyes and throat as she held his gaze with pride and willing capitulation.

"I . . . I didn't recognize you . . . dressed like that," she began, fighting the emotion that blurred her voice.

His eyes looked darker than ever as he limped slowly to the foot of the stairs. "They were short of officers," he told her in a matter-of-fact tone that defied his expression of fierce gladness. "Giles had a hand in it, I suspect."

She forced a smile. "Yes . . . it is the sort of thing he would do." Moving down two steps, she added, "You were hurt?" *He was whole, thank God. Thank God!*

His hand went involuntarily to his face. "They set fire to the great Summer Palace. I was dragged through it to the safety of a lake . . . by a Chinaman. He saved my life. Strange, isn't it?"

It was taut, almost defiant, and she knew as he continued to look up at her that he had gone to war not expecting to return—not *wanting* to return. Now he was here and offering her a challenge. *Oh, dear God, show me what I must do.*

She descended two more steps. "Armand has gone back to France. His father is dying."

A muscle in his jaw began to work. "I thought you . . . I thought you might have gone with him."

She found it impossible to say any more on that subject, and struggled to remain in command of herself. "I . . . I have been dabbling in investments," she managed through a throat thickening with tears. "You will find yourself a wealthy man when you call at the bank . . . and the owner of property on the island." Two more steps. "The Torrington millions are mounting again."

The fire of his gaze blazed up in pride and incredulity. "The Torrington millions? *You* have been handling business affairs?"

She gave a shaky laugh and went down two more steps. "Why not? I have always been the one with a head for business, have I not?"

He had reached the bottom stair and gripped the newel post so hard his knuckles showed white. "Harriet, I . . . why? *Why*?" he repeated in a near whisper.

She was now so close to him she could smell the warmth of his skin, reminding her of so many distant, fast-returning joys the tears could no longer be held in check.

"For you," she whispered back. "For you, as an officer . . . and a gentleman."

"The regiment is posted back to England," he said with difficulty."

"I know."

The air between them seemed to vibrate with the depth of the love neither of them could deny. Then she flung herself against him with a great cry and clutched the smooth cloth of his scarlet jacket as if she would never again let him go.

"Take me with you. Oh, my dearest, take me with you."

His walking stick fell to the ground as he held her with arms that shook and buried his face in her hair. Throughout the fierce ecstasy of their reunion her mind was filled with the words of the old soothsayer: "The fire will burn fitfully but will never be extinguished. Finally, the earth will glow with the fire, and the flames will be borne by the unyielding strength of the earth."